WHAT REMAINS

AN INKED IN GRAY ANTHOLOGY

Edited by

DAKOTA RAYNE & SAN G CROW

Inked in Gray Press

www.inkedingray.com

ISBN 978-1-952969-03-4 (ebook) | 978-1-952969-02-7 (print)

Cover design and art by Covers by Christian

Keep up to date on our upcoming projects by signing up to our newsletter or checking out our website!

If you are interested in reading more works by Inked in Gray, please consider last year's anthology, *The First Stain,* which can be found at all online retailers or on our website at www.inkedingray.com/the-first-stain. The *First Stain* is a collection of works shattering preconceived notions and delving into a dark, grittier world of death, justice, family, redemption, and ugly truths bound in beautiful lies.

Thank you for giving this book a read! We hope you enjoy the mix of stories we have for you. If you are able, we would be grateful if you wrote a review on Amazon, Goodreads, or Indie Story Geek.

Kindest Regards,
    The Inked Team

CONTENTS

FOREWORD

SURVIVAL: *the act or fact of living or continuing longer than another person or thing. The continuation of life or existence.*

Survival is not just about the physical. Mental, emotional, and spiritual survival is more than just the inhale and exhale of oxygen. It is a state of mind, the ability to withstand stress and adapt to a new situation. To persevere, reinvent, reestablish.

Why survival stories? Because survival is something we fear. We fear surviving our loved ones, making choices to sacrifice one thing or person for another, because it means assigning value to something that is priceless. To put it forth makes it real.

Never do I wish for anyone to make those hard choices, but they happen nonetheless. The world is not a safe place and there may come a time when we must make choices we do not want to make, face moments we hope will never come.

What happens when horrific things come to pass is that there are those who seek to forget, those who seek to deny, and those who seek to change. With time comes complacency, and again, the cycle repeats itself.

History repeats itself.

Stories can make us aware of our ignorance, our arrogance,

and of our insecurities. Storytelling helps us remember: we are all imperfect, the choices we make carve the future, cement the past, and dictate our present. Every choice we make affects us and those around us. To do due diligence to our future, we must analyze our present, dig beneath the surface of our past. Sometimes we are the aggressor, stuck in our own way, governed by our own fear. Our struggle to survive is all encompassing. Sometimes there are many in-betweens. Other times, there are only extremes.

How we approach storytelling can help us delve a little deeper into our humanity...or lack thereof. We hope you enjoy this anthology, that it gives you something to think about, chills your bones, and even gives you hope.

With Love,

The Inked Team

P.S. Please read the trigger warnings. They are listed below and prior to each story. Enjoy!

Among Tall Trees: Use of r-slur by the antagonist

Cold: Cannibalism

Threads: Suicide, verbal abuse, violence and domestic abuse, and drug use. Mentions of thoughts of suicide. No suicide depicted on the page.

Old Women: Rape - depicted, but not in graphic detail

A CAGE OF MOONS AND STARS

DAVID-CHRISTOPHER HARRIS

We knelt, as our mothers' mothers had knelt, beneath both moons: sacrificing to one, fearing the other.

"The Suiu clan celebrates this Rising with joy, with caution." As it did each month, Telilal's voice swept through the forest like a current. "We offer the waters of our rivers so that our own lifewaters may be spared."

I slipped my hands beneath the water, rippling its silver surface. Raising cupped hands from our bowls, I joined my fellows in drenching our clothes, our hair, our skin. I frowned, searching among the trees for the other clan. Only Makara, Voice of the Rains for the Mazu clan, stood among my people.

"Where are the rest of the Mazu?" I hissed to Ezili, but she silenced me with a glare. I shivered, dripping, in the shadows. High overhead, the Myst moon's pearled gaze lit the clearing before us.

The Mazu should have been here by now. *Something's wrong.*

"We offer our color so our color may return with dawn's light." We stood along the forest's edge. As Voice of the Rains, Telilal was the first to enter the clearing, stepping into the light. Beneath the Myst moon, Telilal's vibrant rose dreadlocks drained to pale bone, her brown skin darkening to onyx. Unlight—the pearled glow of the Myst moon—stripped all it touched of color. "May the Myst moon above accept this Rising and shield us from the waterless foe."

I wasn't the only one to glance, nervous, at the second moon hanging in the sky. Through the branches, a red crescent grinned. The Embyr moon. Gooseprickles rose along my neck.

Ezili and I hefted our bowl between us to join Telilal in the clearing, the unlight draining all hue from our bodies. Every Rising vessel was painted to reveal new shapes beneath the Myst moon. Stripped of color, our bowl's painted rivers became too-large eyes, the stylized leaves darkened to feathers. A ghost owl emerged upon the clay surface, pale wings flared beneath a field of stars. Setting our bowl upon the slate-gray grass, Ezili and I lowered a leg calf-deep into its waters. Ezili's hand found mine; her pulse raced beneath my thumb.

Telilal's ivory dreads hung wet against her skin. "By the rains within," she whispered.

"By the waters within," a dozen voices echoed. I raised my face to the night. The Myst moon, pearled as an ancient eye, met my gaze. I held my breath.

Silence. The flutter of a Myst moth through the trees. Ezili squeezed my hand. Water dripped down our bare arms, between our entwined fingers to splash into the Rising bowl: *Plik. Plik. Plik.*

Pli—

The falling drops slowed, then stopped in midair.

And then they rose.

Cries of delight filled the clearing as water bubbled off our hair, our clothes, our toes. The droplets rose like glittering grains of sand, wobbling orbs rising from the bowls at our feet. Ezili giggled beside me. Grinning, I raised my free hand to the Myst moon. Water rippled like quicksilver across my dark skin. Droplets slid up my arm, wrist, palm, trembled upon each fingertip before breaking off like glass beads and floating upward. They joined the torrent of inverted rain around us, falling up, up, ever higher into the unlit sky.

I laughed then, joining Ezili and all our fellow Suiu as our glee rose with the waters into the night. Only Telilal remained composed, beads of water floating off her raised arms. Soaked in water, her bone-white dreads hovered around her face like serpents.

Only when the bowls were empty, our clothes and hair drained of all moisture, did Telilal lower her arms. With solemn steps, she walked to the edge of the clearing. Dawn would reveal Telilal's browned footprints in the grass, the human contact that allowed the Myst moon to draw moisture from anything touching us.

Stopping before a great roseoak at the edge, Telilal glanced at a woman with marbled skin. "Makara." Her eyes turned to us. "Ezili. Atlaua."

My heart froze as she spoke my name. Ezili gripped my hand so hard the fingers cracked. We shouldn't be surprised, Source Lusca had declared the names for the Clouding that morning.

Still.

"Something's off," Ezili muttered as we stepped away from our bowl. We joined Makara and Telilal around a single tree. Ezili stood opposite me, the great roseoak's trunk between us. The Myst moon's touch turned Makara's marbled skin into swirls of darkness and silver. She looked worried; the rest of the Mazu clan were supposed to have arrived a day after her to join our Rising. Yet no one had shown. *Yes, something's wrong.*

"Our waters accepted, we now seek shelter from the waterless foe." At Telilal's nod, my companions drew knives. I hesitated before reluctantly drawing my own. Wincing, I sliced my palm. My lifewater bled out thick, clear as a river. The four of us rested our palms against the gnarled, warm bark of the chosen sacrifice. Dozens of cycles old, the roseoak towered to the sky, star-shaped leaves silver in the unlight. My clear lifewater dripped down its bark, the rough surface dark as ink beneath the Myst moon's unlight.

"Grant us protection, pale Myst. Shield us from the Wither to come."

"By the rains within," the four of us spoke as one. The moment the words escaped our lips, a shudder reverberated from the great oak's core, the groan of something ancient jolted awake.

CRACK.

Makara cried out: The earth beneath us shook. The wood screamed. I struggled to keep my footing as the roseoak's roots writhed, thrashed beneath the soil. The roseoak trembled against my palm as its lifewater bled in rivulets along the patterns of its hard skin, every root and leaf and petal shriveling upon itself.

I looked up. A river of water twisted into the air, swelling as the towering oak shriveled to a cracked, desiccated husk. I wanted to pull back, remove my hand, but no—human touch was required. If any one of us drew away, the Clouding would fail. I grit my teeth, but the roseoak's horrifying screams twisted my gut. Tears broke from my lashes, rising in the night to join the torrent in the sky.

Rains, I hated this part.

At last, it was done. Where the roseoak once towered over us all, a Withered corpse no higher than my waist remained. Wispy threads like greyed hairs were all that lingered of branches that had once reached for every star. The roots had vanished. Standing over the husk, I glanced over at Ezili. Her expression of horror matched my own—knowing what would happen had done little to prepare us for experiencing the roseoak's death firsthand.

Far overhead, the great river of the oak's lifewater twisted in the sky until, at last, it began to expand. Like spilled ink, the watery tendrils smothered the night, splitting and fraying until threads fine as spider silk feathered into mist. Soon the entire sky was an impenetrable layer of clouds, the stars hidden from view. Across the sky, the mists covered the red crescent—that was, of course, the point: protection from the full Embyr moon's Thirst. Only the Myst moon's light pierced the shroud—a pearled halo of unlight.

I shivered. *You're never alone, Atlaua,* my grandmother had whispered. *A presence,* she'd said, protects me through the Myst moon's gleam: A god, a spirit, an entire people. *The Myst will always watch over you.*

"Where the rains rose, they again shall fall." Telilal's voice remained steady as ever. "Our lifewater shielded us from the Thirst to come, the falling waters bringing rebirth to the sacrifice made. By the rains within."

The phrase echoed across the clearing in murmurs. It was always the same, the Rising: euphoria at the start, mournful by its end. I licked my cracked lips—the Clouding caused severe dehydration.

We stared at Telilal, waiting, but the Voice's gaze remained fixed on the clouds.

"Telilal." I jumped at the new, but all too familiar voice. Paces away, Source Lusca stood, frowning. The old woman never participated in the Clouding, but as Source of the Suiu clan, she oversaw in silence. The Suiu clanmark gleamed silver on her furrowed brow.

She didn't look pleased.

Telilal tore her gaze from the sky, as if dazed, before frowning. "It's done," she said at last. "Grab your bowls—"

"Makara!" Source Lusca's fury sent a wince rippling across every face in the clearing.

With a slight grimace, the Mazu Speaker set down the bowl she carried and calmly strode past us to stand before the old woman. "Source Lusca."

The graying Source stood nearly two hands shorter than her, but the leader of the Suiu seemed to tower over Makara. "There was supposed to be double our number this Rising. Where in the blooded rains are the Mazu?"

Makara's face was still as a pond. "I do not know."

Source Lusca scowled. "You're their Speaker, girl. *It is your job to know*. Surely Turso warned you of this dela—"

"No." Makara raised a marbled hand, cutting Source Lusca off. "Had Source Turso informed me of a delay, you would have been the first to know. As it is..." She stared at the Source, eyebrow raised. "I don't know."

"Rains, woman's got a backbone of stonewood," Ezili muttered. Even I shuddered at the thought of speaking to Source Lusca so brazenly. But as Voice of the Rains, Makara was Speaker for the Mazu clan: her voice was calm, unoffending.

I frowned. "Source Turso told you nothing?"

Makara shook her head. "The Myst moon swelled over Mazu valley the day after I left. Since we were coming here, he wished to skip our own Rising and shelter with the Suiu." Makara frowned as something caught her eye across the clearing.

"Skip the Rising?" Source Lusca's eyes widened. "Why in the foul waters would Turso skip the—"

A scream pierced the trees, chilled my flesh like an ice drop splashing down my ear. A flock of mooncrests burst from the branches in a flurry of wings and startled *caws*. I turned.

Sprinting across the clearing was a man, an odd lump in his arms. It was a heartbeat before I recognized Ceto, his unlit face wild, panicked. In the frigid night, steam rose from his over-heated body. *Rains, how long has he been running?*

Makara screamed, dashing towards him. "Ebirah!" Her eyes were fixed on Ceto.

Or rather, the corpse he held.

He set it down on the grass before collapsing beside it, gasping for air. I took a step forward but froze, horrified. The corpse's marbled skin and shaved scalp marked him as Mazu clan. But half the torso was collapsed in, puckered, an entire leg and arm little more than bone and shriveled, dried sinew. My knees turned to water, memories flooding my vision.

Tomil's twisted corpse, her cracked flesh shrunken against every bone—

Terrified murmurs spread amongst the clan. I glanced at Ezili over the shriveled roseoak. We knew. Of course we knew. "Wither," Ezili whispered. "That's...impossible..."

But Makara was sobbing, screaming Ebirah's name, her forehead pressed to his. Ceto knelt in the grass before Source Lusca, palms to the ground, chest heaving. "Source," he gasped. "Found him...ahead...hours...I ran...hours..."

But the Source was already unbuckling her flask, jabbing a gnarled finger at Telilal. "See to the Mazu boy. Gentle, now," she murmured as she tipped water past Ceto's gasping lips. "Slow and easy." Another sip, then another. "Are there others?"

Ceto shook his head. "Just him. He'd collapsed on the path, just lying there...I lifted him, but he wasn't breathing...." His voice trembled. "He was so light...rains, he...he weighed *nothing*...."

Source Lusca gently set a hand on Ceto's head. "Shhh. Another sip, there we are." Bright eyes looked up as Telilal rose from examining Ebirah. "Well?" Source Lusca snapped.

Telilal, normally so strong, was visibly shaken. "The Mazu boy's dead. He probably died before Ceto even found him."

Every Suiu in the clearing gathered near, holding their breath as the verdict left her lips: "He's Withered."

No one spoke. The night felt heavy, crushing all sound around us save Makara's sobs. Finally, I gave voice to what we all thought: "That...is not possible. The Embyr moon isn't full for two more days—"

"Quiet, girl." The old woman's eyes could have melted stone. "Vritra," she barked. "Take Amili and run to the village. Warn them what we're bringing. We'll shroud the corpse, but have all children brought inside. Go!"

As they took off into the trees, Source Lusca turned to Telilal. "Source Turso's a fool, but even he knew better than to send a messenger alone. If he sent that poor boy to tell us something, there's another somewhere. Ceto will show you where he found the corpse—from there, Makara will guide you on the paths to the Mazu." She looked troubled. "Something's happened. Go all the way to their village if you have to, but find Source Turso, and pray to the Myst moon this was an isolated incident."

I glanced at the half-desiccated corpse. "Makara said Source Turso didn't perform a Rising. If the Mazu don't come here to our Rising site, there will be nowhere for them to hide from the Thirst." The full Embyr moon's light pierced everything; only moorcat skin and the Rising protected from its thirsty, withering touch.

Telilal frowned. "It's a two-day journey to the Mazu village. We won't make it there before the Embyr moon's swollen."

The age-rivers on Source Lusca's face deepened with her scowl. "Turso, you backwater fool." The Source's hand raised something around her neck—I saw the cord, but whatever it held lay hidden beneath her tunic. I frowned. Something was glowing beneath her shirt.

The old woman stood there, considering, before pursing her lips. "We have no choice," she decided. "If Wither has struck the Mazu, then we must aid our sister-clan. Take the moorcat tents. Put all our provisions and water into three packs—"

"Four." Ezili hissed something at me, but I wrenched my hand away, stepping forward. I prayed my voice didn't betray the thrashing heart beneath. "I'm the better tracker. Besides, if something happens, they'll need a runner. Ceto can't handle another sprint, and Makara..." I risked a glance towards the Mazu Speaker. Her sobs still filled the forest.

Source Lusca bent to retrieve her flask from the grass, rising from her crouch with a wince. For a moment, she said nothing.

The Source's piercing eyes met mine. "Atlaua goes." Relief flooded my veins even as terror rose to replace it. Source Lusca's gaze was sharp. Beneath the Myst moon's unlight, her face seemed lined in stone, dark and deep and weathered. "The Embyr moon swells in two nights," she said. "Do not stop, do not stray from the path. Return here, or rains help me I'll risk the Thirst to end you all myself."

"Whan that wondrous Moone made oure trees bear Fruit, we wondered at the Stone centers byneath the swete Flesh. We tried everythyng: swallowing them, crushyng ynto powder for Drynk & Poultice, cast upon the hot Fyr, placyng byneath the rose light of their mother Moone. Nothyng. What secrets thes Stones hid, they wolde not yield to us."

—Source Yurlungthur, Cycle 27
Scrolls of the Sources: Suiu secret history

Ceto pointed to a spot just off the trail, between three sapling pines. "There," he said, jutting his chin towards a patch of wood sorrel. "He was curled up like...like a child."

I knelt, backtracking Ebirah's steps, but once it was clear Ebirah had used the Suiu-Mazu trail before stumbling off-path to collapse among the clover, Makara took lead on the journey to her village.

By the time we reached where Ebirah's corpse had lain, both moons had extinguished themselves in the night, their light spent. Light now brimmed over every horizon. The night brightened as the land's natural, self-generated light welled into an empty sky. With daylight, came color: Telilal's scarlet dreads blushed back into hue, Makara's marbled skin returned to its swirling browns and creams.

I glanced back at the Mazu Speaker. Ribs poked beneath Makara's clothes, her face haggard. We were all hungry, but food was too precious to waste before evening. Despite the abundance of water, food was scarce.

We hiked well into the night, but found no other Mazu, living or otherwise. I shuddered. Something was driving us, an unspoken urgency to cover as much ground as possible. Still, it wasn't until well into the next day that we finally crossed the Cocyt river into the Mazu valley.

The Thirst came that night.

We stopped beneath a gnarled river yew, well before night. We ate with haste, a fireless meal of pickled ginger root and rivertack, then rushed to set up tents as the full Embyr moon materialized in the dark sky. Makara and I fled into our tent from the red eye above us, sealing ourselves in darkness. Moorcat tents were precious—even the wealthiest clans had barely a handful. Made from the thick, lightproof skin of moorcats, they blocked the Thirst's deadly touch.

They didn't block dreams.

Tomil grins over me, desiccated skin tight against her skull. She sings as Withered fingers wrap around my throat. "Heed not the promises she makes," she rasps. "She takes, my love, you take and TAKE." She laughs while I choke, the Embyr moon's red light revealing the empty sockets of her eyes and she laughs and laughs and laughs—

—Makara, squeezing my hand. My turn to watch over our tent during the Thirst.

I hugged my knees, listening to Makara's snores. *Tomil.* The voices she heard had always been harmless...until they'd been too much to bear. *They want more,* she'd once said in our bed, voice shaking. *Oh, Atlaua, they're always demanding more.* I'd told her to stop being a fool.

The next Thirst, she'd fled the protective clouds of the Rising. We found her Withered remains the next morning, the skin-wrapped skeleton three steps from our home.

Tomil. I sobbed in the tent's darkness, salt-rain streaming down my cheeks. *Forgive me.*

FINALLY, birdsong heralded the morning. Night had fled, and with it the Thirst. As we left our tents, a fluttering by my ear made me turn. My gasp caught the others' attention: Dozens of glasslike moths glittered around us, their delicate, translucent wings refracting prisms to the forest below.

"Mystmoths?" Ceto's eyes widened, rainbows dancing on his face. "I thought they were nocturnal."

"They are," I said slowly. Bathed in prismatic light, the back of my neck prickled. Mystmoths hunted only in unlight. Their wings were an iridescent splendor in the day, but under the Myst moon they were nearly invisible. To see one brought good fortune. To see dozens was unheard of. "They wouldn't come out like this, not in the day. Not unless—"

"They didn't need to hide from their predator." Talilal's eyes narrowed. "Wait here." She strode ahead, red braids swaying behind her. Makara and Ceto's gazes followed her. Whenever Makara visited the Suiu clan, the two often competed for Telilal's attention. Makara muttered something, making Ceto chuckle.

I looked away, a familiar pain in my chest. Ezili had kissed my brow before I left, whispering in my ear as her cheek pressed to mine. *Rains shield you, my heart.* Five dawns ago, she'd lain a marriage gourd at my feet, but even then the image of Tomil's desiccated corpse haunted me. I'd told her I'd answer after the Rising. I expected anger, but Ezili had only smiled. She knew of my past lover, understood my hesitation.

Perhaps there was another reason I'd volunteered for this journey after all.

Makara was back to staring at the moths. "Wings in light, death at night," she muttered.

I frowned. "What do you—"

Thunk. Something slapped my shoulder, bounced to the grass below. Startled, I picked up the object: A...plant? Bulbed and squishy, the lavender skin oddly pebbled."What in the rains..."

"Unlight save us." Ceto's neck was craned, wide eyes staring at the river yew. My jaw slackened. Dozens—*hundreds*—of myst-moths glittered high overhead, darting through branches bearing countless lavender bulbs. The moths swarmed the strange plants, transforming each into a glittering jewel.

Makara eyes narrowed. "These...were not here last night."

Ceto picked another off the ground. He drew his knife and cut the plant open. The flesh beneath was deep purple, an odd wrinkled stone at the center. "Smells like sweetroot," he mused. Shrugging, Ceto popped a slice into his mouth.

"Ceto!" Makara screamed. Ceto's eyes widened.

"Rains above," he breathed. "That...this tastes *incredible*." He blinked at our horrified faces. "What? No dead moths. Seemed safe enough."

I placed a hand on the yew's bark. "It's...food," I whispered. "Like fruit from the nutbushes but...bigger. Sweeter. On a *tree*." But no tree had done this before, let alone a wispy river yew. I voiced the thought none dared. "These came during the Thirst. The Embyr's light...somehow...did this."

"That's not all it did." Telilal had returned, her voice choked. Wordless, we followed her to a ridge.

"No," I whispered, but Makara was already sprinting, a frenzied yell bursting from her lips. I stood frozen on the ridge, my lifewater ice. Mazu valley lie sprawled beneath us, the Cocyt river glittering through the village below.

And at the village's heart, the corpses.

"This earth protects its children. The watersflow through its rivers, its plants, its beasts…neither Myst nor Embyr moon can harvest it. The clans, it seems, destroy this protection. All we touch—a tree against our palm, the grass beneath our feet, our very bodies—moonlight may consume. If the earth protects its own, then, I reach but one conclusion: We are not of this world."

—Thesis, Yemoja Kmuun:
"Human Consumption By and Of Celestial Bodies"
[unpublished: author found Withered before release]

WE HUNTED FOR SURVIVORS: every home and cellar, pantries, wells, casks—anywhere one could hide from the light. Nothing. What remained of the Mazu people lie in the village square, and those remains were crumbling into dust even now.

…all save one.

We found the corpse of Source Turso in his quarters. The Source lay Withered on the floor by his desk, his desiccated flesh whorled as a dried riverbed. Telilal kicked aside fallen books to squat by the Mazu's leader.

"Same as the ones outside…wait. Rains, what *is* this?" Telilal frowned at the stain of something beneath the corpse, a dried pool of reddish-brown. When she poked the corpse's cheek, the flesh crumbled in on itself. She grimaced. "This doesn't make sense."

"You think?" Ceto snapped. Makara was sobbing in his arms.

Telilal shook her head. "The Thirst was last night. It takes at least two days for Withered corpses to disintegrate."

"What're you saying?"

"I'm *saying* these corpses should still be *corpses*, not dust. These people Withered *before* last night."

"…that's impossible." Ceto's words echoed Ezili's from days ago. "How could an entire clan Wither before the Embyr moon bloomed?"

No one spoke, every gaze but Makara's fixed upon the impossible corpse.

"Ebirah," I said at last. All turned to me. "The Mazu you found during the Rising. He Withered two days *before* the Thirst…"

"Which means the Embyr moon didn't kill him." Telilal blinked, turning. It caught my eye, too—a glint in the half-open drawer above Source Turso's skeletal hand. Reaching in, Telilal pulled out a scrap of parchment and a half-covered bundle. Handing me the scrap, she removed the cloth: A radiant stone lay in her palm, glowing just like—

"Telilal," Makara cried out, "your hair!"

We gaped. In the stone's glow, Telilal's scarlet dreads had faded to pale bone. "Unlight?" My skin prickled. "But…that means—"

"It's from the Myst moon." Telilal's eyes widened as her palm's brown skin darkened to onyx. "Atlaua," she said, voice tight, "the parchment."

All eyes turned to me. Trembling, I gazed at the scrap in my hand. I frowned. "This…is old. *Very* old." The ink was so faded I could hardly make out the words. The letters cut off at the parchment's rip:

…& met with the Embyrsayrs. Thusly agreed for the exchange……… eightscore volume coarse water & twoscore refined, & receive thusly via Tradelight……………fore sevenstone drygrain ea. third Rysing…..

And on the back, in a different hand:

…………of three.
And one and one and one need all
The pale, the red, and we.

O love, forsake the pale Myst moon!
Her pale unlight shines Wither'd doom
Heed not the promises she makes:

She takes, my love! She takes and takes.
Beware that folk, the pearly ones
Who plot upon her surface!
Trust not your gaze, you know her face
But not her people's purpose.

I turned the parchment over, read it once more. "Embyr-sayrs? ...rains, this is a *contract*. An agreement between ourselves and...and the *Embyr moon*."

"Slow the current, here." Ceto shook his head. "You aren't truly suggesting *moons* can make trade deals?"

I thought of my grandmother's stories, of a kindly being watching over us through the Myst moon's light: Sometimes it was a god, sometimes a spirit. And sometimes—

"Not moons," I whispered. "*People*." Gooseprickles rippled along my arms. "People living *on* the moons, who use light —*tradelight*—to reach us. Through it, they can take..." I reached into Ceto's bag, removed the pebbled lavender plant. "...and *give*."

For a moment, no one spoke.

"The fruit," Ceto said slowly. "It grew after the Thirst..."

"It's a partnership." Telilal frowned as she read the parchment. "Or...it *was*. Our ancestors performed Risings to trade with the Embyr moon: Food for water. But something happened. We've stopped. We *forgot*." She glanced at the plant in Makara's hand. "The fruit's a message: These Embyr...people...*want* to trade, rather than steal. But they need water. So what we no longer give freely—"

"—they take, each Thirst." I looked up, horrified. "What choice would they have?"

Ceto rubbed his temple. "Let's *say* you're right. Embyr gave food, we gave water." He eyed the glowing rock. "What do the Myst give?"

"*She takes, my love, she takes and takes,*" I whispered. "They give nothing. Why trade? We give them water freely—or someone *convinced* us to, ages ago. And if we don't..."

All eyes fell upon the crumbling corpse, Source Turso's face contorted as his own tightening skin had frozen his horror.

Salt-rain streaked Makara's face. "Source Turso d-didn't perform a Rising. They...*whoever* takes our water in the unlight...we didn't give anything this time."

"And they retaliated." My voice shook. "Just once, the Mazu didn't offer water....and the Myst people must have killed them for it." Bile rose in my throat. "The Myst doesn't protect us," I spat. "We're their *slaves*."

Silence.

"...how could we not know this?" Ceto whispered.

"*He* obviously did." Telilal kicked Source Turso's remains. She raised the myststone, one eye colorless in its glow. "This came from the Myst moon. Something brought it here...or some*one*." She spat at the shriveled corpse reaching for the drawer. "He was working for them. Or..." She eyed the odd-colored stain beneath the corpse. "He *is* one of them." She looked up, eyes cold. "There must be others."

Something glinting beneath the tunic, the light pale—

"I know one," I said softly.

"I cannot shake this feeling. Does Source Chaac not seem strange, I ask? No, all reply, he is as he always was. But tonight four chosen sliced their palms for the Rising as Source Chaac observed...though my heart tells me he once sliced his palm with pride each Rising. My headaches are growing—my memories feel clouded as the sky."

—Unknown

WHEN SOURCE LUSCA entered her study, we were already there. Waiting.

Old eyes blinked in surprise, but the Source gave a curt nod as she limped to her desk. "Took you lot long enough—I was about to send Iri and Nyami to see where in the rains—"

"Forgive me, Source." My knife flashed quick as a needlefish, the same that sliced my own palm days before in the Rising. It grazed the Source's arm—lifewater welled from the cut, dripped to her elbow. Behind me, Ezili gasped.

The lifewater dripped red.

"Source Lusca…" Ezili's voice trembled—I had told her everything. "Who *are* you?"

Bright eyes narrowed in her weathered face, regarding each of us. Finally Source Lusca grimaced, leaned against the desk. "You know, then." She reached in her pocket, dabbed the cut with a handkerchief. "Turso?"

"Withered."

Source Lusca's eyes lowered. "Old fool," she muttered. "To skip an offering…what in the worlds possessed him?"

I thought of Source Turso's corpse, the dried reddish-brown pool beneath. "He's from the Myst moon, too, isn't he? You… you *both* are."

Source Lusca stared at her handkerchief, stained red with her strange lifewater. "Such a delicate thing, our magic," she murmured. "We can reshape memories and voices, cast our heartspells across planets, but amongst *you* lot, with blood clear as glass, a single cut might expose us." She pursed her lips. "Not that you're aware of glass, or heartspells, or…oh. Oh, my children." She looked up, sadness in her eyes. "So much you cannot fathom. And no time to teach you." Reaching to her throat, the old woman pulled out the necklace from under her tunic: Pulsing with unlight, the myststone rendered her face colorless.

"I haven't stored enough energy to reshape all of your

memories. I could Wither half of you to recharge the stone, but that'd cause more problems than solve, and I don't tolerate sloppy work. So..."

The word she spoke was strange, a harsh, guttural sound. But I knew the scream, the lifewater that twisted through the air, the stone's light flaring brighter with every drop absorbed. It was *quick*, too quick, we had no time—

Where Telilal had stood, a husk remained. Ceto cried out, falling to his knees. Source Lusca's age-rivers deepened as she raised the stone, eyes on the fleeing Makara...

We can shape memories and voices, cast our heartspells across planets.
My lifewater froze.

Tomil trembled. "The offerings...they want...more." The voices had been relentless lately, screaming, demanding. "Make them stop, Atlaua," she begged. "Make them stop, or I will."

The voices hadn't been Tomil's invention. Not at all.

Rage, sharp and hot, flooded my heart. I screamed the word that killed Telilal, its shape harsh, the sounds cotton around my tongue. The light flared brighter—I screamed, again and *again*. It took longer, the liquid lazily swirling in the air, but my rage only grew hotter until Ezili's touch jolted me back. "Atlaua!"

I gasped for air, my throat raw.

Source Lusca lay twitching on the floor, shriveled, half her body Withered. "I..." she choked. "H...ow..." The remaining eye widened as I raised Source Turso's glowing stone in my hand.

"Makara figured it out." My voice rasped. "We didn't understand...How could Source Turso Wither in a windowless study? The Myst moon doesn't pierce into homes. But *this*"—I held the glowing stone aloft—"was in his study. When Source Turso opened the drawer, the myststone's unlight touched him, and..." I grimaced. "The result was clear enough."

Source Lusca gurgled. A hand with only a thumb remaining lurched for her myststone. Ceto tore it from her neck with a snarl. We quickly dropped both stones in a moorcat pouch. The danger of the stones' power during a full moon was past, but Source Turso's death proved the myststones didn't have a single master.

Someone else was watching.

I knelt beside Source Lusca, laid a hand on the cracked cheek. "You were our Source," I whispered. "From the headwaters of my mother's womb, you delivered me. You sang the requiem of the All-Sea as we buried Tomil beneath its waves. You loved the Suiu, Lusca. And yet...you betray us."

She could not weep—the stone had stolen her salt-rains. But she trembled, her age-rivers deepening. Her one eye rolled towards the pouch. "Heal...me..."

"Tell us first," I growled. "Tell us how to stop them."

She wheezed, her breath a death rattle. "With...those...you can go...travel across the void." She whispered a word, harsh and guttural. "Say that...to go...to *choose*..."

"What does it mean?" Ezili asked. "The light, the stones... what *is* this?"

"The Myst...our gift. We traded, once...Illuvia's water. Embyr...food. And they...*we*...our magic. It can do things...oh, children, you...can do...*such* things."

"What?" Ceto growled. "Do *what*?"

But the Source's lips were barely moving. "Wonders," she whispered. "Wonders upon...wonders."

WE BURIED their remains in the All-Sea: Telilal, Ebirah, Source Lusca. The waves glinted orange beneath the Embyr's waning light. I stood alongside my people on the black sands, my brow still burning from the Suiu clanmark etched there that morning. As our rain priests waded into the deep, Makara sang our requiem. She'd accepted my offer to join the Suiu clan. As newly-elected Source, I'd led our clan back to Mazu Valley, to properly bury Makara's people alongside ours. Salt-rain flowed down her marbled cheeks as she sang.

Ezili's hand laced with mine. "You will tell them?"

"We'll tell everyone."

"The Myst will know, Atlaua. Next Rising, the unlight will do what they did to the Mazu—"

"No," I growled. "They won't." I glanced at Ceto and Makara, their hands entwined, expressions determined. "We will use the stones. We'll travel across the Void. We will *find* them."

"The Myst will Wither us the moment we—"

"Not the Myst." I looked up. "*Them.*" High above, a red crescent hung faint in the sky. "We'll seek them," I whispered, "and form a new pact. Then, together…we will deal with the Myst."

Ezili shuddered. I said nothing.

The Suiu fell silent as, beyond the shore, the rain priests raised a death-pouch. "I never answered you," I said suddenly.

Ezili's hand stiffened. I turned, kissed her temple. "Ezili," I whispered in her ear. "Yes."

She said nothing, but her arm found my waist, her head rested upon my shoulder. Makara's song floated over us. Opening the pouch, the priest scattered Telilal's dust in an arc over the waves. I closed my eyes, breathing in Ezili's scent, the sea beneath. *Goodbye, Tomil.*

And when those beneath the waves were at rest, and those above had stood before their new Source and learned terrible truths, the four of us stood together, hands entwined.

"Ready?" Makara whispered. Ceto snorted, but Ezili squeezed my hand.

I looked up. Both moons glowed in the void above: waning and red, waxing and pearled. Unlight peeked between Ceto and Makara's clasped fingers, the other stone between Ezili's and mine. "No," I whispered. "…but neither are they."

I took a final breath in this world, and spoke.

Love them. Teach them. Paint their cage with moons and stars,
that they think it the sky.

—Missive #274 [translated]
Magoi Council to Stheno Lusca
Scrolls of the Sources, Suiu secret history

DAVID-CHRISTOPHER HARRIS

David-Christopher Harris's fantasy publications include "Olam Ha-Ba" in speculative fiction and poetry magazine *Arsenika*, "Last Call" in *The Arcanist Magazine*, "Falselight" on *PageHabit*, and "Children of Ozymandias" in *50WordStories*, among others. He received his M.A. in Medieval Literature, which he uses exclusively to teach his cat Latin. He is currently querying.

He can be found on Twitter and at www.dcharriswriting.com

 twitter.com/d_c_harris

MIGRATION

ANDY DIBBLE

Miriam stood hunched near the peak of the sloping cavern floor, driving a chisel against the bone ceiling. A scrim of pale dust coated her shoulders, sleeves, and the front of her vine-weave shirt. Her snarled hair, entwined with blackberry sprigs, fell slipshod to the small of her back.

Rain struck the floor of the cavern above. When last it rained a month ago, the ceiling was khem, dark and porous, so drinking water just trickled through. But the clan had to eat. They planted blackberry in the fertile ceiling, let it grow, harvested.

But nothing comes free. Grow crops in black khem, and it becomes white and unyielding, good for nothing. It becomes bone.

Miriam cursed as the chisel slipped in her sweaty grip. She let her hammer arm drop. This wasn't her job. She had told Sippora to open a route for rainwater a week ago, but the slack woman dodged the work until it was almost past doing. Miriam could delegate to someone who would obey, but they would grumble. That wouldn't do. She was only clan leader until morning. Then her six-month term would be over and leadership would revert to her husband Aaron. Making demands in the eleventh-hour was no way to bow out.

Everyone would rather laze about than do what it takes to survive. Only two others in the clan wore vine-weave. Everyone else flashspun fabric with alkhemy: drawing slip-signs on khem to make it flake into layers and flex-signs to make it hang. Scrawling signs was easy, but why squander khem when there was vine chaff at hand?

More than once, she fancied ordering everyone to wear vine-weave. They'd obey, but only because Aaron would, and then everything would go back to how it was when leadership reverted to him, leaving only her neighbors' grudges to show for it.

Miriam looked over one shoulder and then the other. "Joshua, stay away from there."

Joshua darted back from the narrow passage, the hood of his gratuitously-pocketed cloak flopping over his shoulder, a replica of the Lilah cloak from Aaron's stories.

Joshua peeked into the passage without technically entering.

"Leave the warren *alone.*"

"I wasn't going to go inside." Her son was a terrible liar, but what eight-year-old isn't? Most children believed their parents when told warrens are haunted by the Luminaries—the people who prospered when the world was young and khemical enough to dig new caves by drawing compress-signs. But every sign ossifies khem. Now migration is a way of life: move into a fresher quarter of the world's viscera, grow crops on the dark scalp of khem, then move on when all is wan and fused into the skeleton of the world.

"Just stay close," Miriam said.

Joshua plopped down, fixed elbow to knee and planted chin on palm. He knew better than to protest. But just moments later, he fidgeted, brandished his own chisel and scraped at the gray ground, only partway ossified because the clan hadn't planted so near the warren.

Miriam watched warily as Joshua etched four arcs, the quarters of a circle turned inside out: a four-pointed star. It woke, like a bed of coals breathed upon, lambent beneath ashes. Joshua wasn't sloppy. The surface was just too far gone, so the light from his sign sparked and sputtered. The only way around that was to compact many signs together, but that made khem ossify faster. Joshua gouged the light-sign, and it winked out.

He started on another sign, drawing one lobe and then another. He completed a second arc; the ellipses fused together.

"No heat-signs, Joshua."

Heat-signs ossify as much khem in an hour as a light-sign does in a week. Their clan would migrate tomorrow, so maybe it didn't matter if Joshua idled away a patch so far gone. But he needed to develop good habits.

"Help me." Miriam thrust a callused finger at the bony ceiling. At eight, and small for his age, Joshua couldn't chip the crust. But chiseling would focus him on things that matter.

Footsteps. She knew that gait. "Miriam, can we talk?"

Miriam wiped sweat from her brow and faced Aaron.

He tilted his head to the side toward their tent.

"Joshua, stay there," she said.

She turned to follow Aaron, down the rise where amaranth stalks lay in windrows. With amaranth, from planting to harvest to winnowing, it is all about season. Never harvest when the flowers burgeon in burgundy or purplish ropes, racking the stalk under a sluggish load of blooms. Wait until the petals are a third browned. Then harvest before insects pilfer the seeds.

She and Aaron had a season too, but that season had passed.

INSIDE THEIR TENT, Aaron poured saffron spice into two cups from a canister he kept in his belt. Spices were the product of multi-step processes, which involved not only sweet- and bitter-signs but slip-signs as well. The khem they were derived from had to be virgin, untouched by signs, or the process couldn't be completed. Botch one step and the intermediate product had to be scrapped. It was sport to Aaron. There was even a bit of competition between him and others in the clan to see who could make this or that spice the fastest. But their haste only made for error.

Miriam wanted to refuse, but Aaron was already pouring water from a bone pitcher.

He waited until she took a sip before saying, "I'm hoping you can lay off Joshua, even just through the night. It's New Year's. Let him have some fun."

"I'm raising him right, even if you coddle him. He'll lead the clan one day, him and his wife. And because you encourage him, he pretends he's a storybook character adventuring after an ever-glowing lantern. I think he actually believes he can find it."

"Today it's Lilah, tomorrow it'll be a new game. It's just a phase."

"And what has Joshua's Lilah phase done for the clan? Haven't you heard Sippora call me Gebira?"

Sippora pretended it was a compliment because, in stories, Gebira was a great alkhemist. But the stories also said she was a one-eyed hag too aloof to care for Lilah and her other children.

"Heh-uh." Aaron swallowed his mirth. "No, I hadn't heard, but it's not Joshua's fault. Or mine. If you're a leader, you have to look the part. Cut your hair, clip your nails, shave, wear what they wear."

She planned to do all that when she didn't have to do everything, oversee everything. How long since she bathed or even washed her clothes?

After a primp and fuss, there was no man better-groomed than Aaron, and he got hairy when he let himself go. He kept two flashspun shirts, less than some, like Sippora. But whenever one tore or frayed, he gave it to one of the children and signed a fresh one. Both buttoned-up, an affectation Miriam never understood. But now a method sewed those steely buttons: his brand.

"Look, I'm sorry for coming after you," said Aaron. "Stash the chisel, Miriam. It's New Year's. Get ready for the celebration! There's water enough until we migrate, and once we move on, we'll find more."

How could he be so glib about things that matter but berate her about hygiene? They might not find the next river, not in strange territory so removed from Inside. Everyone would be thirsty after drinking at the celebration. Maybe rain doesn't come with the new year out here. The clan's survival could not be gambled with.

"And just where are we migrating?" she said.

"Farther out, I think. But if you have other ideas, I'm glad to hear them."

Under Miriam's direction, they'd been milling about from cavern to cavern, weaving inward then out again. Farther out, there were Outsider barbarians. Just last migration, they came across the brutes' hand emblems. How long until they found the savages themselves? She could cry dire warnings, but Aaron would just yank them steadily outward like he did during the first half of the year.

"No ideas. Come tomorrow, you're in charge." Her own words proved peoples' grumblings: she lacked vision. Some of the younger generation even whispered that Aaron should lead them perpetually, instead of he and Miriam trading off at Midsummer and New Year's. The traditionalists wouldn't have it, but generations wither as surely as khem ossifies. Maybe she didn't have Aaron's vision, but better no vision than charging into the unknown after a dream.

"You can still advise me, Miriam. Just because tomorrow it's my term doesn't mean you shouldn't speak your mind."

There were virgin spaces here, moist and supple as clay. But those untouched caves—khemical, bountifully black—invariably fostered inedible vegetation and insect life, transforming the landscape into more of themselves and their offspring, their fruitfulness blighting everything. Steady policing almost eradicated these cancers Inside, where khem was scarcer. If they could stoke that vigilance here, these between-places could be their home.

But Aaron wouldn't listen, no more than he had before. "Just how much farther do you think we can go? We're already on the fringes. Farther out there are Outsiders and eventually the walls."

A scowl overset Aaron's features. He thought the walls at the limit of the world were propaganda endorsed by fools, but she couldn't bear the walls in mind without existential compression: She stood within a shadow, one so immense it had no periphery, and it was cast by a vastness, distant but just as huge. It pondered the moment to crush her.

She shoved the thought and its finality aside. "If we turn back, go inward, at least we know what to watch out for."

"But if we go outward, it might be better, with seldom a thing to watch out for or deny us. Have a little hope, Miriam."

"You know the stories. Outsiders scavenging on the margins of the world, godless, guzzling the blood of their enemies. And the walls—"

"Enough, Miriam. You're working yourself up over stories, just stories."

"Just stories?" How could Aaron call any story *just a story*? "How much have you fear-mongered with stories? Were it not for *your* stories, we'd still be Inside."

Aaron scoffed. "Under the benevolent supervision of our Leader?"

"At least Inside, it was safe." Though she didn't believe what she said. The Leader didn't respond kindly to runaways straying back into his fold. That was why she hadn't led the clan inward when Aaron's term ended and hers began.

"Safe Inside?" His lips twisted dismissively. "For now, maybe, but for how long? The Leader just wants to keep everyone in line."

That was the real reason Aaron led them outward. He knew that eventually—ten years? A hundred years?—Inside would be a wasteland too bony to support the clans that pecked at it. Territory skirmishes would ignite into war. There'd be no containing it.

Aaron grimaced. "I know you don't believe his nonsense about renewing khem."

The Leader spun tales about how we could renew the world through devotion to the god Khem, that if folk only drew signs for heat and light, planted frugally, and migrated often, Khem would take mercy and renew the world, turning bone everywhere into khem. That was a pious lie. But why lead everyone outward on another baseless hope that wilderness will house them when civilization can't? At best it was premature, an act of desperation.

"You know I don't trust the Leader any more than you do," Miriam hedged. When they were Inside, she wouldn't have dared say that aloud. "But rushing about is *risky*, Aaron. We don't know the land, whether we're heading toward or away from water. Out here, do the rains even come this time of year? If you would at least insist on conservation, we would have time to plan our next move, instead of just ossifying one cavern after another and pulling up the tent stakes every other month."

"Miriam, you can't lead by always telling people to do things they don't want to do. Austerity isn't a solution."

"And blindly hoping is?"

"It is, if we hope long enough. If we keep migrating and keep hoping."

MIRIAM LEFT THE TENT. Aaron followed her. He flashed a smile. "I figured we'd fetch Joshua together before New Year's."

Joshua wasn't at the entrance to the Luminary warren.

"I told him to stay here," said Miriam.

"He probably joined up with everyone else." Aaron faced the lower stretch of the camp past the well where dry amaranth stalks lay, ready to fuel the New Year's fire. Though summer expired months ago and the harvest was in, ruddy-red petals speckled the heaped stems.

Most of their clanspeople hunched over wafers of drab khem, carving clocks. Miriam could just make out Puah, the oldest woman in the clan, eyes infested with cataracts but dexterous enough to round off her wafer into a circle and engrave ten neat digits around the rim. In the morning, the first day of the new year, Puah would draw a spin-sign on her clock, its sweeping lobes rotated to avoid obstructing the digits. The spin-sign alkhemically compelled the inner circle of the clock-face around twice each day, seven-hundred thirty-times a year.

Miriam knew this could be Puah's last clock, her last New Year's. How many more migrations could a woman over seventy endure, even with Aaron and the other men to support her? That question suffused into: how many more migrations could the clan endure until their luck croaked, and they boxed themselves in and hit a dead-end in a labyrinth of bone and lost their way, like a mouse caught in the deepest pocket of her satchel? They would backtrack, hoping they somehow missed a vital cave. Then they'd fracture, like when they first quit the Inside under Aaron's leadership. The young and foolhardy would cling to Aaron, but a hardy few would stick with Miriam.

Their all-too-curious son had gone where she told him not to. She said, "No, Joshua's not with the others." Miriam wrenched the knob on her lantern, and it flared brighter. Knowing Aaron would follow, she marched into the dim gullet of the warren.

THE LEADER DIDN'T APPROVE of folk scrounging around in warrens. If people wandered the deep roads and galleries—intestines of history—he assumed the inscrutable writing and contraptions would draw them to the same wastefulness that doomed the Luminaries. They were out of the Leader's reach, this far from Inside. But they'd been under his prohibition a long time. Miriam hadn't been in a warren since she was a girl.

She recalled a realm of delicate bone arches and pillars of fused stalactites, a monument to antique glory. This warren was the same, but now the sign-wrought architecture seemed decadent.

She glanced inside a bone crucible for smelting khem into base metals and metals into alloys. That, at least, was useful. Its inside was worked with a dense pattern of intermingled heat-signs. So many! Did it *evaporate* khem? And it was wide, a cauldron really. Surely they didn't need that much metal. Her gut soured further when the path bent into a declining flight of stairs. How many compress-signs did it take to carve those? And for what?

Maybe the Luminaries deserved what they got. She laughed bitterly, prompting a sidelong glance from Aaron. He looked away when she withheld comment.

"What gets me is the smell," Aaron joked.

"The smell?" Aaron didn't mean smell but its opposite, no-smell. Virgin khem is earthy, loam shot through with cumin. It rots as it ossifies; farmers gag taking in the last harvest before migration. But bone—true white-as-death bone—smells of nothing. How long did the Luminaries suck the rot, burrow deeper to escape it, only to nourish it with their compress-signs? How long until they abandoned their homes or at last triumphed over rot by ossifying their livelihood entirely?

Aaron walked briskly on her left, but not so busily as she did because his stride was longer. His gaze roved over the neat rows of writing alongside them, serenely coveting secrets.

Or that was how Miriam assumed Aaron judged it. For her, writing was just more waste. Beneath the indecipherable script were the grayest parts of the warren—the least ossified—but that was only because writing rendered its host surface useless for signs. Why did Aaron care? He couldn't read a lick of it.

When the path leveled and widened into a storehouse, Aaron's pace slackened. Miriam didn't let up. She didn't care whether the weapons about were for battle or ceremony; whether the instruments were for music, science, or torture; or how many pairs of binoculars, contorted flasks, and wardrobes full of gaudy robes leaned atop one another just outside the pool of her lantern light. However genius their alkhemy, the ghosts could keep their treasures.

She needed to find their son.

"Miriam." His voice was tinged with awe.

"What..." The rest shriveled on her lips. Her glare softened, tracked upward, and she beheld the prismatic spray of their lanterns' light.

A statue rose with ozymandian majesty into the vault of gloom above. It wore breastplate, girdle, and flowing cape and wielded outstretched spear, diving headlong into battle. Aaron sighed, twirled his lantern, and the statue's mighty legs flung rainbows that looked like the ribs of an empyrean whale.

Glass like this is possible? The Luminaries crafted spy glasses, spectacles, and—legend said—microscopes keen enough to spot the signs on the husks of seeds. But all those were trinkets, a lens ground this way or that. This monument stood more than twice as tall as Aaron. And it was made entirely of glass.

Aaron gaped again but not upward where rainbow and twinkle tapered into unseeing. He pointed to the warrior's foe, a second statue, greater in dread, no less in majesty, one scrupulously ossified. It was a woman but so wound with snakes, it could be snake and human hybridized. Silvery earrings hung from her ears. She stared past the shoulder of the onrushing glass warrior, seeing some threat the other did not.

And at its base, a heap of shattered clocks. There were hundreds easily, thousands maybe. How many years of clocks? The tradition of shattering clocks on the last day of the year was old, but being in a warren, this mound meant it was Luminary-old.

"That must be Bone," said Aaron, still pointing to the glass woman.

It had to be. Khem's elder sibling, the mother of dragons, the serpents that worm through the fringes of everything, guzzling khem, sapping the world.

"Which makes this one Khem," Miriam added. The god-that-is-the-world, Bone's younger brother, her cosmic enemy. Inside an unadorned khem pillar was marker enough for Khem; a femur or twisting snake or both together meant Bone. But these Luminaries raised grand icons.

Miriam shook the sight off. "Let's get on, or Joshua will get farther ahead." By now, he could've fallen into a crevasse, broken his neck, suffered any number of horrible deaths in the darkness.

"I'll go this way." Aaron pointed past the twin monuments. He was younger than she, his eyes surer. He must see a way she could not.

"We meet back here in an hour," she said. The interval would persist seconds longer. The spin-signs on their clocks ran slow after ossifying for a year.

THE PATH CURVED ABRUPTLY, and Miriam stumbled over a sprawl as wasted as the clocks at the base of Bone's statue. There wasn't much of worth among the insect husks, shreds of vine chaff, razor shards of glass, and mounds of ash, but a slim bone flute caught her eye, whole amidst all the squalor. Why not seize it and use it, just for the celebration? Better that this flute pine and sigh one last time than leave it slumbering here until the end of time.

Taking it wouldn't be grave robbery, more like accepting a baton from a spent runner, like one of a crew dedicated to Khem, sworn to run in a relay for a year and a day. She pictured herself rushing onward—toward...toward what? An image of the walls at world's end erupted with her thrashing against them.

She stuck the flute in her trouser pockets.

Echoes of Aaron's baritone ambushed her. "Miriam, I found him!"

And Joshua's shrill, "Come back, mom!"

Miriam turned on her heel and dashed the way she came, only curbing her pace enough to avoid obstacles and depressions as they zoomed into the range of her lantern.

When the path widened into the storeroom, Joshua was there, gripping his father's hand, smiling guiltily.

Miriam hugged Joshua, lifting him off the ground, the folds of Joshua's Lilah costume bunching in her embrace. Joshua relaxed when no rebuke came.

But she couldn't let him off so easily. "I thought we decided you weren't going to come in here."

"I wanted to find Lilah's ever-glowing lantern." Momentarily, Miriam believed it, could believe anything after beholding the glass monument to Khem. But commonsense set in, and it couldn't be. Maybe there were ever-glowing lanterns according to boy-logic, but nothing could burn forever, nothing could shine or move without ossifying khem, which was finite, however vast the khemical honeycomb might be.

"Did you find Lilah's lantern?" Aaron asked.

Why did Aaron lead Joshua on, coddle his fantasies? Joshua was getting to an age where he had to face facts.

"I think so," said Joshua. He held out a thing of brass and glass, all curves, vaguely lantern-shaped, with a handle. But it wasn't shining. "It needs some work." He regarded Miriam warily. He probably thought she'd make him leave his "ever-glowing lantern" behind.

"Let's get back to camp," she said. "We don't want to miss the celebration."

BY THE TIME the three reached the camp, the New Year's festivities were already underway, dancers whirling in pairs, parting and coming back together. Reuben kept beat on a drum made from a sheet of khem worked over with flex-signs and pulled taut over a kettle. He was the stoutest in the clan, a bruiser who made opposing clans think twice about raiding. But they were Outside now; rivals were scarce. He farmed and supported older folk during migration.

Puah, hunched over, hummed to the ditty that Sippora played on her flute.

Miriam and Aaron approached the celebration, Joshua loping around them. Their feet crunched on stray amaranth stalks and browning flowers.

"They're back!" Reuben shouted, and Aaron hailed him.

Sippora frowned at Miriam but said sweetly, "You playing this year?"

Miriam hadn't considered the flute-shaped bulge in her trousers. "Did last year." But she wouldn't play, not tonight. Sippora was a better flutist than she was.

"But last year was before Aaron set us on our path."

Aaron planted himself between them, hands raised to ward them back, though neither advanced. "You two sure you want to go through New Year's like this?" A command formed on his lips but fizzled. He wasn't leader yet.

Sippora snapped erect.

Miriam offered her hand. "How about we bury the hatchet?"

Sippora regarded it as though it wasn't attached to a human appendage. Her grimace slipped when she caught Aaron's eye on her.

She shook Miriam's hand, hard. "I won't have to take orders from you until Midsummer anyway."

So much for forgetting old wrongs on New Year's.

Miriam surveyed the feast, a spread of brown-speckled amaranth seed patties fried in amaranth oil on a bed of maroon-veined amaranth leaves. Beside was a spiced garnish of pulped blackberry. Aaron pried the seal off a pot of blackberry beer, brewed last New Year's. It had been nestled in the clan cart since they left Inside.

The clan's table was indistinguishable from the ground until they reared it with emboss-signs, much like the feast was just pliant khem until it burgeoned from the walls and ceiling. They'd let the blackberry crop ripen thoroughly so that it encrusted the cavern ceiling into a skull. The berries weren't any more nutritious, but they were plumper, juicier, singularly sweet. After chiseling for more than an hour to pay for the luxury, she might as well enjoy it.

Miriam watched Joshua over with the children, muddy khem smeared on his face. He scrawled light-signs in the muck on his cheeks, conjuring an ailing neon glow. After sprinting up the incline, he launched his palm-sized clock over the descent. It arched, plummeted, and burst on the cracked ground.

Joshua sprinted back down the slope, knelt down, and set upon gluing clock shards together with khem. He formed them into the shape of a man holding a slender shard, a spear. He picked at the end of his fraying Lilah cloak, tore free a gauzy layer, punched a hole with his finger, and tied it around the man's neck. Next he assembled a winding snake, a dragon. He set the man upon the dragon, struggling in front of the firelight, like a puppet in a philosopher's cave. When the dragon was rubble, he raised the victorious slayer high. But its shadow on the cavern wall was skewed.

The dancers—Sippora, a few others of her generation, and a gaggle of children—looked dizzy from whirling. The musicians exchanged wry smiles, then picked up the tempo. The dancers faltered as the tempo picked up again, but at last succumbed with a flight of breathless giggling.

The musicians rose to fill their plates. As they returned, Aaron signaled he was about to begin a story. Everyone quieted.

"Who wants to hear a story about Lilah and her ever-glowing lantern?"

All the children cheered, Joshua loudest of all. He giggled and flailed his limbs, even after other children had quieted. Come morning, Miriam would have to talk to Aaron again. So what if it was New Year's? It was time for Joshua to grow up, and Lilah stories weren't helping.

"It was New Year's in Lilah's clan," Aaron began. "All their old clocks were shattered, just like ours. But in her clan, they called it the Timeless Night because they know what a New Year's without clocks can do. In fact, in her clan they had a rule against drawing spin-signs on the Timeless Night.

"Now, Lilah's clan was further on in the evening, the musicians had stopped playing, everyone was full to bursting and all the storytellers were too tired to spin another yarn. With the fire down to embers, everyone staggered to their tents squinting in the dimness, because by then, night mellowed over all light-signs, binding them until day." Aaron flashed an infectious smile. "Do you think that Lilah went to bed too?"

"No!" all the children shouted.

"And why's that?"

"Because she has an ever-glowing lantern," one of the children cried.

"Because she didn't want to waste the *magic*," Joshua said.

"You're both right," said Aaron. "Anyone know about the magic on the Timeless Night, what magic there is *tonight*?"

"People can run really fast, like a river," said one child.

"And you can climb without falling."

"Compress-signs press faster, so you can burrow through a wall in no time at all."

"Right!" said Aaron. "On the Timeless Night people can run like a river, climb like they're moseying from one cavern to the next, and signs work faster." Which was nonsense, of course, but that didn't stop him. "But the problem is that no one can see. Even with all the magic, it's night, and light-signs don't shine, and by morning the magic will be spent." His fingers spread like smoke.

Everyone knew what would happen next, even those who trusted Aaron's flair for innovation.

"That is what made Lilah's lantern so special. She just turned the knob on it, right here." He lifted his lantern and flicked the mechanism. "And it glowed bright as day. Even during the Timeless Night." His voice dropped. "But that was her secret. No one else knew about her lantern.

"Hidden by her cloak with a dozen pockets, Lilah scampered off, turning her lantern on when she was out of sight. Infused with the magic of the Night, she sped into the next cavern and leapt into another. Beside her was a waterfall streaming through the air like a ribbon.

"She noticed the fire of another clan and stopped. By the cheers, they weren't through celebrating. Maybe she could join them. But when she got close, she saw ogreish men sharpening spearheads. Women were drawing sigils of war on the mens' chests, not with amaranth dye but their own blood. Their crafty one-eyed leader bound a thrashing serpent to a ribcage altar and said a prayer to Bone, who knows all endings. He sliced the snake open and unwound its innards. He declared the omens for the coming year good. Tomorrow they would go reaving."

Most of the children were too young for this talk of blood omens and reaving. Miriam ground her teeth, just short of the requisite chutzpah to upend his story.

Aaron took another swig and said, almost offhandedly, "As Lilah scampered off, she saw their banners. They bore the pillar emblem of the Leader."

Some of the parents leaning drunkenly against one another gasped. Folk weren't ready to be party to vilifying the Leader, even if only through a children's story. Those much younger than Miriam—Sippora and the rest—couldn't remember life outside the boundaries set by the Leader, his bureaucrats, and police.

Aaron didn't acknowledge the airy outcry. "Lilah hurried back to the tents of her clan to warn everyone. Even come morning, no one believed her. Lilah was just a silly girl, and no one imagined the Leader could be close.

"But Lilah knew that the Leader's agents were fast approaching. She'd overheard their plans. They would slip rogue-like through the adjacent cavern, and come first light..." Aaron thrust down, impaling an imaginary sleeper with an imaginary spear. "Lilah couldn't sleep, only laid awake in her bedroll next to her father, flicking her lantern on and off beneath the blanket.

"She had to do something. It was still hours before morning, so the light-signs on everyone else's lanterns and staves couldn't shine. She bolted up and raced through camp, her ever-glowing lantern shining as brightly as she could make it shine. 'Wake up, everyone!' she cried. People woke, some protesting because it was early, but then they saw light outside their tents. That proved it was day. And that is how, when the Leader's men attacked, everyone was ready to fight them off."

"I THINK MIRIAM SHOULD TELL A STORY," said Sippora. "What's it you say, Aaron? 'Everyone knows at least one story'?"

Aaron didn't answer. He glanced sidelong at Miriam, trying to know her thoughts.

"She didn't at Midsummer." Sippora shook her head. "Not last New Year's, either. Show us we're going to miss you leadering."

Aaron shot Sippora a hard look. That was uncalled for, even on New Year's, even though Miriam was only clan leader for a smattering of hours.

"No need to twist Miriam's arm," Aaron said.

She could refuse, but she was still clan leader. She couldn't back down. "It's all right, Aaron. Sippora's right. Everyone knows a story. But not just any story. Everyone knows a *particular* story."

Some could even guess it, the story told in one shape or another from the Mother of Waters in the heights to the cimmerian shores of the Downsea, where all rivers flow. In the seclusion of the family tent, every mother tells this story to her daughter when she thinks her mature enough, every father tells it to his son. It is told only once, and not publicly.

But after Sippora's goading and so much frivolity on the cusp of migration, everyone needed a hard reminder about the way the world *really* worked. Lilah's flight in the Timeless Night shuddered before her mind's eye. Wasn't New Year's a night for daring?

Miriam drew herself up. "The world was new, once, when Khem was young, because the whole world is Khem's body. Back then, no one had to migrate, but everywhere was lush and fresh." This was lore, but no one needed much convincing that it was also history. They saw a whitening world with each migration. It must have been pristine, once. "But Khem could not be innocent forever. His older sister would make him wise." Miriam inhaled the smoky air. She respired. "That sister was Bone. That sister was death.

"Bone wrested Khem and overpowered him because who can wrestle death and win? Held in a stranglehold, Khem surrendered. 'Survival will cost you,'" Miriam rasped, but her imitation was poor. She let up. "Bone, the Broodmother, demanded tribute, food for her young, the innumerable dragons that worm through lush places, sapping the world.

"And so Khem created man from himself, a clever beast creeping through his caves, his insides and outsides. At first the man knew only dark and groping, but he discovered signs for light and heat, for stretching and spinning, and one for transmutation. And so Khem became white and stark and unlistening. Khem became Bone.

"The man woke in the night, his food stores frothing with maggots, the land around desiccated, a desert of chalk. And fumbling, contending by the feeble light of early-morning light-signs, he migrated outward.

"A dragon ambushed him, but it was young, unaccustomed to the hunt and frailty of its prey. The man fled, tossing aside his pack and walking stick. Truly lost, he tripped into a deep well. He only just clutched an outcrop as he fell. With his free hand, he found a moist knob, not new but new enough, *mercy* from Khem."

A few bitter chuckles tinkled in the audience. They knew how the story ended.

"The man drew a light-sign and squinted into the depths of the well. A dragon raged below, roused by the dim sign, more terrible and aged than the whelp above. It thrashed in the water, inpatient and indomitable.

"There might be a way up, if he tore his hands bloody on the climb or if he, by alkhemical wit, molded the knob into sticky putty, or stakes, or a fierce light to guide his way. But whatever he did, the dragon whelp at the top would nab him as he escaped. And if he dropped into the depths, the aged dragon would devour him at once.

"A fragrance brushed his nostrils. Beyond his reach, blossoms hung like grapes on a vine. He edged along the outcrop and did not consider the vine and the khem it sacrificed to the beauty of the blooms. He should destroy the root at once. In time, it would overtake not only the knob but crumble his handholds. He did not think. He only leaned deep into the blossoms and foolishly stuck out his tongue for a drop of nectar."

MIRIAM JOLTED AWAKE. She expected trouble, given the indiscretion of her story, but it wasn't even morning. Aaron's breath washed over her from above, and the heat of his body snuck into her vine-weave bedding.

Aaron had shaken her awake.

"Joshua's gone," said Aaron with intemperate worry.

"Gone? What?"

"He's not here." Did Joshua believe that fiction about Lilah's ever-glowing lantern and Timeless Night abracadabra? He wouldn't have dared run off if not for Aaron's ridiculous story.

She couldn't see his face in the dark. But he would picture anger blossoming on hers. So she pictured sheepish guilt on his face.

"What time is it?" said Miriam.

"Almost morning, I think." If Aaron's was right, they'd be able to see farther than their own feet, if they packed light-signs tightly.

"Did anyone see him leave?"

"I'm not sure yet," Aaron said.

"Ask around! Talk to Sippora first. If Joshua's not in camp, past her tent is the only way out." A grim possibility, but one that couldn't be ignored. "Unless he went back into the warren." If Joshua wandered down there, by now he could be anywhere in that maze.

She couldn't see, but she knew Aaron paled. Her husband was charismatic, a genius storyteller, visionary, maybe even wise, but he was worthless in a crisis. "You think he would go back in there?" he asked in a rush. "He knows we have to migrate today."

Migration could be delayed another day. But only one. There was little to drink and nothing to eat after last night's splurge, nothing not already earmarked for migration, and scant khem to grow anything, even if they could linger for another harvest.

Sippora and her friend, a shrew-faced woman named Zippa, had stayed awake all night, swilling the last of the beer and gossiping in the dark.

They told Aaron about hearing someone slip past her tent. She hadn't gone out to figure out who it was, but no one else had been out in the night. It must have been Joshua. Aaron ordered her and Zippa to check the warren, just to be sure. Zippa protested but obeyed. Sippora took it for what it was: reproof.

Aaron ordered Reuben and Puah to tend to the children and wrangle them into loading the cart. Aaron, Miriam, and the other eight adults went to search for Joshua as well as ten could.

They went the way they came when their clan migrated last, leaving their encampment through the only exit other than that which led into the warren, so Miriam had a feel for it. Or she thought she did.

The path branched again and again—more times than her memory testified. Each time they called for Joshua, and each time only echoes came back. When an offshoot was too curved to scout at a glance, Aaron ordered one of their number to investigate. They'd regroup at day's end.

Before long, it was just she and Aaron rushing along the main way, following the slashes they'd left when they last came through here. Aaron glanced around, squinted at shadows as the darkness shifted around the globule of their lanterns' light. With the others about, he had put on a front. But now the veneer was gone.

The passage widened into a cavern. "Joshua! *Joshua!*" Again, no response.

An etching of an upright hand as tall as Aaron confronted them. When last they came by here, Miriam had guessed this sigil a warning. Aaron thought it was swearing an oath. Whatever its meaning, it was alien, an Outsider thing. Last time, Miriam had taken them the other way.

But now going the other way meant turning around with Joshua unfound.

"Now do you regret filling Joshua's head with stories?" she asked.

"If you hadn't scared him with that hopeless story, the man trapped in a well, maybe he wouldn't have run away."

"You think he's afraid? Our son's reckless enough to wander into a warren alone, why would he be afraid?"

"Joshua's gone. He's *gone*, Miriam."

His helplessness severed her own. Blame was useless. They wanted the same thing, and her husband was just flung wayward by the upheaval of his mind. She had to help him through that. They would find Joshua. Then, they would migrate.

Gradually, as though Aaron might skitter, she embraced him, breathed deep, exhaled. Breathed deep again and exhaled. He imitated her. His hyperventilation eased.

As if putting themselves in order could put the world in order, astonishingly there was Joshua, rushing to them. For a moment, he seemed more spirit than boy.

"Joshua," said Aaron, blinking, tears fleeing the corners of his eyes. "Where were you?"

"I fell down a hole, and they found me."

A dark-skinned woman approached them, her eyes piercing, seeking. She was astonishing but not a spirit; she was too solemn and solid to be fiction. She sported elaborate jewelry, some piercing the cartilage of her ears, a ring through her left nostril. Silvery loops bit through the skin of her upper arms and shoulders, like a thing mechanized, a relic of a Luminary warren.

Inscrutable tattoos framed her forehead and cheeks, wound down her neck and past the collar of her flashspun smock. It was vibrant, dyed in flowing bands of amaranth-red and maroon, lush greens and ocher, dyed colors Miriam couldn't name—colors she hadn't seen, except maybe in the iris of another's eye.

"I am one of the People." The People? She hadn't really thought they would call themselves Outsiders, but something fearsome, surely. Stories said Outsiders were faithless, clanless, vying with dragons in the wilderness, dueling with one another, gulping the blood of their enemies. But stories never told of Outsider women.

Aaron found his voice first. "The People?"

"Yes. What do you call yourselves?"

Aaron shrugged. "Haven't met another clan in a while, not much need for a name."

The woman cocked her head. "We hoped to leave you alone, but your son fell into a well outside our camp, and unused wells are often the nest of dragons."

"Dragons?" she and Aaron said at once. Was that a joke? But the woman's face didn't admit even an uptick of smile.

"An old nasty dragon?" said Joshua. It seemed he'd rather wait in a well until a dragon made his acquaintance than be rescued and miss the opportunity.

The woman made a toothy smile, no different from how anyone smiles at the things children say. "A young dragon. They migrate outward as they age to where the land is newer and able to sustain them."

Miriam was about to pry, but Aaron said, "I'm Aaron. This is my wife Miriam and my son Joshua. I lead a clan of refugees from Inside." He held his hand out in greeting.

The woman looked like she didn't know what to do with it, but she grasped it with both hands and shook vigorously, not even letting go once she began to speak. "My name is Ashera. It is good to meet you." Still shaking Aaron's hand, she added, "I didn't think your people were comfortable touching strangers."

Noting Aaron's unease, Ashera released his hand.

"We will learn each other's ways," said Aaron.

"This word 'refugee,'" said Ashera. "I am not familiar with its meaning."

"It means that we migrated to escape a political challenge where we lived. 'Politics' do you know that word?"

"I believe everyone knows what 'politics' means." If anything, Ashera's smile was wider than before. "My clan and I celebrate New Year's this evening—"

"This evening?" Miriam said. "We consider the new year already here."

"We prefer to anticipate." Ashera frowned, finger to her lip, as if waiting for the right word to surface. "We prefer to *look forward* to the new year and pass over the last in silence. Would you celebrate it with us?"

"Unfortunately, our clan must migrate today," said Aaron. He seemed genuinely saddened, and perhaps he was.

"So soon?" Asked Ashera.

"'Celebrate much, migrate soon,'" said Aaron. His mouth slung open, mute recognition that she might not have understood the adage.

But Ashera smiled wanly, nodded. "You are welcome to our celebration."

"We can't leave our clan during migration," said Aaron.

"Please understand," said Ashera. "My invitation does not extend to your family only but to your entire clan. Celebrate New Year's with us, then migrate tomorrow."

"There are many of us," said Aaron. "And we do not have much to contribute."

"You would be our guests. All of you," said Ashera.

Miriam said, "Your clan must camp in a lush place if you can accommodate another so easily."

"We would not extend this invitation to just anyone. Your son did a noble thing by running off."

"A *noble* thing?" asked Miriam. Did Ashera really mean "noble," or was that just another word mangled?

Joshua chimed in before Ashera could explain. "It was the Timeless Night, and I thought that with a lantern like Lilah's I could run far enough and climb high enough to find a way through the walls at the end of the world, so that you wouldn't have to worry so much and fight with dad." Joshua held his "ever-glowing" lantern out. "But the lantern didn't glow forever. I tried to run back, but I fell into a well."

"He did what the best of my people do. We look for a way out."

"You've seen the walls?" asked Miriam.

"Walls? What walls? There is only a world becoming bone, and that world cannot sustain us forever."

THE PEOPLE'S camp was mostly children and the very old. Younger men and women were scattered about, tending to the children or finishing preparations for the feast, but too few for this many youngsters. Everyone wore flashspun clothes, dyed-yellow or amber or florid pink—a mosaic of color. Most had piercings—signs of rank?—though none so many as Ashera. The color was too much, garish even, but many were laughing. No one was gaunt or reserved.

If so many of their adults spent their time in the outer wilds, searching for this "way out," it was a terrible waste of labor. But they were a different people from her own, with different values, and Miriam couldn't deny they'd done well for themselves. They hovered above the daily struggle.

Ventilation was poorer, so the fire was not as large as that of the night before. The feast was grand: a hearty stew of root vegetables, amaranth patties spiced with turmeric and saffron, and succulent salmon. Inside, salmon was almost extinct due to overfishing, and the Leader reserved spices for those nearest him.

Many of the People held bone flutes or lyres in their laps, but no one played. They waited for Ashera. "This is a story familiar to my people," she began. "Though I will tell it again, for the sake of our guests, and for the sake of us all. It tells of the search for Sky."

A few sighs of realization breezed among the People.

"What's Sky, mom?"

"Shh, Joshua, let our host tell the story."

A MAN OF OUR CLAN, newly come of age, went to seek Sky. He vowed not to return until he found it.

Bone did not wish for anyone to escape her domain. She boasted to her brother, "I'll dissuade him."

Khem regarded his most ancient enemy with a condescending smile. "Your persuasion kills. *I'll* dissuade him."

With only his shadow to measure himself against, the man climbed into a high cavern that belched forth molten khem and ashes. Khem erupted before him in volcanic splendor. His eyes blazed like thrice-mingled light-signs, and a mane of fire wreathed his face. He plucked the man from the heaping ash and said with a voice like thunder, "You presume to search for Sky?"

The man sputtered, but Khem's question could not go unanswered. "I swore I would."

"Words are wind." Khem breathed whirlwinds. "Turn back!"

The man figured he'd be dead already if Khem sought his life. So he said, "What kind of person would that make me?"

"A prudent one." Khem's grip tightened perilously. "Your mortal years are too few to find Sky."

The ashes stirred and sighed, breathed laughter like falling sand, and said, "*My persuasion kills?*"

Disgraced, Khem withdrew into the earth.

The man hurried on, but the ashes stirred and followed him wheresoever he turned.

The cavern path contracted, grew hoary and wan, but the man loathed to backtrack. Everything behind was known; Sky could only be farther out. So he went on, and came to a warren of our ancestors. At the threshold, the ashes trailing him knit into a winding sheet. A woman filled the shroud. Her eyes stared without focus, and her skin was like porcelain.

"Sky can wait," she said.

Her sheet unwound and wound around them both. She caressed his check; that touch lent sweet repose. She kissed him on his neck, and even that was high delight.

But her breath smelled of nothing, and her tongue was forked.

The sheet fell as he drew back, and he beheld her entirely. She was pale, powdered, like the corpse at a wake. And behind the pallor, she was dead.

"Stay," she wailed. "I can give you children. For Sky is too far away for you to find. Only your children will have enough years to find Sky."

"Lady," he said, retreating. "I do not think our children would have any years at all."

From his deep place, Khem saw his sister's failure and grinned. He broke from the ground, but flameless, his glory veiled.

But Khem's lantern shined merrily. How could that be? It was night; every light-sign was stoppered. This lantern was brass and glass, a core of muddy khem, a simple thing. How could day cling to it alone?

"Trade?" said Khem. "My lantern for your quest?"

The man's clan would marvel if he brought this wonder

home. But his honor overburdened that vision: the shame of giving up was greater.

Khem plucked a glass shaft from his cloak. "This prism sprays darkness. Look."

The man touched the tender darkness surging from the prism and shivered when it touched him back.

"Lantern and prism are yours, if you give up your quest."

"My honor for two trinkets?"

Khem smirked. He knew his mark was almost won.

From her secret place, Bone saw that smirk. She roused her dragons. With haste, they might slay the man before a bargain was struck.

Khem offered a spyglass to the man. "This glass is keen enough to spy the subtle signs on the husks of seeds. Look."

The man spied the secret of seed growth. With study, he could rear a harvest five or ten times heartier. There would be more than enough for everyone.

But no sign comes free. He might grow more with less, but less isn't nothing. He might conserve, but every year the world would still be a little whiter. Everyone might conserve and still plod toward that final bony end.

"This is wondrous," the man said. "But it isn't an escape, it isn't Sky."

"Man of khem, do not shrug off my aid so rashly. Know that my sister sends her brood to claim your life. I could be your champion, if you give up your quest."

"How odd. The Khem I hear of is noble, merciful. He'd never stoop to ultimatums. You must be another, some pretender."

Khem unveiled his glory. His eyes blazed again; fire wreathed his face. "I have mercy on whom I have mercy." The man would plead, for every mortal fears death.

The man lifted his chin. He did not look away.

"I will save you this once," said Khem, "but only to prove our enemy is the same."

Khem whisked them to a lush place. He plucked a lump from the cavern wall, pressed a mesh of signs into it, and let it writhe and form itself into a soldier on the cavern floor. It hammered its signs into the mud, replicating itself.

When the dragon brood rumbled in, they met the spears of the golem army. Khem charged into the fray, and the man ducked after him. They stood shoulder-to-shoulder, spears everywhere, skewering the web of serpents. Their killing was clean, all-at-once. Not Bone's degradations, her rasp and whimper.

At the end, Khem pumped his fist triumphantly and clapped the man on the back.

"Renounce your search! Then my armies are yours." His golem army reassembled. "You will never be defeated."

Victory was sweet, but the man saw the golem army was stiffer, bonier than when it was born. He remembered: never is a long time. "Giving up would be its own defeat."

"Your choice is to be a victor or a corpse! Sky is held from you."

"Let me be a corpse that sought Sky, rather than a victor standing alone among corpses." The man turned his back, put the desolation behind him.

That evening, Bone slipped into the man's shadow and unstuck from his heels. "You've taken me to and fro about the earth, and I've never given you anything for your trouble."

"That so?"

"I can make you see truth and lie plainly, without any penumbra at all. You only have to do one more thing for me."

"Give up on Sky?"

"That's right."

"And why would I do that?"

"Because then you'll know Sky when you see it. How will you find it otherwise?"

The man was done with her. There was no point in haggling

anymore. He turned his back again.

His shadow flitted to a broad cavern along his path, so vast even the light of a thousand lanterns would be lost in mist and distance.

The man reached that broad cavern and spied a marker above the entrance. It read: "Sky." He went to tell his clan of his success.

***

THE PEOPLE CHUCKLED or hollered as Ashera finished the story. Some suppressed their mirth until her last word. Reuben and two others of Miriam's clan followed, but their chuckles were throaty and delayed.

Miriam would have scoffed were it not for her hosts. The man in Ashera's parable was a fool, declining boon after boon even after he knew that his fabulous goal was unattainable, and then at last he was tricked by a word? Was that the moral, that even the most principled can fall prey to naiveté?

Ashera didn't chuckle or acknowledge the approval of her clan. She waited for her guests to respond.

Joshua spoke first. "So Sky isn't a really big cavern?"

"Why do you say that?" Ashera said, like that was just the question she'd been waiting for.

"Bone tricked the man into thinking a big cavern was Sky, so it can't be," Joshua said. "That's what the story says, right?"

"I think I and all my clan would like to know what your story means, Ashera. We've never heard of Sky before," said Aaron.

"Not every answer comes easily, Aaron of Inside. Allowing only what the story tells outright, maybe even Bone and Khem don't know where Sky is. Maybe they just said things to trip him up."

Miriam thought Ashera more of a straight-talker, but evidently, not when it came to this story. "You say answers don't come easily, but you must have an interpretation. What do you think Sky is?"

Ashera paused, considering her words. "Sky is a place where everyone can live and no one has to migrate. It's out there." She motioned toward the wall that was furthest from Inside. "Beyond, like the realm in which stories unfold."

Miriam's eyes narrowed as a thought condensed. "So the man really believed that if he just kept going eventually there would be no more caverns and he'd be...*somewhere*?" Miriam motioned too but awkwardly. She couldn't find the words. "Like you said. Beyond."

Now it was her clan that chuckled, though many stifled it. Her people judged it absurd—and well they should. There's no such thing as a place outside a cavern. *Cavern* is just part of what "place" means.

"Beyond" meant a backside to the walls. And beyond that plane...what? A void? She pictured a breeze tickling a serpent's back, swaying as the snake undulated. The walls undulated too, and they were not khem but a cosmogonic dragon constricting everything, Bone wrestling Khem into a stranglehold.

"What the man really believed isn't in the story," said Ashera without acknowledging the tittering of her guests. "But I'll tell you what I like to think."

Everyone quieted.

"I like to think Sky is the far side of that last big cavern, lost in mist and distance. Bone tricked him just in time. Because I say he didn't give up, he turned his back on Bone and denied her offer, so he didn't know the truth of Sky just when he was on the cusp of success."

Miriam recalled how much the man gave up: technology, victory, truth. And he didn't even understand Sky well enough to see it when it was only a little farther on. The man wasn't a fool. Not exactly. She pitied him.

Joshua leapt up from between his parents. "I think he found

Sky. Bone told him with the marker above the entrance. There was *something* in that last big cavern that the story forgot. That's Sky."

Some of the People gaped at Joshua.

"That is...interesting," said Ashera at last. "You think that Bone told the man the truth?"

"Um, maybe," said Joshua, inspiration gone with so many eyes upon him.

Miriam added, "Maybe he stopped searching after all, turned his back on his search, and so Bone gave him the boon she promised, so that he would always know truth from lies." That wasn't so much of a stretch, was it? The story hadn't said straight-away whether he'd given up or not. "He knew Sky when he saw the marker."

"Ha!" said Aaron. "He found Sky just when he gave up looking."

Whether he'd given up or not, whether he succeeded or not, he deserved praise. She could trust that he knew when to keep trying and when to ease back because, maybe, easing back meant his goal would come upon him when he least expected.

Pity for the man in the parable transmuted into hope. What is this? Some higher alkhemy beyond signs and a calcifying world. The walls retreated, cracked like cheap facades. Were there even walls? Wasn't it better to pursue a goal, a thrilling beyond, rather than dread circumscription?

She had the flute from the warren. She'd play it tonight, ably or not. Let Sippora jeer as she will. Tomorrow will be the first day of a new migration, but she wouldn't let that trouble her. It might be three days or three weeks until her clan trudged into a cavern lush enough to call home, but lightness sloughed off even that burden, a molted skin. There might be dragons or drought or hostile strangers, but not this night. This was New Year's, a second night apart from time. She could check her clock in the morning.

ANDY DIBBLE

Andy Dibble is a healthcare IT consultant who lives in Madison, Wisconsin. He has supported the electronic medical record of healthcare systems in six countries. His work appears or is forthcoming in Writers of the Future, Star*Line, Sci Phi Journal, and others. He is Articles Editor for Speculative North magazine.

He can be found on Twitter, Facebook, and andydibble.com.

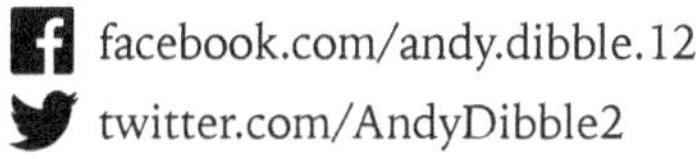

facebook.com/andy.dibble.12
twitter.com/AndyDibble2

CATHURANJALEE

DL SHIREY

S parse weeds and low, thorny shrubs survived the blistering anvil of the ancient lava flow. Not much else. Even insects retreated from the place Sheikh Khalwa came to pray. It was not as if they fled from him as a general rule, only during the ritual known as Djaanum-el. And since Khalwa trekked to the crown of the Bayuda cinder cone at least once a week, perhaps the animals simply tired of constant evacuation and made nests elsewhere.

Khalwa, The Holy One, made the trip each Sabbath; not on Friday as it was for Muslims, or Sunday as Christians observed. Khalwa's Sabbath was decreed by the wind on any day of the week, whenever the breeze shifted north and smelled of orange.

The scent on the wind was not citrus, but the color orange. A lifetime in the desert had done something to Khalwa, to his senses. While some mystics saw auras, Khalwa smelled them; at least, that's the way his mind interpreted differences in the wind. Green came from the Nile, blue-black an approaching sandstorm, and the Sabbath called with orange.

Khalwa inhaled deeply, infused by color. He ordered his sister, Cathuranjalee, to bring the mule and heavy riding blanket.

Cathuranjalee was the only woman in Khalwa's life and the last of his family. She and two other sisters had been born for the purpose of serving The Holy One, each ten years apart in age. Anisah and Uzmay had died here, leaving Cathuranjalee, at twenty, as the remaining attendant to her brother. Like her sisters, Cathuranjalee could hear Khalwa's thoughts as if his words were spoken aloud. His commands were powerful and harsh, and he was unconcerned that Cathuranjalee felt assaulted by them. His sister existed only to serve.

Cathuranjalee felt a tint of orange enter her mind moments before the words invaded. She could not smell colors as Khalwa did, but his thoughts were powerful enough to transmit a feeling of color an instant before the words came. Cathuranjalee braced herself for the onslaught and, more importantly, hid her true feelings behind a river of happy thoughts.

"The Journey is upon me. Fetch my animal and blanket while I dress."

Cathuranjalee got up from her cushioned chair and strolled out onto the sunbaked earth of the compound's courtyard, seeking the boy to ready her brother's mule. As she searched the storerooms and stable for him, villagers moved aside to let the Sheikh's sister pass. She found Amaal feeding the livestock.

"There you are. Ready the Master's mule and don't forget the special riding blanket."

"Yes, Rahiba."

She smiled at the honorific; the word meant *sister*, but with a more devout meaning, as a nun might be called sister. Cathuranjalee basked in the respect, but she could only enjoy the adulation for a moment before the whiff of orange entered her mind again.

"I am ready. See to it that I am not left standing in the courtyard waiting for my animal."

A river of happiness jumped to the front of Cathuranjalee's mind, a reflex she had learned in her years of servitude. But today, on Khalwa's Sabbath, she was secretly excited; only when her brother left the compound did Cathuranjalee dare let down her guard and drop the barrier of pleasant thoughts that masked her true desires.

Since she was a child, Khalwa punished Cathuranjalee, Anisah and Uzmay for impure thoughts. Unlike her sisters, Cathuranjalee learned to survive his pious intrusions with her own trick: she imagined a River flowing with happy, obedient thoughts, hiding the dark longings and dreams that could free Cathuranjalee from subservience and bring an end to the poverty she despised.

Cathuranjalee could not imagine the consequences if Khalwa ever saw past the River. She protected her secrets at all costs, letting the waters part only when her brother was away. To wade past the River, Cathuranjalee could slip into hope and feel it soft upon her skin, let desires wash over her and wear them like a veil against the endless grit of sand, drab surroundings and malignant probing from her brother's mind.

The boy and mule were waiting in the courtyard when Sheikh Khalwa emerged from the residence, plodding with slow, uneven steps. He had changed from his everyday, checkered headcloth. His long, white hair was wound in shiny black fabric, tied by a more-formal front knot. An old, tattered riding shawl hid his matte-black prayer robes.

Talk from the crowd turned to whispers as the faithful noticed what The Holy One was wearing.

Those who had walked the ten kilometers from Berber to Khalwa's compound had a choice: return to town or make camp outside the wall, where shade grew in the afternoon. Khalwa would hold no audience before the journey.

The Sheikh crooked his finger and pointed at three men closest to him. They bent forward and gave thanks for the honor of carrying provisions and following the mule to the edge of Bayuda.

Cathuranjalee remained out of sight. She wanted nothing more than to have her brother's full concentration on the journey ahead. When the mule and rider diminished into the distance, she peeked out from the stables and summoned Amaal. She gave him 20 qirush in coins and a note to be delivered to her seamstress in Berber. The seamstress would pass the message to her new Bedouin friends.

Cathuranjalee stepped out into the sunlight, watched as the believers shouldered jugs of water and followed Khalwa into the Nubian Desert. She envied the faith that drove them but was disgusted by the poverty, theirs and hers.

She went into the residence and traded her old crêpe abaya for an even older garment, the one made from cheap, scratchy, sand-colored cloth. Cathuranjalee hid a bota of water and a small pair of binoculars under her clothes and casually strolled out into the courtyard.

She paused at the open gate until she was confident her brother could not feel her presence. Then Cathuranjalee followed the tracks out into the desert.

CATHURANJALEE DIVERTED from the trail of footprints, climbing a tall dune downwind from the Bayuda cinder cone. The soft sand gushed down the steep slope as she struggled to the top. Careful not to be seen above the crest, she crawled the few remaining meters on her belly. As her eyes cleared the top of the dune, she had gotten closer than she intended. Now she had to be extra cautious. Cathuranjalee cleared her mind and didn't move until she was certain her brother was deep in meditation, undistracted by anything other than his preparations for prayer.

She knew the ritual by heart. The mule had already been tended; it munched grain from an oat sack. One of the three followers was helping Khalwa keep his balance as he rinsed his feet. More hands steadied the old man as he stepped from the plastic basin of water onto the riding blanket that had been laid on the very edge of the dark, volcanic rock. As the Sheikh regained his balance, the attendants turned their backs to Bayuda and began chanting.

Cathuranjalee was close enough to hear the deep-throated voices, but still needed the binoculars to accomplish her mission. She was careful not to let the setting sun reflect off the lenses as she pulled them to her eyes. She focused first on the attendants, adjusting the magnification to see their dirt-smudged faces and ragged edges of their wind-worn clothing.

Cathuranjalee then trained the glasses on her brother. It was as if she could reach out and touch him. As well as she knew

Khalwa's face when he worshipped, when no outside influence would break him from this trance, Cathuranjalee was still apprehensive at the illusion of being so close. She pulled down the binoculars to remind herself it was the lenses that thrust her into intimate proximity, and watched unaided until Khalwa bowed to each of the four horizons. Only then did Cathuranjalee raise the binoculars once more. The ritual her brother called Djaanum-el was about to begin.

At the edge of the cinder cone, where black rock met brown sand, stubby, twisted stems found purchase. Khalwa sat cross-legged on the blanket and studied the plants, selecting two shoots. He snapped off the stems, took a deep breath and smiled at the scent. Khalwa raised the twigs one at a time toward the setting sun, placed both between his teeth and bit down. As if on cue, Cathuranjalee heard the attendants' voices raise an octave. She glanced over to see their arms linked at the elbows, swaying as they chanted.

Snapping the glasses back to Khalwa's face, Cathuranjalee adjusted the focus. She could clearly see the yellow, fibrous strands held in her brother's teeth a moment before he started chewing them. He sucked at each hollow stalk then cast the stems out into the sand. She watched him stand. If she hadn't known him to be her brother, Cathuranjalee would have sworn this a much younger man rising to his feet. The limberness belied the old knees and hips that usually affected Khalwa's gait. And he spread his arms to the heavens, arching his back that he so often complained was stiff and sore.

From her perch in the dunes, Cathuranjalee pulled the binoculars away from her dark eyes. She withdrew a hand-drawn map from the pocket of her abaya and unfolded the paper. Her Bedouin friends had given her a precise outline of the cinder cone and she penciled an X precisely where her brother now stood. From her pocket she next pulled a photocopy of the four plants hearty enough to survive at the edge of Bayuda. Cathuranjalee identified the one Khalwa used and scratched an X next to it.

Her hands shook with anticipation. Her new friends would pay handsomely for these two Xs and offered her much more if she would follow her brother to the exact spot where he performed his prayers. Cathuranjalee had rejected the second task because no payment was worth the risk. If she laid foot on Bayuda, Khalwa would sense her—of this she was certain. And now it wasn't anticipation that caused her hands to shake, it was what her brother might do to her if he ever found out.

She gazed at the heavens as her brother often did and said a little prayer. The constellation Sayylad, the Hunter, hung just above the horizon, just south of the Bedouin camp. Cathuranjalee would use the stars to find camp and arrange payment for information about the plants. Hopefully, it would be enough money to throw off the rags of poverty and regret, dip past the River and feel the fabric of her dreams come to life.

* * *

Khalwa brushed his fingers through the stiff, crooked tendrils of the sacred raiha'an plant, searching for stems that had recently bloomed. He rubbed dead petals off two twigs and pressed the inch-long pieces between his thumb and fingers, rolling them back and forth to loosen the pulp, and the golden scent began to fill him. The overwhelming color of raiha'an reminded Khalwa of the first time he was allowed to set foot on Bayuda.

His father first brought Khalwa to the sacred cinder cone when he was ten. The old Sheikh hadn't prepared his son for the event, telling Khalwa nothing about the ancient rite, only that it was a task passed down from father to son. Rituals and mysticism were everyday occurrences for the boy, as common to him as smelling colors and reading minds. That the villagers held his father in reverential esteem wasn't strange to Khalwa, nor that his many aunts, instead of having families of their own, fawned over the old Sheikh's every need. This was the way Khalwa was raised, the only household the boy knew, so a father-son trip to Bayuda seemed like any other family outing. Only later would Khalwa learn about his family's great powers, after he survived Djaanum-el.

The old Sheikh showed Khalwa the proper plant, which stem to choose and how to suck the pulp. The smell was a trivial shade of gold compared to the taste. Color exploded in Khalwa's head and bleached his senses to a dull gray. The boy panicked at the sudden colorlessness of his world, as someone might if suddenly stricken deaf or blind. He remembered turning to his father for explanation, but the man no longer stood beside him. The old Sheikh had joined the three attendants out on the sand, their backs turned to Bayuda.

Djaanum-el had to be experienced alone. And even though he was now an old man, there was still a twinge of apprehension when the color disappeared from his mind. Unlike the first time, Khalwa knew the color-scents would return.

He stared down at the intricate patterns of the riding blanket on which he stood. Streaks of electricity shot from his feet and into the maze of threads. Like a thousand tiny tubes of neon, brightness channeled through the woven designs, seeking the earth beyond. The rock absorbed the firebolts, and the ancient lava flow seemed to glow from within, revealing striations of dark basalts and mottled granite. A vein of obsidian stood out from the illuminated creases of rock, jagging helter-skelter up the slope to the crest of the cinder cone. Khalwa placed a bare foot upon the volcanic glass.

From within the obsidian, bright torrents of light pooled around Khalwa's feet as if each step attracted subterranean lightning. He walked heel to toe, a slow, purposeful progression that allowed the power of the earth to fill him. As the path inclined, so did Khalwa's senses; the blur of his old eyes sharpened and he could hear the papery grit of his calloused feet on dusty volcanic glass.

Only at the summit of the cinder cone did his sense of smell return. The surrounding of stars above him shone white to a magnitude of brightness that never ceased to amaze Khalwa. And each time he inhaled, the brilliant pinpoints increased their numbers a thousandfold. Every breath embroidered another layer to the constellations above him, embodying the starry skeletons of Sayylad and Dukaar with form and musculature and sheaths of white skin. Nahrelaam, the constellation of a river, was now woven in its own snowy landscape. Khalwa filled his lungs until there were only specs of night-black around the white marble sculptures crowding the sky.

Another deep breath and the bull Dukaar lowered its head, pawed at the firmament as if about to charge. The stars in Nahrelaam rushed down the riverbed, its whitewater spilling up over the banks. Sayylad, the Hunter, lowered his club and stretched the stiffness from his body.

Sayylad looked down, his blank, white eyes finding the mortal atop the cinder cone. As Khalwa watched, the Hunter leaned down, his colossal face eclipsed the sky, lips coming close to whisper in Khalwa's ear. Words in fiery magenta colored Khalwa's mind and filled him with shame. He closed his eyes, not wanting to believe his sister's treachery, but the Hunter had seen it from his perch, high above the desert. And Sayylad never lied.

When Khalwa opened his eyes, his cheeks were wet with humiliation, but he knew what had to be done. Once more, Khalwa glanced at the heavens to give thanks, but the stars were unraveling. Sayylad was reverting back to a disembodied string of stars, but Khalwa saw him pick up his stellar club. And just before he rejoined the pantheon of stars above, Sayylad pointed his mighty weapon eastward.

Khalwa faced east, the night sky again dusted with meager flecks of light. He cleared his mind with one more breath and caught the rot-brown scent of betrayal.

***

NO MOON AND FLAT SAND, a walk like this always reminded Cathuranjalee of childhood. Nighttime was when she and her sisters, Anisah and Uzmay, would play, when their brother slept and they weren't required to serve him. A favorite game was tadur wanuqta, spin and point; it was the reason Cathuranjalee knew where she was in the desert after dark.

The three sisters would find a flat stretch of desert with no discernible landmarks within sight. Next, they held hands— Uzmay, usually, in the middle—and spun around, faster and faster. When the world became a blur and it was all Cathuranjalee could do to hold on, Uzmay would let go and the sisters would fly apart and topple into the sand. To win the game was to be first to stand and point to whatever way she faced, then shout out the correct direction. Stars were the only clues. As the youngest, Cathuranjalee could get away with shouting any of the four cardinal points. Anisah and Uzmay had to be more precise and identify the points in between, like northeast or southwest.

The best part were those few seconds before Uzmay released her sisters, when it was hard to hold on. There was an exhilarating attachment between them, and Cathuranjalee could draw strength from her sisters simply by holding their hands. No matter how fast Uzmay would spin, Cathuranjalee's grip seemed to multiply when the three were linked.

Even now, if Cathuranjalee concentrated hard enough, she could feel Anisah and Uzmay in her mind and visualize that unbreakable bond. She held out her arms, to recreate the moment, to will them to stand beside her in the desert. A mental picture began to form of the three sisters at play, but the reverie was broken by a sound in the distance.

In the silence of the desert, Cathuranjalee heard the rumble of a generator long before she spied the lights of the Bedouin camp. She rounded a dune and saw the strings of bare bulbs; they glowed anemically, but bright as beacons against the pitch-black landscape. Six small tents were illuminated, flanked by a windwall of carpets, strung and staked in the direction of a moderate breeze.

Cathuranjalee trudged across the sand flats, purposely making noise with each step. Even though the Wahr al-Asad was not a warrior clan, Cathuranjalee did not want to startle anyone who was on guard. She entered between two tents and at the center of the encampment saw a man squatting by a low fire. Unlike the windwall, the carpets surrounding the fire pit were of the highest quality. Cathuranjalee cleared her throat, but the man did not stir.

"I have come as promised," she said finally.

The man turned his head. Even in the dim light, Cathuranjalee saw how the fabric of his head cloth billowed, characteristic of fine-loomed cotton. He faced the fire again, calling out a name. After a few long seconds, he barked it again, louder. Cathuranjalee knew better than to move unless invited.

A petite figure emerged from the largest tent: a woman, her hands the only skin showing. She knelt by the man and nodded intently at the words he whispered. She rose and accepted a small, wrapped bundle the man pulled from beneath his robes. With a quick bow, the woman turned from the fire pit and walked toward Cathuranjalee.

"I am to inspect the papers," the woman said. She clicked on a tiny penlight, and the aura from the bright beam illuminated the coverings on her face.

Though the night was warm, Cathuranjalee shivered with envy. The woman was fashioned in a dream: her chiffon abaya literally glowed, a sheen as soft as the fabric no doubt was. An expensive sheila scarved her head, adorned with arabesques of tiny black beads, sewn with an intimate precision that only hours of handwork could render. The woman's mask was the definition of decadence; it mimicked the shape of a falcon's face, so that below her eyes, the nosepiece peaked in a stiff crease and tapered down to a feather-like lace, bordered with dark jewels.

"The papers?" the woman said, this time with impatience.

Cathuranjalee withdrew the map and plant photos from the pocket in her own abaya. The rough fabric scratched at her wrists. When the woman flicked her eyes down and narrowed them, Cathuranjalee knew her poor, tattered outfit was being judged.

The woman snatched the papers and shone the penlight across both sheets. Even behind that lovely mask, Cathuranjalee could see the woman's thick brows, fashioned to match the angles of a falcon's. Her hands were soft and exquisitely manicured. Cathuranjalee couldn't tell how young the woman was, but her husband or father kept her in finery. Jealousy consumed Cathuranjalee now that she had a picture of what her life could become. She could see herself clothed in these exact raiments, and in this disguise make her escape from Khalwa.

The penlight clicked off. "Go now," the woman ordered.

The bundle was thrust into Cathuranjalee's hands, a fine linen handkerchief wrapped around a stack of U.S. twenty-dollar bills. Cathuranjalee watched the woman return to the man, the folds of her abaya rippled in lavish waves as she knelt before him once more.

The falcon turned in profile from the fire's backlight. "Go!" she screeched.

CATHURANJALEE RETURNED FROM THE DESERT. The morning sun, just above the flat horizon, was shrouded by the static of a distant sandstorm. It diffused the intensity of the light, but did nothing to quell the suffocating heat.

A tint of long shadow painted the sand off the compound's western wall as Cathuranjalee strolled through the gates. They were always open, as if to welcome those who sought Khalwa's counsel, but the dozen people who waited would not enter until invited. A few nodded to The Holy One's sister but Cathuranjalee did not reciprocate; she was searching for signs of her brother's return. The inner courtyard was still, save for the small sounds the servants made in preparation for the day.

"Amaal," Cathuranjalee called, her voice just above a whisper, but loud enough to bring faces to the open windows and increase the bustle inside the residence. The boy's face emerged from the darkness behind the stable doors. "The Master, is he up yet?"

"No, Rahiba. He has not yet returned from where he prays."

Cathuranjalee had asked the question in pretense, it was obvious her brother was not at home or she would have known. Khalwa radiated thought as a dust devil swirled sand, and the closer his proximity, the easier it was for Cathuranjalee to feel his presence. She could not read his thoughts as much as she could glean Khalwa's frame of mind and smell the colors he was feeling an instant before he invaded her mind.

Her presence was always required at his daily audience with the locals, where Khalwa would give spiritual advice and practical counsel. Cathuranjalee would sit quietly, listening to the verbal exchange, and at the same time sense Khalwa's true sentiments; he adored being respected and dispensed guidance in an effort to help, not for his own personal gain. Khalwa was sincere in his affection for his followers and resolute in his faith. It was the one thing Cathuranjalee admired about her brother.

"Can I get you anything, Rahiba?" Amaal repeated,

motioning for Cathuranjalee to relieve herself of the objects she carried.

She handed the empty water bota and binoculars to the boy. Amaal held his hand out for her other bundle, the one wrapped in the fine linen handkerchief. Cathuranjalee tucked it under her arm and dismissed Amaal with a nod.

"There is porridge for breakfast," Amaal said. "What fruit and cheese we have is being held for the Master. Cook says she will go to town later. It's Market Day, you know."

A smile lit the boy's face as he trotted happily toward the residence to put away the bota and binoculars. Market Day was a twice-monthly holiday and everyone in Berber attended. It would also mean a slower day for Khalwa, with fewer visitors seeking counsel. Perhaps that was why Khalwa stayed longer in the desert, lingering in prayer instead of rushing back.

Cathuranjalee fingered the fine linen that wrapped the bundle of money. She wished there was such finery at the market stalls in Berber, but knew that to find the kind of fashion worn by the falcon woman, Cathuranjalee would have to make the long trek to Atbara or Khartoum. But this was part of the plan. Although it would give her great pleasure to wear fine garments, it would also serve as a disguise. The next time her brother went to Bayuda to pray, Cathuranjalee would escape. She would cover herself, head to toe in elegance, board a train to Port Sudan, then a boat to Cairo. She would finally be free to find her own life, free from her brother's expectation of servitude.

A dark twinge colored her mind. She scanned the courtyard and cast her feelings for signs of her brother's approach. No, the twinge she felt was her own anxiety; she knew better than to entertain thoughts of escape openly. If Khalwa should return, get close enough to probe her mind, unguarded thoughts such as these would be her undoing. So, she washed away all her dreams and plans behind the River of pleasant thoughts and piety.

With a contented smile, Cathuranjalee walked to the residence, keeping the screen door from banging as she entered the narrow hall. Her eyes adjusted to the dim light, and she saw a flap of white cloth as it disappeared around the corner ahead of her; a servant, no doubt, giving way to The Holy One's sister. Cathuranjalee stopped at the toilet to wet a cloth in the basin of fresh water. As always, she held her breath in the room; even a basket full of pomegranate peel did little to mask the stink from the pit in the tile floor. She tucked the precious bundle under her arm, wrung the threadbare handcloth, and took it to her bedroom down the hall.

The room was spare, only a small bed, wooden chair and a plain armoire no taller than Cathuranjalee. There she undressed, down to her underthings, using the hand cloth to wipe her face, neck, armpits, and crotch. She tossed the handcloth on the floor next to her sand-colored abaya, intending to have them washed. In the armoire hung her two black garments—one for special occasions, the other worn every day. On the armoire's floor lay neatly-folded bolts of inexpensive fabric, too colorful for Cathuranjalee to wear, but hoarded there like secret wishes. Next to the fabric, a pair of sandals and her worn-out dress shoes.

Her entire wardrobe was worth less than that one square of fine linen binding the stack of money. She unbundled the bills and brushed the handkerchief against her skin. She let it lick against her naked arms, as Cathuranjalee imagined the clothes she would soon wear, loomed from materials finer than this.

She grew wary again; Cathuranjalee was so close to fulfilling her goals that she was getting careless. It was hard not to daydream, but perilous to do so. Once more, she brought her River of happy, obedient thoughts to the front of her mind. This was her best protection and had worked for her since she was a child. Her brother would regularly scrutinize Cathuranjalee's thoughts, intrusions accompanied by physical discomfort that could induce pain if Khalwa was angry. But with the River in place, all he would find was a constant flow of contentment and tranquility.

She concentrated on the River while placing the stacks of money in the armoire, between the folds of colorful fabric. Quickly, Cathuranjalee donned her workaday *abaya* and a ratty headscarf. She scooped up her dirty laundry and dropped it in a pile just outside her door.

A square of shade remained on the porch in front of the residence. It was where she took solitary meals. Cook or Amaal had placed there a bowl of porridge, garnished with shavings of almond. It was tepid, but Cathuranjalee was hungry.

All around her, the compound was more alive now, a few villagers milling impatiently outside the gates. She spooned up the last lump of cereal, her mind dipped below the River to review her actions since her return this morning. With her brother's imminent arrival, Cathuranjalee wanted to make sure she'd covered all her tracks: Amaal had put away the bota and binoculars, the clothes she'd worn were in the laundry, her reward safely hidden away, and the handkerchief…the handkerchief.

What had she done with the handkerchief?

"Why do you daydream in the shade while my faithful wait outside the gates and in the sun?"

Khalwa's voice rang clearly in her head as if he was speaking on the porch next to her. His words startled her and the bowl and spoon tumbled into her lap. He was close. Usually a color-smell preceded his assault; this time, angry magenta permeated *after* Khalwa's words clawed their way into Cathuranjalee. She choked off the panic and let the protection of the River flood every crevice of her mind.

"I didn't know you had returned," she said aloud.

"You were not meant to know."

Khalwa had the ability to shut his mind if he chose, but he rarely did. Cathuranjalee could remember only one or two instances when Khalwa stopped his mental trespass, out of respect to a person of importance.

Cathuranjalee didn't force herself to make her voice calm, the River did it for her. "I shall circle the courtyard on my hands and knees in penance, if that pleases you."

"Why would you concern yourself with scraps of linen when I should be attended to? Take a seat in the sun, open your mind with prayer and I will decide punishment for such indolence."

The sharpness in his words made her wince, as much for the knife-like intrusion as the certainty of his eavesdropping. How long had he been listening in, and why hadn't she felt him doing so?

Cathuranjalee set the bowl and spoon back on the table, enduring the after-ache of his incursion. She flooded her mind with the River of happy thoughts, hoping the waters would soften the edges of the next attack. She submerged every speck of guilt and fear beneath a rush of fidelity and kindness. Then she stepped off the porch and into the sun toward the benches just inside the gates of the compound. Cathuranjalee would take a seat and pray, just as instructed.

Her confidence grew with each measured step. She could feel Khalwa's mind now, judging her, wading into her thoughts, measuring them.

"Tell the faithful I will see them now. You sit and wait."

This time his words stung less, the harsh magenta faded to lavender. It would only be a few more steps, then his believers would swarm in, and Khalwa's mind would be otherwise occupied. She allowed the muscles in her neck and shoulders to slacken ever so slightly.

Then from the corner of her eye, Cathuranjalee saw her brother emerge from the shadows inside the stable, hand resting affectionately atop Amaal's head. What was that the boy was holding? The handkerchief? Cathuranjalee's breath caught and her steps faltered. She jerked her head towards Amaal, seeing accusation in his black eyes and the white linen he held.

The River in her mind changed course, a boulder dividing the current. For a moment, everything she tried to protect was laid bare. Khalwa's mind plunged through, tearing deep into Cathuranjalee's thoughts. She stumbled forward, catching hold of a sun-bleached bench that sat against the compound wall. The villagers outside the gate peered in as Cathuranjalee pulled herself up onto the wooden slats.

"What is it you're hiding?" His words ripped at the walls of her consciousness.

Cathuranjalee imagined her brother wading knee-deep in the water, thrusting his hands to the riverbed, trying to claw through to the bottom. She summoned a tide of reverence and devotion, causing the River to rise. Khalwa still stood in the water, but she flooded him with nothing but admiration and kind wishes until Khalwa was up to his waist. Cathuranjalee wondered if she could suffocate her brother in pleasantries, make the River overflow its banks and force Khalwa out of her mind before he drowned.

She imagined the water rushing higher, up to Khalwa's neck. It had been a long time since Cathuranjalee felt such happiness. Then, in her mind, Khalwa raised his hands overhead and an enormous fist of white marble thrust from the heavens, crashing through the River, draining the protective waters.

"The stars foretold your betrayal. But I want to know why." With each word came a thrust, ripping to the back of her mind, as Khalwa grubbed for pieces of her memory. Cathuranjalee tried to redirect the River, pouring as many pleasant thoughts as she could muster, but Khalwa waded through the deceit with brutal force.

Cathuranjalee gripped the bench and pressed her back against the wall to brace herself against the onslaught. In her mind's eye she caught sight of each memory Khalwa exhumed, like pages torn from a photo album: the sand dune with binoculars, photocopies of plants, approaching the Bedouin camp, the woman with the falcon mask.

There was a pause. *"Ahh. You thought this a sufficient disguise? Nothing you could wear will hide you. Nothing will keep you from serving me."*

Then she could picture it, the final thought Khalwa had snatched from her subconscious. Not a memory from real life, but something from Cathuranjalee's own imagination. She was wearing the delicate chiffon abaya, a matching scarf with beaded arabesques, and sensual burqa mask with its feathering of lace, boarding a ship in Port Sudan.

The image didn't move from her mind. For as long as Khalwa held it in place, Cathuranjalee was blind to the rest of the world. In a panic at being rendered sightless, she tried to stand, sweeping her hands in the air to locate any obstructions before her. What she found was a boy's shoulder, his arm stiff and soldierly at his side.

"It is Master's wish you do not move," Amaal said, "There are faithful waiting outside the gate, and His Holiness will hold counsel with them before dealing with you."

The boy grabbed Cathuranjalee by the hips and forced her to sit on the bench. Anger rose along with the color in her cheeks, and she pushed Amaal away, struggling again to her feet. She could see nothing but the portrait of herself dressed in finery, but she could hear the villagers talking among themselves. They were only a few meters away. She would run to them and beg for help. Surely one of them would take pity.

"Do not move or pay the price."

Cathuranjalee started to rise, but a fist thudded against her cheek, a blow coming from the inside out. The portrait in her mind bent: her face, cloaked in its luxurious adornments, snapped to one side, the falcon mask knocked askew, revealing her frightened eyes.

She collapsed onto the courtyard bench, reeling from the blow to her mind and body. After a few shaky breaths, she leaned back against the wall, still blind to everything but the now-damaged picture in her head. She saw purple-red bruises, her eye swollen shut and the lovely arabesques shattered from missing beads. She didn't know which ache felt worse, the blow from her brother or her dream ruined.

"Bring the faithful in. Now." The words were for Amaal, but Cathuranjalee still felt them in her head.

She heard one person after another file past, eager for Khalwa's counsel. She heard Amaal making small talk and the villagers' scorn when the boy told of Cathuranjalee's punishment. From the number of voices and shuffling feet, the crowd moving past her was quite large. A slow drip of hope trickled into her consciousness as she realized her brother would be busy for many hours. And without having Cathuranjalee to assist him, Khalwa would be immersed in ministrations to the congregation.

Cathuranjalee decided to do precisely as her brother had asked: she would not move, not show a trace of resistance, and keep Khalwa's mind occupied elsewhere. She had a plan and with it, her hopefulness surged.

Concentrating on the brutalized portrait wedged in her mind, she willed the River to build behind it, until water seeped at the edges and trickled down from the top. Soon rivulets poured down the surface, healing the bruises and mending the arabesques. Overflowing with joy, Cathuranjalee imagined the water rise and carry the falcon mask away from the portrait. She would no longer need to hide behind it.

Her image was whole again, and the resurgent River washed the portrait free from its moorings, allowing Cathuranjalee to see once more. She looked about the empty courtyard to regain her bearings and let the possibility of freedom fill her to the brim. Any physical movement would bring back her brother's wrath, so she would need an ocean of pleasant thoughts to inundate Khalwa when he invaded her mind again.

Cathuranjalee searched her past for when she was truly happy, and her sisters' faces appeared. Anisah and Uzmay, her fondest memories; just the thought of all three sisters together made Cathuranjalee smile. She recalled what it was like to be with her sisters again, playing tadur wanuqta once more.

Cathuranjalee rose from the bench and walked to the center of the courtyard. She raised her arms, hands reaching out to either side. In her mind, she grasped her sisters' hands; Anisah on the right, Uzmay to the left. This time Cathuranjalee was in the middle.

The smell of magenta was immediate and overwhelming. *"I warned you not to move. You dare disobey me?"*

Cathuranjalee began to spin. Slowly at first, then faster. Khalwa penetrated her mind, but he hesitated, seeing all three of his sisters at play. The girls were laughing, whirling with happiness, ignoring Khalwa completely. He tried to break their grip, only to be immersed in his sisters' glee; Cathuranjalee flooded her mind with the River, only this time there were three tributaries. And as the sisters played tadur wanuqta, the spinning became a maelstrom, pushing out wave after wave of bliss.

Cathuranjalee envisioned Khalwa's counsel chambers, all eyes stared at him. She felt his body go rigid as he gripped the arms of his well-padded chair. He stood, staggered forward and made his way to the compound.

In her mind, Cathuranjalee could see Khalwa fighting the tide, but the man floundered before her. He wobbled against the wall of water, the waves of sisterly love crashing against him. Khalwa thrust his arms upward to summon help from above.

Instead of bracing for retaliation, Cathuranjalee continued to laugh. Even the marble fist pummeling down from the heavens could not break the bond between her, Uzmay, and Anisah. The god's arm shattered as it struck down at the center of the whirlpool and the power of three Rivers swept the debris away.

Khalwa fell back onto the sand of the courtyard. Amaal pushed past the stunned villagers, rushing to attend the Master. The old man struggled to breathe. Amaal caressed the old man's face and watched Cathuranjalee slow her spin; her fists softened into fingers and she seemed to be waving goodbye to someone. She stood in the center of the courtyard, blew a kiss in one direction and another to the side opposite. Cathuranjalee didn't look at Khalwa or the boy, simply turned a heel towards them.

She pulled at the hem of her old, black abaya and took long strides out the gate and into the desert. Night would soon be upon her and she would use the stars to point her way to Port Sudan. Cathuranjalee no longer needed the Bedouins' money to get to Cairo. She had herself.

DL SHIREY

DL Shirey lives in Portland, Oregon, where it's probably raining. Luckily, water is beer's primary ingredient. His stories and non-fiction appear in 60 publications, including Confingo, Page & Spine, Zetetic and Wild Musette.

You can find more of DL Shirey on Twitter and at www.dlshirey.com.

 twitter.com/dlshirey

AMONG TALL TREES*

DAMIR SALKOVIC

.

Trigger Warning: Use of derogatory r-slur by antagonist.

The young boy races for the ridge, a good twenty feet ahead of Jeff. With every painful breath, the distance between them grows. If the boy wanted to, he could already be out of his sight, halfway up the mountain that rises ahead of them, a blue-gray bulk topped with first snow, deep into the thick evergreens. But the child is holding back, glancing over his shoulder every now and then without missing a beat, without interrupting the purposeful elegance of his stride.

Save yourself. Go.

Jeff shouts none of this to the boy, whose thin arms are pumping up and down, skinny legs effortlessly swallowing the punishing grade of the mountain as if unfettered by gravity. Jeff is too busy wheezing, hauling in lungfuls of frosty air, trying to hear his own frenetic thoughts over the pounding of his out-of-shape heart and the tidal roar of blood in his ears. Trying to keep his burning lungs from falling out and keep his feet, clumsy in heavy boots, trudging one in front of the other. Every misstep, every stumble and pause for breath, erodes their already thin lead on the men who hunt them.

They are slow, too, these others: some weighed down with age, like Judge Crenshaw, who is eighty if a day. Some by sloth and neglect, like Big Mike Bragg, who weighs well north of three hundred pounds. Fear herds them together, and a mob is only as fast as its slowest man. But determination drives them, a remorseless singularity of purpose.

Although Jeff can't see them, they aren't far behind, marching through the leafless, scattered hardwoods down by the road, fanning out in a rough semicircle to cover as much killing ground as possible. So after a too-brief break, the boy catches Jeff's eye—he has an uncanny way of looking up at just the right time, or somehow making Jeff do so—and flicks his head.

He doesn't speak, but Jeff understands. Up. Up the mountain, into the pines. Their mad scramble resumes. Down here there are gaps in the treeline, patches of open ground between thickets and dense scrub, and open ground spells trouble.

Not that the boy seems concerned. Or what to all intents and purposes resembles a boy: a pale, scrawny slip of a kid, eight- or nine-years-old, maybe a small ten. Scabbed knees and elbows and bright green eyes, dirty blond hair cut in an unfashionable bowl around a pinched face. He bounds up the slope in easy strides, each as long as two of Jeff's faltering steps, looking to the rest of the world—if there was anyone up here to see him—like any one of hundreds of identical, small-town American kids indulging in a bit of horseplay before going inside for dinner.

Except Jeff has seen those arms lock around Clyde Garver. Good old Clyde who Jeff had played high school football with and who fixed cars at Dan Laurie's garage in town. The boy had grabbed Clyde and wrenched his head clean off his shoulders like a papier-mâché piñata, with no more effort than Jeff twisting a cap off a bottle of Miller High Life.

Except it's late November in the Great Smoky Mountains. Snow weighs over the town like a judgement, but the boy's wearing nothing but pants and a thin T-shirt and his feet are bare, and he's giving no sign of feeling the cold.

Except the horseplay they're indulging in will end in death. They can cheat it for a while, draw out the inevitable, but the men behind them aren't about to give up. Good men, or so Jeff used to think. Men he's known all his life—fathers and husbands and brothers. Men who piled into their trucks and four-wheel-drives without hesitation to hunt Jeff and the child. Men who are not going back down without their prize.

There's only one end Jeff can see. But he keeps running, up toward the trees under the lowering sky.

JEFF HAD FIRST SPOTTED the boy less than seventy-two hours ago: a blurred, pale face peeking behind the trunk of a towering oak tree, moving too quickly for him to be sure what he'd seen.

The crew was hanging drywall in the half-finished cabins a group of investors out of Gatlinburg had hoped to transform into the Pine Estates vacation community. Jeff had gone down to the truck, rummaging through the back for a screw gun and the extra saw, sweating despite the cold, thinking how good a beer from the cooler would taste at the end of the day. He hadn't been sleeping well lately—not since he and Jen split six months ago—and last night had been worse than usual, in bed by eleven and up at one-thirty in the frozen dark, the red eyes of the alarm clock staring him down, the silence of the house weighing down on him like a tombstone.

It took his tired brain a moment to catch up with the information fed through his eyes, by which time the kid was gone, vanishing back into the forest.

Jeff stood by the truck, feeling slow and heavy, his gaze going from the trees to the alien objects in his hands. Then realization set in: the kid had to be one of the vandals. A few days ago, someone had broken into one of the houses, ripped down the tarps stretched over the holes of windows and defecated in one corner of the structure. Jeff's money was on meth-heads from the trailer park down the road, while Pearly, the foreman and owner of the construction company, was sure it had been local kids on some dumb internet dare.

Whatever the reason for the vandalism, the crew had to put an end to it. The job was already over budget and behind schedule, and Pearly was already muttering darkly about cash flow and liquidated damage clauses. Every setback brought on angry calls from the developer, drained the already dwindling bank accounts. Jeff and the other men had not been paid for weeks, and it seemed only a matter of time before their services were no longer required.

Anger flared as Jeff thought of his empty house, the takeout boxes scattered around his recliner, the unopened bills piled on the kitchen table. Now a bunch of little assholes were holding the job up, messing up his life for their own amusement. The anger felt ugly and wrong, but it was the first emotion he'd felt in months. On some level he knew his rage had little to do with the kid and the messed-up job site, but feeling something—anything—was good. It meant he was still alive. He fanned the spark into a blaze, let it warm him from within.

Pearly and Gus were in the frame house closest to the road, measuring and cutting drywall, handing the sheets to Beezer who was hanging them from a stepladder.

"Someone's up in the woods," Jeff said from the doorway, before he could change his mind. "Some kid," he added as all three faces pivoted toward him. Already he regretted saying anything, but he couldn't take his words back now.

The atmosphere in the unfinished room shifted, as if a cold breeze had wafted through the doorways. Pearly's face darkened, his lips vanishing into his beard. He lowered his tools slowly, let out a long breath that steamed in the cold.

"Fucking punks," he mumbled under his breath. "Time we taught them a lesson."

Jeff saw Gus and Beezer exchange a quick glance, then avert their eyes. Pearly dug through the rolling toolbox in the back of the room, came up with a baseball bat. He handed the bat to Jeff, the movement revealing a shoulder holster under his anorak, an automatic nestled within it. Pearly wasn't a gun nut, but he had started carrying after the trouble at the site. Suddenly the gun looked a lot bigger, bigger than the room itself.

Jeff's heartbeat rose into his throat. "Hey," he said, his voice a weak croak. He glanced from Beezer to Gus, but both men had found something on the wall to stare at. He was on his own, this was none of their business.

"Just to give them a scare," Pearly said. "Put the fear of God in them." A strange smile hovered on his lips as he spoke, making his face seem colder, his eyes distant. Like the other three, Pearly depended on the job paying off without further delays.

Unlike the other three, Pearly was deep in hock to the bank, over-leveraged and barely keeping up with the interest payments. He couldn't cut his losses and walk away to try and find other work. The construction business was all he had to support his family—a wife and two kids, with a third on the way —and having something was often worse than having nothing. It demanded constant sacrifice, an unflinching singularity of purpose.

Jeff realized he'd made a mistake. He didn't want anyone to get hurt, definitely not killed. But the look in Pearly's eyes told him that that ship had sailed. Feeling like a man in a dream, he hoisted the bat and trundled after his boss.

They trekked uphill, two burly men with rolling midsections already out of breath by the time they got to the treeline. Jeff was ready to say he couldn't remember where the kid had gone, or lead them in the opposite direction, anything to prevent Pearly from cracking a few heads, or worse, when the other man grunted and pointed at the muddy ground. A trail of small footprints led into the woods, disappearing into the shadows.

Pearly cracked his knuckles and set off, silent on his feet, a hunter tracking prey. Hoping that the kid had had the good sense to get lost, Jeff followed.

Something bothered him about the prints, and almost immediately he knew what it was. They had been made by bare feet. Who would let a child ramble around the forest, this high up the mountain at this time of year, without any shoes on? He was starting to have a bad feeling about this. Wished he was back down at the site, or sitting his truck with that after-work beer.

It only took a few moments for the woods to cut them off from the daylight, for silence to isolate them completely, as black branches obscured the sky. This high up, the oak and hickory and basswood thinned out, made way for pitch and white pines. When Jeff had been a boy, the treeline had started right outside town. Logging and construction had forced it to retreat upward, but successive economic downturns had put a stop to that retreat. Jobs had dried out, moved to urban centers and distant lands.

Now the town was trying to rebrand itself as a mountain resort: skiing in winter and the lakes in summer, cheap permits during hunting season. As far as Jeff could tell, it was a lie. One nobody bought. A run of bad winters had chased away developers; the construction of a new highway had diverted the already scant summer crowds elsewhere. The town shrank to a scatter of houses along two streets, empty allotments dotted with rusty trucks, another lost place travelers sped through on their way to more vibrant destinations. Only the mountain remained, eternal and defiant, the forest spreading to reclaim abandoned properties with terrible vitality, as if thriving on the misfortune of those who lived in its shadow.

The trees opened up, a patch of blue sky shining into the darkness. Pearly halted, his hand reflexively going to his pistol. Here the mountain fell away into a narrow ravine, like a gash in bare stone. A few yards from where they stood, a series of caves yawned darkly in the cliff face. Jeff thought he could hear noise, or voices coming from the nearest opening, but it was just wind whispering through half a dozen stone throats. His bowels quivered, and he wanted to turn back, but Pearly was already halfway down the slope, walking into the darkness as it swallowed him whole.

Again, Jeff had the sensation of the world growing thin,

somehow less real, even as his feet carried him forward, into the vast gaping mouth of the mountain.

"Holy shit."

Blasphemy was appropriate to the occasion. The inside of the cave reeked like an animal's cage, shit and damp fur and slavering carnivore breath. In spite of his misgivings—or perhaps because of them—he gripped the baseball bat tighter, a troglodyte clutching a club against the claws and teeth of night. Pearly stopped ahead of him, craning to peer farther into the cave. Not that there was anything to see. A few paces from the entrance, the darkness reigned absolute. It pressed on Jeff's senses, a cold black tide filling his eyes and ears.

Something clicked, and strong electric light flared up, a bright beam probing the nullity. Pearly swept the Maglite over the rock walls before pausing over the shapes in an inner chamber of the cave. Letters, or symbols of some sort, painted on the rock in hues of ocher and brown. They reminded Jeff of footage he'd seen on National Geographic, pictograms on stone unearthed somewhere in the Mexican desert or a cave in Europe, but not quite the same.

Almost unconsciously, the two men wandered farther in. The chamber opened into another one, much larger. Here the flashlight beam seemed no wider than a pencil, failed to reach the far walls. With every step, the symbols proliferated, painted so thick in places that Jeff couldn't tell the color of the stone underneath.

Murals depicting strange beasts and even stranger humanoid forms covered the base of a great column. A scene of worship, or slaughter, or something between the two. Some of the paintings looked ancient beyond the count of years, but others were fresh, the colors vivid and thickly layered, as if they'd been touched up recently.

Deeper in the cave the animal smell was stronger, hot and rank in Jeff's sinuses. Did anyone in town know about this place? It seemed impossible that something like it could be kept secret, that the mountain wasn't covered in teams of archeologists digging up the remains of a long-gone era.

Amazement and sheer terror fought within him. Scratching noises came from the darkness, the soft patter of feet on stone. Were these echoes of their own footsteps, his ears playing tricks on him, or was something watching them from the lightless depths, its shape not yet revealed? He wanted nothing as much as he wanted to leave, but the dimensionless space around him, the seeping, living dark, stole his sense of direction. When Jeff turned round, he could no longer find the tunnel they had come by. The eternal night squeezed tighter around them, the blade of light narrowing as they stood.

His throat seemed to narrow with the light. Was it already flickering, or was it only his imagination? The battery would eventually run out, and when it did they would be trapped in the dark.

Trapped, but not alone.

Jeff felt his mind lurch toward claustrophobia. A scream fluttered at the back of his throat, but he couldn't gather enough breath to expel it.

He jerked as Pearly's beam swept around, fragmenting the cave into a confusion of planes and shadows. "Come out," the foreman said, his voice like a roar in the silence, followed by the sound of the pistol being unholstered.

The beam danced unsteadily, settled on a pale figure on the floor of the cave. Next to Jeff, Pearly grunted something incomprehensible. The boy looked up at them from a pile of bones and rotted hide. Small and thin, white arms like sticks, dark eyes under a mop of blond hair. Naked, other than a dirty plastic sheet draped over his shoulders. One of their sheets, Jeff realized, the clear kind they stapled over the windows. The expression on the boy's face was wary, his eyes darted from one man to the other, narrowed against the light.

"Don't get too close," Pearly said, but Jeff had already lowered the bat and was inching toward the child trying not to look threatening. Agile like a cat, the boy pivoted to face him and bared his teeth, very white, very sharp in the beam of the Maglite.

"What's your name?"

This elicited no response, other than a darting glance into the darkness, a short step out of Jeff's reach. The kid was scared out of his wits, probably a little feral, the offspring of transients or junkies looking for a place to spend the winter. But where were his parents? Jeff's balls tried to crawl up into his stomach as his imagination populated the maze of tunnels with meth addicts hopped out of their skulls, maybe armed.

"Kid's some kind of retard." Pearly lowered his gun, but didn't return it to the holster. Probably shared some of Jeff's apprehension about the tunnels. "At least we know who messed up our construction site. Better get out of here before his parents come home."

"We can't leave him here." What did the boy survive on up here, naked and alone in the frozen wilderness? Jeff tried to visualize those small hands snapping open padlocks, breaking two-by-fours in half, and couldn't quite do it. "No one's been taking care of him. He looks like he hasn't eaten in days."

"Not our problem." Pearly moved the flashlight from side to side, watched the boy's head follow the beam, a savage confronted with strange magic. "We done all we could. This is a job for Chief Hedlund and his boys now." He took a step closer to the boy, gingerly prodded a bone with the tip of his boot. "He's a meth-head kid. Look tat him. Drugs burnt his brain before he was born."

Jeff removed his waterproof jacket, shivering in the chill of the cave. Carefully, without sudden moves, he closed the distance and held out his jacket. The child's eyes turned up to him. In the dim light, they were black pits, glassy and flat. His head twitched back and something like a growl rumbled in his chest, but he allowed the garment to be placed over his thin shoulders. Under the jacket, his bare flanks were grimy and caked with dried excrement. Jeff's apprehension gave way to pity, then anger.

"I'll take him to social services in Gatlinburg. They'll know what to do with him. Maybe he's already in the system. Got relatives somewhere."

"Nothing but trouble," Pearly said, but he dug through his pockets and found the remains of a Payday candy bar. He tossed it at the boy, who eyed it warily before picking it up and sniffing at it. "He's probably better off up here in the woods than in some foster home."

Jeff straightened, picked up the baseball bat. The shadows at the edge of the light seemed to slink along the ground, making his neck hairs stand on end. "No one in their right mind would do this to a kid. No one human."

"He'll be alright." The foreman made as if to ruffle the boy's hair, then pulled his arm back. "Get him fed and cleaned up, and he's no different from my own two boys. Or any kid in town. Except this one's never seen a candy bar before."

They watched the boy stuff the bar in his mouth, bite through it, then frown and spit out the wrapper, his dark eyes flitting from one man to the other.

<hr>

THE BULLET WHIZZES over Jeff's head and caroms through the trees a moment before the report catches up with him. He hunches his shoulders instinctively and keeps running, trying to keep up with the boy, who is moving even faster now, flickering through the sparse foliage ahead. The space between his shoulder blades tingles in anticipation of the next shot, the killing round that will sever his spinal cord or punch through his lungs.

In spite of all the signs, Jeff did not expect it to come to this —chased and hunted like a beast of the woods, run down and slain in the wilderness. He grew up with many of the men now pursuing him. The thought reverberates through his brain as he scrambles over deadfall on all fours, a meaningless echo that prevents him from focusing on survival.

There's no time for him to scan every face, but he's pretty sure they are all locals. Not just locals, but folks whose families have lived in town for generations. Pat Duplass, the class clown in Jeff's senior year, whose dad Alan taught history and whose lineage probably goes back to the first fur traders to settle in the area. Judge Crenshaw, whose ancestors fought in the Chickasaw Wars. Even old Doc Williams, who delivered Jeff just like he delivered Jeff's father. All eager to do their part in the hunt, to bracket Jeff's existence from cradle to grave.

It's a well-rehearsed drill: the summons spreading through town subtly and efficiently, the participants mobilizing right away. No hesitation, no questions asked. Jeff has never had any inkling of it, but he now knows this sort of thing has happened before, with the same actors, or their forefathers: a bloody game repeating itself through history for as long as men have lived in these mountains. The verdict always passed unanimously: death for the boy, and death for the man who has picked the wrong side, sealed his fate.

Shots spray black dirt behind Jeff, in front of him, shear off branches and smack into wet, rotted stumps. He's almost at the top of the ridge, a single inhalation from exploding, his heart and lungs a solid knot of white pain, when he notices the boy stop and crouch on all fours.

The forest has lied to them, lulled them into a false sense of security. Ahead, the tree cover thins out, exposed rock bares its teeth, rises in a forbidding wall. Below the ridge, in the ravine, more hunters are moving through the trees, not bothering with concealment.

Jeff curses himself for not thinking about the ambush. Their pursuers have split up. While the first party chased them up the mountain, the others have circled up the old sawmill road to cut off their prey. Plenty of time to drive around the ridge ahead of their two targets on foot.

On his own, the boy could have outrun both ambushes. He could have danced up the ridge and down the other side, disappearing into the thick, unbroken blanket of trees before they'd had the chance to head him off. But he had not wanted to leave Jeff behind. Either out of duty or impulse, this creature has already shown more humanity than its pursuers.

The gunfire behind their backs has waned, the barking of the dogs diminished. No sense in wasting bullets from a distance. The hunters know their prey has nowhere to run. This story ends the same way it has always ended. The townsfolk knew it from the start, as had their fathers, and their fathers' fathers. Man deals with the unfamiliar the only way he knows how—through subjugation or destruction. Jeff stares at the boy, but the boy isn't looking back at him. His eyes are roaming the cliff face, scanning the cracks and seams in the rock.

Then his deceptively thin arms reach up, his fingers dig into the rock like pitons, hauling him upward.

"No," Jeff says, shaking his head. But the shouts of the hunting party are getting closer, the baying of the dogs—Matt Wendell's hunting hounds, which Matt won't shut up about—louder. Without conscious effort, his mind is making back-of-the-envelope calculations, his tired muscles tensing for the climb.

The body wants to live. Even when faced with certain demise, its faith in its own survival is monumental and unwavering. Jeff is afraid of heights, has been all his life, but he knows he will try. Anything to put off the inevitable, to earn another breath, if only for a second or two.

The sun is hidden by the near peak, the wall of rock awash in blue shadows. They'll be sitting ducks up there, lined up as in a shooting gallery. But even a slight chance is better than none.

Jeff finds a grip in the precarious handholds, fixes his eyes upward. From this vantage point, the cliff is as treacherously smooth as glass and goes on forever, right into the sky. He grits his teeth and starts after the boy.

NEITHER OF THEM could guess the kid's age, but Pearly had clothes of all sizes; boxes and boxes of them gathering dust in the attic. His wife was not a believer in hand-me-downs. The shirt and sweater Jeff settled on were a little baggy, the trousers stopping above the boy's ankles, a length of rope for a belt. But they were clothes, and they kept the boy warm.

Jeff fed the kid three cans of Spaghetti-Os and planted him in front of the TV set while he retreated to the kitchen to think. The boy had not spoken a word and met every attempt to address him with bland indifference, his stare going right through the speaker, unfocused and glassy. Only the small twitches of his facial muscles, the slight jerking of the head to every sound, betrayed the ruse. Like a cat, alert under his torpor, coiled tension ready for release. It made Jeff uncomfortable, almost like what he'd felt when in the depths of the cave. He couldn't swear to it, but at moments the kid looked almost inhuman, alien in some indefinable way. There was a barrier between them, and every attempt to overcome it only seemed to drive the child deeper into himself.

After he'd put the boy to bed—or rather onto the pull-out sofa in what had once been designated as the nursery room, now used mostly for storage—Jeff got a beer from the fridge and sat at the kitchen table without drinking it. The TV was blaring in the background, but he had no idea what was on. He gazed at his big, scarred hands, then at the darkness outside, without seeing either.

He ought to figure out what to do about the boy, but his mind kept returning to the dark, vague place where he went whenever he tried not to think about Jen. The empty house, the unruly back yard littered with tools and projects he'd started then abandoned. Unfinished, like most things in his life. Two years of college had left him with debt but no degree and a marriage that was over as soon as it started, but had kept going for years on fumes of resentment. The online vocational retraining classes he'd stopped taking after the divorce. There was a sort of masochistic pleasure in enumerating his failures. At least he was accomplished at screwing things up and feeling sorry for himself.

Pearly had called the boy retarded, but Jeff wasn't convinced. Feral, beyond a doubt, and developmentally challenged, starved both physically and for human contact, abandoned by his parents. Probably the same druggies who had messed up the construction site, then either moved on or overdosed some-where in the woods, leaving the boy on his own. Every new season seemed to yield a fresh crop of homeless with it— addicts, or mentally ill, or simply people who had given up on trying to cope with the world as it was. More and more often, Jeff wondered how long it would be until he joined their ranks.

He didn't need the extra headache. Tomorrow he'd feed and dress the kid, then drive him down to the social services center in Gatlinburg so he can be someone else's problem. Pearly might dock him a day's pay, but that didn't bother Jeff much, seeing as said pay was in no danger of making it into his pocket anytime soon.

Turn the boy over and be done with it. Another unfinished project, another responsibility dodged. Jeff stared at the beer bottle for a long moment, then picked it up and poured its contents down the sink before stalking off to bed

He woke up in the bleary gray of dawn, frozen stiff, every bone in his body aching like a rotten tooth. At some point in the night he must have migrated from the recliner to the couch, draped an old blanket over himself. The heat had gone out in the middle of the night and the house was bitterly cold, the window next to him fogged over with his exhalations.

When he got up to go check on the oil heater, the boy was standing in the doorway leading to the kitchen, naked but for a pair of old briefs. Head cocked to the side, unbothered by the cold, eyes staring at Jeff with an almost alien inquisitiveness.

"Jesus." Jeff shivered so hard his teeth clicked together. He draped the blanket over the kid, who remained as motionless as a marble statue. "Aren't you cold? Here. Let's get you something to eat."

The boy showed no interest in Cap'n Crunch and milk. He chewed on a spoonful carefully, spat it right back into the bowl. Jeff frowned, dug through the sparse contents of his fridge. A package of bacon elicited more of a response. The boy raised his head and sniffed the air.

"Good choice. Bacon and eggs are more my style too."

He slit the package open, dug through the cabinet under the sink for a pan. "Goddammit." He'd run out of coffee filters again, which didn't matter because he was also out of coffee. The silence in the kitchen made him nervous, eager to fill it with words. "Want some water? That's the only other thing I got. Well, that and beer, but we can't have you stinking of booze when we roll into the city. Social services ain't gonna appreciate that."

Jeff turned round, almost dropping the pan. The boy had torn the package off and was gnawing on the raw bacon slices, gobbling them down in chunks. He looked up at Jeff and smiled through shreds of meat and gristle, his lips shiny with grease, his teeth very white, very sharp.

———

BLACK SPOTS DANCE in Jeff's vision as the boy helps him over the ridge, hauling him up by the arm like a sack of feathers. The men at the bottom of the cliff have opened up a cannonade, rounds pinging against the rock. He feels a sharp kick in the calf as he drags himself over the top of the cliff, like in a playground scrap.

When he lifts his head, the boy is gone.

Jeff watches the trees, but the pale figure is nowhere in sight, only branches and dry leaves whispering in the breeze. If there's a message in their whispers, some secret salvation, he can't understand any of it. All he understands now is the exhaustion in his long-neglected muscles and the dread of being hunted.

He rolls up the leg of his jeans, already soaked with blood. There's a tiny hole about halfway up his calf muscle, but the bullet passed clean through. Blood beads from the wound, dark pearls in rhythm with his pulse. The pain is not too bad, not yet, but when Jeff tries to put weight on the leg it doesn't hold him up. His running days are over. In all likelihood, so are his living days. He hobbles a few steps before collapsing on a flat rock. Below, the shooting has stopped. The posse must be circling the cliff, looking for a way up to join the advance group, who should be arriving any moment, clambering up from the road.

Jeff wonders if the boy managed to get away. He wonders which one of the pursuers will pull the trigger. If there'll be remorse in his eyes, or only hatred and determination. If they'll bury him on the mountain, or toss him into a crevasse and let the elements and animals dispose of the evidence.

A sudden rush of terror tightens his throat, making it hard to breathe. He has thought about death a lot, more often in the past six months, but thinking about the certainty of it couldn't be more different. Worst of all, he's afraid that he'll piss himself when he sees them coming, leave the world with that final indignity.

Brush snaps underfoot, and Pete Clegg emerges from the trees, scratched up and out of breath. In his hands is an old over-and-under Remington. His eyes are bright with anticipation. Jeff is reminded of a kegger in Redman's Wood, of Pete—then eighty pounds lighter and with a thick head of brown hair—bragging about getting into Kayla Conlon's panties the night before. The same expression lights up Pete's face as he sees Jeff. Incongruously, he nods and smiles a little, as if the two of them had just run into each other at Sully's, nursing a couple of cold ones. Slowly the barrel rises, the muzzle looking as wide to Jeff as a highway tunnel. Frozen in its dead blank gaze, he turns his head away and raises his hands, as if to deflect the killing shot.

AFTER FINDING THE BOY, no one wanted to talk about him, but Jeff sensed the change. Pearly and Gus did their best to pretend that nothing was amiss. Beezer, on the other hand, was having none of it. He worked alongside the other three in hostile silence, communicating in nods and grunts and sullen looks. Jeff had seen the older man act like this before, usually after an epic bender at the end of a payday, but this time it seemed personal, almost hateful. When he tried to bring up the boy, he was met with a shrugging of shoulders and averted eyes.

"Beezer, his family's old in town, man," Gus said, as if this explained anything. He chewed his bologna sandwich thoughtfully. "You know? His granddaddy built that house he lives in, and *his* was granddaddy here before him. All the way back to the Civil War, or something." He stole a glance at Pearly, who shot him a look of such force that Gus stopped talking and stared into his lunchbox.

"What's that mean?" Jeff said. "We all grew up here in town."

"He didn't mean nothin' by it." Pearly's tone implied the discussion was over. "Beezer's just being Beezer. More ornery'n a bear with a toothache. He'll sleep off whatever's eating him in the back of his truck and be fine by noon."

Jeff didn't think so, but he knew better than to push the issue. Something had settled into the space between them, an invisible wall with Jeff on one side and Beezer on the other, the other two men careful not to take sides.

If he was being honest, he understood the gist of what Gus was saying. The town was an old town, and many of the families currently inhabiting it had lived here for generations. Just a small podunk place, no better nor worse than dozens of others in the area, yet industries had come and gone, times had changed for better and worse. Those deeply rooted in the land never left in search of better job or educational opportunities, never wondered what lay beyond the mountains.

"There's families here as old as the Boston Brahmins," Jeff's father would sometimes say when he was in his cups, an unreadable look in his eyes. He had moved to town to work in the long-defunct lumber mill, having met Jeff's mother, herself a mere second-generation newcomer, at a dance in Sevierville. "Just as closed up, too. We're not part of them, and we never will be."

Belonging to the town's old families conferred no material advantage or protection from the ravages of economic downturn. There were descendants who lived in the trailer park down by the state highway and those who inhabited the row of decaying mansions built during the brief lumber boom of the thirties. In times of plenty, newcomers outnumbered them by as much as three to one, and even in the lean years, they never made up more than half the town's population. But the gap had always been there, now that Jeff thought about it; a subtle sense of who was old in town and who was just passing through. A bond stronger than blood or land, stretching back centuries. Secrets were passed down to son or daughter, but never to the new blood.

Which was why Jeff was only mildly surprised to see that someone had gone through his house while he was at work, careful not to break things but not enough to conceal their tracks, or even bother trying. As far as he could tell, nothing was missing, and the intruders had left the place relatively neat. Of the child he'd left in the living room, there was no trace. He turned the deadbolt in the lock for the first time he could remember. Then he sat in the dying light of the day, trying to make sense of what was happening.

Had someone come and taken the boy? There were no signs of struggle, no suggestion of forced entry. Jeff found it hard to believe that a child who could survive alone in the wild for days would allow themselves to be taken just like that. Perhaps the boy belonged to one of the old families, the offspring of an embarrassing secret dalliance, or a disabled child kept out of sight, like people used to do with ill relatives in bygone days. He tried out several other answers, discarding them one by one. The strange behavior up at the construction site seemed ominous now, a sign of worse to come.

Something about the child had turned the Old Bloods against him, and the rest of the townsfolk, newcomers like Gus and Pearly, would be of no help. Whatever was happening had nothing to do with them. Maybe they had seen the same thing play itself out before and knew better than to get involved. Too long settled into their roles as spectators, they had lost the ability to assert themselves, used their indifference as a shield from the incomprehensible.

Worst of all was the knowledge that he had brought this

upon himself, sentenced the boy to death by bringing him down from the mountain. He had done it out of the best intentions, but best intentions only counted in fairy tales. He was out of his depth, an unwilling participant in a game with unfamiliar rules.

Beyond his reflection in the window, all was night. Lights coming on in the few houses across the road, the sky a smooth expanse of black volcanic glass. Stars sparkled in their thousands, cold, hard diamonds, many of them already dead, extinguished millions of years ago. Whoever had searched his house would be back, and soon. Jeff went out on his porch, lit a cigarette and waited.

He saw the lights before the sound of the engines reached him, blazing eyes coming up the road, one after another after another. Briefly he thought about going upstairs and getting his gun, before realizing how hopeless the situation was. He had known these men all his life. No matter how bad things got, Jeff didn't have it in him to harm them. As he stepped into the blinding glare of the headlights parked on his front lawn, shielding his eyes, he realized that he was outnumbered.

Six of them. No. Nine. Faces he knew almost as well as his own, or had thought he did. Rifles and shotguns cradled in their arms, not pointed at him but not lowered either, expressions darkened by the shadows.

They faced off across the lawn, the headlight beams drawing a line between the house and the trees, neither side speaking a word. It was probably the adrenaline, but Jeff didn't feel afraid, only anxious to find out what would happen next. Without knowing how or why, he had transgressed against some rule he'd never been made aware of, and now he was about to be punished for it. The stances of the men, the lack of interest from his neighbors all spelled this louder than words ever could.

A small, pot-bellied man took a step forward, tipped his hat either in salute or in preparation for what he was about to say. Jeff recognized Tom Hedlund, the chief of the town's three-man police department. "We're here for the child," he said, sounding almost apologetic. Jeff barely registered the words through the flood of relief. So they didn't have the boy: they could not have harmed him.

"He's not here." Jeff tried to see the reaction of the others, but the bright lights made it impossible. "I don't know where he's gone. Thought you had him."

"You're lying." Clyde Garver came forward, and there was no mistaking the fury and hatred on his face, the way his fists knotted around his Winchester rifle. A sudden rush of memory —the two of them sharing a Lucky Strike under the stadium bleachers, trying to look up girls' skirts, struck Jeff like a physical blow. Clyde stopped right in front of him, raised the rifle. "Get out the way. I want to see for myself."

"We already been in the house," Tom said, his unnatural calm making Jeff's head swim. He sounded as though he'd just caught someone doing sixty in a twenty-five zone and was about to hand out a speeding ticket, and his matter-of-fact voice was somehow more frightening than the guns in the hands of the men. "He ain't there. No point in looking."

"He knows more than he's lettin' on." Clyde pointed at Jeff with his weapon. "Why else would he bring that thing into town? Maybe he's got a deal with 'em. Some kind of pact."

Jeff felt a surge of anger at these men, this mob, menacing him at his own doorstep. "What do you want with him? He's just a kid."

"That don't concern you none," the chief of police said. "If you know where he is, tell us right now. Or else keep your mouth shut."

"He ain't done nothing to you."

"You don't know what he did or didn't do." Tom Hedlund rubbed his face with his free hand. "This has to do with the town."

"I was born here, too," Jeff said. "Just like the rest of you."

"You're *from* town," Tom said, his voice softening, as if speaking to a child. "But you ain't *of* the town. That makes all the difference."

He made a wary gesture, and the men started getting into their vehicles, as if awakened from a trance. "Go inside and stay there. Don't open the door. No matter what you hear out here."

"It's my town. My house. My land. It doesn't belong to you."

"It don't belong to none of us," the chief said. Lit by this truck's inner light, he looked tired and scared, as did the rest of his men who cast nervous glances into the darkness. "Not the town, not the land it was built on. Not the mountains. Never has, and never will. All we can do is hold onto it for as long as we can."

The cars and trucks started up and roared down the empty street. Within moments, the curves of the mountain hid them from sight. Silence fell again, leaden and unbroken.

Jeff went inside and closed the door. Sat down before his legs had a chance to betray him. His hands were shaking; he held them clasped together until he felt strong enough to get up and walk around the house.

The boy must have realized what lay in store for him and gotten away. But where could he have gone? Jeff went to the kitchen window, gazed out at the back yard. The night was absolute, a living thing, a total absence of light. Clouds must have rolled in, hiding the stars. A thin fingernail of the moon showed through, shedding a silvery glow on the slopes and peaks. He tried to put himself into the boy's shoes and quickly gave up.

A pale finger rapped softly on the glass, and he nearly jumped out of his skin. The boy stood outside, still wearing yesterday's outfit, dirt smeared all over his face and hands.

Jeff rushed out, dragged the boy inside. Wanted to hug him, to cry out with joy, but stopped himself.

"Where?"

The boy pointed to a beat-up Dodge truck resting on cinder

blocks next to the tool shed. About a year ago, Jeff had bought the wreck for cheap and gutted the interior, with the vague plan of selling it through an online forum for demolition derby enthusiasts. Like most of his projects, this one had gone unfinished, but had left the truck with several hidden nooks between the seats and the bodywork the small boy could easily fit into. Even if his pursuers had thought to check the truck, they would not have searched beyond the cabin.

Jeff went from room to room, switching off the lights, leaving on a single bulb in a windowless closet. His mind was working, making quick calculations as he layered warm clothes on himself and the boy. An hour to Gatlinburg, maybe two if he drove with the lights off and kept the speed under thirty. He could navigate that road blindfolded, and the darkness would hide the car from prying eyes. The Old Bloods would be looking for them, but there were few of them and too many square miles of rough terrain to cover.

"We can't stay here." He had no idea whether the boy could understand him or not, but he didn't care. "They'll be back for you. Sooner or later they'll find you. I can't keep you safe."

He gazed down into the boy's face, and a strange sensation took hold of him. For a second, for half an eye-blink, the child was no longer there, it had changed shape, and what was standing in front of him—

Jeff recoiled, put a hand on the wall to steady himself. The boy was just a boy again, a small figure swamped in an oversized jacket, looking up at him.

It don't belong to none of us. Never has, never will.

Carefully, Jeff knelt and placed one hand on the boy's shoulder. "I don't know what to do," he said. "But there are people in the city. Social services. They'll figure out who you belong to. Who you are. *What* you are. That's the best I can do. Okay?"

He didn't expect a response, and he didn't get any. But when he got up and went into the kitchen, the boy followed close on his heels. Jeff put a couple of water bottles into a backpack, tossed in a bag of chips and some energy bars. Went to the sash window and watched the dark street.

There would be no coming back from this, but he realized he wouldn't miss any of it. The house was just another house: a box with walls and floors and ceilings, filled with the debris of a shattered existence, of a life half-lived and purposeless. He wouldn't miss the grim little town with its smell of failure and defeat, the blood he now knew had soaked the land since time immemorial.

"Right," he said, more to himself, as he opened the door. "Right. Here goes."

GASPING, Pete Clegg parts the thick brush, checks the cliff's edge, every nerve thrumming. The downed man is on his side, trying to get up. But he can't see the creature anywhere. It's probably dashing through the trees, fleeing toward the second group of hunters. Pete feels guilty relief; though he knows what it is, and what it's capable of, it still *looks* like a little boy, and he doesn't want to be the one to gun it down.

The man on the ground, however, is a different proposition altogether. Pete tries not to think of him as Jeff, his drinking buddy, someone he's known for years. Just a man who's found himself on the wrong side of a law older than either of them, and who has to pay the price. *It's not your fault,* he thinks as he sights down the barrel. *Not really. I promise I'll make it as quick and painless as I can.*

Before Pete—a responsible gun owner, a man who hunts for subsistence, not out of sadism—can get his finger inside the trigger guard, a flutter of movement rustles the branches to his right. The boy leaps down from the tree and rushes at him, arms and legs pumping, hands hooked into claws. There's plenty of time, in spite of the child's speed, for Pete to take careful aim and take both targets out at once. But Pete is scared. Pete has seen what was left of Clyde Garver, and he grew up on stories about the things that stalk the woods. For no longer than a split second, Pete hesitates, and that's all the boy needs. Faster than the eye can follow, he scrambles up Pete like a jungle gym, hooks his legs under the man's armpits, pulls the head back and sinks his teeth into his exposed throat.

Pete tries to scream, but all that comes out through the gush of blood is a gurgle. There's blood everywhere, running down the front of his jacket, splashing on the ground. His hands flail around as the thing clamped to his upper body continues to chew and tear.

HORRIFIED AND REPULSED, Jeff feels the last of his strength leave his legs, his arms, his back. The boy raises his head, bright red and steaming in the cold, and drops from the thrashing corpse, already listening for the others. They're close now, the dogs barking in a frenzy, the men shouting and hooting.

Jeff drags himself away from the cliff edge, limps over to the dead man and picks up the gun. To his exhausted muscles, it feels like it weighs two hundred pounds. He points it toward the noise, raises the barrel higher and fires into the canopies. Waits for the report to spread, fires again.

Abruptly, the forest goes silent. Jeff crouches down and filches Pete's pockets for shells, reloads the shotgun. Next to him, the boy licks his hands, passes them over his bloody face. He's looking at Jeff with something akin to confusion.

Jeff picks a position behind a stout trunk, lets off another shot into the trees, closer to the ground now. He can't hold them off for long, but he thinks the boy might just make it. At least he'll have the opportunity to try.

"Go," Jeff says, but in his delirium isn't sure if he has spoken out loud. It doesn't matter. When he turns to repeat his entreaty, the boy is no longer there. A tremor of branches, a shadow skittering through the ranks of boles, and he's gone, like he never existed.

The light filtering through the branches leaches color from the day. Fog invades his mind, his senses. A dog yelps and whimpers somewhere in the trees. Jeff imagines the animals straining their leashes, Matt Wendell struggling to hold them back. Matt has paid a good deal of money for those hounds, money that could have gone into fixing his trailer or his beat-up truck, or into the alimony payments he almost lost his driver's license over.

Jeff stands up, rummages through the corpse's pockets for shells. Breaks and reloads the shotgun. Pain has woken up inside him, everywhere at once, a volcano spewing fire up his leg. In the movies...in the movies it's always just a flesh wound. Someone laughs, and he realizes the raspy sound is coming from his own mouth. He fires over and over, aiming high and wide to scare off the hunters, praying that he doesn't hit anyone.

The forest explodes with gunfire, and Jeff drops to the ground.

His face buried in cold mud, he curls instinctively to make himself into as small a target as possible. Angry buzzing fills his ears, the thump and thwack of bullets in old wood. The rifle is gone, forgotten; it could be within reach or a hundred miles away for all the good it will do him.

Head ringing, Jeff rolls over and tries to crawl away just as the dogs reach him, compact bodies slamming into him, raking his arms with their claws. Damp, steaming breath and sharp teeth find his sleeves and trousers and unprotected skin, fighting for purchase.

He screams and kicks out with both legs, feels the killing jaws rip away, taking shreds of fabric and flesh with them.

Grabing a piece of wood, he slams it into the nearest dog's snarling face, brandishing it at the others like a caveman.

The gunshot and the impact barely register. All he knows is that his muscles aren't holding him up anymore and the ground is rushing at him, darkness tunneling his vision.

⁂

THE BARRICADE HAD BEEN ASSEMBLED from sandbags and scrap lumber, all but invisible in the darkness. Jeff had plowed into it at no faster than twenty miles an hour, and that alone had saved his life. At the last moment, he had hauled the wheel to the right and the truck's front end came to rest in the ditch by the road. His nose was bloody and his sternum ached like it was broken, but he seemed to be otherwise unhurt.

"I want to see your hands," said the silhouette approaching from the left, its words underlined by the cocking of a trigger. Jeff nodded slowly, pulled the door handle and raised his hands. He pushed the door open, struggled out of the canted seat. Beside him, the passenger door cracked open, just enough for something small and lithe to slink out into the night.

Clyde Garver walked into the light, hunting rifle pointed at Jeff, a terrified expression on his face. "I knew you were lying," he said, with a nervous chuckle. His eyes traveled from side to side, straining to penetrate the moonless night.

Jeff leaned on the truck, tried to get his bearings. They were at the turnoff for the old football field, long overgrown and succumbed to trash. On closer inspection, the sandbags were half empty and the wood was black and rotted. He could have stepped on the gas and driven straight through it.

"Where is it?" Clyde must have read his next thought. "Where's the thing?"

Thing. That is what the boy was. Something that could look

like a human child when it wanted, or like something altogether different.

"No idea."

"Hell," Clyde said. "I don't like doing this any more than you do. But it's got to be done. For our children. For everyone in town."

"They leave us alone." Jeff took a step toward the other man, who shouldered his rifle, but kept looking into the darkness. Out of the corner of his eye, Jeff caught a hint of movement, a deeper shadow across a field of pitch black. "They're not the ones hunting you right now. Or me."

He moved closer, and Clyde did exactly what Jeff expected him to do—aimed the gun straight at him, squinting against the truck's light.

In an instant, the boy was on him, hands and teeth closing around Clyde's scrawny neck, a lion taking down a Cape buffalo on the scorched savannah. Clyde yelled out, more in shock than pain, dropped the weapon as he tried to fend off his attacker. His feet tangled and he went down as the boy twisted his neck. Blood sprayed across the grass, black and shimmering in the headlights.

Sickened, Jeff crouched behind the truck, his stomach heaving. He clamped his hands over his ears, but there was no escaping the noises, the rip and slap of gristle and wet meat, the crack of bones, the tattoo of the dying man's boots in the dirt.

Time passed, but Jeff was unaware of it, buried in a nightmare of red and black, of claws and flashing teeth, of yellow eyes shimmering in the dark. When he dared look up, the boy was standing in front of him. He had shed the outer garments and cleaned up his hands and face, but there was still blood on his hands and in the corners of his mouth.

Jeff became aware of two things. The first was that the sun was coming up, a reddish glow through rifts in the clouds, tendrils of fog dragging across the empty fields. The second was that he could hear vehicles approaching from the direction of town. Clyde must have called for reinforcements before approaching the truck.

There was only one way out and it was up over the mountain. Into the woods. Their pursuers wouldn't follow them into the caves. This he knew without a doubt. The boy and his kind belonged up in the mountain, just like the Old Bloods belonged in town—an old law that laid down boundaries neither side could overstep, on pain of death.

He got up and set off after the boy, into the blood dawn spilling over the mountain.

SHAPES SURROUND JEFF, blocking out the trees. Across a vast distance he hears Matt Wendell calling the dogs to heel, patting their wet flanks. Already Jeff feels his breath getting shallow, his heart quickening as it strains to pump the leaking fluid through his body.

His body jerks in the mud as if someone has just kicked him in the side. Mike Bragg's jowly face swims above, red and contorted with rage.

"Where did it go, you sonofabitch?" Mike asks. From the expression on his face, he's ready to stomp Jeff's head to a bloody pulp, but Tom Hedlund restrains him with a hand on his massive arm.

"You got no idea what you've done," Hedlund shouts to Jeff. The faces of the other men are darkened. Either the sun has moved behind the trees, or Jeff's vision is fading from the fatigue and loss of blood. He pulls in a breath, realizing there's nothing to say.

Hedlund spits on the ground, points his rifle at Jeff's face. "It's us or them. Today and tomorrow, going back hundreds of years. Maybe more. You can't understand that. Or you do understand, and this is your choice."

Jeff squeezes his eyes shut, waits for the blast. When it doesn't come, he peeks through and sees Hedlund walking away, his rifle slung over his shoulder. The others follow without so much as turning to look at Jeff. He's as good as dead now; even if he could drag himself back to town on shattered legs, he has made himself into an enemy, a monster, a thing to be hunted down and shot without mercy.

The last of the voices fade. Now there's nothing but the hum and creak of the forest, the silent song of the wind. Nothing but the pain and cold, death stalking the landscape, patiently waiting him out.

By the time Jeff crawls and stumbles his way to the cave mouth, the sun has already passed its zenith and is making its way down the indifferent sky. He's cold everywhere, in his bones, in his head, a deep lake of cold brimming in the center of him. There can't be much time left, if any.

It's dark in the passage, but he feels his way to the painted chamber, lies on his back, rough stone digging in through his clothes. The drawings and symbols glow dimly, as if generating their own light. He traces their shapes in the air with his finger. A story of death and destruction and rebirth, written aeons ago. A story he'll never understand and doesn't feel he needs to.

They press closer around him, the eyes bright in the darkness, watching him, waiting. He has upset the balance, broken the rules in some incomprehensible way. With his last strength, Jeff pushes himself upright against the cave wall, allowing tension to drain out of his spent muscles. The blank periods behind his eyes are getting longer by the minute and it's harder and harder to snap out of them. He's tempted to let go, to slip away and let the warm embrace of darkness carry his pain and fear away. But he wants to see them. He wants to know.

Winter is almost here, and spring will follow. Then summer

and fall, another turn of the cycle in the bright world above. Down here, everything will stay the same, just as it always has. Down here, where the tunnels lead into the real, secret heart of the earth, where time stands still. Some small part of him will always be one with the darkness.

He goes away for a moment, returns to soft caresses on his face and arms. In the gleam of the symbols, they are beautiful: long bodies and angular skulls, lips smiling, showing more teeth than any human mouth can hold. The boy is somewhere among them, reverted to his true form.

A sharp talon rests on his neck, right over the jugular vein. Jeff can feel the pulse under the skin, the pressure. There aren't many of them in the cave, and they are starved. They will survive. They always survive. But their feedings have been further in between than ever, and a long, hungry winter lies ahead.

Jeff catches an amber, vertically slitted eye. Throws his head back and takes hold of the talon, gently pushes down on it until he can feel the skin part under the razor-sharp edge.

In the short instant before the darkness invades him, he feels like he belongs. Finally belongs.

DAMIR SALKOVIC

Damir Salkovic is the author of novels Kill Zone and Always Beside You. His shorter work has been featured in the Lovecraft eZine, Dimension6 Annual Collection 2020, and in multiple horror, science and speculative fiction anthologies.

TAYLOR MANOR

LT WARD

T ucked away in the rural town of Craine, there was a castle with stretching, manicured gardens of tightly-cropped grasses and bursts of blooming flowers, the edifice erected to tower over the farmed fields and riverbeds. Elegant, majestic, perfect.

A juxtapositional domain for the opulently-lifestyled, located at the edge of the mortgaged farms and small-town businesses. For Craine, Taylor Manor was the lifeline that saved its failing economy after the Great Depression. Years of hard weather—floods one year followed by droughts the next—left Craine with one fiscal option to save their citizens: tourism.

So Taylor Manor became a destination for those who wanted to visit an American castle, to stroll the grounds and imagine the wealth it took to have called such a place home. For nigh a century, the residence remained inherited property down the Taylor lineage. Each generation leased the land and the buildings to the village. The estate earned a pittance of what it was worth, as the family couldn't find a buyer with enough wealth, nor one who was willing to live hundreds of miles away from the nearest city.

Then Edi Fera, the pop star, decided she was desperately overdue for a year-long hiatus. She and her husband Michael sought somewhere away from the chaos of stardom. Of course, they *were* music royalty, so when an online search showed Taylor Manor was on the market for a steal, Edi called their realtor and had him bang out the paperwork.

Move-in day, all hands were on deck to help unload and unpack the many Fera possessions. Edi, swathed in a silk blouse, fitted slacks, and impractical Gianvito Rossi stilettos, stationed herself on the upper landing of the sweeping foyer staircase, directing her staff with a lilting voice trained to carry perfect acoustics over packed amphitheaters.

After the California king bed was brought through the double doors, Edi descended the grand staircase. She turned to monitor the two movers who carried the oversized black wooden headboard, followed by the two with the footboard. At the base of her staircase, she gazed upwards with a squint, her eyes scouring the walls. The mahogany panels rose to greet the vaulted ceiling, but the shades of stain varied ever so slightly.

"Odd. The space looks like it should be filled with something."

Michael, passing through with a head bowed to the phone in his hands, stopped beside his wife. "Did you say something?"

"There." She pointed to the landing. "That empty space. That whole wall. It's odd that nothing's there, right?"

He looked up and agreed. "Maybe there's something in the attic. The historical society kept a bunch of the Taylors' items up there. Maybe they forgot about it."

Not knowing what they wanted, but certain they would know it when they found it, Edi and her children rummaged through the manor's attic. With flashlights in hand, they lifted and searched under dust-covered cloths and inside trunks with creaking, rusting hinges. The children's flashlight beams crissed and crossed the elongated room, bouncing over the misshapen drop cloths draped over artifacts left behind from the Taylor family. Ghosts of the original family, waiting for the new manor owners to unveil them. Brave and curious, Lion and Vivre split from their mother's side to search deeper in the attic.

"Mama!" squealed Vivre. "Look at me!" A plum velvet cloche on her head, Vivre's small hands flipped her fine brown waves over her shoulders. She cocked her head side to side as a model peacocking her newfound hat.

Lion joined his sister. "You look like one of those steampunk femmes."

"Thank you," Vivre beamed. She turned back to the trunk and pulled out a sable woolen bowler. After brushing away the dust, she handed it to Lion. "Here. This one is yours."

Lion rolled his eyes and placed the bowler onto his head.

"There," he said. He posed with one arm folded across his belly, the other across his back, and bowed. "Ma'am."

Vivre giggled and clapped her hands.

"Well, aren't you both the dapper pair?" Edi said, raising her head from peering into a cardboard box on the floor. "Okay, you two, I need help. We're looking for portraits or paintings. Something that's big enough to fill that space on the wall at the middle landing."

"Why do we want their stuff?" asked Lion. He walked the trail between the Taylor artifacts.

"It was first the Taylors' home and now it's ours. They designed this place."

Lion stopped his stroll before a few museum placard stands and red velvet ropes clumped in front of a sheet that covered something flat and tall. Edi walked over to her son. Vivre stayed on her mother's heels until she found a vanity with a time-melted mirror, the glass tarnished and wavy, to inspect her new look.

"According to their Wikipedia page, Taylor Manor took two years to build. They started just after the birth of their second son Louis and lived here during some of the construction. Kind of how we're living here with the renovations.

"The Taylors clearly loved this place and so do I. I think it would be a wonderful homage to hang whatever paintings they had up, don't you think?"

Lion nodded. He studied the organized clutter, stepping closer to the sheet-covered treasure he found leaning against the wall.

"Looks like you found something. Those are about the right size." Edi smiled at her son.

Together, they tugged a side of the drop cloth to slowly reveal a stack of paintings. The first a massive oil painting of the original Taylor Manor matriarch. Edi peaked behind the painting. Another painting. The patriarch. Nestled behind their parents' portraits were two six-foot paintings, each of a young boy smiling and posed similarly to his parents. The crown princes.

The Feras had hired contractors to renovate some of the rooms from storage spaces for the Tourism Board into variously-purposed rooms—bedrooms, offices, banquet hall, recording spaces, toy rooms, and more. Edi took two of the workmen off their jobs and ordered them to rehang the Taylor family portraits above the landing.

With the first family on display in the mansion again, Taylor Manor became home.

DURING THE FOUR weeks it took the Feras to close on the manor and prepare their family to move across country, the Law Offices of Hughman, Shifrin, and Brown sent notice on the Fera family's behalf to Craine's aldermen and tourism board that Taylor Manor was indefinitely closed to the public. This unexpected announcement caused disbelieving mutterings to circulate around the small town.

The official placard affixed to the wrought iron gates was met with furious screams.

Without the draw of the castle, who would come and willingly spend their vacation dollars? Trinkets, magnets, and apparel featuring the manor would go unsold. Huge diner and restaurant orders from tourists, determined that calories do not exist while on vacation, would go unordered. The rooms of the hotels, motels, and bed and breakfasts would remain empty until the holiday season saw an influx of traveling family members.

Taylor Manor was the lifeblood of Craine's economy and the Feras were transient vampires here to drain the town.

However, this was unbeknownst to Edi and Michael, who fell

in love with online images of the quaint town, excited for the solitude that could never quite be found within their city homes and certainly not in the hotel penthouses.

Only five staff members from the Los Angeles hills traveled across the country to move to Craine—Edi and Michael's personal assistants, the children's nannies, and a live-in chef. The rest of the household staff was comprised of local hired help.

Craine's residents were reluctant to take anything from the Fera family. They weren't from Craine. In fact, unconfirmed rumors circulated that they were only using the manor for a year, then abandoning the property for world tours. If true, they were long-term visitors, not residents. Unwanted, selfish guests. In one year's time, the damage to the local economy would take years to recover from. If the Feras didn't reopen the land to the public, even longer.

Unbeknownst to Michael Fera of his pariah status in Craine, he called Hibbert Landscaping, the only landscaping company in town, to contract them to care for the grandiose gardens. After nearly three decades keeping Taylor Manor lush then let go once the Craine township lost control over the estate, they had been the first business to head towards the red. The Fera rehire contract would put them in the black, but Caleb Hibbert was conflicted.

Until Alderman Fetterman showed up in Caleb's office.

"We need you to get close to the family," the alderman said. He'd been closely monitoring the goings on at the manor as he was one of the few privy to the documents handed to the Tourism Board. His political campaign had rested upon Taylor Manor's previous years' successful income. Now that his cash cow was no longer public, his position as Craine's most powerful alderman was being called into question.

"What the hell do you mean 'get close to the family'?" Caleb's eyes flicked to the screen; the Fera contract lay opened and waiting for his digital signature. The tab had sat open for several hours, the words a blur in his mind.

Alderman Fetterman cocked his head, his mouth quirked into a smile. "Not close like sharing Thanksgiving dinner bullshit. But close enough so the Feras consider you someone trustworthy."

"Trustworthy?"

"Someone they would never question to be on their property."

"Wouldn't this be siding with the enemy? If I work for them?"

"It's not them you'd really be working for." For as long as Caleb had managed his inherited company, Alderman Fetterman had held his political seat. He was as much a staple on the city council as Taylor Manor was its honeypot. He was not one to be questioned, his motives clearly driven by Craine's best interests.

Alderman Fetterman walked around the desk and slapped a hand to Caleb's back. "Think of it as being an underground hero. The man who helped save Craine from music industry trash. Trust me, Caleb."

Squelching the last of his reservations, Caleb Hibbert signed the contract.

Along with the groundskeepers, the Feras hired two full-time and two part-time employees from Maid for Perfection. Alderman Fetterman made time to speak with all four new hires before their first day at the manor.

Despite Michael Fera hiring the staff, he left the home management to his wife. Edi was the domestic head of their family, and Michael was pleased to support her in that vein. He dutifully greeted his employees, then apologized for being called to work in the refurbished west wing, where the his and hers recording studios were located. Meanwhile, Edi issued the day-to-day directives to the employees. Vivre, followed by her nanny, trailed behind Edi. The child echoed her mother, crossing her arms when her mother did, pointing when her mother did, nodding when her mother did.

Caleb Hibbert took notes from the new homeowner about the land he'd cared for since he'd inherited the business from his father. Wanting to tell Edi where to shove her suggestions for landscape changes, but it was Alderman Fetterman's words that made him hold his tongue. Actually, it was those words that curled his lips into a placating smile.

The Fera children stayed indoors most of March, but as April approached, their tutors insisted Lion and Vivre spend more time outdoors, freeing the house staff of the incessant questions and indifferent messes that are part and parcel with having children. For Lion, the thirteen-year-old dragged his electronics onto the stone lanai, donning sunglasses and headphones to drown himself into the familiarity of the digital world.

But Vivre, in all of her eight years, had never known the freedom she found on the grounds of Taylor Manor. Her parents' careers required visibility, accessibility, in order to make their record and tour sales. She had become one of their commodities, and although Edi and Michael protected their progeny from the public with walls of bodyguards, nannies, and an entourage, Vivre still hadn't experienced true privacy.

However, her parents loosened their reins on their daughter, allowing her to run wherever she pleased as long as it was within the confines of the stone walls outlying the Manor's property.

"Just be careful," Vivre's nanny told her as she escorted the young child through one of the sitting rooms. It was an odd room, one renovated and out of sync with the rest of the domicile's style. The nanny hated it without cause, always feeling even more of a chill there than in the other rooms, but its doors led to the expansive lanai and the great outdoors of the backyard. It was the fastest means through the main floor to the courtyard.

The April sun baked the damp, mowed lawn, turning the air into a blanket of humidity. Vivre inhaled a deep breath of earthy air, her young lungs swelling with the promise of adventure. Her first exploratory stop was the gatehouse. The building at the front gate mimicked the style of the manor with limestone blocks and metal-paned windows.

Vivre stood on her tiptoes with flat palms on the dusty windows, her nose pressed to the dirty glass. Having been renovated into a gift shop, rows of stands lined the room, each overflowing with notecards, posters, and history books. The walls were racked with more merchandise, sepia images of the Taylor family splayed throughout.

Vivre's face pinched. She did not want to explore anything that sold someone else's life.

She turned, disgusted, and marched across the massive grounds. One of the hired groundskeepers—Peter, Vivre thought his name was—bobbed to a beat only he was privy to, his head entrapped by oversized noise-canceling headphones. Vivre watched for his gaze and darted away to the backyard without ever being seen.

The hedged walkways and low rolling hills spilled towards a small forest—an untouched clump of nature within the estate's property lines. Vivre hurried her gait until she reached the shadows at the forest's edge. Her steps slowed as her eyes widened. The mess of maples and oaks and pines loomed, but there was a beaten path with ground so packed and so smooth, she felt the hardness through the rubber of her Nike soles.

The boughs of the forest folded over one another, blocking the light to envelop the child in midday darkness. Just as her nerves began to best her curiosity, sunlight gleamed bright and yellow onto the path. Vivre marched into the light's warmth. It wrapped her with reassurances that she was safe, even as she stepped into a small graveyard.

Vivre squealed, clapped her hands, and jumped several times.

She rushed inside the stone walls topped with wrought iron swirls. Granite stones laid at the head of sunken beds. The girl ran between the gravestones, reading the names and dates, before finally planting herself at the foot of a gray monument that was taller than her father. Two smaller headstones rested on either side of the statue.

Ansel Rotham Taylor
Sadie Nottingham Taylor
Malcolm Rotham Taylor
Louis Elias Taylor
Beloved family, angels stolen from Earth

Vivre fell to her hands and knees and crawled back and forth from one headstone to another. They all cited the same death date—*21 October 1926*. She sat back on her heels and calculated their ages in her head, tapping her fingers to hold onto the numbers. Ansel was forty, Sadie was thirty-two, Malcolm was thirteen (like Lion), and Louis was eight (like her).

With a pouty lip, she asked, "What happened to you?"

No one answered. No one *could* answer. Instead, the sunlight hugged Vivre as she rose to collect dandelions and laid a fuzzy, yellow bouquet at each of the headstones. When the shadows shifted and the air chilled, Vivre shivered, bade the stones good-bye, then headed home to her castle.

THAT EVENING, Vivre told her family at their formal dining table all about the little graveyard. "And there was a family with the same name as our house. And they all died on the same day. And there were two little boys. Malcolm and Louis. Or is it

Louie? Louis, right?" She took a breath and shoveled a forkful of buttered carrots into her mouth, waiting for someone to answer.

"We bought dead people?" Lion dropped his fork with a clatter onto his plate.

Edi reached over, covering her son's shaking hand with hers. "No, honey. We didn't buy dead people."

"Well, we kind of did." Michael chuckled. His wife shot him a look, her eyes darting to their son, then back to her husband. He rolled his eyes.

"We didn't buy dead people," Edi said, a warning to Michael embedded in her steady voice. "We bought their home. A home they loved so much, they wanted to be buried here."

Vivre said around the vegetables in her mouth, "I want to be buried here when I die."

Edi's face flickered, a wince, then smoothed into softness. "That won't be for a long time, but if that's what you want."

"How did they die?" Lion asked, looking to his father. Against his electric green locks, the teen's face blanched to a sickly hue.

"There was a fire," Michael began. "Back during the Great Depression, people didn't have furnaces like the ones we have. They used fireplaces to stay warm. One night, the kids slept together in one of the downstairs sitting rooms but, from what the brochure on this place said, a few sparks flew onto the rug.

"Their parents woke up to the housekeeper screaming about smoke. The parents ran for the kids. They got out, but the family later died due to smoke inhalation.

"All of the live-in staff made it out. The manor was saved. The damage being in mostly that room and a bit in the nearby ones and that hallway."

Vivre set down her fork. "Those poor people. That sucks, Dad."

"It does."

Lion said with a tremor, "After they died, who lived here?"

"No one, honey," his mother cooed. "The Taylors' extended family inherited the manor—one of the brothers, I think. But they didn't want to live here. They renovated it, then tried to sell it but couldn't. For years, it's been a tourist destination, because they could lease the property to the village."

"Which was why it was a steal for us to buy." Michael ripped a chunk off his biscuit and popped it into his mouth.

The Feras finished their meal in silence. Edi rubbed Lion's hand, eating slowly, watching her son out of the corner of her eye.

After Shanna, one of the Maid for Perfection's full-time staff, cleared the dishes, Edi escorted her children up the grand staircase. She paused at the landing, the preserved faces of the Taylors peering down on them.

"Do you think they would like us, Mom? If they knew we're the ones living in their home?" Vivre asked.

Edi looked down on her daughter, then up to the first Taylor Manor matriarch. "If they could know how much we love this home, I'm sure they would."

As Edi tucked Vivre under her plush blankets, she sang her child a lullaby.

Ears once deafened by death, six feet below the ground, encased in a mahogany box and fertile dirt, awoke and listened to the mother. The matriarch's voice filled with love, a siren's call to rise.

NIGHT FELL as Caleb drove the Hibbert Landscaping truck down the Taylor Manor driveway, tires grumbling against the gravel. He parked it off to the side of the circle drive, in the designated service staff lot.

He slammed his driver's door, coughed emphatically, then walked towards the back of the property. Along the way, Shanna came out the service entrance with the other house servant, Brian.

"Hey!" Caleb shouted, waving his arm high. Beyond the reach of the front and rear lampposts of the property, the soft yellow light streaming through the mansion's windows shone down on the stone walkway. He tipped his head towards the windows, searching the lit ones.

The threesome met halfway.

"Isn't it too late to be working?" Shanna asked.

"It's crazy dark, man," said Brian, with his hands in his jacket pockets. "What the hell are you doing here at this time of night?" The frogs croaked songs interspersed with splashes from the garden pond, veiled in the darkness of the cloudy night. Their conversation boomed over the tranquil evening sounds.

"Fetterman asked me to stop by."

The housekeepers exchanged a look. Each replied with a smile.

"The big project?"

"You know it," Caleb bellowed. He hacked a faux wracking cough into his hand. A peek to the windows.

Nothing.

Raising his volume, Brian said, "Any big plans for the grounds this year?"

"Not sure yet." Caleb's voice was a steady shout. "The Feras insisted I keep them looking like last year's, but some of the hedges are nearing the end of their life cycles. It might be time to pull them. Plant something new."

"They're listening," whispered Shanna.

At a second story window, Vivre pressed her hands upon the glass. She waved at the staff below. As the groundskeeper and housekeepers waved back, the child's nanny appeared behind her. She curtly nodded, then tugged the child by her shoulder and away from the window.

In voices hushed for their ears alone—even the frogs were

too distracted to hear—the conspirators spoke for several more minutes before parting to their individual vehicles.

Yet past the garden and its pond, across the vast lawn, at the edge of the woods, four charred shadows heard every word.

IN THE EARLY EVENINGS, as the daylight stretched to make way for the coming long summer days, the family drove into Craine to dine at the various local restaurants, an effort to connect to their new hometown. When the Feras first moved into Taylor Manor, there were seven restaurants offering a variety of options. But by the middle of May, three had shuttered permanently.

The spring break tourists hadn't bothered to come. The behind-closed-doors purchasing of the manor had managed to keep the looky-loos away with the exception of one lone paparazzo who couldn't capture a verifiable picture of the Feras as the family rarely strayed from their castle.

Aside from the Craine denizens who worked at the manor, the locals shunned the celebrity residents. Bitterness led to cold shoulders, and unrequited greetings followed the Feras. Edi and Michael, unaccustomed to the brush-offs, nixed the nightly outings, much to their children's vexation.

As May waned into June, the family locked themselves away on the mansion grounds, ordering food and necessities online to be delivered to the front gate. Discomforted by even those familiar to them, the Feras released their personal assistants and live-in chef to an extended summer break. Pleas from Lion and Vivre to keep their nannies on staff worked, barely.

Without fans and an entourage, Michael and Edi found themselves living in a world of silence. Taylor Manor's silence was so thick, their skin itched. It whispered at them. It gnawed at their peace.

When Edi spoke, her songbird voice startled her, foreign to her own ears. She had nowhere to go, so she swapped out her designer business wear for couture sweatpants and tank tops, her hair no longer needing to be styled beyond a messy bun, and her makeup limited to a tinted balm and mascara. Lonely, the naturally extroverted creature attempted to befriend her hired groundskeepers and house servants, but they expressed no interest in friendship, abruptly ending conversations as soon as her directives were given. Edi resigned her days to streaming television and YouTube videos, hours in the manor's new workout room, or singing with her husband in the west wing.

Meanwhile, Michael's ambivert nature initially thrived with his evenings free to spend alone with his wife and children, the nannies dismissed to their own devices. His days in the recording studio propelled him to be weeks ahead on his next album, having found Taylor Manor to be a fortuitous muse.

Even so, as Edi's shining spirit dwindled—rekindled briefly during their daily practice time together—his own spark began to fade. Over the weeks, Michael, unnerved by the quietude and his wife's transformed demeanor, found himself withdrawing from all but his music, his children, and Edi. Whenever the staff approached the patriarch, a sharpened glare silenced them until they scurried away.

Adding to the restless quiet, an irrepressible heat loomed within the castle. No matter the open windows or forced air conditioning units employed, spending too much time in any given room would bring perspiration to one's skin and thirst to their throat.

On the good weather days, to encourage Lion and Vivre to escape the unexplainable warmth within the mansion, the nannies banished the children to the outdoors. Vivre bounded across the property to the little graveyard where she placed dandelion bouquets on the graves of her new friends.

Lion joined his sister reluctantly. He put on a brave face,

pretending that like his younger sibling, he had no fear of ghosts. After a few weeks of visitations to their deceased friends, Lion's nerves faded to a peaceful expectation. The siblings traipsed to the private cemetery, bringing with them stories to tell the undead. One child wore her purple cloche; the other wore his woolen bowler.

The elder Feras faded from the rest of the world. Phones and tablets were abandoned at charging stations in the bedrooms. Calls and emails were left unanswered. Their publicists, agents, trainers, bandmates, and friends worried at the disappearance of the Feras, but Edi and Michael made the obligatory proof of life social media posts, dismissing any further communication as superfluous and distracting. Their immediate solitude seeped into an imbalance where they pushed all others away as the manor drew them in with an alien serenity to which they were desperate to embrace, faithful the zen would come.

The shift from extreme extroverts to a family of hermits worried those outside of Craine, but pleased the locals, who whispered behind their hands that soon, soon the town would see the eviction of the Feras and a return to its natural order.

However, the Feras did not belong to Craine. They didn't even belong to the world anymore.

They belonged to Taylor Manor.

IN JUNE, more businesses closed. After the tourist traps, it was the dry cleaners, the bowling alley, the car dealership, the coffee house, one of the gas stations.

Unemployment soared.

Faith in Craine's aldermen fell, and those around him began to question his regime "It's unacceptable. Those bastards are taking Craine's inherited tourism," Alderman Fetterman growled into his phone.

"I'm not sure what you really want me to do." Caleb Hibbert was chomping at the bit to do *something*. His wife had lost her job at the IGA. The grocery store had initially salvaged jobs by cutting the employees down to part-time, but the lower sales weren't enough. Four clerks were let go and Catherine Hibbert was one of the unfortunate few.

"Nothing illegal, right?" he asked of the alderman.

"No, nothing illegal. You've been invited onto the property. Shanna Dunker has keys. It's not trespassing, if that's what you're worried about." Alderman Fetterman did not enjoy having doubt laid upon his plans.

Alderman Fetterman leaned into his political voice, the one he used to sway the voters. "Just scare the Feras a bit. They have an old American castle. Let those pansy ass musicians know what it means to live somewhere that's old, with a history and a past."

"Ghosts?"

"You don't have to be dead to scare the shit out of someone."

CALEB REACHED out to those he—and, to a lesser extent who Fetterman—trusted. Peter, Shanna, and Brian readily volunteered to accompany him. Shanna and Brian, familiar with the reach of the security cameras, worked out where the dead spots would be.

Two hours into a Wednesday morning, the four parked outside the front gate. With a sliver of moon overhead, Caleb opened the iron gates. The gatehouse watched quietly as the intruders wove themselves across the massive lawn, dodging the sights of the cameras.

As they approached the manor, they regretted the ski masks and black garb they'd chosen to wear. The night air failed to stave off the June day's heat. Sweat built up, trapped between fabric and skin, adding to the urgency to get through the intended jape as quickly as possible.

Once inside the back door, Shanna padded in the keycode, silencing the alarm system. Slinking along the walls, they made their way to the foyer, turning the tchotchkes on the decorative tables to apparently wrong directions. Small, noticeable touches.

Beside the grand staircase, nestled into the curve on either side of the steps and below the barristers, two life-sized marble statues—Morticia and Gomez Addams—overlooked the entry-way. The foursome huddled around the first statue, preparing to turn Morticia around. Crouched, lining around all four sides, they readied themselves to maneuver the stone. However, their hands were slick with sweat and slipped inside their gloves, none of them able to achieve a solid grip on the marble.

"Fuck," whispered Brian.

"Shh," hissed Caleb. "They might hear you."

Brian stood with his hands on his hips. "Well, what the hell are we supposed to do? It's hotter than Hades in here. We can't risk prints on anything and I can't get a grip for shit."

Caleb dabbed at his masked forehead with his sleeved forearm, doing little more than squeegeeing sweat from his ski mask into his eyes. The heat inside the castle was worse than outside. For all the times he'd visited Taylor Manor as a child on a field trip or as a volunteer with the Taylor Manor Historical Society, Caleb never felt hot inside the mansion. If anything, he'd always been cooler inside the manor. Cold, even. The stone and brick usually captured the chill with an oppressive hold.

Before Caleb could render a decree, the chandelier above came to life and footsteps lightly padded the staircase.

"Go, go, go!" whispered Peter, ushering everyone out the way they'd come.

After they'd escaped to the front lawn, the barest evidence of a few erroneously turned knickknacks left behind, they ripped the ski masks from their heads. The wash of tepid air cooled the intruders immediately.

Shanna looked back. Just a glance. The lighted windows trailed from the second story east wing, down the foyer, and toward the kitchen. Someone had woken for a snack, maybe a drink of water, Shanna could not be sure. But she was sure of the anger boiling inside her. The Feras were interlopers, interfering with Craine by their very presence. Too much wealth. Too many blessings. The Feras had more than anyone should expect in life, yet they took that which belonged to Craine. As Shanna fled with the others, the last of her doubts and permissiveness towards the obstinate family dissolved within her anger.

Taylor Manor deserved better than the Feras.

---

21 October 1926

A COLD SNAP frosted the grounds of Taylor Manor. The last of the autumn blooms and vibrant leaves that had yet to fall from the trees were painted in a frosty glaze. As the full moon beamed brightly, illuminating the glittering frozen ground, Hamish Tund took a swig from his flask.

The former farmer glared at the mansion, muttering profanities under his fogging breath. Hamish's blood ran hot and fast through his veins, making his threadbare jacket sufficient against the icy outdoors. He drank until he emptied his flask, the last of his bourbon. Rage heated him to his core—the alcohol tagged along out of habit, not necessity.

The Taylors. God's curse to Craine.

After two hard seasons of drought and winds that ripped his struggling crops from the ground before they could flourish, the Craine Savings and Loan foreclosed on Hamish, leaving him, his wife, and his children without a livelihood and a home. It wasn't Hamish Tund who sold his family's home to the Taylors. No, they purchased the land for their mansion by swooping in as vultures, buying it on the cheap, well below market value from the bank.

Evelyn Tund left her husband and ran away to her family in Missouri with his children. She was a bitch who blamed him for the failings of the farm. It was not his fault that the winds pulled the seedlings from the parched ground. It was not his fault the bank refused to excuse the missed payments on their mortgage. It was not his fault that bourbon, whiskey, and moonshine were the only things that kept him sane.

A year ago, the divorce summons arrived. *Impotence.* His soon-to-be ex-wife actually had her attorney declare him impotent so that she could take the last of his legacy from him—his family.

The humiliation bore into him until Hamish lost his days to a drunken stupor.

As he stood before Taylor Manor, eight years of restrained rage sobered him. Had Ansel Taylor not stolen his land, Hamish would have managed to find the money to reclaim it. He'd just needed time. But the mansion was erected in the blink of an eye, his home lost forever when his ancestral home was torn down and the foundation for the mansion poured.

Hamish Tund stormed towards the mansion; his unsure steps found footing in his determined motives. The glass windows reflected the moonlight, streaks of silver brushed between the brick.

He jiggled the lever handles on the double doors that led from the lanai. Locked. Hamish cupped his face, pressing against the panes of glass. A fire murmured in the resplendent fireplace of the sitting room. The audacity of affluence, that the Taylors heated an empty room while the rest of Craine struggled to survive the collapsing economy. Despicable.

Slipping his fist inside his jacket sleeve, Hamish punched the glass beside the handle. He unlocked, then opened the door.

Careful to avoid stepping on the shards—momentarily remembering the hole in the sole of his left shoe—he skulked across the sitting room towards the fireplace. The low flames hugged the logs, their heat thawing Hamish as his fingers screamed.

He held his hands towards the fire and flexed them. The dry skin, perpetually nicked and scraped. His right pinky knuckle, a warped knob from having been broken and reset numerous times until it no longer fit with the rest of his hand.

A working man's hands.

Fuck the Taylors.

The man who used to be a farmer reached for the iron tongs. He plucked one flaming log, flung it over his shoulder. Then another. And another.

The Taylors' good fortune would end tonight.

A young child's scream stopped the intruder.

Hamish spun to find the two young Taylors under a mound of blankets as a makeshift bed on the rug. The fire had crawled from the wood at their feet, up the wool and cotton. The boys' laps were aflame. They frantically tried to escape their bed covers, but the fire clung to them, melting pajamas to flesh. Each boy shrieked as he slapped fruitlessly at the flames. Sparks jumped and their hair caught fire. They writhed together on the rug, entrapped by the luxurious bedding.

Horrified, Hamish could only watch.

"Fire!" shrilled a maid from the hall.

Hamish's faculties returned. He ran for the door in which he'd entered to escape the growing inferno behind him.

The fallen Tund had had no idea the children were there.

"Father, please forgive me for what I have done," he murmured, his hands clasped together over his heart as he ran.

"Forgive me, forgive me, forgive me." His footfalls paced to the words of his prayer.

Inside the mansion, the staff rang the alarms. The house servants rushed out to the well house to relay buckets of water to squelch the flames. One maid dashed to Ansel Taylor's office, her first use of the newfangled telephone, and called the fire department before all of Taylor Manor burned down.

They hadn't known the master and mistress had allowed the children to sleep in the sitting room. But the parents remembered.

Ansel and Sadie, hearing the screams of "Fire!" sprang from their beds, chilled by fear as they raced past their servants to the sitting room. Pausing at the doorway, they searched for their children. There was no sign of them. Black smoke blinded and choked as they called for their sons.

"Malcolm!"

"Louis!"

Crackling, popping, whooshing instead of their children's voices.

The frantic parents rushed through the darkening room, finding their way to where they knew they'd left the boys. The fire nipped at the hems of Sadie's nightdress and Ansel's union suit. The parents found the mass of flames—their sons rolling in agony. Alive.

Sadie grabbed little Louis while Ansel seized Malcolm. As they bolted for the lanai doors, they smacked at the flames dripping off the children and spreading to their own bodies. Staggering, coughing, panicked, the Taylors made their escape into the outdoors. They laid each boy onto the frost-kissed lawn, before collapsing beside them.

The blaze inside Taylor Manor was doused, the gray smoke billowed an ominous fog over the rear lawn. When it cleared, the bodies of the once-auspicious family were found—a mother, a father, two sons, just outside the home they loved.

"Taylor Manor belongs to Craine," said Alderman Fetterman. The minutes of the town council meeting were noted and ready to be filed officially, but the aldermen stayed in their seats. "Craine is quickly disappearing. Business here has turned to shit. The farms aren't bringing in money, at least not until the harvest. Hell, they're not going to be able to save our asses, if things keep going as they are. How long until our people start to move out? The harvest will render some work, but those will peter out before winter." Alderman Fetterman, palms flat stamped on the conference table, leaned towards the others conspiratorially. "Projections show that houses will go on the market, but without jobs, foreclosures are our future. There's no point to our seats on the council if Craine is a ghost town."

"I'm not sure I'm okay with this." Alderman Benaji, the newest to the elected position, fretted by chewing their lip. "I mean, they have small children. Do we really need to harass them?"

"It didn't even work the last time," said Alderman Dampling. He'd held his seat for eleven years by keeping closed lips, always voting on the side of Alderman Fetterman. "The Feras aren't like normal people. They don't get that they're not one of us."

Fetterman rose from his chair. His gaze sought—and connected with—each of his fellow council members until they shied away, unable to challenge the man.

"It'll work this time." His fist punched the table. "It fucking has to."

"Fetterman's right," interjected Alderman Stevens. "Do you really want to lose our town because some strangers moved in?" Her words were met with shaking heads. "Hibbert and his crew aren't going to harm the family, just mess up their stuff so they know they and their kind aren't wanted here."

Benaji and Dampling shared a look. Each acquiesced with a

nod. They knew the stakes if the Feras kept their hold on the manor; it was their job to do what was best for Craine and hold their tongues.

With Alderman Stevens's support, Alderman Fetterman watched his cohorts individually accept his plan. Satisfied, he said, "Now. Let's vote. Who agrees, it's time to haunt the Feras and take back what's rightfully Craine's?"

The unrecorded votes were unanimous.

CALEB HIBBERT HUNG up with Alderman Fetterman, their phone call a few terse words. The rebellion's lieutenant briefed the dozen volunteers, then ordered them to load into the two Hibbert Landscaping trucks and two Maid for Perfection vans. Assured of his crew's loyalty, the caravan brazenly drove the country roads before turning onto the Taylor Manor lane. Caleb entered the keycode at the iron gates to allow his people access to the grounds.

Private Property.

He raised his middle finger to salute the placard as his truck crawled between the electronic gates.

The bruised July twilight masked the trucks and vans under shadows. The lampposts took their cue from the impending darkness, simultaneously flicking on, their glow warming against the already hot evening. The vehicles parked in their usual spots to the side of the manor at the unusual hour. Caleb mass texted his crew to wait another hour. If his reconnaissance was accurate, the younger Feras would be tucked in for bed, leaving their parents and nannies vulnerable.

He wanted them out of the way this time. They weren't there to play ghost; they were there to make sure the Feras knew they were unwelcome, and to give them cause to leave the manor.

As the lights beyond the mansion windows one by one fell

dark, Caleb sat. His cohorts whispered nervously, but his spirits rose. Not immediately—as no one should risk legal ramifications by being named for what they were about to do—but eventually, what was about to transpire would become heralded folklore. They were Craine's saviors and he their fearless leader. Fetterman's part would be lost in the retellings as he deserved. No risk, no reward.

But Caleb Hibbert was going to become a local hero.

When the entire first floor fell dark and but a few smears of light gleamed from the second story windows, Caleb dispensed latex gloves and gave the signal. Released from the air-conditioned vehicles into the muggy night, Shanna led the party to the back door. With her key and the security system passcode, she ushered the rest into the manor.

Caleb swapped lead with Shanna. A series of hand gestures and the crew split into foursomes, Shanna and Brian each in charge of their small groups.

They broke from one another. The plan was to reconvene by the back door within a half-hour. They had thirty minutes to put the fear of hell into the Feras. The cardinal rule was to protect the manor. Everything—and everyone—else were fair game.

Shanna's group was tasked with damaging the recording studios. Pocket what they wanted, but their mission would only be a success if they destroyed the Feras' livelihoods.

Meanwhile, Brian and his crew headed downstairs to the cellar. What was once a storage space for casks of wine, now functioned as a home base for Taylor Manor's security. The naturally cooler temperatures of the stone walls and floor were ideal for the massive server providing the upgraded electrical needs for the vast grounds. The Taylor Manor Historical Society originally repurposed it, paying for the renovations via Craine's tax dollars, but even their modifications were nothing compared to what the Feras had done.

A towering gray box in the corner sang a mechanical *hum*.

Two of Brian's crew stood guard at the bottom of the cellar stairs while he entered the security room. He stood behind Margaret as the Craine High School technologies teacher took her seat at the console.

Twenty green and black screens campused the grounds, their scotopic light illuminating the otherwise dark room. Screens 16 and 17 showed the nannies in their respective rooms, each readying for bed while they watched television. Screen 14, Lion stared at a laptop, headphones on, while Screen 15 revealed a sleeping Vivre. Screen 18, Michael lay on his bed in only boxers, reading something on a tablet.

"The bathroom door's closed," Margaret said. "Edi's probably in there."

Brian murmured agreement as his gaze roved the other monitors.

Shanna's team moved from Screen 4 to Screen 8 as they made their way through the halls. Once they reached the recording studios, they would appear on Screens 6, then 7. On Screen 2, Caleb's team stood at the base of the grand staircase. With a wave to his party, he barreled up the steps where he and the others disappeared from the view of the camera.

"Um, Edi." Margaret tapped Screen 18. Edi, dressed in a sheer babydoll negligee, sauntered across her bedroom. Her husband rose from the bed to embrace his wife.

"Shit. We could snap a pic and sell that to make back some of the money if Hibbert fails." Brian raised his phone to the monitors. Margaret smacked his hand away.

"Pervert." She shook her head as she looked through the desk drawers for tape and paper. She covered the monitor, not before stealing a glance at the bulge that was Michael's erection, secreting that memory away for herself.

While Margaret wiped the desk of everything she touched with the hem of her shirt, just in case, Brian watched the monitors. He flapped his collar to force a breeze down his chest. "It's getting hot in here, isn't it?"

"Serious perv."

"Mags, first off, fuck you. Second, really. It was actually cold down here, but now, now it's like a damned sauna."

As if on cue, a trickle of sweat ran off Margaret's brow, tickling her cheek.

The monitors blinked. "Shit. Are they overloaded? Is the air conditioning crashing?"

"It shouldn't matter. We're underground. These old cellars are meant to stay cool enough to store food."

Brian and Margaret looked to the wall of screens. Green and black images blitzed and rolled across the monitors. The distorted recordings simultaneously, and without flourish, darkened.

The glass reflected the gawking expressions of Brian and Margaret.

"Did you touch something? You weren't supposed to touch anything!" Margaret gasped.

"Of course, I didn't. You did."

"No, I didn't. I just sat down. I hadn't started anything yet."

"Yes, you did." Brian reached over Margaret and ripped away the taped paper over Screen 18. Shaking the paper in Margaret's face, he said with a panicked pitch, "Did you touch anything else?"

Margaret's mouth opened for argument, but she and the room's darkness were interrupted. As though a lit match had kissed the corner of the sheet in her hand, a flame skittered across the paper.

Brian shrilled, dropping the burning paper just before the fire reached his fingertips. He stomped the fire out with his boot.

"This is fucked up," he said, his voice a shaky whisper. "I don't know what's going on, and I don't care how much Hibbert and Fetterman want us to do this. We gotta get the fuck outta here."

Margaret held up her phone in flashlight mode towards the security room door. "Tyler. Jackson. Go to the van! We're aborting the mission."

The two guards turned to peer around the doorjamb. Instead of Tyler and Jackson, a man and a woman, clothed in night-clothes from another era, strolled into the room. From their sooty faces, black orbs where their eyes should have been glared at the intruders.

Margaret stopped in her tracks. Brian bumped into her from behind. Her light shook, and it was only her reflex to hold onto anything that could be used as a weapon that kept the phone in her hand.

"No, no, no, no," whimpered Brian. He dug his fingers into Margaret's shoulders, where he pinched a nerve, causing her to drop the phone.

Stooping for the device, she stopped when a small hand reached it first. The screen's light shone through the tissue and blood. Bulbous yellow blisters covered what remained of his blackened flesh.

Margaret raised her eyes to the melted face of the small child. She croaked, "Thank you."

The boy's mouth opened wide. A scream.

An encore of his last sound.

THE FOURSOME AT the security room were of no consequence to the Taylors, their snooping an annoyance.

Voyeurs. A disgusting side effect when one lived—or lived after death—as an outlier.

It took little more than a smile and gesture of kindness by entities they did not understand to scare the intruders away.

Sadie and Ansel allowed the uninvited guests in the security room to pass. The first two had run off at first sight of the scorched family, leaving behind those whom they guarded.

Sniveling ninnies.

It was Louis's proper etiquette that scared away the other two. Despicable peons who ran from a child's politeness.

It was not the boy's fault his words were stolen from him, leaving him with a voice of screams.

After the first group escaped to two of the vehicles, the Taylors moved through their home to find the others.

Holidaymakers had come and gone through the manor over the decades, but an ethereal pull from the homeowners had called the Taylors from their eternal unrest. The Feras. A family within the Taylor home.

Sadie and Ansel's home.

Their children's home.

Their forever home, which was always intended to be a place for family.

Regally moving through the halls, the Taylors sought the rest of the trespassers. Sadie parted from Ansel in the foyer, their children in tow. Ansel tasked himself to the ones breaking apart the rooms where the elder Feras made merriment, where joy sang freely and smiles were shared. Memories made.

The first room was a loss. But just as the criminals broke into the second room, they were startled quickly by the rise in temperature. Ansel was cautious to not touch any of the odd instruments in the room, and certainly not the beloved mansion's bones.

Fury at the intrusion to the safety of the manor and its occupants raged within him as the first patriarch opened his mouth. A bellowing cough drew in the attention of the burglars.

Moonlight and lamplight streamed through the windows, resting peacefully upon the fragmentary Ansel. Despite being garbed in only a union suit undergarment—one riddled with burn holes, torn from his failed attempt to save his children—the former man held himself tall with dignity.

The trespassers ran for their lives, their ungodly screams of terror echoing through the halls as they attempted to escape from the ghost.

Meanwhile, in the foyer, Sadie marched up her staircase, Malcolm and Louis on her heels. At the middle landing, a group of four worked together, slicing along the inside edges of the gilded frames to remove the immense portraits of the Taylors. Thieves on top of being desecrators. Malcolm and Louis's likenesses were already rolled into tubes on the floor.

The lady of the manor pointed towards the east wing, giving her sons a shooing gesture. The brothers trotted up the steps to the top landing without notice. Little as they were, Sadie held confidence her children were more than enough to protect the Feras and their caretakers from any harm the miscreants might intend.

Once her sons were out of sight, she opened her mouth. A wracking cough emitted from her lips, startling the thieves. The lead man turned and dropped his jackknife.

"Holy—" he breathed.

"Caleb," whimpered one of his brethren. "Who is that?"

Sadie's blackened lips grinned. She raised her elegant arm to point with a long, blistered finger at her portrait. The four obeyed her directive to look upon her painting. One corner curled down, covering half of the lady's face, but they held no doubts that the non-corporeal being standing on the landing with them was the first matriarch of Taylor Manor.

Another of Caleb's henchmen shrieked, then ran past Sadie and descended the staircase at a full run, risking a fall in order to escape unknown consequences from the ghost. When she opened the front door, the mansion's alarm system clicked on and a siren screeched warning. The piercing sound shook the others free from their paralyzed status. They sprinted downward and met up with the rest of their party.

And Ansel.

He allowed all but Caleb and Shanna to pass through the front door. The master of the house grabbed the pair by their sleeves, his hands singeing the fabric. They frantically screamed and twisted away from his heated grasp. Ansel readjusted his grip to his captives' forearms. Their shirt sleeves having burned away, they were trapped within the heated manacles of his hands, flinching to avoid blistering their flesh yet too fearful to pull away.

His wife descended the staircase. Mrs. Taylor strode with confidence, her charred head held high. Her black orbs surveyed the entrance to her home. Decades away from her station, Sadie still owned whatever room she was in.

Elegant, majestic, perfect.

Reaching her husband, she laid a hand on his shoulder, then kissed his cheek before turning her ominous gaze upon Caleb and Shanna.

"I...We...We were only trying to get those people out of here,"stuttered Caleb. "They aren't like us. They aren't like you. Taylor Manor wasn't meant for them." He winced as Ansel's hand tightened. The undead's caustic fingers pressed into Caleb's arm and the man gave a soundless scream of pain.

Sadie led the way outside. Her husband released their captives, and forced them to follow under threat of touch. She crossed the lawn, barefoot. Her steps sizzled against the dry grass.

At the front gates, Sadie Taylor stopped. Caleb and Shanna hesitated, looked to one another, then back to Sadie. Caleb, too captivated by the horror, stood aghast as her black lips peeled back over her sooted teeth and Ansel grabbed Shanna from behind. His body pressed against her back, the woman howled in agony as her flesh cooked. Sadie stepped closer. She puckered and blew into Shanna's gaping maw. Her breath was a black smoke, tinged with odors of the grave—rotting tissue, old earth, and must.

Ansel released Shanna, then shoved her across the property line. The woman with her back bloodied from the burns, hacked and coughed. She stumbled into the darkness, towards the country road and Craine.

CALEB'S FATE was the same as Shanna's. After he was scarred by Ansel and inhaled Sadie's breath, he staggered along the gravel shoulder of the cracked, paved road back to town, chasing after Shanna. Lunacy edged his mind, and the want of home forced him forward.

He caught up with Shanna, and the pair wandered towards central Craine. Their muscles seized, yearning to recover from their burns, but it was the smoke blown deep into their lungs, leaving them unable to catch a full breath, that caused them to slow their gait.

All thoughts focused on making it home, to their warm beds and to their loving families, they took an ill-fated shortcut through the cornfields. The stalks towered over them, and no one knew where they'd gone, so when they collapsed, still gasping for air that could not save them, they were buried among the cornstalks above ground.

Months later, the farmers harvested the fields and discovered the bodies with no flesh left on the bones. Animals and elements had stripped the pair clean; their causes of death remained unknown.

The Feras and the two resident staff members had woken to the screech of the alarm system. At first, they thought a fire had been detected. The bedroom doors had been hot to the touch, but once Michael and Edi risked the sweltering heat of the hall, nothing was found out of place. They, along with the nannies, whisked Lion and Vivre out of the manor until the police and fire departments arrived.

The security footage revealed the twelve perpetrators and the damage they caused. Only Shanna and Caleb were identified, their passcodes snitching on them. But they were not to be found.

Whispers turned to rumors about what happened that one July night.

Most prevalent was ghosts. The dead had risen. Taylor Manor was haunted. Implications that Caleb and Shanna were murdered by the undead ran rampant.

The aldermen met. They discussed but failed to come up with a plan to salvage Craine's economy. Pitches to embrace the local celebrities and to lure tourists to gawk at the Feras from outside their private gates were immediately squashed. Edi and Michael canceled their hiatus, jetsetting off to one of their penthouses in Chicago.

The Feras were irate with the town that had dismissed them, suspecting it was locals who broke into the recording studio and ruined the Taylor portraits. They discredited the theory that ghosts had ransacked their home—a poppycock explanation for vandals infiltrating their privacy.

A lease to Craine was not offered, even though Taylor Manor did not go on the market. Edi and Michael had invested too much into the property with the renovations. A sale would be too much of a loss. Besides, one day, maybe after the next tour when the normalcy of their high-octane life wore them down again, they might return. At least, that's what they promised Vivre and Lion, who had fallen hard for the manor.

Yet, a forgotten resource came forward. Quiet, then loud, then viral. The teenagers of Craine posted on social media about the horror stories their parents told, embellishing the tales as one is wont to do. The voyeurs came under the guise of tourism, revitalizing Craine's economy. The businesses that had folded added an air of yesteryear to the ghost stories.

As all of this unfolded, the Taylors returned to their unrestful sleep. Despite the manor remaining closed to the public, the original family were disturbed every now and again, woken by looky-loos who snuck onto the grounds seeking the apparitions. The Taylors greeted their unwelcome guests, spooking them away faster and faster each time, until word got out and no one crossed the gates.

Taylor Manor was a place designed, not as a business, but around family. It had needs to be satisfied—a craving to have children's laughter, shared memories, love within its walls.

Until the Feras returned, or another family replaced them, the Taylors would keep their spectral watch. They could wait. They *would* wait.

Time was inconsequential, unable to be forced into expectation.

Another family would come.

LT WARD

LT writes mostly speculative fiction shorts and novels while spending her days raising her children and satisfying her never-ending thirst for knowledge through reading, meeting people, and first-hand life experiences. She has short story publications with Dancing Lemur Press, Me First Magazine, Jazz House Press, and forthcoming with Black Hare Press and Cardigan Press. She currently volunteers with WriteHive, a nonprofit literary organization.

She can be found on Twitter, Instagram, and at ltward-writer.com.

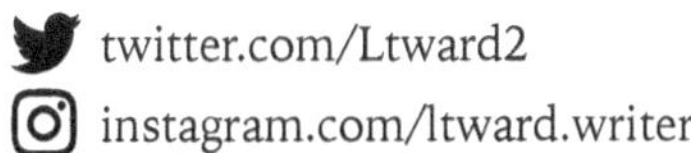

twitter.com/Ltward2
instagram.com/ltward.writer

ESCAPE FROM THE HOUSE OF ASHER-FELL

MAXWELL I GOLD

I

A terrible shroud of silence, fat and heavy, weighed down on the House of Asher-Fell, built of poor decisions and empty dreams, where puppets and platitudes hung in the cobwebs of the dim, dreary home, occupied by my great-aunt Hellan. She was the most awesome of lunatics—lovable and ecstatic, neurotic and ever the brilliant recluse.

Despite being raised in a bubble of obscene wealth, dripping with predestined routines, social graces, and ritualistic humdrums, Hellan loathed the established customs of her social class. Even more since the death of my Great-Uncle Abraham.

Uncle Abe's death had propelled Aunt Hellan into a maelstrom of sadness, forcing herself away in a profundity of grief-stricken mania. Gossip sprouted, contagious and malign, through the family as to the true nature of Uncle Abe's passing. Rumors scurrying in the silence, like scratches, those awful fucking scratches. Though, they remained as such in my mind: a story for another time.

The fresh rains painted a muddied canvas of bristled gravel specks along the tires of my car, lumbering with heavy drones as the exhaust sputtered and coughed.

The real nature of my visit remained unknown, save for a mysterious envelope delivered to my residence prior. Aunt Hellan requested my help with matters pertaining to the family; the tenor of her letter was unusually cryptic and oddly rambling, its incoherencies filled with chasms of dead thought.

"To my dearest great-nephew:
The stresses of life, the estate, and my own health grow to become
burdensome, too burdensome with each and every day. There's
nothing else I can say, no more, no less.

The rest of the family sees my condition as without recompense, kaput, beyond the pale. You name it. Vultures! Probably wish me dead! Not you though, darling! You were always different, understanding. Please, at your earliest convenience, take a trip to the family estate, and I'll explain when I can see you face to face. Time is short, the doors are closing."

Our relationship was predicated on notions of curiosity, as Aunt Hellan acted more like an estranged parent or eldritch grandmother. As a child, I could remember her gliding across a marbled terrazzo floor. Her Dior heels would click and clap, the worn taps underneath on the verge of falling off as the rhythm of each step approached me, like a ghost from old Hollywood suddenly brought to life. Aunt Hellan loved to cocoon herself in silk treasures, with cubic zirconia and ostentatious costume rings weighing down her dainty fingers. Thick, brown mascara was always overdrawn, the caterpillars penciled in to cover sagging lines and dead memories, and fake eyelashes unevenly attached above her brows. Oversized pearls dripped from her dainty earlobes, crowned by an obnoxious cream turban, hiding strands of silvery hair conjuring some past life in a Billy Wilder film.

"No more, no less, darling," I'd remember her saying.

She was hypnotic, like a car crash, bracelets, bangles, chains, dancing along those bony wrists as she swayed. Clicking, clacking, tapping. Thankfully, no cat food or zombified manservants were involved, at least to my knowledge.

This wasn't the first letter she'd sent me; I'd amassed quite the collection. Prior to making a conscious decision to come to Asher-Fell, her last letter caused me worry, fear, and concern that something was truly wrong.

"No one answers my letters anymore, darling. My loneliness grows as the doors swing behind me, heavy and unaware of the puppeteers in the shadows. I swear, the days are growing shorter, and the doors are closing. There are only so many doors. Everyone has deserted me, love. They've retreated, leaving me to this bastion of languor. This hell of crystal and tapestries. I hate it most days, you know that? There're piles of junk everywhere, dust and dander, it's wretched. Perfectly horrid, though I digress. Please, come see your Auntie, I promise, no more letters. No more, no less."

The air was stale and unwelcoming, filled with a heavy silence followed by the crumpled soft thunder of my car door closing behind me. A familiar sensation cupped my shoulders, almost as if an ominous shade, itching with hunger, was preparing to eat the last shreds of light.

Aunt Hellan must have been expecting me. Immense wooden doors lined with ironworks and crystal cracked ever so slightly, exhaling sawdust and ash from the bowels of the great mansion. While the outside remained an Edwardian edifice, the inside was a Gaudian labyrinth, where wild tessellations of corridors melding against windows and bleeding into chandeliers was something out of a dream, or a nightmare.

The floorboards moaned; crystal trinkets bunched together on dusty hutches trembled. Memories of dead things floated through the air. Strange feelings, familiar sensations grew in the pit of my stomach as the rotting wooden jaws clamped shut.

"Darling? Is that you?" The shrill, operatic composition of Hellan's doting voice made its way down the stairwell in a glissando of hurried notes.

My skin curled. "Yes, it's me Auntie."

I'd arrived in parlor, unaware, unusually tense as the tapping from her heels thudded against the terrazzo marble. "I've been waiting. What took you so long? I thought you'd never make it.

Thought those wretched family members filled your head with more superfluous lies about my *lifestyle.*"

"Never, Auntie," I said. "You were always like my other mother, especially after, well, you know—"

"Yes, it was terrible, my darling. And they were in such good health too." Her dusty tone scratched the air. "I only wish I could have done more, short of taking you in. Though a life trapped here in this old place would have been akin to being trapped in a house of wax figures." She cackled. "Your late great-uncle, bless his poor heart, spoke to the tune of needing to escape on good days before he passed. Strange, right? He always took life too seriously for my tastes. Some days it was like he was clawing at the walls to get out." She took a pencil and attempted redraw over the uneven heavy lines under her eyes, and of course, she missed.

"I think that's why we made quite the pair. The yin to my yang, the sun to my moon! The Eros to my Thanatos! The Beauregard Pickett Burnside to my Mame Dennis, the..." She paused to adjust her caftan. "Well, you get the idea. Balance, my darling, no more, no less."

The ebb and flow of red, gold, and blue silk washed over the bannister where I stood under the guise of her hazel orbs. "I couldn't imagine the pain, Auntie. Now, what's the matter? By the tone of your last letter, you seemed, well...distraught."

"That's not important now. Come, I've prepared a supper in the dining room for us," she said.

"But, Auntie..."

She clapped her hands, bracelets dancing. "No more, no less. Now, come, let's eat."

My stomach churned. "Since when do you cook?"

"Oh, ever since Great-Uncle Abe's death, my darling. I've become a whole new woman! I've studied horology, botany, wood carving, welding for that matter! I cook, clean, even purchased a loom where I weaved this magnificent garment.

Don't worry, you won't starve." Her voice rose to climax, then quickly died. "It's not like I'm feeding you cat food!"

"Right, of course not." I sighed.

Well, it could be worse.

II

AUNT HELLAN slunk her way into the immense dining room, big enough to house an Olympic-sized swimming pool. Bone china dishes imported from England, with blue, white, and amber geometrical patterns layered throughout, aged silverware lightly-coated in a layer of dust. The entire table looked as if it had been staged, left for some macabre dinner party. Another crystal chandelier dangled high above, looming with a sense of awesome uncertainty as Aunt Hellan crossed me, taking a seat at the head of the table.

"Come, sit, darling," she offered.

The table itself measured somewhere near twenty feet long, not your average dining room arrangement, though Aunt Hellan was far from average.

"You set all this up? What happened to Shaeffer and the staff?" I asked.

A cooky grimace slithered across her lips as some hair creeped out from under her turban. "Oh, I laid them off years ago! Mostly after, well, you know," she said, stuffing the silvery strands back up inside the ball of silk. "Life was difficult at first, doing things *on my own*, but I endured. It was a little bit of an escape for me. I even managed to find all the silverware. I didn't even know we had *this much*! I'd no idea where Shaeffer hid them all these years, so many drawers. You could hide a body here, but once I found them, I just left the table set."

Picking up a knife, scraping a visible layer of dust on my finger. "For how long?"

"Oh, who knows. Time is all a construct anyways; it's as phony and made up as the clothes on our backs. Another one of humanity's great inventions." Her face contorted into a sneer.

"So, you don't remember?" I pressed.

"Years? Decades? Why go through all the hassle of putting it away." The obnoxious array of bracelets and bangles clinked against one of the crystal goblets as she pressed the glass to her lips. "Put it all back and do it all over again? Besides, I haven't really had company in some time, my dear. Seems pointless to get caught up in ridiculous mundanities like that. Why put anything away? Just makes the place seem bigger than it already is and me more alone. And I can't have it. I won't. No more, no less."

I watched her uncover a dish near the edge of the table, revealing the most overcooked bird, charred potatoes, and soggy vegetables. Though, her eyes lit up as if gazing upon an immaculate feast for kings. It looked hideous, but maybe not. I should've given Auntie some credit. Plunging my fork into the blackened beast, it almost bounced like a piece of rubber. One bite was enough, chewy as if I were eating a cooked ball of rubber bands seasoned with salt, pepper, and ash. I wanted to throw up, but ceaseless hunger captured my instincts, and I was ready to eat anything, even this. It had been a long day's drive from home.

"You cooked this, Auntie?" Cringing a little, breaking a smile, struggling to swallow even the smallest of bites.

"Doesn't it look fabulous?" she asked

Tearing off another piece of the blackened chicken, faithfully swallowing it. "Tastes delicious," I lied.

"Oh, goodie. Then take some more. Can't have you on an empty stomach."

The disgusting excuse for a dinner carried on for near a full hour, lopsided candles dripping wax excrement onto a poorly sewn doily with cold chicken, sour wine, and broken conversation.

I eyed the bowl of fruit in the center of the long table. It had rotted, flies taking their spoils from the discolored apples, browned pears, and moldy citruses lying in their porcelain grave, while the tablecloth had slowly been eaten away by moths, edges falling apart. Normally, my aunt was an excellent conversationist, her wooing aristocratic charm carried on at parties like soft music. Something was different though; something was out of place. The silence and static clawed through every other phrase, gleaning some part of her humanity in the voids between words. This was not the person I grew up with.

"Auntie, I've had it!" A pronounced slam from my silverware clanked across the table. From the crystal glasses, dust floated in the trembling light.

"Concerned?" She paused, her eyes moored against every word with a sincere naïveté bleeding down her cheeks. "About what?"

"*About you! You* are making me concerned. We've been talking about God knows what for the last hour, everything on the planet from horology to your new obsession with jacquard scarves. The family thinks you've gone off the deep end—at least the family that I've been able to get in contact with. And so far, I'm not seeing anything telling me otherwise. When was the last time you left the house?"

Her demeanor changed, sudden and swift. "It's hard to tell. You're the first to see me in so long. I rarely get visits from the rest of the clan anymore. It's like they've all disappeared. I don't even hear from my children! Nobody. It's the strangest thing. I get so lonely in this dusty old house; I can only find so many hobbies. It's like they"—she began to cry—"don't want to have anything to do with me anymore. Like I've become some monster! Am I a monster, my little love?"

"Auntie, you're not a monster," I said, consoling her, watching the mascara run down her cheeks.

"I just can't bear the loneliness any longer. No more, no less. It's a dreadful condition. Perfectly dreadful, my darling."

"Well, you're not alone anymore," I said.

She finished her glass of wine and wiped the black ink from her cheeks. "Doors between decades, love. Escape grows impossible as the decades dwindle, and loneliness looms taller and vast, and those doorways become smaller and smaller. It's hard to explain, but your Uncle Abe understood it best, I think. It's why we were meant for each other, sweetie. You see, we passed through the same door, at the same time, but I wasn't ready. I wasn't ready to go. I couldn't let him leave without me, so I had to do the only thing I could. What was necessary. No one else in the clan really understood, but you were always different. I remember you had that music in your eyes as a boy."

A long hard pause weighed on the conversation, an uneasy tension pressing against my soul with some deadly trepidation, like manicured nails clawing underneath the tablecloth.

"Darling?" The breathy alto voice crooned through my daze.

"Sorry, I was in a haze for a second," I said.

"It's a lot to take in, I know, but you'll come to understand, like Abe did. It's like music. You'll just have to learn to hear it sometime," she said softly.

As she spoke, my leg, right below the linen tablecloth, began to itch. Something had bitten me. Rolling up the wrinkled cotton of my pants, I found, to my horror, scratches on my leg. My pale skin marred by the red and puffy claw-like marks.

"Are you alright?" Aunt Hellan said, standing up and clearing some dishes. "You look as if you've seen a ghost, or worse!"

"Worse, I think." I sighed, attempting to hold my terror back.

Aunt Hellan, leered over the edge of the table and, noticing my shock, cracked a signature grimace, her voice whirling. "Oh my! It must have been these awful chairs. God knows when the last time they were refinished. They're probably older than I am. Not to worry, stay here, and I'll go grab some peroxide for that little knick."

This all felt like a dream—a confusing, upside down Dalian dream. Send in the fucking clowns and pour some melted clocks into my wine glass, and the setting was complete. *Jesus Christ, what did I get myself into?*

Sitting in the vast empty dining room, silence once more my companion, the uncertainty of why, how, and what if traversed the maddening stairwells of my thoughts looking for answers to my Aunt's unnerving sermon. The wound was irritating me as my skin bubbled red, quickly scarring as the same pain suddenly flared up on my other leg. *Fuck, did she have some kind of parasite or God knows what lurking on these chairs? Who knows how dirty this place is.* It took every last piece of me to hold back from screaming as my fingers squeezed the linen tablecloth.

Through the kitchen doors, I heard a terrible music, like someone singing a lullaby or a broken aria. Aunt Hellan's out of tune raspy alto carried into the dining room, and I could smell the decades of cigarettes, bourbon, and Chanel waft in from the kitchen. Her song felt unnervingly orchestrated to my scratches, floating from behind the doors as the intense writhing traveled up my leg until it jerked, slammed into the underside of the table. The China and crystal tumbled to the floor where shards scattered on the terraced flooring, eliciting a pang from behind the kitchen doors, interrupting my Aunt's aria.

"Darling? Are you alright?" she called.

"Yes! Yes, Auntie, I'm fine," I cried. The pains grew worse, but something inside warned me against telling her. "I just spilled some wine. Not to worry, I got it."

Aunt Hellan continued rummaging in the kitchen, humming that awful melody, probably preparing something she considered to be coffee, maybe sludge. God only knows. Heat slowly transitioned into an icy paresthesia on the surface of my skin, the pain dissipating and my thoughts clearing.

"I've got to get out of here," I said.

THE TWO GALLEY doors at the end of the dining room swung open, my Aunt Hellan gleefully pushing a small decorative cart, dainty cups surrounding a silvery pot and creamers.

"I hope you weren't trying to run away now, my little love." she winked.

"What? Of course not. What gave you that idea?" It was becoming harder and harder to hide my apparent terror as she lifted the tray, pouring the simmering black liquid into a cup by my seat.

"I've been around the block a few times, deary. Besides, you really can't leave just yet."

"No, it's not that Auntie. I had plans back in Eastwind I needed to get to, and I thought there was actually something wrong."

Aunt Hellan's bone china cup clanked abruptly against its saucer. "Well, of course there's something wrong. No one else believes me." Unnerved, afraid, uneasy couldn't describe the awful bodily sensations churning throughout my entire body as I painfully gulped the rest of my sludge. "I knew nothing would change your mind about how the rest of the family saw me. Not even your poor Uncle Abe believed me." She paused again, her long, manicured nails tracing the gold rim of the porcelain cup.

"Alas, what is a woman to do? Remember the doors? The decades are closing my sweet nephew, even my own door will close soon, and goodness knows where I'll end up. I don't want to go there alone, so I figured I'd take someone with me." My scars were starting to burn again, watching her trace the rim of her cup. "Sometimes, you have to find your own way out, when all other doors are shut."

"Auntie, I don't understand," I said, my hands clenching both legs now. "And what happened to Uncle Abe?"

Silver wires flopped from her silk cocoon as a wild symphony of laughter erupted, echoing in the great hall, Aunt Hellan's fingers clawing at the linen tablecloth attempting to control her rather gruesome cackle. "I told you, remember? I had to make sure I could take someone with me when the doors shut."

Silence returned. Deliberately, methodically, with purpose, Aunt Hellan plucked a sugar cube with her bony fingers, the sweet crystals dissolving into the black sludge. Quiet, deathly quietness washed over us both, my terrified consciousness trembling through brain matter and blackness through each stir and clap of her spoon. She didn't adjust her hair; more silvery strands continued to creep out making her look more like the loon she described.

"Auntie?" I said.

A gentle tone blushed through those ruby-red lips. "Yes, darling?"

"About what you just said? The door?" Shaking, setting down my cup, I watched her remove the turban, a mop of snake-like black, grey, and silver bounced in the amber glow under the chandelier as if Aunt Hellan had scalped Medusa's hair, simply to procure it for some bizarre collection.

"What? Doors? What did I say about doors, darling?" she said, looking genuinely confused. "How's your coffee? I made it myself. Why, I even broke a nail getting the damned package open."

Silence composed with sips and slurps, orchestrated under sinister thoughts, consoled me as I rubbed my scarred legs.

III

Aunt Hellan requested, or rather insisted, I stay the night. And of course, she had room to spare. Maybe it was the guilt, or the unnerving sensation nagging at the back of mind telling me something was off kilter that made me decide to stay. The entire world pushed merely an inch out of place, enough to create some bizarre, twisted imbalance.

Needless enough, it was still necessary to understate the sheer vastness of the House. My quarters were located in the *Fell Wing,* the original apportionments of the estate where only family were allowed. It was a wretched building.

I found myself under the unfortunate guise of furious, waxy facades, spilling out from the viscera of the shadowy blackness, pouring down from the rafters. From deer heads to raccoon paws, lynx teeth to cougars, followed by darker more exotic tastes: rattle snakes, elephant tusks, two Komodo dragon scales, and even some species unrecognizable to human anthropology—mangled skulls with slack-jawed teeth and jagged nails. Aunt Hellan indulged in the strangest, arguably macabre interests.

I followed her through hallways cleaved from massive sandstone bricks and limestone columns, faceless dress figures followed me the entire way down. Lidless and dead, the fabric bodies of hundreds of mannequins stood like a horrid reminder of what might lay beyond these endless doors. Their linen nakedness hidden away under haphazardly woven caftans, incorrectly layered and sewn, a vomitus saturation of ambers, chartreuse, burgundy, and teals. Stitched together in wild patterns without any care or thought, random tatters of string, mismatched tassels, and assorted buttons hung from the cloaks in a most unsettling manner.

"Just a little farther, darling!" she called out.

Doorways. That's all I could think about. The countless doorways lurking in my peripherals, and whatever was behind them. Places lost, or buried away from my Aunt Hellan, traumas so great and terrible, but growing ever smaller as history marched forward.

"What is all this?" My head whirled, attempting to take in the unnerving sight.

"Do you like my collection? The taxidermy was *mostly* Uncle Abe's, though I've added to it slightly over the years." She smiled. "The caftans are all mine, I made them all myself. Even the dress figures. In my loneliness, I was able to really *dig* into my work," she said, her nails flexing for effect. "They're the only clothes I wear anymore. Don't they look stunning?"

"Yeah, stunning." Speechless, unable to truly muster the courage to speak, I continued gawking at the terribly crafted clothing.

"Yes, they are. Ignore the scratches on the figures though, I always get frustrated whenever they don't turn out how I want them to." She meandered towards one, gently stroking a tassel with her long nail, highlighting a gaping abysm trenched into the neck of one mannequin. "I never fixed this one. It always gave me so many issues, but maybe one day I'll come back to him."

"Him?" I said.

"Oh, yes! They all have names, stories. It helps me pass the time. I even sing to them. I think it helps them with the loneliness too. No more, here's your room," she said, stopping in front of a scratched wooden door and jiggling the rusty handle. "It's a little dusty but it'll do for tonight. Oh, and stay out of that closet in the corner."

My mind piqued, I peered into the room and saw a tall oak door, tucked away in the dark dressed in cobwebs. "What's in there?"

"Oh, nothing. It's where I keep the dress figures that kept giving me issues." She laughed. "Now, you have to promise me you're not going to just run off in the middle of the night, now are you?" She smirked, a nail raised towards my lip.

"I wouldn't dream of it."

"Good. I'll see you in the morning. Try not to wander too

much. It's easy to get lost in this dreadful place. We wouldn't want to find you lying around somewhere or lost in a closet." My spine rattled as her broken cackle resounded throughout the hallway, foreboding machinations pressing against my mind.

"Good night, Auntie," I said.

"Good night," she returned. Lasting images flashed across my eyes of silver strands and manicured nails slithering from behind the cracked doorway as her heels clapped in muffled thuds over the carpet.

The mind-nagging anxiety transformed into a painful itching, failing to placate this weird terror, growing out of control, further destabilizing my nerves. "Jesus. Fuck, I have to get out of here." I panicked, my breath hushed and soul terrified as the realization of my situation began to settle in. Something wasn't right, though my attempts to understand her behavior have proved pathetic exercises in futility.

Manicure tools, more faceless unused dress figures, piles of silk, and strands of silver twine cluttered the guest room. Sleep was a fantasy, a dream as I paced maniacally in my luxurious dungeon chamber. Anxious pangs deep in my chest throbbed with an incessant nervousness as I schemed, wondering how to get out.

"Dammit," I cursed.

The growing danger and fear were more apparent. Muffled thuds from the carpeted floor outside, starting and stopping until they finally disappeared altogether as silence appeared by my side once more.

My legs no longer irritated me. The marks lingered, ten healthy scars on my thighs, red and scabby, a woeful ruin of something evil. The wood recesses in the ceiling sank into the liquescent darkness. Shuffling creaks and moaning iron vents were the only sensual comforts as I sat on the musty bed; not even my own thoughts gave me any commiseration. An incessant itching erupted from my wounds, as if some bleak infection had taken hold of my body.

"Fuck, what in God's name is going on!" I cried, unable to stop myself from itching, scratching, wishing to tear my flesh right off.

Falling to the ground, as quickly as the pain began, like lips to a candle gently extinguishing the flame. It was over. The scars were gone. It was as if nothing had even happened, and my mania derived from a psychosomatic paranoia.

"I don't care anymore. I'm getting out of this place. One way or another. I can't stay in this…" I stopped, my ears perking up hearing off-key singing floating down the halls… "Hell?"

As I reached the door to find the source of the almost inhuman music, a clatter near the corner of my room slapped the back of my head. My gaze turned towards the forbidden oak door. I walked over, fingered the dark oak stained with images of ornately carved dragons, laurels, and other seemingly fantastical creatures slithering along the doorframe like some fabled gateway to a distant world.

The smells of musty oak, moldy wallpaper and rusty wall fixtures adorned with limp wax creatures yanked at my nostrils; pulling me closer. Hesitant, afraid, brimming with primal curiosity the door swung open and an avalanche of useless junk, fabric corpses, and satin floral hat boxes spilled their defame, rotted, putrid contents over me. Dismembered limbs wrapped in silk and silvery twine marinated under a heavy carrion fog throttled my ability to scream, coughing phlegm and bile as the horrendous choppy waling continued in the background, the disgusting music filling my ears.

No more. I ran as fast as I could. Away from this lethiferous pit to anywhere else in some hope that I might escape. Decayed flesh sunk into my pores, the awful scent mixed with the aromatics of the dusty building as I ran down the hall, following the antithetical singing. Doors on top of doors emerged like geometric malignancies from infinite corridors spewing confusion as the only signifier illuminating my path was that haunting music. Past the marble orangutans, over Siberian tiger rugs, gaudy houndstooth chairs, and assorted knick-knacks probably pulled from a Lewis Carroll story.

I passed underneath the hungering gaze of an Italian oak grandfather clock, carved in the form of a hideous crocodile, teeth snarling. The music grew in furious crescendos. I must be close. I carried on farther, until one of the dizzying corridors spat me out at the mouth of the immense dining room.

To my dismay and terror, I saw her, confirming my worst fears. Aunt Hellan, wailing over the table performing to an inanimate audience of mannequin heads, scattered across the elephantine table as if to please their failed ingénue, watching her moan and dance in a theater for the dead.

Upon my arrival, Aunt Hellan's concert came to an abrupt halt. "Can't sleep, darling?"

My legs felt tighter, the gripping paresthesia returned, as if a thousand knives pierced my skin. "Oh, I just, I was going to get something to drink from the kitchen," I lied, standing opposite of the galley doors, wincing in pain.

Aunt Hellan turned away from her audience, adjusting her turban. "Don't fight it, dear. The pain goes away after some time. Funny, the rest of the family never struggled as much as you. Not even Abe. He managed to put up the least resistance; he was my favorite you know? Being the most stoic, oh-so-serious, makes for the most freeing garments to embrace lonely bodies." She paused as my eyes glazed over, feeling heavy and plastic. "Am I rambling again, darling? Sorry, I'm merely overjoyed that now, I'll never be alone."

I tried to move, but couldn't pull my legs away from the breathy terror of Aunt Hellan's smokey vibrato as she drew me closer, manicured nails tracing my neck. Her yellowed toothy smile leering down through wiry hair. "Sit." I obeyed, my control over my own bodily functions gone.

"Listen, can't you hear it now? Can't you hear the music? The silence, my darling?" Unable to compose words, I watched aghast as she mounted the table, kicking her heels off without a care, her caftan swaying in the dark like some Hadean thing, as she wailed and moaned in ecstatic delight. My body felt tighter, breathing more difficult as her singing intensified with monstrous glissandos whizzing up and down, touching scales no human ever heard before.

Dizzying revelations of doom and puppetry flooded the pitiful ruins of my consciousness as the deadly concert, the last scars of humanity twisted themselves into wood, worry, and silver twine.

"I hear it, Auntie. I hear everything." I coughed bits of bile, blood, and sawdust, my pleading eyes met hers as the terrible shroud of silence, fat and heavy, weighed down on the House of Asher-Fell, built of poor decisions and empty dreams.

MAXWELL I GOLD

Maxwell I. Gold is a Rhysling Award nominated prose poet, focusing on weird and cosmic fiction. He is a regular contributor to *Spectral Realms*, edited by Lovecraft scholar S.T. Joshi and his work has also appeared in *Weirdbook Magazine, Space and Time Magazine, Startling Stories, Baffling Magazine*, and many others.

His debut prose poetry collection, *Oblivion in Flux: A Collection of Cyber Prose* is forthcoming this August from Crystal Lake Publishing.

Maxwell can be found on Facebook, Instagram, Amazon, and at www.thewellsoftheweird.com

facebook.com/TheWellsoftheWeird

amazon.com/Maxwell-I.-Gold/e/B07L2HQ378/ref=ntt_dp_epwbk_3

COLD*

R.A. BUSBY

Trigger Warning: Cannibalism

The gentleman at the head of the table picked up his knife. "I hope you know," he said, "that you will always be part of this family. A most valuable addition."

"Oh, I—" the younger man began awkwardly, dabbing his lips with a linen napkin. "Thank you, sir."

"Father." Mr. Limos smiled politely. "Please. Sylvia has been a peerless daughter, but I have long wanted a son. I do hope you shall allow me to regard you not just as Sylvia's husband, but as my own flesh and blood."

Around them, the shadows were diminished by the candelabra, but not even the crackling fire of the great hall banished the winter creeping into the stone. Against his will, the young man shivered.

"Cold, William?" The older man's face assumed an expression of solicitude, and he rang the small bell at hand. "I can have Packer put on another log. Best do it before the servants take the evening off." At the door, a manservant appeared, silent as a cat, and soon the room blazed with greater light and warmth.

After the dishes from the dinner had been cleared away, the two men retired to the comfort of the parlor with its deep leather chairs and unobscured view of the tree-lined avenue leading to the mansion. The road stretched to the east for many miles, and the young man shuddered again, keenly aware of their isolation. In the distance, he heard the wind rise, its voice a wordlessly whispered hiss.

"Cigar?" Mr. Limos extended an inlaid box of Spanish cedar to William, who waved a hand in polite demurral. "Ah. You do not smoke? A pity. I have found no virtue in abstaining from life's great pleasures—smoking, to be sure, but eating most of all. That is the primal pleasure, the first we ever feel."

The young man blushed and accepted a brandy with a respectful nod. "I am so sorry Sylvia could not join us for this excellent meal."

"Ah, yes." The tip of Mr. Limos's cigar glowed, a single red eye in the gentle lamplight. "Called away, you said?"

William nodded. "Yes, and gone by the time I received your kind invitation to dine. I sent a man after, but he could not reach her train, so I am afraid Sylvia will have to join us later, sir." He coughed and corrected himself. "Father."

Mr. Limos rang the bell, but when no one appeared, he peered out the window with a slight laugh. "Ah, as I supposed. See that line of cars? The servants wasted little time in taking their leave. The wind has quite blown them away. Now we must rough it for the night alone." With a chuckle, he gazed at his elegant fingers. "Rough it. As a boy, I could never have imagined possessing hands so smooth. Long after I acquired my fortune, my fingers still bore the tinge of the dirt ground into them for nearly two decades."

"Sylvia once described you as a self-made man," said William as he eased back into the velvet wingback chair. The panes rattled with a sudden gust, and he jumped. "What did she mean, if I may be so bold?"

Mr. Limos smiled slowly. "A self-made man. What an odd expression. As if one is both Adam and his God. But my crude American story is—well, surely of no interest to you, a gentleman raised in the comfortable environs of inherited English wealth."

"No, rather the opposite," the young man interjected. "I have often asked Sylvia to relate the history of her family's rise to prominence, but she has explained little, and being a stranger to these parts, I cannot even rely on..." William broke off, gesturing to the vacant road in the distance. "On the local village gossip."

"Oh, I could tell you the tale," said Mr. Limos as he turned to the window. "But I think it might not be—well, to your taste. And as the night appears to be growing increasingly wild, perhaps it should be savored another day." Even as he spoke, a sudden gust arose, setting the trees along the drive to a frantic dance.

"The weather has been changing for several days now," Mr. Limos continued. "It puts me in a melancholic mood, this wind. At such times, the pull of the past is exceedingly strong. Gray hands clutching upwards from a grave."

The young man protested. "Oh, I do wish you would tell the story, sir. What a pity Sylvia could not come." He chuckled. "Why, she does not even know that I am here. She shall be jealous, I am sure, for it sounds quite the tale of adventure."

"Adventure?" Mr. Limos turned away from the glass, his face twisted into an expression of dark amusement. "It was. Yes. I suppose it was. Very well, then." With a sigh, he settled himself in his chair.

———

"PERHAPS YOU REMEMBER," he began, "those tales of gold discovered in the West? The reckless rush of would-be fortune hunters, ill-prepared pioneers throwing themselves at prairies and deserts and mountains with little or no knowledge of the exquisite terrors of those places—you have read of them in your neck of the woods?"

The young man nodded.

"The tales," Mr. Limos said, "are true. My father was one of those fortune hunters. Though a minister, he was a greedy man, ripe for temptation. Naturally, he became a willing gull for a Mr. J.R. Macready, a guidebook author who claimed he alone knew a secret pass through the mountains that ended in a veritable valley of gold. I remember him pulling out a small leather bag from which he drew a misshapen nugget the size of a thumb-tip. 'Common as pebbles!' Macready proclaimed. For a mere exchange of banknotes, silver, or the family jewels, he'd take you to that place himself."

William's blue eyes grew wider. "Oh, dear."

"Father gave him the small salary he'd scrabbled together, nearly all our wealth, and together with a caravan, we set out. By the time our party reached the mountains, it was late in the season, deep into October, and though the deserts had boiled us in Hell's own heat, the white breath of the peaks chilled us even as we approached their first slopes. It was…" Mr. Limos shook his head. "A mistake."

"What sort of mistake?"

The older man's lips curled sardonically. "A grave one. After a leg-shredding push up a particularly punishing rise, I remember staring upward at the stark granite cliffs, the landscape stabbed by high green fingers of fir and pine pointing to a sky so blue it seemed almost black along the edges of the trees. Silently, I watched the wagons slip and fall and fail on these steep and rocky ways trod only by the Washishiw. And we were heading into a territory those wiser souls did not choose to cross.

"One by one, members of the party turned back until only a few men and horses remained with whatever they could haul or carry. We were among the men that stayed, my father and I. And Macready."

"But surely—" William frowned, then stopped. "Surely you could not have been more than—" He stared at his father-in-law. The man's brow was nearly unlined, his movements fluid, his carriage upright like that of a man only a few years past mid-life.

"More than?" Mr. Limos's eyebrows raised.

"Well," William began, his face flushed, "this happened so many years ago. I mean to say that you—well, you bear your years quite lightly."

Mr. Limos smiled. "Clean living." He held aloft his snifter of brandy. "And a healthy diet."

William nodded apologetically. "Please forgive me, sir. Heading into winter, you said?"

"Indeed. By then, only ten men remained. Through the early part of the season, we pressed on, Macready leading us from ridge to ridge, farther up each day. I recall a signal moment when we broke above the timberline, and in all directions lay nothing but jagged peaks. I knew then we had ventured deep into the maw of a monster, caught like meat between its pointed teeth. And I knew then something else."

"What was that?"

"It was alive. This mountain. In its very earth-flesh, I could feel its buried glee. Above us, the dark earth was patched with white snow, and from the very rocks, I sensed that this land *wanted* winter, waited with granitic patience for summer to slip away before assuming its real form, its true shape. The shape of cold.

"It was then I recalled Macready mentioning that this country was known as 'the trackless lands,' and when I asked what that meant, the man laughed and said that not even the Washishiw went there. That *no one* went there."

William nodded. "Except you."

Mr. Limos's expression was shadowed by the failing firelight. "Except us." He paused, and in the silence, the men hearkened to the steadily rising hiss outside.

"Funny," William remarked with an idle laugh. "You can almost hear voices in it. That wind."

Mr. Limos's eyes sharpened for a moment before he turned to the fire. "Yes. And I do." A log crackled, collapsing into squares of molten gold.

"Before long," the older man continued, "the bare track on the mountain became increasingly impassable, for an early storm a week before had brought thick snow to the approach of the pass. In the distance, we could see it. The pass. It lay along the skyline, a gentle saddle for a giant rider, and beyond, I swore one could almost catch the scent of green growing things in this world of frozen white. Ever more white. Ever more cold. And at last—" Mr. Limos broke off, shrugging.

"At last what?"

"Well. We had made camp that day alongside a small escarpment, a place where the granite rose in a forbidding wall, but the irregular projections of the cliff offered at least some meager protection. When we awoke the next morning, though, Macready had simply vanished." Mr. Limos laughed. "Into my father's sleeping hand, he'd slipped a letter which the men read aloud. 'Going for help,' the message said. 'Crossing pass with aid of horse. Will return 1 week. Wait.' It ended with the man's florid signature."

William shook his head. "And you waited."

"We did. And one week passed. Then two. Silently, the men began cutting trees and stacking them against the escarpment wall. No one ever said we were making plans to winter in that place. Not out loud. When we looked at the other men, we recognized the bright tinge of fear in their eyes. As in our own.

"Then came the desertions. First one stole away with a horse, and then another. Finally, over the western ridge of the mountain, we saw our certain doom: a storm cloud dark as sin with a white edge feathering the air above the distant pass. Hastily, Father and I chopped down even more trees and branches, covering them with canvas and hides that once contained our meager possessions. In a frantic rush, we cut green boughs, layering the hard ground with wood too warped to be walls, and lashed the structure with the horses' ropes and halters. The lean-to held—but barely."

"Good God," said William.

"I am less sure than you of His goodness," replied Mr. Limos with an ironic grimace. "The days that followed are—unclear. Hunger made our eyes sharp and tongues sharper, but our quarrels soon diminished to angry glances, murmurs. Hunger gnawed at us. We were losing flesh, and with it, the will to fight. At length one morning, my father and I started awake at the commotion of the other men departing with the remaining horses, but though we struggled upright, they had already gone. We had eaten the others by that time. First the meat, then the hides. Then we cracked the bones for marrow and when we'd eaten that, we licked the insides and sucked on them like dogs.

"When at last the sound of their leaving died away, we sat in silence. A very long silence." Mr. Limos's black eyes grew unfocused. "And then once more the snow began to fall. At first, it hissed across the new-cut wood and sent shining sparks flying up into the winter sun. Soon, though, the snow crept into corners, piled along the walls, covered us in a shroud. And by that time, we were too weak to do anything about it."

The man had been staring out the window, but now he turned back. "In some ways, I believe I'm still on the floor of that shelter. Did you know that?" Mr. Limos asked. "I wake in the middle of the night and stare into the dark and feel entirely certain that this—" he gestured at the elegant parlor, the old carved mantlepiece— "was nothing more than a fever-dream, and the only truth is the whisper of the snow and the wind.

"As it happened," Mr. Limos continued, "I had chanced to lie before the firepit built against the edge of the escarpment. At first, the pit bore a bit of residual warmth in the stones from the fire, and to my disordered imagination, it still seemed so. Before my eyes was a square grey stone with a vein of quartz running across the center like a strip of fat through a piece of well-done meat."

He closed his eyes and took a deep breath before opening them again. A solemn darkness descended over his face.

"Meat. That was what I thought on, day after day, with an obsession that allowed no other focus, no other god. Staring at that stone, I thought of meat, the slick-salt feel of cooked fat bursting on my lips, the rubbery pressure of muscle bitten by teeth, the coppery tang of fresh blood. We call it 'juice,'" he remarked, "but we know it is blood."

"Yes—ah. I suppose. Of course." William shifted in his seat.

"I lay on that dirty shelter floor and stared at that rock and dreamed of nothing else. The hunger ate me from inside, gnawed on my veins, sucked the marrow from my bones. Hunger was my alpha and omega, flesh of my flesh, blood of my blood."

William frowned. "And what did you do then?"

"From time to time, I imagined groans beside me and told myself I was not alone, but eventually from the corner on the other side of the firepit where my father slept, no sound came. He had not moved in days. But I heard whispers. So many whispers. Soon, I began to fancy that those sounds were more than dreams."

"More than—"

"It was the voice of the land. The land spoke to me, as it had on that mountaintop." Mr. Limos paused in thought. "It began with the wind. Lying on the floor of that shelter, I believed that if I listened attentively to the hissing wind, I could make out words."

"Do you mean—"

"The land spoke to me. It told the history of a thousand times a thousand years, the story of each grain in the rock, its fire-birth, the tumble to dark earth enrobed in flakes of snow." Mr. Limos gave a quiet laugh, but the sound was without amusement. "I listened to the forest, to the verminous curls of roots that writhed beneath my ear pressed to the floor. And do you know what the trees whispered?"

William's face had grown pale. "I have—I have no idea."

"They said, *You lie upon our bones*, and I asked, 'How so? I sleep on the shelter floor,' and they replied, *You lie upon the bones of our fathers, the bones of our mothers. Their flesh was promised to us for our eating, as our flesh shall feed our seed.'* And then they told me what to do."

Mr. Limos ran his hands over his face. "I had lain for days in a state of weary inanition. Only my hearing and taste remained sharp and keen. From that position, staring at the rock of meat, I needed no vision to tell me I was alone. I could smell the truth, you see." As he spoke, his eyes closed, but his nostrils widened. Across his face came a look that was nearly beatific.

"How unimaginably foul," William said.

"Oh, yes," Mr. Limos replied abstractedly, but he licked his lips as he said it. "God had taken them all. At the same time, God had left one. For me."

"But you cannot mean—"

The eyes that fixed on the young man were black and unfathomable holes. "God provided the prophets with manna in the desert that fell as frost and snow upon the ground. Manna. I had to eat it soon, though, for like manna left untouched, it would breed worms.

"The scent rose through my nose, my mouth. I raised my head for the first time in days. In the murmuring of the wind, a voice cried, *At dusk ye shall eat flesh and in the morning, ye shall be filled with the bread which the Lord hath given you to eat.*"

William swallowed hard. "Dear God."

"Indeed. From a deep reserve, I gathered strength to push myself to my knees, and in time, I reached the fuel the men had piled in the corner, the pitiful remains of pinecones and bark, torn clothing for kindling, a few logs. And the flint. With that, I kindled fire. The flames danced in the hearth and made that broad strip of quartz glisten as if it were hot oil. I ran my fingers along the stone and half-expected it to drip."

"And then?"

His eyes softened. "How did Mr. Longfellow put it? 'Then hunger did what sorrow could not do.'" As realization swept over the young man's face, Mr. Limos's mouth twitched upward in a delicate smile.

"Near me was a foot," Mr. Limos said, his black eyes shining in the firelight. "I clawed off what was left of the boot. Easily done. We'd eaten the leather already. His feet were yellow-white, the color of old parchment. On his big toe grew three dark hairs. His right toenail, the one in front of me, had a small chip on the outer side.

"With what strength remained, I dragged him nearer, saying to myself, *God took him, God left him, God took him, God left him.* At last, he was close enough. I hitched his pants as far as the knee and heaved his leg into the flame."

William had grown pale.

"The hairs on the toe singed first. The flesh around the nail blackened and peeled away like the skin of a pepper. With a gasp, I tore the toe from the foot with an effort, the tendons white and curled as frightened worms. Though it burnt my tongue, I put it whole into my mouth and ate it, bones and all. The sole—I could say it was tough as leather, but having savored that delicacy already, I assure you the skin was far more tender. Like veal. Yes, distinct from any other flesh I have eaten before or since, but most resembling delicate, well-grown veal. I ate it, then ate more. In all that time, my eyes stayed fixed upon that vein of shining quartz."

William drew a breath and pressed his fists into his stomach.

"It was as if I reeled from a wild and heady wine, a galvanic force that trembled through my frame. I do not exaggerate when I say it gave me new life. Indeed, it has given me more than that." His eyes focused on William for a moment. "To this day, I have only a vague memory of saying, '*Except ye eat of the flesh of the son of man and drink his blood, you have no life in you!*' Or perhaps I screamed it. Yes. I think I did." He smiled slightly and poured a measure of brandy into his glass. "It was the best meal I have ever had."

"I—I cannot imagine," William answered.

"No. I suppose no one can. Or very few. We are a select confederacy."

"Thank God."

"I did. With every bite."

"But—" William began. "How did you find rescue?"

From his position in the armchair, Mr. Limos stared back at William with a flat, black gaze. "If I have learned one thing, young man, I have learned that help most often arrives too late. Or never. Rarely when most wanted. And so it was with me." He tented his fingers before his lips. "Several days later when— well, when my supplies were running low—I caught the sound of breaking branches and the snort of a horse. I peered between the gaps in the lean-to walls, and I saw him. Macready. And I knew what he wanted."

"What could he possibly want?"

"Gold. I had seen his eyes sweeping over my father's vest, the place he concealed such treasures he retained—my mother's golden cross, their wedding rings, his wallet of banknotes."

"So it was a trap. To leave you desperate. Or dead."

"It was."

"What did you do?"

"I had been sleeping under a filthy tarp I now drew over my —the remains of my meal. I could not let Macready see. Or not too soon. In the shadows, I huddled on the ground beneath the tatters of my father's coat. In my hand, I clutched a rock from the pit.

"Outside, Macready shouted, 'Halloo the house! Anyone there?' I held my breath, and for once, the wind was silent. Then came a jingle as Macready tied the horse's harness to the logs of the lean-to, pulled the canvas aside, and stepped within.

"As the scent struck him, the man recoiled, coughing, his hand before a patchy beard white with ice. His eyes, I knew, were adjusting to the dark as mine were to the light. I had lain in darkness so long I did not remember it. The light. I stayed still as the corpse, careful to make no sound.

"Macready began tossing aside those possessions piled against the shelter walls, searching for whatever valuables remained. From my father's vest, discarded on the floor, he plucked the leather bag with my mother's rings and cross and gave a satisfied grunt. Then beside the fire, Macready saw the bundle I had covered with the tarp.

"'What's this, then?' he murmured, and bent to uncover what lay beneath. As he drew it aside, he whispered, 'Oh, Jesus.' That was all."

"So you—"

"Three blows with the rock. One in the back of the head that struck through the bone. I saw a dirty clump of his hair sticking to the pink jelly in his skull and hit him once again. When Macready rolled onto his back, eyes wide in sightless surprise, I brought the rock down a third time on his forehead so God would know the mark of his sin. And then I was alone."

"But then..."

"But then I knew what to do. I stripped the man of his coat, shirt, mitts, and uneaten boots. In doing so, I found golden prizes everywhere. The hems inside his pants. A bag tied about his neck and concealed in his armpit. A hollow place carved into both his inner boot heels. A leather wallet shoved into the split of his ass. Another wrapped behind his withered balls." Mr. Limos chuckled. "I ate those first."

He paused, contemplating the fire. "You have asked how I made my fortune. This was how. In my hands, I held the golden seeds I grew into great wealth. I suppose you could call me a consummate consumer."

William found himself unable to speak.

Mr. Limos nodded as if William had spoken. "I shall not detail the events thereafter. I took the remains and with some effort, shoved them over the cliff for the earth to eat. And it did.”

“A good thing,” murmured William. “Anyone seeing the bodies could have known immediately what—what had transpired.”

“Agreed. But at least with the first, not many remains remained to be seen. Waste not, want not. But I digress. With the horse—and God be praised, the supplies it bore in both saddlebags—I followed Macready’s tracks across the pass and into safety.”

“It must have taken incredible effort,” William remarked with slow deliberation. “To do that. To dispose of the bodies. To ride so far in the snow.”

Mr. Limos laughed. “Not at all. From that moment—from that initial bite—I felt a vigor I cannot begin to describe. A richness. A potency. I confess, dear William, that the first time I tasted that flesh, I did so with a cock as hard as a railroad tie.”

The young man drew in a breath. For a long time, the two sat watching the flames. A knot in the pine wood cracked, and William started from his reverie. “There is so much I do not understand,” he said at last, “but one thing especially.”

Mr. Limos let out a broad chuckle. “Ask now. I venture I shall never speak of this again. And you will not be telling Sylvia.”

William nodded. “You had been through—” he broke off, trying to find the words, “an unimaginable trauma. And yet you stayed out here, in the West.”

“I did so.”

“But why? With your fortune, you could have lived—well, anywhere. New York. Paris. Even London. You have visited England, I know. Sylvia told me.”

Mr. Limos did not answer immediately. “This land grows on you,” he said. “Never say I didn’t warn you.”

“Warn me?”

The older man rose and placed the brandy gently on the

table. Venturing to the window, he looked out onto the snow that already covered the porch and piled up in little stacks on the leeward side of the columns that held up the roof. Flakes of it clung to the windows in swirling, patternless feathers of ice. "As I have said, when I was in that makeshift cabin, I hearkened to the voices of the roots, the trees, the earth itself. They spoke to me in the wind, in the conspiratorial whispers of the pines."

In the silence, the howling grew louder.

"The wind speaks to me now. Listen, William." Mr. Limos nodded, and lowered the wick of the lamp, a fussy thing painted with riotous English roses. "Can you hear it?"

William's face had gone gray.

"I do. I hear it. And at such times as these, it seems as if I am still inside that shelter. I feel the cold within the marrow of my bones. I see the line of thick white quartz. My nose fills with the sick-sweet stench of death, and my own dying flesh above all.

"I hear that call," Mr. Limos said. "Sometimes softly. Sometimes…more. Then the hunger comes. That strange and ceaseless hunger that has never really left me." He smiled. "And then it tells me what to do."

The wind screamed and hissed, and below the sound arose a lower tone, a drone like the sound of summer bees. Within that drone were words.

Whispers.

William tried to utter a sound, but his throat would not open. He glanced about the room wildly, understanding at last the absent servants, the dark and featureless causeway, the distance from those places of light and safety he would never see again. He had ventured much too far from home.

The silence in the deserted house was, he realized, so very loud.

So very cold.

R.A. BUSBY

An award-winning literature teacher and die-hard horror fan, R. A. Busby is also the author of "Bits" (*Short Sharp Shocks #45*), "Street View" (*Collective Realms #2*), "Not the Man I Married" (*Black Petals #93*), "Holes" (*Graveyard Smash, Women of Horror Anthology, Vol. 2*), and "Cactusland" (*34 Orchard,* forthcoming).

"I was always instructed to write about what I know," she states, "and I know what scares me." In her spare time, R.A. Busby watches cheesy Gothic movies and goes running in the desert with her dog.

She can be found on Twitter and at RABusbybooks.weebly.com

 twitter.com/RABusby1

DICEY PROPOSITION

THOMAS CANFIELD

Colfax3 was an insignificant little planet well out on the fringes of the galaxy. It had known a brief period of prosperity, attended by an influx of settlers, then had begun a long, slow decline into hardship and deprivation. Corporate interests had exploited the planet's mineral resources, despoiled the environment and looted the treasury. After having taking their fill, these vultures abandoned the planet to its fate. It was an old story, played out many times, so common and predictable that it no longer even stirred any outrage.

The population that remained was split into two distinct political entities: Wetside and Dryside. Wetside was an ineffectual, petty tyranny, with a ruling clique that was brutal, self-indulgent, and vindictive. They maintained a tight lid on dissent and asserted the supremacy of the regime over every other consideration. They won few adherents and many critics. For the critics, escape was the only option. And escape, of course, entailed crossing the Slough.

To cross the Slough, to make it to the other side and emerge alive, the services of a guide were indispensable. Finding one who was trustworthy and reliable, however, was the problem. They were men who, by the very nature of their profession, operated outside the law. As a rule, they tended to be bold, cunning, and without scruple. They had to be, in order to survive. To place one's life in their hands was to hazard everything—and sometimes to lose everything. Yet such was the desperation of some to live again as free citizens under a free government that they risked the crossing all the same. So it was that men such as Thorn flourished.

"How do I know there are Rasps out there?" Higgins gestured at the dark with one hand. A flicker of red static danced along the far horizon. The scent of the swamp lay thick in the air. "You say there are. But I don't know that. It might be you're lying."

Thorn pulled at one earlobe, frowned. His eyes were as black as the night and thinly-veiled menace. "Stay behind, if you like. That would be one way to find out."

"I'd be a proper fool to do that. And you know it." There wasn't an inhabitant on Colfax3 who hadn't heard tales of the Rasps, nor any that didn't live in mortal terror of them. "But if we do as you suggest, it'll take twice as long to get clear of the Slough. We can't afford that!"

"I was retained as a guide for this expedition." Thorn planted his feet well apart and hooked his thumbs over his belt. "And I'm telling you: the one chance you have of coming out alive on the other side is to do as I say."

Higgins did not trust Thorn. The guide put on a big front about acting in the best interests of their company. But it wasn't anything more than that—a front. They had lost three of their party already, and the question that preyed on all of their minds was: Who would be next? Higgins *did* know what Thorn had said was true: None of them would get out of the Slough alive on their own. Thorn was the only one with the expertise and the knowledge to make it happen. *If*, that is, he was of a mind to do so. The guide was playing his cards close to his chest. And Higgins was doing the same. Some secrets were not meant to be shared.

"What about Hodges?" Higgins said, motioning to the man leaning against a boulder, cradling his leg.

Thorn shrugged. "What about him?"

"I think we ought to leave him behind." They would have been clear of the Slough had Hodges not been stung by a Wicket. The barb had caught him in the thigh and his whole leg had gone numb. They had taken turns supporting him as he hobbled along. Even then, their progress was slow and halting.

Higgins looked at the remaining members of their company huddled together like a clutch of pack animals. A pall of fear hung over them, fear and desperation, as though they were condemned men, only waiting for the axe to fall. They were men who talked boldly and complained loudly, but in the event, proved themselves timid, cautious, and indecisive. Higgins could no longer stand the sight of them.

"Not a chance!" Thorn was emphatic. "He's coming with us. That's final."

"He's dead weight!" Higgins protested. "He can barely stand, let alone walk. Better one of us goes under than all of us."

Thorn offered a brief, caustic smile. "I never was much good at that kind of math. Some people, they've got a head for it. They can weigh a person's life and assign a value. Me, I'm not that talented. I figure everybody pretty much deserves a chance. That includes Hodges. So, until I decide otherwise, he comes with us. Is that clear?"

Higgins frowned, a hard knot of rebellion forming in his stomach. "It's clear, alright."

"Good. You spell Reinhardt for a while. If you're so eager to ditch Hodges, talk to him and see how *he* feels about the matter." Thorn turned to the others. "Reinhardt, take the rear. Brevard, you're up front with me."

Higgins eased in next to Hodges and helped him to his feet. Hodges smelled of despair and stale sweat. His eyes were dark pits bored into his skull, reflecting no light. He trembled and shook with fever before draping an arm around Higgins's shoulders. "What were the two of you talking about, Cody?" he asked.

"Nothing."

"What do you mean, nothing? You looked like you were about ready to start throwing punches. Both of you."

Higgins stared off into the night. Streamers of mist wound through the desolation of the swamp. The mist collected in hollows, emitted an eerie green radiance that bathed the land with light. Odd chittering noises surrounded them, accompanied by the trilling of insects. The ground squelched underfoot.

"Cody?" Hodges shifted his weight. "What were you talking about?"

Flashes of static along the horizon hinted at an approaching storm. "Thorn wanted to leave you behind. Figures we won't make it if we have to carry you."

Hodges's mouth twisted in a bitter grimace. "The son of a bitch. I knew we couldn't trust him, knew it the moment I laid eyes on him. Throw me over like I was so much ballast." Hodges's face burned with resentment. "He doesn't give a damn. What's it to him? But you stood up for me, Cody. You told him how it is?"

"That's right." Higgins offered a tight smile. "I let him know exactly how I feel. He doesn't have any doubts about that."

"The son of a bitch," Hodges repeated. He hobbled forward at a great pace, intent on proving he was not a burden. Higgins concentrated on the night sounds, wondering which of them were harmless—and which signified imminent danger and death.

They slogged along for what seemed like hours, on the alert for any sign of trouble. The mist grew thicker, drawing in around them and blurring the line of the horizon.

Ahead of them, Thorn froze, turned and walked back.

"Where's Reinhardt?" he demanded.

Reinhardt had been only a few feet behind, so near that Higgins had felt man's heavy aura of nervous tension. Now he was gone.

"He was practically stepping on our heels."

"Well, he isn't there now." Thorn unsheathed a knife hanging from his belt. "Wait here." Thorn stalked back along the trail, disappearing into the mist. No one spoke. Hodges slumped, his face haggard and grey. Higgins shifted his feet to better bear the weight. His back burned from the strain.

When Thorn returned, he was cleaning the blade of the knife, wiping off a film of blue-black ichor.

"He's gone. There's no trace of him." Thorn peered into the mist, his expression grim. He turned to Hodges. "How you holding up, Hodge? You going to be alright?"

Hodges was slumped with fatigue but snapped erect under Thorn's scrutiny. "I'm fine. The leg's fine. Anything we got to do, I'm up for it. You don't need to worry about me."

"Good. That's good. Another couple of kilometers, I figure. The Slough is tricky. You can't ever tell exactly where you are. But, come daybreak, I think we'll be free of it." Thorn turned to Higgins. "Brevard will spell you for a stretch. You take the rear."

"Nothing doing!" Higgins scowled defiantly. "That's a dead man's post. I'm sticking to the front with you."

Thorn's face remained expressionless. "Somebody's got to take the rear. Who do *you* think it should be?"

"I don't give a damn who it is. I only know it's not going to be me."

Thorn ran his thumb along the blade of his knife, measuring Higgins with his eyes. "Hodges can't take the rear. I can't. Brevard is helping Hodges. That leaves you."

"That leaves nobody! I already told you. I'm not taking the rear."

Thorn pressed the blade of the knife against Higgins's abdomen. "There are many ways to die in the Slough. Few are either quick or merciful. In your case, though, I'm not certain mercy is called for." Thorn punctuated these words with a thin smile. "I'd kill you myself if I thought it would accomplish anything." Thorn slid the knife back into its sheath. "*Both* of you help Hodges. That way nobody is in the rear and we ought to make better time. Don't fall behind. One false step, and it likely will be your last."

Thorn pushed on ahead, leaving Higgins and Brevard to follow with Hodges.

"Did you hear him? The son of a bitch threatened to kill

me." Higgins spat. "He's a mad dog, is what he is. You can see it in his eyes."

"We'll all die, every one of us," Hodges hissed. "Only Thorn will walk out of here alive." Any man whose services could be purchased, after all, could sell them to any party he chose—or, as happened only too frequently, to both parties.

"I swear he can see in the dark." Brevard shot a look at Thorn's back. "Make out things that you or I, normal people, would never see."

"We were fools to think we could trust him." Higgins drew one arm across his forehead, wiping away the sweat. "We ought to have known better." They slogged through the mire, Hodges flagging and growing more feeble with every passing minute.

A chill settled over the Slough. The chittering noises grew more frantic. Mist shut them in on every side, weighing upon their spirits, infecting their thoughts with visions of death.

Brevard lurched forward suddenly, his leg sinking in the ground up to his thigh. He gave a blood-curdling cry.

"Merciful God!" He twisted back and forth, eyes clenched shut in agony. Blisters began to appear on his throat and face as the heat of the thermal coursed through his blood.

Thorn came running. He plunged his knife into the ground, hacking away at the waterlogged turf. A foul, grey exudation bubbled up out of the earth. The blisters on Brevard's face grew larger. His whole frame quivered.

Higgins backed away, Hodges clinging to him like a shadow. Both watched to see what Thorn would do.

Thorn stopped digging and remained motionless a long moment then swung the knife up in a long, fluid arc and brought it down hard. Brevard's skull split apart with a sickening crack. He slumped forward.

"He would have died anyway." Thorn's voice was devoid of emotion. "That's a bad thermal. Caught the whole leg. Better to take the easy way out."

"You should have warned us," Higgins whispered, his eyes never leaving Thorn's face. "You should have said something."

"Sure I should have—if I saw everything and anticipated everything. It doesn't work that way. Even *you* ought to know that much."

"I know we started out with seven men in our party." Higgins thrust his face forward. "Now there are only two of us."

"That's right," Thorn acknowledged. "And the longer we stand here talking, the better the chances there soon won't be any. Is *that* what you want?"

"There might not be any no matter what we do. The way I see it, that'd suit you just fine."

"I can think of one person I wouldn't mind being rid of." Thorn's grin was an open taunt. "But I figure that's not up to me."

Hodges grabbed at Higgins. "Look!" he exclaimed, pointing over Thorn's shoulder.

Amidst the swirling banks of mist and swaying reeds, two points of golden light stared back at them. They blinked with sleepy malice and slid sideways through the fog.

"Rasps!" Higgins said, his voice thick with horror.

Thorn tracked the progress of the Rasp through the fog. Its lithe, cat-like movements conveyed only the merest hint of its power, of the coiled ferocity waiting to explode. "I make out one of them. One, I can handle. But if the entire pack catches up with us, we're done for. You and Hodges go on ahead. Don't get separated and don't stop, no matter what. I'll catch up with you."

Higgins looked at Thorn then at the menacing silhouette of the Rasp, employing the mist as cover to approach closer. He was not certain which he would rather take his chances with.

"Let's go, Cody. Let's move!" Hodges pleaded. "Now, while there's still time."

Higgins stepped toward Thorn. "You'll catch up with us?"

Thorn tugged at one earlobe. "I said so, didn't I?"

"Yeah, I guess you did." Higgins draped Hodges's arm around his shoulders. They hobbled off into the mist together, not looking back.

They covered a long stretch of barren ground, never knowing what lay up ahead or what might be creeping up on them from behind.

Hodges stumbled, collapsing to the ground, cradling his leg with both hands. "I can't go on, Cody. I'm spent. There's no feeling at all in the leg. Even my spine has gone numb. I got to rest."

Higgins wet his lips. "I can't stay with you, Hodge."

Hodges blinked. "You'd leave me here? Alone? You wouldn't do that!"

"I got to, Hodge! There's only so much I can do. You don't expect me to stay here just so the two of us can die together. You're not asking me to do *that*?"

"I'm only asking you to wait. Once Thorn catches up..."

"Mother of God!" Higgins cried. "Thorn's not coming back. Open your eyes! He's cut us loose, like we knew he was going to. He's bailed on us. It's every man for himself now."

"You can't do it, Cody." Hodges's voice trembled. "You're not like Thorn. You've got a conscience."

"Yeah, well, I'm fixing to lose it." Higgins tightened the straps on his rucksack. "In fair weather and calm seas, you can afford a conscience. But not now, not under these circumstances."

"Thirty minutes! That's all I'm asking." Hodges's voice cracked. He bowed his head, wiped at his eyes.

"Can't do it, Hodge." Higgins's face was chiseled out of stone. He had jettisoned all the trappings of civilization, all the bromides about what was owing and due to others. The only obligation he recognized now was to himself and to his own survival. "The Rasps will be all over us. Besides, thirty minutes, five hours—it won't make any difference. The only way you'll make it out of here is if somebody carries you. I got to look out for myself." Higgins hesitated then turned and walked away.

"That's what you're best at, isn't it, Cody?" Hodges called after him. "Looking out for yourself!"

Higgins kept on walking. There was nothing more to be said, no more he could offer. A quarter hour's hard hiking, panic pressing at his back, brought him to safety. The foul miasma of the swamp lifted. The fog thinned and scattered. The ground no longer squelched underfoot. Higgins staggered up an incline and sank down upon a boulder. The shifting, treacherous terrain of the Slough lay behind him. He had escaped, alone out of them all, he had escaped. He slumped forward, hands dangling between his thighs, too tired to feel anything at all.

Gradually, the sun pushed above the horizon. Light washed over the land, banishing the dark, and with it, the sense of nightmare. Higgins lifted his face, let the warmth soak down into him and salve his bruised spirit. He had just begun to relax, just begun to take in the reality that he was going to survive, when a grotesque, misshapen creature with a humped back came charging out of the Slough.

Higgins vaulted to his feet, groping at his side for something to defend himself. An acute sense of despair gripped him when he realized the figure was none other than Thorn. Slung over Thorn's back was the broken, rag doll form of Hodges. Thorn lay Hodges on the ground, examined him with quick, deft movements of his hands, seeking a pulse.

Higgins hesitated. He stared off into the depths of the Slough a long moment, filled with resentment. He had thought never to have to face this moment, never to be confronted by the consequences of his own actions. He had hoped to bury it all, and the memories along with it. Finally, he walked over to Thorn, whose face and clothes were streaked with muck, his eyes sunken with exhaustion.

"Is he alive?" Higgins asked.

Thorn wiped his arm across his forehead. "Look for yourself."

Hodges was almost unrecognizable. His face was bruised and swollen, his lips torn and split. He had an ugly, open wound across one temple, crusted black with blood. Higgins could not detect any sign of respiration.

"He was alive when I found him," Thorn said. "But only just. He'd fought off an attack by the Rasps. How, I don't know. But his luck finally ran out on him." Thorn paused, stepped over to Higgins. "*You* were supposed to stay with him."

"I did so for as long as I could. Right up until he finally collapsed. He couldn't go on."

"So you left him to die?" Thorn rested one hand on the haft of his knife.

Higgins eyed the knife. "I left him because if I had stayed, we both would have died. It's that simple."

"Is *that* what you tell yourself? That makes it easier, I suppose. I would have brought you out. Both of you."

"Maybe." Higgins watched Thorn's hand, waiting to see if he would draw the knife.

"Oh, but I would have. I brought Hodges out, didn't I?"

"You brought him out dead." Higgins's words did not rise above the threshold of a whisper.

Both men looked at Hodges. The multitude of wounds covering his body proved that Hodges had fought desperately for his life. Higgins tried to muster some feeling of solidarity, some measure of empathy. But he could not get past the fact that Hodges, with his lame leg and his fading strength, had endangered them all.

From the moment the Wicket caught him, Hodges had been a dead man. The poison from the barb was slow acting but, in the absence of medical treatment, nearly always fatal. With his political connections, with his intimate knowledge of the ruling regime's many crimes, Hodges had been a marked man from the get go. To be caught helping him to escape was a death sentence. Higgins knew it, and had governed his actions accordingly. And Thorn, for all of his fine talk, had been playing both ends against the middle, never committing wholly to one outcome or another.

But if Thorn had played a double game, so too had Higgins. From the very outset, he had maneuvered to abandon Hodges, to strand him in the Slough. Only thus could he ensure his own survival. They were all of them compromised in a sense, all of them corrupted. The poison of tyranny engulfed everyone.

The two men measured each other in the silence now. Each recognized much of himself in the other, detected an affinity of spirit and outlook. Neither was pleased with the resemblance.

At length, Thorn lifted his shoulders in a gesture of resignation and disgust. Higgins cast one last look into Thorn's eyes, turned and walked away, walked away from all of it—Hodges, Thorn, the Slough, all of it. He could only swallow his shame, could only try and convince himself that he was, in some quantifiable fashion, better than Thorn, somehow different. Knowing all the while that he was not.

THOMAS CANFIELD

Thomas Canfield lives in the mountains of North Carolina. His phobias run to politicians, lawyers and TV pitchmen. He is still trying to plumb the logic of the sales pitch: The more you buy, the more you save. It never quite seems to work out that way in the real world. Canfield occasionally reviews books on Goodreads.

SLEIGH 54

BEN ARMSTRONG

orty-seven, Forty-eight, forty-nine, fifty. Jack counted as each sleigh, led by eight flying reindeer, lifted into the starless sky on their way to the Outerworld—the human one. Jack quickly looked back down at the beasts in front of him and made sure the crupper was on properly for the fifth time that day.

Each sleigh held five elven soldiers. Close to Jack's right stood Ross, the sleigh leader, who itched his evenly trimmed beard. Behind Ross sat the navigator, Ronald, studying notes and maps that crinkled beneath his fingers; he had joined Sleigh 54 a year before Jack. On the left and right side of the sleigh leader stood the two young lads, Kevin and Jermie, who both eagerly gripped their crossbows.

Fifty-one; three left. Two left. Jack watched as the fifty-third sled and its reindeer took off into the air right as the bend of the his sleigh's runner touched the wooden launch pad. His reindeer stomped and snorted, their visible breath filling the air. Jack flicked the reins and the reindeer began to trot, canter, then gallop up the large wooden ramp, their hooves thudding against the planks until they were off, the sled following shortly behind.

The large circular elven city below was surrounded by an army of lifeless thousands, the meaties: tall skeletal thralls of elf or human remains, with red tissue still clinging to some areas of their rib cages. Not to be confused with undead that dwelled deep within the Mortuus Forest, meaties would come from the deep south once a year to try and penetrate Christmas town, whether it be to feast on warm elf meat or something else was unknown to Jack. When he was young and still in school, he heard that expeditions went south to find the origin of meaties. His teachers told him that the explorers came back bearing stories filled with magical tales of endless waterfalls and caves made entirely of sweet desserts. As Jack aged, he learned that the stories were a lie, and that the explorers never did come back.

Jack could hear the shouts of elven commanders as they battled the dead below, a flaming trench surrounded the city, ashes billowing into the sky from the hundreds of burning corpses piled atop each other forming a bridge of bones where the meatie army flooded towards the city walls. As they reached the structure, they began to pile on top each other, one, two, three, four, until they looked like ants atop a sugar cube. There were less this year than the last, way less, though still a site to behold.

"Jack," Ross said in his calm voice. "Eyes ahead of you lad, keep your hands on the reins. The soldiers have their job and you have yours."

Jack nodded and fixed his gaze ahead of him where fifty-three sleighs flew, dumping pails of boiling tar atop the dead army. He heard Jermie and Kevin chuckle as they did the same. In the corner of his eye, Jack saw Kevin chuck his empty bucket down upon the horde followed by Jermie copying the older elf.

"Aye, Jermie," Kevin laughed. "Do you think my bucket hit any of 'em buggers down there?"

"Hope so," Jermie chuckled. "Otherwise it'd be a waste of a bucket."

"What about you, Jack, do you think we could hit a meatie from here?" Kevin asked the deer master.

Jack grinned as he stared ahead. "I don't know."

"Well, it all depends if you injure the feller first or not," Ronald said, not looking up from his maps and paperwork on the humans they were going to visit that night. "What's the point of irritating the creature with a falling bucket if you don't at least take it out of the fight?"

"Well of course I injured one," Kevin said. "You see, Ronald, a meatie's skull is different from a human skull, it's...it's softer."

"Ronald, have ya ever killed yourself a meatie or just

humans?" Jermie asked. "Or do you just not like fighting the scrawny devils?"

The navigator smiled, finally looking up from his papers. "When I kill things, I like to know they understand that they're meeting their end," he said.

Jermie gave an uneasy laugh, and the five sat in cold silence. The killing had never been hard for Jack, since all the humans they slaughtered every Christmas Eve had been guilty of treachery, rape, or murder. Jack didn't enjoy the way Ronald spoke of it, though

They continued away from the trenches and walls of the city and off to the gateway to the Outerworld: the Door.

Jack glanced down and saw a few towering bipedal beasts covered in white fur moving along with the dwindling dead army…ogres. A meatie scurried around it, looking about half the size of the larger creature.

Jack heard that ogres could smash the walls of Christmas Town into rubble and squash an elf like a bug, which made him glad he didn't have to fight them. He had heard a tale from Ronald that Ross had slayed one before, but the leader had never admitted to it.

"Only thirty this year?" Kevin asked as he looked at the papers Ronald sheltered with his body.

"Yep," Ronald said. "Seventeen nice, and thirteen naughty."

"Who's our big one this time?" Jermie asked as he took a paper from its safe haven and into the ripping wind. "Adrien Banville," he read. "That's our big one this year? Looks like this guy doesn't even have guards. *Lamar*? Where's that?"

"It's a town near *Normandy*," Jack said. "We were there six years ago, though you were not with us then."

"Hey, do you think I can go with you guys, and someone else can stay with the reindeer?" Jermie asked with an air of hopefulness.

"No," Ross said, looking down at Ronald's paperwork. "You can go on the big one next year."

"You said that last year," Jermie complained.

"I lied last year," Ross said.

"He's just worried for you, son." Kevin patted Jermie on the shoulder.

"You'd think meaties would be more dangerous than a little noble." Jermie scoffed.

"I wish," Kevin began, "that I could still distribute coal to the humans who have been exceptionally 'kind' to another member of their strange race. All the 'silencing' of humans has really gotten tiring." Ronald gave a small chuckle at Kevin's lie.

"Speaking of which," Jack said. "We're halfway to the Door, so get prepared for a meatie reunion." The skeleton army beneath them had all but faded away, leaving only footprints and corpses of unlucky animals who got trapped in their path.

The air became cold and damp as they flew through a large cloud. Jermie and Kevin each took hold of the large crossbow mounted to the side of the sleigh. Ross strapped on his helmet while Ronald sat undisturbed, studying his lists and maps. The conversing of elves dwindled. Slowly, one by one, each of the three hundred and fifty sleds led by Santa fell into a dead silence. The only sound was the soft pants of reindeer and a light jingle of Christmas bells. In the distance, the faint noise of chattering teeth accompanied the sound of rattling chains.

The meaties were near.

The first sled of death crashed through the clouds above on the right side of Santa's sleigh formation. It was led by eight thrall reindeer—a bit of blood-soaked flesh still clinging to their bones—and large black chains haphazardly connecting them to a tattered sleigh. The sled was followed by countless others that shared its resemblance. The congregation dove into the wood and steel of their civilized enemy, while the elven sleds struggled to stay in formation. The dead deer crashed into the left side of one of the sleds on Santa's southern flank sending bones and meat showering down upon the snowy battlefield a hundred feet below.

Bolts from crossbows began to let loose from all of the right-sided elven archers. Kevin pulled the trigger on the crossbow and cursed as his bolt missed its target. Jack just stared ahead, gripping the reins tight in his cramping hands. More and more of the meaties' sleds burst from the night crashing into elven sleighs.

"Grab the damn bow," Ross shouted at Jermie who was aiming his crossbow into nothingness on the northern flank. The young man fumbled as he tried reaching into a compartment inside the sled. He took out a bow and quiver only to drop in his struggle.

The sleigh to their right broke formation and started to dive towards the ground to avoid a collision with a dead reindeer pulling a broken down sled. Jack shifted their position, giving the sleigh more space to maneuver.

A sleigh full of meaties slammed into the side of Sleigh 54. Jack fell, dropping the reins, which he quickly grasped again before the reindeer veered off course. Kevin was able to get one last shot off, catching a meatie in the ribs and forcing it off of the sled.

"Prepare to be boarded!" Ross shouted to his unit. Jermie scurried to the back of the sled while raining arrows upon the meatie reindeer. Ronald finally looked up from his papers as they rustled in the wind before stuffing them in a pocket and unsheathed a long sharp dagger. Ross gripped his sword with clammy hands, prepared to greet the invasion.

"Come here, you buggers," Kevin screamed with excitement as he took a hatchet from his belt. Jack still stood, hunched like a frightened rabbit, as he held the reins, his nose burning from the dead stench.

The first meatie smashed into sharp bone fragments by

Kevin's hatchet. The second swung at Jack with a short rusty sword but was deflected by Ross's own blade. In the corner of his eye, Jack saw that the bits of red meat on the skeleton seemed to pulse as the creature went to attack Ross. A third meatie gaped as Ronald leaned over the edge of their sleigh and thrust the blade up into its jaw. Jack swore he heard the chatter of the meaties teeth over the sound of blade on bone.

While the melee was in progress, Jermie had managed to shoot down three meatie reindeer. The uneven weight of the dead deer soon pulled the meaties' sled down to the snow.

During the scuffle, a reindeer died and Sleigh 54 veered off balance. Jack stared at the limp corpse dangling from its reins; they would have to land and cut it loose.

"Hey." Kevin chuckled. "Was that your first meatie, Ronald?"

Ronald smiled and opened his mouth to reply but was cut off by the screams as another enemy sled crashed into them, this time smashing into the reindeer. Both dead and living deer struggled, wailing and biting into one another. Bones, teeth, and antlers tangled.

Meaties began to jump from their sled towards Sleigh 54, though many could not make the jump and fell into the hungry clouds.

With the two sleds entwined together, Jack didn't know if 'twas the meaties' sled diving toward land or his own dead reindeer dragging them down the ground that started the crash. It didn't matter. The white expanse grew closer and bigger.

"Prepare to land!" Jack yelled. His heart hammered in his chest as the terror overwhelmed him, the sled coming closer and closer to its demise. Jack's eyes watered as the snow-filled wind attacked his face.

The elves connected themselves to the sleigh with red straps around their aching shoulders. Jack grasped the reins with all his might trying to untangle their sleigh from the meatie reindeer. The meaties, who didn't have the luxury of straps or reins to grasp, tumbled off the sleigh. Jack had gone through this drill plenty of times, but never in a real crash.

Ronald had been in a crash once, ten years ago; his whole unit died except him. That's when they transferred him to Ross's unit. Jack didn't know how Ronald kept his sanity during the ordeal, and Jack hadn't even crashed the sled yet. He wanted to turn his head and see Ronald's reaction to the chaos, but couldn't force himself to do it. His neck was locked in place.

The meaties' sled hit the snow tumbling up and over a hundred times, coming untangled from Jack's sleigh until both sleds collided again. Jack let go of the reins before jumping into the soft but freezing snow.

Both sleds came to a stop after flipping and turning a storm of weapons, coal, and scrap metal into the air. Coughing, Jack stumbled to the wreckage. Bones and dead meaties scattered the ground about him, the screams of dying reindeer pierced the air. Jack passed by a caribou who had snapped free of its harness during the crash, but doing so caused it to snap its neck and mangle its legs; one of its legs was barely attached above the knee by tendons and muscle. Jack forced himself to look away from the site and to his comrades who lay injured before him.

He found Kevin and Ross struggling to get on their feet. Together they located Ronald, who had fallen out of the sled half way through chaos, somehow uninjured. They finally came upon Jermie, his breathing heavy, a grin spread across his face. His breaths were too labored, Jack noted, as if Jermie was trying to suck air from a small tube. There was something wrong with Jermie; his brown shirt started to grow dark and wet.

"Are you okay, Jermie?" Kevin asked, eyeing the wound.

Jermie looked down to his belly and the joy melted from his face to the cold snow. He grew pale as if he had just noticed the wound was there. Jermie gasped and began to cough.

"Oh" was all he could say as he collapsed to the ground. Kevin caught him before he hit the white powder.

Jermie coughed.

"You'll be alright Jermie," Kevin said with a choke in his voice. "Look at me, you'll be fine."

Jermie coughed again.

While he was distracted by Kevin's words, Jack and Ross tore open Jermie's shirt to reveal a nasty cut. It was an uneven and jagged laceration. If Jermie moved the wrong way, his guts would spill out of him like a bloodied waterfall.

Another cough. A ragged rasp, a smattering of blood.

"You'll be alright." Kevin's eyes turned to pools of sorrow. "You'll be alright. You'll be alright. You'll be alright." It was a lie of course, but before he could comprehend the lie, Jermie's coughing ended.

Kevin's tears warmed the corpse he held, still repeating the words. It was the first time Jack had seen an elf die this close up —four years ago he had witnessed the death of an uncle from old age, but that was not the same. Jack felt an emptiness and chill envelop his body, he suddenly became afraid.

The meat that Jermie's gash revealed was a darker red than the tissue that clung to meaties. It leaked small trails of blood down Jermie's stomach like the tears that fell from Kevin's eyes. Even when they killed sinful humans, they made the death as clean and quick as possible. *So that's what the inside of me looks like.*

Ross squeezed Jermie's hand and got up. "We will search the wreckage for supplies," he said. "Then bury our dead."

Jack, Ross, and Ronald searched what was left of Sleigh 54. Jack put a few daggers and a hand mace into a sack, along with the quiver of arrows Jermie had used and slung the bow around his shoulder.

Kevin searched the meaties' sleigh. "They're all dead," he said, the sadness in his voice replaced with a harsh, stern tone.

It didn't take them long to dig a hole. They laid the corpse in its new home and buried the young elf with snow.

"We need to bury the deer," Jack gazed at the eight brown bodies that lay strewn and mangled in the red snow.

"We aren't burying the deer," Ronald replied.

"We need to bury the deer," Jack repeated, giving no heed to Ronald's words.

"I said we aren't burying the damn things," Ronald's voice grew loud as he spoke.

"Now calm it, the both of you," Ross interrupted. "Ronald's right. We don't have the time or energy for that; let's be thankful we at least got Jermie in the ground." He then gripped Jack's shoulders with each hand and spoke softer. "I know what they mean to you, and what they mean to us. At home, we may have given each a funeral, but in these circumstances, we can't. Remember your training. When we make it back, we will mourn, but now, we fight." Jack smiled in agreement and forced his eyes away from the animals.

"What now?" Kevin asked, still staring at the mound of snow that covered his friend.

Jack spoke up. "I say we head towards the Door. We can wait for passing sleighs there."

"No," Ronald replied. "We need to head to the outpost near the Wailing Mountains."

"Ronald's right," Ross said. "If we go there, it'll be warm and they'll have food and drinks for us. Plus, most likely there's meaties at the Door waiting for elves to reemerge."

"Ok," Kevin said. "How will we get there?"

"I went there last time," Ronald replied. "I know the way." Ross looked at all of them and nodded. They nodded back. "And so we're off," he said.

Ross and Kevin traded their steel armor for a warmer solution made with the fur of ryngess. Ronald kept his leather armor though grabbed a coat to keep warm. Jack rarely wore armor, so he threw on the same thing everyone else now wore. The group raided the inner compartments of their sled for coal for the humans on the nice list. They gave one last look and then left the corpses to be swallowed by the sea of snow.

"Say Kevin," Ross spoke up after a bit of silence. "Did you make it to fifty-four."

"What?" Kevin looked up, confusion clouding his eyes.

"Last year you said you were on your fifty-second kill," Ross replied. "Don't tell me I got your two kills this year.

"No, no, I got 'em." Kevin gave a small laugh. "Three, actually. Which puts me past fifty-four and up to fifty-five."

"We 'otta throw you a celebration when we get home." Ross patted Kevin's shoulder. "We ever throw you an event for your fifty-fourth, Jack?" Ross looked at the young assassin who hadn't been paying much attention.

"I don't keep count that much," Jack said. "Either way, I doubt I have over thirty."

"You had to have gotten at least ten more." Ross grinned. "With that little wreck you caused." Jack felt something cold run up his spine as he started to think. *Nineteen if you count Jermie and the reindeer.*

"Don't be so down, Jack," Ronald chimed in. "I haven't hit fifty-four yet as well."

"You haven't?" Kevin and Ross both asked, the surprise evident in their tone.

"I haven't, but like I said," Ronald smiled. "I don't count meaties."

"Then if you're counting humans," Ross wondered. "Do they count for more, the bigger they are? Big as in powerful? Which in that case, most of the powerful ones are also physically large as well."

"Very true." Ronald laughed. "I once saw this clan leader, he had grown fat with age. Bastard could barely get out of his chair before I cut him. He must have been of good health in his youth, I don't believe he was part of any monarchy."

"Yes, most of them do run at first, I guess," Ross began.

"This one quick little worm just killed his father for a throne, he did. He was able to run down the halls screaming as he was, alerting all them guards. I threw a knife, but alas, I was sloppy, the butt of the blade hit his head, so I had to finish the work. The poor guards though, they did nothing wrong. Just trying to earn shelter and food where they could." Jack and Kevin did not speak, but instead let the older elves tell their stories.

"I remember that one," Ronald remarked. "Nearly slaughtered half the fort that day. I got me some three, maybe five guards. All came at me with spears. At different times, of course."

"Jermie was never able to go on a run," Kevin said, breaking the mood. "We said he would next year, but there won't be a next year for him, or maybe any of us."

"Don't let the gloominess take hold of you," Ross said to Kevin. "I think he would want us to make it to the Outpost and cherish his life, not mourn his death." Kevin gave Ross a warm smile, and the group fell into an uncomfortable silence once more.

It did not take nearly as long as Ronald had predicted. After six cold hours, they finally saw their destination. The outpost was indeed at the foot of the Wailing Mountains—a hundred miles of peeks, thousands of feet high. The Outpost was a tower to keep an eye out for any disturbance, supplied monthly by sleighs, but now it looked dark, lonely, and empty.

When the men pounded their frozen fists against the doors, there was no answer. They knocked again. Nothing. After about five long minutes, Ross pushed against it. The heavy wood swung open.

"Unlocked?" Ronald's confusion echoed into the eerily empty foyer. "Last time, I waited here ten minutes before the lazy bastards decided to open up."

The room was dark, and colder than expected. It took a while for their eyes to adjust and when they did, they revealed thirteen dead bodies strewn about the cobblestone floor. Ten were meaties, two were elves. Though what surprised them more than meaties being this far north was the muscular humanoid that was taller than any elf but not as large or muscled as an ogre. It had brown fur and frozen red blood stuck to its thick neck. What scared Jack was the two large ram horns protruding from its skull.

Ronald adjusted the creature's face with his foot to get a better view. "A tog."

"A tog?" Kevin asked fearfully.

"Yep, it's a tog," Ross said, tilting his head to study the face and horns.

"I thought those went extinct over a thousand years ago," Jack said, still not knowing what to think of it. Last time the smarter togs invaded, Christmas Town had been lost for weeks before the elves reclaimed their land.

"Well, they're back," Ronald said. "We must tell Mr. Claus."

They crept from room to room. There was not one part of the tower unmolested. The room they found the least bodies in was the armory, which had only one elf; a knife had dug a hole through his heart. His now dry, pale eyes stared blankly at weapons that lay cluttered on the floor.

The dining room held one large table and forty corpses—elves, meaties, and togs. Some bodies of elves looked as if in a deep slumber, Jack had never seen something so peaceful in the Innerworld. Others bodies were different; some had gashes across their throats that had caused them to choke on their own blood. Intestines and organs were spread across the room.

The worst corpse had to have been the body of the largest elf, though one could only estimate the size of its body, for its clothing, flesh, and meat had been hacked to shreds; the enemy must have wanted to make sure their work was done. You could not see the elf's face or even skin tone, only small red flaps of skin that hung loosely from its body. A few of the other elves had chunks of meat torn from their face by some sort of teeth. Another had one arm nearly flayed, all the flesh eaten down to the bone.

"May we leave this room?" Jack asked, feeling his stomach lurch. *And I thought Jermie was bad.*

A loud *crash* echoed through the fortress. They followed the sound wishing to find survivors. When they made it to the wooden door, they were disappointed to hear the rapid chattering of teeth. There was a hole in the wood door where at an angle one was able to see in. Jack saw five meaties. One sat hunch over an elven body, picking meat out of the elf's stomach with its sharp, bony fingers. This one was much bigger than the others and more meat filled its body that seemed to pulsate to a hidden rhythm.

The other four meaties walked around the room occasionally glancing at the larger one. One of the smaller ones got too close to the dead elf. The giant meatie grabbed hold of a rusty jagged sword, sprung up, and swung at the transgressor who reeled away from the blows making loud teeth chatters in return.

It angered Jack more than frightened him to see this elf desecrated, even though he never knew the feller. After each member got a good look through the hole, the elves started to conceive a plan. Before they could finish, they noticed that the sound of the chewing of flesh had stopped.

Two quick footsteps echoed in the room before the door was thrown open. Five meaties charged the elves who tried to form a countercharge. The first meatie to come at Jack was weaponless, clawing at the elf with its pointed-bone fingertips. Jack dodged the blows and was able to get his short sword out in time to thrust through meat and bone. The meatie chattered and slumped to the ground. Before Jack had time to relish his kill, the large meatie, who had apparently lost an arm during the scuffle, lifted Jack with surprising ease and threw him at the concrete wall.

Jack crashed to the ground and grabbed his stomach, begging for air. When he looked up, he saw the six and a half foot skeleton charging at him. The meatie towered over him, its breath reeked of rot and dead flesh. The meatie tried to chomp down on his leg and chattered. Not knowing what to do, Jack jammed his ring finger and forefinger into the eyeless sockets of the meatie; the creature didn't seem to notice until Jack's fingers reached warm meat. The meatie's teeth chattered violently as Jack dug his fingers deep into the stiffened muscle. The meatie's mouth still tried to find Jack's throat when Kevin planted his hatchet into the creature's skull with a loud crunch.

The four living elves sat staring wide-eyed in their direction, none of them speaking; the only sound to be heard was loud gasps from each assassin.

"That thing nearly gutted me," Kevin stuttered through ragged breaths.

"Yep," Ross said. "Those are the big ones. I say the remaining togs left, leaving the meaties to feast."

"That's why that snot waffle was so difficult," Kevin replied. "Would you ever count that one, Ronald?"

"I'd say so," Ronald smiled. "But alas, you were the one who got it."

"That one must have been the greedy bastard who kept the elf corpse to himself," Jack said as he picked meat out of his finger nails. "When I was in school, the kids would share a rhyme, 'Jog like a Tog' and 'Greedy as a Meatie.' I guess the rhymes were the one accurate thing we learned as children."

"Well, what I learned as a child"—Ross stood up—"is you never get anything done by sitting on your arses; let's get a move on."

The last room that laid unexplored was a small office where an elf lay dead beside a tog and three meaties. Frozen blood painted the elf's cold lips. Its eyes were foggy and lifeless as it stared at the elves as they cleared the bodies from the room.

They made a fire to eat some untainted food Kevin had found. While he ate, Ross started to read a piece of paper he had found in the dead elf's hand.

"It says there were thousands of togs and meaties that stormed the fortress," he said. "They got to him before he finished."

"Well, they're about to get to us too," Ronald said as he stared dully out the window. Jack glanced through the glass and saw a horde of dark spots moving down the slope of the mountain.

"You had to say it." Kevin laughed. "Jog like a tog."

"Well…" Ronald took a deep breath. "No point in staying here, let's gather all the supplies we can hold and try heading for home."

"I say we can hold them," Jak said. "From the ramparts. Give me a quiver and bow; bet I'll take down more than a dozen before they reach the bottom of the hill."

"No," Ross replied sternly as he shoved the paper in his pocket. "That is just a small unit of togs arriving. A larger force is most likely behind them. Anyway, they won't just scavenge the fort then leave it. These are togs. They're not the brainless meaties we are used to; they will come with a strategy and means to take this fort for an outpost with what I can only guess to be an army to take back the land we chased them out of all those years ago."

"Well, we could put up a fight," Kevin said.

"And die?" Surprise and confusion swirled in Jack's blue eyes.

"It'll be a story for the ages," Kevin defended.

"But who would live to tell the story?" Ronald chuckled again. "Besides, we're gonna do a lot more good getting this news to Claus. I don't know if they forgot to teach you about the togs that all died years before the first Saint Nick even showed up. You've heard of Krampus though, right? He was one of them togs, and he nearly tore down the Innerworld during the war he created."

"Agreed," Ross said. "We must find a space to hole out far from here. We will have to travel the edges of Mortuus Forest."

"Don't the Mortuus Witches dwell in that place?" Kevin asked with concern.

"Well, yes." Ross smiled. "It *is* called the Mortuus Forest."

"So do wolves, undead, giant spiders, and other unspeakable creatures," Ronald stated. "But meaties generally don't venture through there, and it is an easy landmark to follow home."

"As for now," Ross started, "we must find the forest."

The elves began to rush around the fortress, gathering all the food and water they could find before they left shelter and plunged into the bitter cold once more.

"Don't venture far into Mortuus, there are creatures as hungry and as rude as meaties in there," Ross warned when they made it to the forest's edge. "We shouldn't need to worry about meaties anyways, for they rarely travel near these parts."

"Well ,they also never traveled to the Outpost either," Kevin remarked.

"That is true, let's get digging," Ross commanded. "Then we wake up early the next morning and continue our journey."

Jack had taken first watch to guard over his comrades. He stared into the dark wood that lay west of him, when in the corner of his eye, he saw something orange. He stared at it, hundreds of bright eyes stared back. Jack saw the outline of a plump, round shape clinging to a tree, though it was hard to tell what it was in the dark.

They gazed at each other for what felt like ages until the loud sniffing of what sounded like a large dog resounded around them. The many orange eyes quickly turned towards the sound then, with the loud creak of limbs, the body scattered off.

THE CREW WOKE to chattering the next morning.

The sky hadn't even begun to grow bright as they left their hole to whatever had followed them. The chattering soon grew closer and closer until the shallow sound of howling pierced the air.

Though they were in a rush, the elves stopped and listened as the howling was replaced with low, rumbling growls. Soon the shrill cries of dogs were heard along with the crack of bones. The chattering ceased and the sharp crunching of the wolves' feast echoed throughout the forest.

"Poor bastards don't know what's good for them. Never seen meaties, most likely," Ross said. "They'll be dead from the tainted meat within a week."

They trudged onward through the snow. "I wonder," Jack said after a while of walking. "Why don't the meaties ever gobble up any ogres. I heard they eat anything that pumps blood."

"That is a question for the philosophers, Kevin," Ross replied, his eyes still ahead of him. "All we know about the ogres is they come from the south. And yes, they do bleed red, I should know."

"I heard," Ronald began, "that human's call 'em yetis."

"Humans?" Jack asked. "I thought the only living beings able to get through the Door were elves and reindeer."

"And humans," Kevin remarked. "How do you think 'ole Santa gets through each year?"

"Then in that case, did a human happen to stumble in and see some 'yetis'?" Jack looked towards Ross for an answer.

"No, the only ones to get through are the Clauses," Ronald replied instead. "And the wife each son chooses whilst inside the Outerworld."

"Maybe," Kevin theorized. "One of the upcoming Santas told some human friends about the ogres while looking for a wife in the Innerworld."

"Possibly," Ronald agreed. "But then how'd they get the name yeti?"

"It's also very possible a human stumbled upon the corpse of an ogre that somehow got through. We shall never know," Ross admitted. "You do know other creatures can make it through the Door, just not alive?"

"I guess I did," Kevin stated. "Just never thought of it that way."

"But be cautious to never bring any to the human world," Ronald warned. "The humans, other than the Clauses, of course, haven't developed any immunities to the meaties. That's why Mr. Clause has to not see the missus for two days after Christmas."

"Why thank you for the lesson, Mr. Ronald," Ross joked. "Can't wait for a new one tomorrow." Ronald grinned and they began to walk in silence once more.

They finally made it to a stopping point and dug into the snow once more to sleep. When they finished, their fingers burned of impending blisters and the hole was as tall as Jack and wide enough to fit five elves. Ronald took watch as the rest began to slumber.

It took about thirty minutes for Jack to finally fall into a deep sleep for the roughness of the terrain made him twist and turn. He had barley drifted into a dreamworld when the sound of footsteps—eight footsteps to be exact—forced his eyes open. They sounded different, inhuman, like eight javelins being thrusted in the snow.

Jack climbed up the side of the hole when a hand from below grabbed him by the collar and silently dragged him back into the shelter. Ronald had a finger to his lips, motioning for Jack to be silent. They woke Kevin and Ross before scaling the hole. It was still dark outside, and the snow was covered with round puncture marks.

"What in the devil," Kevin said. There was a loud squishing

sound followed by a grunt from Ross.

When they turned around, Jack's eyes went wide. Ross stood, wobbly on his feet, a large black spider leg stuck through his chest. It slid from the elf's body with a hollow squelch, and Ross flailed to the ground.

Jack dodged as the spider took stabs at him. Kevin's hatchet swung at the tar black legs. Blood dripped from Ross's lips as he tried and failed to suck in air, as the spider stared at Jack with a hundred demon eyes. Jack swung his blade, cleaving two dark limbs, painting the snow with yellow puss. Ross began to roll, gasping and grunting as the fight raged on above him.

Ronald dug his dagger deep into the side of the spider. It proceeded to hiss and claw at Ronald, who dogged the blows but stumbled into the deep hole. The spider aimed more strikes at Jack. He backpedaled, then tripped, landing in the soft snow. The spider's backside hit the powder as Kevin hacked off the rest of its back legs.

As Kevin went in for a killing blow, the spider bounced back up, knocking him to the side. Before the arachnida could make another move, Jack pounced on it, straddling the creature's back. His fists grew red and sore as he smashed them into the spider's body, which seemed to irritate it more than harm it.

The spider thrashed and bucked, trying to relieve itself of Jack. Kevin came up from the side and dealt a blinding blow to the monster's eyes. The spider gave an ear aching *hiss*, stumbling as it tried to locate its prey. Jack had by now fallen off the spider and grabbed his short sword.

With two hands tightly gripping his blade, Jack pushed into the spider's skull causing a satisfying *crunch*. Kevin embedded his hatchet into the creature's brain. Jack yanked the sword from the body, and without thinking, striked the spider again. Kevin, doing the same, lifted his weapon and swung it down for a second blow, eliciting another *crunch*.

By the time the two were done, no crunches came from the spider for it became a soft, yellow, and mushy corpse

Kevin panted, his breath coming in gasps as he fell against the huge spider's back. Jack rushed to Ross whose eyes had closed. A finger pushed under the sleigh leader's hood. His pulse was gone. Jack felt hot tears warm his face as he held Ross's limp body.

"Jack, get over here," he heard Kevin call. Jack reluctantly lets Ross slip from his arms as he rose.

He found Kevin and Ronald in the hole, Ronald laying on the ground, his foot twisted the wrong way. Jack stumbled down and helped Kevin get Ronald up. With a few grunts and pulls, they finally got the injured man out of the hole. Ronald almost fell backwards, but was caught by Kevin.

"Ross is gone," Jack said, looking at his feet in shame.

"What do we do now?" Kevin asked, his tone more angry than sad.

"We do what we were already doing," Ronald said through heavy breaths. "We'll be safe once we get to the outskirts of home. But we must hurry."

Ronald removed his boot causing him to clench his teeth in pain. They examined the wound; the outer edge of his foot had grown dark brown and swollen. He stuck his bare foot in the snow for a bit, groaned in relief, then took it out and with even more effort, put it back in its sheltering boot.

What little food they had with them had been with Ross and tainted by the spider, leaving them hungry. They buried Ross in the hole they had previously made but left faster than when they buried Jermie. It wasn't long before they began to hear howling from within the wood.

They walked in silence this time; it was different without Ross. Lonely. Ronald seemed to walk fine, though he winced with each step. Soon Kevin had to put Ronald's arm over his shoulder to keep him steady. When Kevin became weary, Jack took his place in supporting the navigator.

None of them saw any form of life as they walked. They stopped to go to sleep early that night. Jack woke to lights, beautiful lights. He had seen the purple and green wonders in the sky many times before, but, for some reason, this time they made Jack feel happy and warm. Soon Ronald and Kevin woke and joined Jack to stare dumbly at the bright sky.

They left before daylight, the chattering of bone teeth in the distance.

At times, walking had become so unbearable their bodies forced them to stop and rest.

Kevin was the first to spot the reindeer. It was an old, scrawny, feral-looking creature.

"Give me the bow," Ronald whispered.

"You're not gonna shoot it," Kevin replied in shock. "One of us could ride it back and get help."

"You're not gonna be able to ride that one, kid," Ronald replied. "The moment he sees us, he's gone. Now give me the bow."

"You can't be serious," Jack said.

"You boys have two more days till you make it back home," Ronald began. "Starvation will just make you weary, and with an army of meaties and God knows what on our tails, I don't like the sound of weariness. Now give me the damn bow."

HOLES WERE DUG in the snow for shelter and insulation. A small fire was made with coal to produce heat and cook the reindeer meat. Jack did not enjoy the taste or texture of it one bit. He had heard many stories of humans eating and hunting reindeer in the Outerworld, but for the Innerworld, elves ate ryngess, large fat and plump cow-like creatures covered with layers of fur the elves then used for warmth. Reindeer were sacred and prized; even the ones born flightless were cherished. Surprising though, was how little meat Ronald had eaten for he was the one who had the idea.

"Aye Ronald," Kevin asked, "why ain't you eating?"

"You guys will need the nutrition," Ronald replied.

Jack immediately understood. "But why?"

"My ankle is all messed up. I'll just slow you down."

"Nah Ronald," Kevin said. "Come with us, please."

"Ronald, not you too," Jack begged.

"Leave me a bow and quiver; now go on before they get here," Ronald commanded.

"Ronald," Kevin began.

"It's okay, lads." Ronald grabbed Jack softly by the shoulder. "I'd rather go out this way then pissing my sheets as an old man." Ronald smiled and his eyes began to puddle though he wiped them away fast to hide his shame. "I guess this is what you call karma." He laughed, which was received by odd looks from Jack and Kevin. "Since we didn't bury the reindeer, now I shall lay, unburied." He looked at the sky, and Jack tried not to notice the new tears in the older man's eyes.

"Hey," Ronald said joyfully. "At least I've seen a tog, now what modern elf has done that."

"Only two others." Kevin tried to laugh, but it came out forced.

"You better tell 'em stories about me." Ronald chuckled. "Ronald the Great. Damn, I should have written a memoir about my first crash. Anyways, this time was much more exciting." Loud howling interrupted their conversation, followed by the consistent crunching of snow from the woods.

"Best you two lads get going." Ronald sat up and knocked an arrow. "Hey, I'll miss you guys." They both squeezed Ronald's hand and gave him the best of wishes. Jack tried not to look back as he and Kevin ran, but he found himself doing exactly that until the veteran was blotted out by trees. And when he couldn't see Ronald any more, Jack wished he had looked back more times.

THE TWO TRUDGED through snow with weapons and dead reindeer meat at their sides. It was quiet when Kevin began to talk, even the wind had stopped its constant screeching.

"I have been thinking about something, Jack," he said. "About Jermie, the way he…the way he reacted when he found out about his wound. Before he noticed, he acted like nothing was there, but then I told him, and he got all pale and…and this was his fifth year. Only fifth. He was not even twenty, yet; now he's dead because of me."

"Now, that's not true," Jack said. "We did everything we could."

Kevin just nodded and kept walking. They continued in silence, each seeming to be content with their own thoughts.

Just before dusk, they heard the chattering from the inside of the woods.

This time they couldn't outrun it.

A small group of meaties burst from the trees and sprinted towards them. Three came at Jack with rusty swords. He parried two with his own, but the third sunk its blade deep into his side. Kevin struck down another meatie and began to drag Jack away from the oncoming attackers.

"Stop," Jack gasped, drool and blood dripped from his mouth. "Go! Run!"

"No," Kevin choked. "Not you too, don't leave me. I can't— not alone."

"It's okay," Jack said in a softer voice. "Don't be scared; fear is just an idea."

The chattering of teeth was replaced by the rapid rhythm of

hundreds of feet crushing through snow. Jack gave Kevin a light shove. Kevin cursed and began to run.

Jack stumbled to his feet and wrapped his fingers around the cool hilt of his sword. Jack slew the first meatie before it could lift its weapon. The second one wielded nothing but its claw. Jack hacked into its soft head but was too slow to retrieve the blade before he felt a sharp pain in his side. It burned up his body. Jack grabbed the meatie by the eye sockets, pulled back, then drove his sword into its skull.

Another burn engulfed his neck as a meatie's blade hacked through the top of his shoulder. The next moments were a blur of fire and agony. He could not feel the wind on his face or the fourth sword impaling his body. And when the fifth weapon struck him, he was not afraid and in fact looking forward to laughing with Jermie again, brooding with Ronald, and reveling in the sweet sound of Ross's stories as they flowed into his ears.

The elf didn't have time to notice the rusted blade careening towards his neck. His body slumped, lifeless, and numb to the hundreds of teeth that began to gnaw at his skin and flesh.

***

KEVIN RAN, and when he could not run, he crawled. Even when he was out of harm's way and could see the elven city, he still stumbled as fast as his body would allow. The snow around the city was all slush, painted black and red from a freshly-made battlefield. Parts of the surrounding walls were torn to rubble, unburied ogres lay as evidence beside the heaps of stone and mud.

An elf on a flightless reindeer rode out to meet him.

"What's your name?" the elf asked.

"Kevin from Sleigh 54," he croaked back. "Take me to Claus, now."

Instead of being taken to their human leader, Kevin was brought to a room that held an elf of great stature.

"General," Kevin gasped. "The Outpost. Meaties. Togs."

"Slow down, son." The General spoke in a deep but soft voice. "Let's start the story before we finish it. From what I heard, you're part of the List Checkers. You should have been nowhere near the Outpost."

"Yes." Kevin gulped at a mug of water he was handed.

"Okay then." The General sat up and crossed his fingers. "Start from the beginning."

Kevin told them how they crashed and quickly skimmed over Jermie's death. He remembered that Ronald had been in a crash once and then revealed that to the General. He spoke of how silent the Outpost was when they reached it and of the strange horned creature that had laid dead. If Kevin was expecting any reaction from the General, he got none, for the ranked elf just sat there, listening intently with an undisturbed face. Kevin spoke of what he saw running down the mountains and the Mortuus forest. He spoke of the wolves and of how far west the meaties were. He skimmed over Ross's death as well and skipped the part of the reindeer they had to slaughter. Kevin ended the tale with, "I lost the last two before I made it here."

The General sat in silence as if digesting the tale he had just heard, then spoke. "That sounds like quite the journey. Are you injured in any way? I know you told the guards that you needed no medical assistance."

"It hurts," Kevin forced a laugh.

"What hurts?" the General asked.

"Everything." The tears felt like lava in his eyes.

IN THE CENTER of Christmas town stands a small golden statue of a sled and five passengers. Two passengers hold crossbows, one looks young and excited. The other grins, a bucket held in one hand. The navigator stares intently at maps and papers. One passenger smiles, golden teeth glistening in the sun as he guides his men. The last one looks scared, excited, and curious all at the same time as he smiles at the reindeers in front of him. Below the statue a plaque reads:

The Heroes of Sleigh 54

BEN ARMSTRONG

Ben is a young author who has been writing stories for over six years now. Recently he has been published in his town's newspaper.

THREADS*

LAWRENCE WEST

Trigger Warning: Suicide, verbal abuse, violence and domestic abuse, and drug use. Mentions of thoughts of suicide. No suicide depicted on the page.

I don't want to die.

I don't want to die, but I hate being alive.

This is my first thought each morning when I open my eyes. My morning prayer. I'm dangerous to everyone and everything around me, and no one knows it. That's why I'm here, sleeping in my car as far from civilization as I can get. A danger made safe.

I roll over in the backseat of my car, dreams fading to vapor, and lean down to dig for the little plastic baggie I keep hidden under the floor mat. My Oxy. The only thing keeping me alive in this fucked up world. I find it. It feels empty but isn't. *Only one left. Shit.*

The windows of my home carry a heavy film of condensation. It must have gotten colder during the night. Soft morning light filters in through the glass, diffused and golden. Faint threads of color sway and eddy on the currents of the air. Just a few bright lines the width of a hair dancing around me. What are they connected to? I don't want to know. I don't even want to acknowledge them. Nope. Not gonna look at them. I shut my eyes tight. Not gonna see them. They are not there. I am not crazy.

The threads are still there though. They rub against the skin on my arms and chest. Even through the thin sheet I use as a blanket, I can feel them. Where they touch me, they burn, and tiny flashes of what they are and what damage I could do, flood my mind.

Don't touch them, Theodore. *Don't touch them.* Move carefully. *Slowly.* The ritual must be completed. As slowly as I can, I reach trembling fingers into the baggie and grab hold of the small pill. *The last.* A thread hums against my arm. *Fuck, Teddy.* People could die. What the fuck is wrong with you? *What the fuck is wrong with me? I can't do this. I can't. I can't I can't I can't I can't.* Tears well up as my frustration mounts. *Why does everything have to be so hard? I don't want this. I don't want to hurt people.*

Breathe, Teddy. *I have to breathe.* Come on. You can do this. *I really can't.* A single thread of red light drifts down and rests itself against the length of my arm singing the soft skin and filling my car with the scent of burning flesh. I can see its light through the membrane of my eyelids. Just this tiny touch affects the thread. Shifting the thread's course.

The welling tears fall, wetting my cheeks. In my head, I see them stained red with innocent blood. I have to stop. This thread. These threads. Burning me like a brand.

I follow the red line on my arm. The thread is attached to a little bird. Its feet *tik tik tik* across the pavement. Its feathers rustle in a faint shift of the air. The little thing is hunting for food, water, life, survival. If I move again, the thread on my arm will waver, and the bird will die. I've already done too much, changed the bird's luck. Its thread has gone from vibrant red to a muted pink. The bird will linger, pecking at a food wrapper that provides no sustenance instead of simply taking wing, and because of *that,* it will flutter away on different currents than it otherwise would have. My mind fast forwards to its fate: six days later the bird will meet a hawk it would have missed and die.

I need my pill. I need it. To make the threads fade away. So I don't see or touch—even by accident—any of the other threads that have listed in my direction and destroy even more innocent lives. I've already damned one soul; I won't have more blood on my hands.

Slowly. I inch my hand across my lap making sure to keep my eyes squeezed shut. I know it's childish. It doesn't help. The pill is a piece of reality. A stark contrast to the heat of the thread on my arm. My muscles twitch, shifting the thread resting against it. Fresh hell surges through my mind. A swirl of possibilities. I'm trapped. I'm completely trapped.

I don't wish I was dead. I just wish I wasn't alive. I can't do this anymore. I don't want to hurt things. I don't want to kill things. I just can't seem to help it. *Please God. What am I supposed to do?* God is silent. The pill is still in my hand, trapped by lines of death. My last one. I need to swallow it. I know I need to. I know what I need to do. But I can't.

Fuck it. *Sorry, bird.* I lift my hand to my mouth. The thread sears my flesh. I stifle a scream of pain. The pill lands on my tongue; it tastes like love and slides easily down my throat.

My hand drops back down, and I freeze in place. I risk a glance and open my eyes. The pink line dances inches away like nothing has happened to it or its owner. But I know the truth. Fresh tears escape me, growing to sobs, until my chest heaves with suppressed misery. It's all I can do while I wait for the pill to hit me and wipe the world clean. Make me safe again.

"I'm sorry," I mutter to the unyielding universe. "I don't want to be bad."

Most addicts do drugs to get high. I do them to get sane. *Yes I do.* It clears the head, sends the suffocating threads away. High, I'm safe. Sober, I'm dangerous. Sober, I hurt people. Sober, people could die. When I'm sober the threads are everywhere, a rainbow of light connecting everything alive or inanimate to everything else, and when I touch them, things change. Always for the worse. But in the cloud of Oxy, I can't see the threads, and if I can't see them, I can't touch them. I can't change things.

The threads fade before the sadness. I'll be safe again soon. At least while the drugs remain in me.

The car itself is clean and organized. No food or drink is allowed in the car. That's a rule. My clothes are folded neatly on the front seat. Keeps them fresh longer. A couple swipes with the sheet cleans away some of the fog on the widow. It's a cool, crisp autumn morning. Beautiful. Peaceful. It makes me smile to see it. Even if it is just an empty parking lot in an industrial park at the edge of town. For the night, it was my little slice of heaven. I see the bird I'd doomed extend its wings and fly away.

It could have been worse. The thought comes unbidden and my stomach drops instantly. *I really am a monster.*

Naked, I step out of the car and walk the few feet to the tall grass behind the building. Not ideal, but it's too early for anyone to be around. The body is meant to squat when you take a shit, so this location is perfect. I use the last of the TP and leave the empty roll behind along with my mess.

Two minutes later, I am dressed again. I give a cursory sniff to the clothes. Fresh enough, but I'll need to wash them. I spray some Axe on to help, just in case. I don't need my boss questioning my hygiene. Not again. I like this job.

I fold the bed sheet and put it away in the trunk. I put my sole towel into my gym bag with the body wash and shampoo, set the bag next to me on the passenger seat and drive away.

Ten minutes later, I pull up to the gym. It's busy for a Tuesday morning, which is perfect. No one will notice me. I'm just another person. I go in, walk past the employees behind the counter and head right to the showers. I quickly wipe off the grime and sweat, shave and brush my teeth. By the time I leave the gym, the burn from the thread that morning is just a faint line on my arm. It matches perfectly with the others—my growing collection of scars. I know if I concentrate I could find the old, lingering threads that connect all things together, but I don't. The drugs dull me enough that I'm just a guy. Just a guy. Not a murderer. Not a threat.

I don't remember when the threads started. So much of my life is a hazy blur. They have faded in and out of the periphery of my awareness as far back as I can remember, growing in persistence as I grew in age. A part of me knows that they finally solidified at the age of twelve when I hurt my mom, even if I try my best not to think of that day. It was the moment I admitted to myself that they were real. That it wasn't just my imagination.

What would my life have been if I hadn't found Oxy?

I had learned about the pills when I was eleven. My mom had given me an Oxy left over from her back surgery to dull the ache from breaking my toe, and the relief from pain it provided was nothing compared to the side effect. Laying on my bed, high as a kite, the threads faded. The world became bland again. I've never felt more in awe of something than I did in that moment. For those few hours I felt sane and human.

I've been chasing that high ever since.

After what happened with my mom, I knew I needed the protection the Oxy provided, and I didn't have to wait long to find a supply. Mike Stilson had made sure of that. He was a local kid. His mom was a junkie who liked to hurt herself so she could get her pills. I knew this. Everyone knew this. No one talked about it, but we all knew. So when my mom's leftover Oxy were used up, I went over to play video games, but really I went to snatch the pills. I had to do something. If I didn't find something to keep me from hurting someone again, I would have to take more drastic action to protect others from myself.

In between games I excused myself and went to take a piss. Mike had told us all where she hid them, so I lifted the tank lid after flushing, pulled out the baggy with her bottle in it, hidden so her boyfriends wouldn't find it. I took the whole bottle, popping one before I left the bathroom.

It hit like a freight train. The fear of moving faded. The threads vanished. If I couldn't see them, I couldn't affect fate, and I wouldn't have to worry about the consequences if I did. I could live a little longer without adding more guilt.

Mom wasn't a mistake, though. Even now, at twenty-six, I know this. No, Mom was on purpose. That's why I'm still carrying the guilt. Mom was proof that I couldn't be trusted. A lesson I needed to learn. Like that first burn you get when you touch something hot on the stove. I knew—or at least guessed— what the threads were even then, and I did it anyways. She and Dad were—are—good people. They loved me. Did everything they could for me, but how could they understand? They couldn't see what I could. They had said as much when I tried to explain the threads I see every moment I'm sober. And if they couldn't see—if they couldn't understand—how could they grasp what I was capable of if I got angry?

It happened because of a fight. Just a fight between parent and kid. Fourteen years later I can't even remember what the fight was about, but in that moment, when she was standing over me in my bedroom—me shouting at her, her back at me, both of our faces purple with rage—I hated her. I saw her thread clear as day for the first time. A crystal blue line, milling with hundreds or thousands of others infesting my room, but burning bright with limitless potential energy.

I reached out, wrapped my hand around her thread and pulled. One quick tug. It burned like acid. The mark is faint, but the scar is deep, and I can still see it clearly all these years later. A constant reminder. I knew immediately what I had done was wrong. I wanted to take it back, but the die had been cast. I choked on the shame of it, my throat tying knots around the words.

My mom had huffed at me, threw up her hands and stomped out of the room, slamming the door behind her. She walked down the hall, and when she got to the stairs, she tripped. I just sat there on my floor where she'd left me. I sat there, rooted to the spot, and listened as she crashed down the steps and cried out for help from the bottom. Dad came home ten minutes later and took her to the hospital. Her collar bone had shattered, as had her forearm and three of her ribs. I heard my dad tell her that if she had landed just a little differently she would have broken her neck. It was a miracle she was alive. But I knew differently. It was my fault. I had made her fall.

That's why I need the drugs. If I had tugged on my mom's thread harder, or held it longer...just by the tiniest bit, she would have died. It had been that close, and I couldn't—can't—let it be that close again.

In my car again, I drive off. Always without thinking. My mind is a slurry of memory and regret. Some time later, I pull up to a house on Mason street. My brain knows what I need even though I haven't told it where to go. This is my dealer's house. Tam's house. Tam is short for Tamborine. I have no clue why he goes by this stupid fucking name; it's probably because Eric doesn't strike fear in the hearts of his buyers. Still, Tam isn't any scarier, but I keep that knowledge to myself.

I knock on the door three times. My recently cashed paycheck—thank God Walmart cashes checks—is now a neatly-folded wad of twenties burning a hole in my pocket. The door opens. Nick, a beefy troll of a man, fixes me with his trademark dumb expression for a second, then steps aside. I walk in, and he shuts the door behind me.

I pull out the stack of cash I'd separated from the rest. Four hundred bucks. The price of forty pills. Enough for ten days. Ten beautiful days. B-E-A-UTIFUL. Yes, sir. And that, my dear fellows, is why I live in my car. Nick shakes his head and gestures down the hall. *What the fuck?*

This is as far as I've ever been in the house. I've never needed to go deeper. Not in six years. But I need my pills, and if I have to walk down this hall and actually see Tam to get them, I will. There was a time when I could have gotten my pills elsewhere. Oxy isn't hard to find, but Tam's price is best, his product is pure, and it wasn't worth the risk of pissing him off by buying elsewhere. Tam has a reputation, and that alone means I ain't worth another dealer's time. That didn't matter though. My money is good, and I have extra if I need it. At the end of the day I'll go back to selling plasma and semen if I need the extra cash. Whatever it takes to keep me from making another mistake.

The hallway is dark and lightless, like a throat. It feels like the house is swallowing me. I reach the end of the hall and stop in the archway leading into the living room. Unsure what to do next, I knock on the wall three times. Better to be safe, than sorry.

"Enter," he says. I cross the boundary, reaching out to get a bearing on what I'm stepping into.

The living room is large and empty except for a couch, coffee table, two bookcases, and a mini fridge. A TV hangs on the wall with a video game system on the floor beneath it. Tam sits on the couch with his arms slung over the back, a big Nazi flag on the wall behind him. He's a big guy, tall, and muscular, with a thick head of curly black hair. He clearly spends too many hours at the gym, and uses lots of steroids. It probably means his dick has shrunk, but I'm not dumb enough to say that to his face. Sitting next to him is his girlfriend Penny. My heart sinks. I don't like this. It's too weird. Different. "'Sup Teddy? How you doing, my friend?"

His words bounce around in my head as I stare at Penny's pallid face and tired eyes.

I've known Penny for years. I was seventeen when we met, already living in my car and dealing to support myself. I was loitering outside of the high school when I saw her. She was just as beautiful then, but her eyes aren't as bright anymore. I introduced her Tam, but I've regretted it ever since. At the time, I just wanted to help my friend when she was kicked out of her home. I didn't understand what Tam was, or what he would do to her.

You could say I love her, but that word has never felt like enough. Love is way too simple. Way, way too simple. Penny's perfect. Her hair, her smile, her laugh, but most of all the way she didn't look at me like a freak. Everyone else did, but not her.

Now she looks a shell of what she was. Her eyes are red and the left side of her face is puffy. *Warning!* She is looking anywhere but at me. *Warning!* Why won't she look at me? My heart leaps in my throat, and I realize I should have turned around at the door, but it's too late now, and I'm running out of time til the Oxy wears off. This whole thing scares me. Not the Nazi shit. Yeah that's scary, but in my life, I put up with what I have to put up with. No, that look on her face—it's the look that says something bad is going to happen. I have five hours until the Oxy is out of my system. And I'm out. So bring on the shit, and let me go.

"Fine," I say, looking away from Penny and back to Tam. Based on his grin, I'd glanced for too long. "Nick pointed me down here."

"Yeah. Yeah, he did," Tam says. He moves his arms off the back of the couch and leans forward. "How long have we known each other?"

Eyes that blue shouldn't look that dead. Having him look at me like that makes me want to shit myself.

I lick my lips and say, "Six years. Give or take."

"Give or take. I like that. I give, you take. And yeah, six years. Long time. And man, you are consistent. Every ten days like clockwork. I like consistency. I like loyal. I know you could buy from others. Maybe get a better deal on the Oxy, but you stick with me." He looks over to Penny who forces a smile. "I like that. Loyalty. I like you too, Teddy. You're a good guy."

Tam stands up and walks across the room to one of the bookcases. They're the only things out of place in the room. Tam doesn't look like he reads. He pulls a book off the shelf and opens it. Inside are dozens of baggies. The sound of literal angels fills my head. A year of my life. A year as a human is inside that book. A year of safety. Tam pulls out one of the baggies and then a second before snapping the book shut and putting it back on the shelf.

Tam turns back to me. "You know Paul, right?"

Paul? Black hair, beard, fat. That Paul? "Yeah," I say.

"Good. Cuz Paul went away. Got caught beating the shit out

Megan. She was stepping out on him." Tam shrugged like this was a justifiable reason. "So I need legs on the south side. You work on that side of town, right? At that gas station?"

I nod. I don't like that he knows this. Penny must have told him; she's the one who helped me get the job there.

"Well, I want you to be my legs. Push product."

"No thanks," I say without thinking.

The fake smile falls off of Tam's face. Anger flashes, then the smile is back.

"I don't want an answer right now. You're gonna listen, think it over, and *then* answer. Got it?"

I nod again.

"Not good enough. I need a yes or no."

"Okay," I say before quickly adding, "Yes."

"Alrighty." Tam laughs. "So here's the deal. You'll have from Brady to Park, and Center to 27th. On top of your cut, I'll give you a discount on your own product. Half off. Skinny little white boy like you, all clean cut and innocent. No one will ever suspect you. And since you don't have a dick, I don't have to worry about you popping some bitch and ending up in jail. Or trying to fuck me over. You need balls for something like that."

That—that made me take a step back. Mentally. When I do, the threads rise up in a forest all around me. Faint, but very much there. Did you know that every person has a little instinct? It's probably a carry over from our cave dwelling days, when we needed it to suss out danger and keep us on our toes. With time, that need dwindled, but a little nugget remains in all of us. Some people have more than others. I have a medium amount, but I have honed that little chunk of instinct like a knife, and it's telling me to run. *Screaming* at me to run. It is so loud that it's even giving me a way out.

The threads.

A thousand colored hairs teeming around me, coming from every surface and every direction. Tam's thread isn't hard to make out amongst the others. Green as a poisonous jungle snake. All I have to do is reach out and yank, and my Tam problem would be gone. Can I though? Can I really murder someone? Even an abusive, racist asshole like Tam?

In the periphery of my vision, I can see the bookcase. The book. The pills. Like a magnet, they pull at me. I need them, and in spite of what he said, he is all I got. I'm not loyal. I'm a junkie. Not for Oxy. I'm a junkie for being human, and I'm not dumb enough to cross Tam.

His smile widens, and I can see the yellow teeth of his grimy sneer. Behind him, Penny's whole body shakes, but she never looks up. Vivid splotches of purple bruises litter her arms.

Tam catches me staring again and turns to her; when he looks back his smile is wider.

"She and I had a wild night. Don't you worry about her. She likes it rough. Just think about what I said." He tosses the two baggies onto the table in front of the couch and pulls a smaller one out of his pocket. There are three pills in it. He dangles the bag in front of me.

"Three for now. Enough to get you through the day. On the house. You decide you're in, you come back tonight. I'll give you both of those," Tam says, motioning to the baggies taunting me from their spot on the table. "Free. A little loyalty on my part. You decide you're out, well, you can find someone else to buy from." Tam laughs. Nick, who is in the archway leading into the hallway now, laughs with him. Only me and Penny remain quiet. Tam looks at Penny and frowns.

"What the fuck am I going to do with you? You lost your ability to laugh? Huh?"

Penny forces a listless chuckle.

"I don't want a pity laugh. I want a fucking answer." The last is a growl. He walks over and stands so close her nose touches his stomach. "An answer. Now."

"No. No, I haven't."

"So I'm just not funny then?"

"No. You are." Penny is crying now. Silent tears flow down her cheeks.

Tam growls again. "Do I need to teach you how to laugh?"

What the fuck does that even mean? What the fuck is wrong with this guy? My instincts are playing like a marching band now. Run is on the drums, Hide on the trumpets, Kill Them is on the Cymbals. The last scares me. Kill them. I can. I know I can. The threads are faint, but I can summon them if I need to. How much would I need to pull on Tam's for his death to be immediate?

That thought stops me cold. I need a pill. I need the haze of humanity again. Not the distillation of adrenaline.

"No, sir," Penny squeaks out.

"Good," he says and smacks the side of her head. Penny's head rocks, her hair falling down, blocking her face from my view. This is good. Very good. If I had to see her face for one more second, I know I'll do something stupid.

"Come on," Nick says.

I almost jump out of my skin. How is a guy that big so easy to forget? He waves his hand and I follow him out of the room, leaving Penny with Tam. Abandoning her. My stomach sinks and my skin crawls. This is worse than what I did to the bird this morning. But I can barely save myself. What the fuck can I do for her? Trying and failing would just end with both of us dead. Would that really be better for her?

Maybe.

I'm in my car again. Nick had grabbed the pills from Tam when I had been lost in my contemplation and had handed them to me at the door. Just three. Enough for the day. *Tam, you fucking asshole.* They were his insurance policy. We both knew it. I'd left my stash at a friend's house and tried to buy Percs a few months ago, but Jerry down on 5th refused to sell to me. He wouldn't say why, but I understood. If I wanted my pills, my sanity, my humanity, I would have to go back to Tam. Or leave town.

And if I didn't come back to him, leaving town is exactly what I will have to do. Tam won't let me wander about knowing as much as I do. Fuck. I could call the cops, rat on Tam, and they would roll up and take him down. The image warms my heart. Until Tam makes a call from prison to one of his goons, and I wake up to someone busting in the window of my car. Alive just long enough to see the gun and hear the shot. I sigh. Yeah. Cops are out. So, it's take the deal or run.

Why am I fucking cursed? I put the car in gear and drive. I need to get to work. Twenty minutes later, I pull into the parking lot behind the Lapis Street Pantry, take out the Axe Body Spray, douse myself, then pat my pocket. The pills are still there. The Pantry is a good job, pays well, and my boss Tim is a good man. The best part is that my coworkers are pleasant and leave me alone. I've had a lot of jobs over the years because my parents always had a habit of finding out where I worked, and when they did, they would show up and beg me to come home. Then I'd have to break their hearts and move on. The last time I had seen either of them was when I had fled my job at McDonalds, leaving my father crying in the parking lot. I didn't even risk going back for my last paycheck. It was too risky.

The hardest part of being what I am is watching it slowly kill my parents. I thought it would be the shrinks, the endless questions, diagnoses, changes of diagnoses, but no, it was my parents. So I got good at pretending and took the Oxy. Eventually, when I got older, my parents had me committed. I was sixteen, and they'd had enough. The doctors there tried like all the others. It was hard there. I didn't have access to my pills, and so I had to contend with the threads.

Three nurses and two doctors had accidents. Trips, falls, and one car accident that had all resulted in broken bones and lasting pain. And no one believed me when...when I explained that these 'accidents' had been my fault, they tried to give me different pills. Pills that turned me into a zombie but did nothing for the threads, or the accidents, and I realized that they didn't give me the meds to make *me* feel better, but to make *themselves* feel better.

The secret was in their smiles, the way they looked relieved as I drooled on myself. That's a hard truth. Most of the time, when people tell you to 'get help,' it isn't because they want to see you better; it's because they can't handle seeing you unwell any longer. It's too much for *them*, and they either want you to be normal or go away. This is just as true for doctors as it was for anyone else. Once I learned this, I accepted that I had to pretend to be normal for their sake. Nine months later they let me out. Pretending had gotten me that much, but I couldn't do it forever. So when I got home, I packed a bag and left. I haven't been back since.

That was ten years ago. Ten years of learning. Ten years of figuring out just how much my parents loved me. Ten years of slowly peeling away every aspect of my life with them until they were all gone. No friends. No social media. No phone numbers. No comfort of my old neighborhood, because Mom and Dad would strike at any blip of me that cropped up on their radar. The last had been a year ago, when I had been working in the back of that McDonalds. Now I'm here on the South Side. In the slums. No one my parents know would be caught dead down here, and so far none of them had. I make enough to buy my humanity with enough left over to eat well and have a savings if something comes up. But like everything in my life, the other shoe has dropped, and Tam is holding a gun to my head.

Fuck.

At around four in the afternoon, I am leaning against the counter, idly watching the traffic outside. I'm alone in the gas station, and my replacement won't be in until five-thirty. The door chirps, and I look up to see Penny skulk in. Thick coat on covering her bruised body and big sunglasses masking the ones on her face. She smiles when she gets to the counter.

I try to smile back but can't manage it. The Oxy makes me human, but it doesn't make me happy. Seeing her should do that, but it doesn't; not this time. Seeing her now has the feel of a funeral home—quiet, solemn, and smelling of death.

"'Sup," I say.

I wait for her to say something, maybe buy a pack of cigarettes. I am already half turning to get her a pack of Marb Reds when she does talk.

"Hey." I stop and turn back.

"Don't go back tonight."

Maybe she is a mind reader, but I'd already decided I was going to take Tam's deal. I had dealt before, and Tam is right, I am good at it. I don't like it. Something about enabling actual drug addicts is unpleasant, but I am the pot, and I refuse to call the kettle black.

"It'll be fine," I say. That's not true. It won't be fine, but my home is right between a rock (my pills) and a hard place (Tam).

"It really won't," she says. She takes her glasses off. A fresh bruise envelopes her eye. "I got this after you left cuz I begged him to take it back."

"I appreciate the concern and all, but don't get fucked up on my account." I stop, lean close and whisper, "I've dealt before. It'll be fine. Eventually he'll find someone better than me, and it'll go back to—"

"No," she whispers back, then looks around like she expects to see Tam or Nick standing behind her. "No. Just no. Just don't go back." She turns to leave.

I sprint around the counter to get in front of her before she can get to the door.

"You gotta do better than that. I need my Oxy. You heard Tam. It wouldn't look very loyal if I turned him down and got my shit from someone else. I don't want to get dragged out of my car in the middle of the night and shot. This is all I got."

"Tam doesn't give a fuck about you. Or anyone. He's bad. Worse than you know. Don't get in deeper than you already are. Head out of town tonight. Get away."

I laugh. Genuinely. Just run. *Run where?* "That isn't going to happen. I got enough to get me through the night, and then what? What about tomorrow? Who am I gonna buy from? I got a good job here. Life actually doesn't fucking suck all the time. And you want me to just, what, go back to zero?"

"Better than being dead." She doesn't look at me when she says it. Her glasses are back on, but she is looking past me now.

"What the fuck do you know about wanting to be dead? Dead would be a fucking relief for me. A *godsend*. Guilt and obligation are the only things that have gotten me this far. I'm not afraid of being dead."

"Suit yourself," she says with a shrug. Her voice is faint, and something in the tone makes me stop. *What? Pity? Anger?* When she walks around me this time, I don't try to stop her. Suit yourself. What the fuck is all of this about? Penny is my friend. Maybe my only friend. Why is she suddenly all about 'saving me'? She doesn't have a problem with me living in my car or drowning myself in a waterfall of white pills, but me actually taking a step into the realms of financial okayness—that was where the line was?

Well, golly jeez, ain't that grand.

My replacement, Booker, shows up late, like he always does, and I don't make it out of work til seven. I still have an hour til my next dosing and that should honestly be enough time to talk to Tam and get to a place to bed down for the night. Penny's warning still bounces around my skull. *Suit yourself.* I'd had hours to mull it over, and now I am pretty sure there is something she hasn't said. Something behind the words. I put my car in drive and head not towards Tam's place, but back to my parent's home. I drive six blocks in this direction before I realize what I am doing and have to course correct. *What the hell?* As I drive in the right direction, I wonder if I am making a colossal mistake. I remember my thoughts about being cursed. Am I fucking up?

Probably. Definitely. But what I said to Penny was true. I have no other choice. If I go home, I would just kill my parents more quickly, maybe literally. I knew a couple of dealers in Madtown that could get me through a couple of days and maybe actually put me in contact with someone who could get me as much as I needed. But it was too big a risk. I wasn't going backwards. I would rather die, and if that was what I was driving towards, then so be it.

It was 7:45pm when I pulled up to Tam's block. I park two houses down the road even though there is space right in front. I don't want them to see me park, but as I turn off my car and the headlights make the darkening street seem even more menacing, I realize how stupid this is. The shitty-looking structure looms on the nice street like a dead tooth. The porch light is on. *Come on in, Teddy*, it says. I get out of the car and walk down the road towards the house, before cutting across the lawn up to the porch.

Knock. Knock. Knock.

Silence. A long silence. This is wrong. I always come here during the day, and the street is creepy at night. It's too empty and every dark window feels like it has some unseen person watching from on the other side of the glass. I raise my hand to knock again when the door opens. It isn't Nick. Or any of the goon squad. It's Penny. She doesn't smile or say anything but swings the door open farther and gets out of my way so I could walk in. The sunglasses are still on. *Why? Did he hit her more?*

"I—" I begin, but Penny turns her face away. This isn't right. I shouldn't be here. But what choice did I have?

The hall is quiet except for the soft tap of my shoes on the floor. Like a moth to a flame, I flutter through the black on trembling wings. The short walk takes ages, twenty feet stretching miles. Could it be because I know what is waiting in the soft lamp light ahead of me? The faint sound of music hits me as I finally reach the archway outside the living room. I have no clue what the song is. Some shitty country tune, but it doesn't matter. I just need my pills, my instructions, and the exit.

Tam is laying on the couch, an arm slung over his eyes. *Should I say something? Clear my throat?* The pill baggies are still laying out on the table. Should I just take them and leave? An old ass flip phone is sitting next to them. A burner, of course. Penny walks past me and sits on the couch by Tam's feet. She is making a point not to look at me.

"Teddy! You came," Tam said moving his arm off his face. "You know ,we were going back and forth about you. I didn't think you had the balls to show. She knew you would. Even if she didn't want you to." He swung his legs off the couch and stood. His back cracked as he stretched. "Weird, ain't it? I'm delighted to be wrong, and she's miserable to be right." He laughs and the sound drowns out the music. It is not a happy sound. It sounds like a threat.

"Any idea how she could possibly know you'd be here?" he asks.

I hesitate and resist the urge to look at Penny.

"Never mind. It ain't important."

"Where is everyone?" I ask.

"Out on a supply run. It's better this way."

He twists his neck land rolls his shoulders. I can hear the pops and cracks.

"You know, I don't normally like being wrong." Tam closes the distance between us, and I step back til my butt hits the wall. He smiles like a tiger eyeing a gazelle and slaps my shoulder, then bends around me and opens the mini fridge near my calf.

"Beer?" he asks, pulling a can out. He puts it in my hand before I can answer. "'Course you do."

He pops the top on his and stalks back towards the center of the room. The cold can feels slimy as the condensation grows on the aluminum. I want to chuck it across the room. Tam gulps his down in a series of mechanical bobs of his Adam's apple. A belch explodes out of him when he is finished.

"What was I saying?" he asks, looking first from Penny then to me. "Oh yeah. I hate being wrong. But not today. I didn't think you'd have the sack to come back. I'm always underestimating a junkie." He picks up the baggies and weighs them in his hand. "I could get you to suck my dick, and then charge you money for the honor of it if I wanted, couldn't I?" His eyes bore holes into my skull and his lips curl into a vicious sneer. "Couldn't I?"

Am I supposed to answer? He takes a step closer to me. "Couldn't I?" His zipper goes down easy and a second later his ugly cock was poking out, soft and spongy.

Can I go now? Keep the pills you dipshit. Then I eye the pills in his hand. "Yeah," I say. "I guess."

"You guess? What's to guess about?"

Fuck you, Tam. Put that thing near my mouth, and I'll bite it off. My face turns red and the room grows hot. Tears pool at the corners of my eyes. Don't cry, you weak piece of shit, Teddy. Don't give him that. *Fuck you, Tam. I'm not letting that thing anywhere near me.*

My knees bend. *I have to.* I'm looking at the pills in his hand and not the cock hanging limply inches away from my face. *I'm disgusting.* I think of all the people I've hurt. All the harm I've done. Tam barks a laugh and then tucks himself away. He doesn't pull up the zipper.

"You were really gonna do it. What the fuck? Stand up and act like a man."

My body obeys his command without my consent. Based on the temperature of my skin, my face must be as red as a stop sign. I'm going to kill him. It's so strange to really want to kill someone. To really mean it.

"I don't get it," he goes on. "Can't believe the little slut has a thing for pussies. I thought she enjoyed real men. Do you enjoy real men, or pussies like this guy?"

Before she can answer, Tam is back in front of Penny. His fist shoots out and slams into her face. Her nose shatters, her sunglasses go flying and are lost behind the couch, and her head smacks the wall.

I move before I realize what I'm doing, closing half the distance to her before Tam holds up his hand to stop me. "Don't move a fucking muscle." His voice is the low command of God, and I freeze. Penny sobs and clutches her broken nose. Blood seeps from between her fingers. Tam cocks his hand back and then slaps her across the face. The impact sends her flying. She hits the cushion like a sack of mud before rolling off with a soft thud. *Thud.* Blood pools around her face like a red shadow. *Thud.* Why can I only hear the sound of her hitting the floor? *Thud.*

Tam makes a noise like a broken garbage disposal and hawks a phlegmy glob of spit across the room. It lands heavy on Penny's face. *Splat.* Penny doesn't move. Is she dead? When he turns around he is smiling again. I can see red on his knuckles. Blood. Penny's blood.

"This is what they call a teachable moment, Teddy." Tam's voice is low and steady. His eyes are bright, alive for the first time since I've known him. "A two-fer actually. See, I need you. Want you. This bitch...well, this bitch has lost her way. The only reason she ain't dead already is so you can see." He wipes his hand onto his white t-shirt leaving a bright red stain and then walks past me. I stand frozen, unsure of what to do. My instincts are on fire again. Run and Hide aren't here anymore though, only Kill remains, playing a high, piercing note on its trumpet. The fridge shuts with a bang. The snap of beer can opening. Tam walks around me again. He smiles as he takes in my frozen state.

"Like I told you this morning, Ted. I like you. You got good genes; you're loyal, and I understand you. You'll be right as rain on the team."

"But Penny—" I start. The rest of the words shrivel to dust under Tam's gaze.

"Remember what I told you about Paul?"

I nod once. I don't like where this is going, but then I think of Penny helping me get my job, of risking Tam's wrath to come and see me earlier.

"The difference between me and Paul is that I'm not gonna wait for my bitch to step out. If the lessons I give aren't enough to smarten her up, then she ain't ever gonna be smart enough. Penny is one dumb bitch. Always blabbing about you. Wouldn't shut the hell up. So I gave her a lesson. Reminded her why she was with me. Then Nick and Johnny reminded her too. But that bitch still tried to go after you. Stupid. Bitch must really feel something for ya."

His words are barely audible over the hammering of my own heart. Threads reemerge, dance all around us. I welcome them; for the first time in my life I *want* them. I see Tam's swirling between us. It is a vivid green. The color of poison. My throat clicks dryly when I try to swallow my fear.

"So she has to go. And unlike Paul, I'm not dumb enough to leave her around to call the cops on me. Nope. That's why you're here. So you can learn what happens to people who stop being loyal." My eyes meet Penny's. She hasn't moved at all. Are you ready to die? Or do you just see how pointless fighting would be? Why did you have to try and help me?

He gently pats my face. Vomit and bile rise up my esophagus. Tam turns and picks up the baggies again, takes the still unopened can of beer from my hand and drops the pills onto my empty palm.

"It's good to be in business with ya, Teddy."

Business? Me? I don't understand. He is going to kill Penny. Because she is my friend. He is going to kill her. Kill her. She tried to warn me. Why? Did she know what she was risking? I could have listened to her. I could have agreed to run, told her to come with. I should have—

The baggies slip from my hand and hit the floor, spilling the contents and sending the pills rolling in every direction. My fingers tighten into a fist. My arm pulls back. Slowly. So slowly. Trumpets blare in my ear. *Don't. You can't. You need the pills. Penny did this to herself. You aren't responsible for her fuck-up.* I swing my fist with every ounce of strength I have.

Tam's eyes go wide, his jaw slackens. He steps back casually and my fist sails past. His fist rockets forward landing in my gut. All of the air is ejected from my lungs as I'm sent flying backwards. I hit the wall. My skull slams against the plaster. Lights pop in my vision and my ears ring. Tam is on me, his hand wrapping around my throat. His hot breath is on my face. His dead blue eyes are glaciers, so cold they burn.

"What the fuck man? Are you this dumb? You gonna die for this worthless fuck toy?"

I try to talk, to nod, to beg, to scream, but my throat can't work around the fingers crushing it. *This is it. This is how I die.* The world grows hazy. Gray creeps from the edges of my vision. This is it. The last thing I'll see are his dead eyes. *I guess it was always going to end this way.*

Brightest green stands out amongst the blandness of death. A line. A thread. *Really? It's come to this?* Tam mumbles on, but his words are inarticulate noise. Can I really murder someone? Is my life worth more than his?

What about Penny, you fuck? *Penny?*

My vision swims, the gray almost overwhelming. Do it. Just grab it. I reach until I feel the thread burn against my palm. *I'm not crazy. This is real. It has always been real.* It burns. Like holding a live wire and hot metal rod all rolled into one. The pain is welcome. Let me burn.

Thin tendrils of smoke rise up as my skin cooks. I pull. The tension and the pain crescendo together until they reach a high keening note. Flashes swirl around me, visions of days that will never happen. Moments I am about to steal from Tam. Decades recede to years, to months, to weeks, to days, hours, minutes—

The thread snaps. It fades, no longer green, but a burnt orange. The tail of it flails limply. Like a dying snake.

My body jerks with the force of the snapped thread, and Tam's grip slips from around my throat. Suddenly bereft of energy, I collapse to the side. My head strikes the top of the fridge. I can hear the smack of my skull connecting with the metal but not feel it. My lungs are filled with broken glass. *Stay conscious.* Tam steps back. His lips are moving. What is he saying? Why does he look scared and confused? I watch. I already know. I've already seen it. Tam steps backwards. *I can't stop it.* Do I want to? *I caused it.* His foot lands awkwardly on the full can of beer, the can crunches and his ankle twists. For a moment I think that will be it. Tam will stumble, only to finish what he started. *I'm just a crazy addict. Delusional. I don't have any power.*

Then he begins to fall backwards. Time slows like we're in a movie. Face shocked, arms thrown out to the side, Tam has no idea what is rushing up to meet him.

I'm glad I can't hear the sound his skull makes when it cracks the corner of his coffee table. The sharp metal edge crunches bone.

The room goes still. Tam's body twitches and shakes. I wait. Any moment Tam will roll over or stand up. Seconds tick by into minutes. I wait. The pain in my head swells and eventually overtakes the pain in my seared hand. The world grows in color and vividness with each fill of my lungs. Fresh air replaces broken shards of glass. *Is it over?* The last faint glimmer of orange fades to white before flicking out like a spent candle. The thread is gone.

Somehow, I make it to my feet. I sway. My stomach gurgles. My bowels are liquid. I fear that I might shit myself as I close the distance to Tam's limp body. I know he's dead before I reach him. His thread is gone. Blood spreads about his corpse, crimson and vile. There is a wound in the back of his skull, and beneath the flow of red, I see white bone and gray—

I did it. I killed him. *Murder.* I look at Penny. Her faint blue line still dances and moves in the air. Relief floods my body and I have to swallow the vomit that explodes in my mouth. *You're a monster. Murderer. For her?*

"Thank God," I say over the taste of acid and regurgitated gas station chicken sandwich. *What now?* Tam is dead. I killed him. I need to escape. I need to get in my car and drive. Never look back. Penny. What about Penny? Even broken, she is still beautiful. *Leave her.*

I gather up the scattered pills, leaving the ones already drowning in the pool spreading out around Tam. I shove them all into the pockets of my jacket and pants. I take the other baggie off the table and move over to the bookshelves. My heart stops. So much is here. I find three thick stacks of bills in the book next to the pills and another set of three stacks in the book next to that one. And more pills. Almost more than I can carry. I take off my jacket and pour everything into the center before pulling it closed like a sack.

I turn back to the room. My eyes land on Penny. I shift my jacket and move towards her. *Leave her.* I try to wake her but she only groans. Leave her or take her? Is that really a question? *Don't be a fucking idiot. The others will be back anytime now.* Finally, with the rising smell of spoiled meat filling the house, I do the only thing I can think of.

It's harder than I expect to sling Penny over my shoulder like a fireman, but somehow I manage it. My knees threaten to buckle with the added weight of Penny and the heavy sack, but adrenaline is still my friend, and I only have to get her to my car. *Dear God, I hope no one is watching the house. If they are, there is nothing I can say to explain this.*

I am at the front door before I know it. Now the hard part. Somehow, I open the door and step out into the crisp evening air. With every step I take, I expect to see one of Tam's thugs roll up in their car, or jump out from behind a tree, or start shouting at me. But none come. I am alone with the night. And the threads. Thousands of threads dance around me, a rainbow gauntlet lightly burning my skin with each touch. Images and catastrophe fill my head. I know I've caused damage I can never fix. I will be scarred from this walk. I know it. Scars that will go deeper than flesh. But for the first time since I caused my mom's fall, I don't care.

Then I am at my car. The long steps were a blur, but I'm here. We are here. Nearly free. I lay Penny on the backseat. Sweat covers my aching body. My skin is on fire, my head throbs, and I can feel the slow swell of grief in my chest. From the front seat, I watch Penny in the rearview mirror.

I pop an Oxy from my pocket and begin my wait for the slow build of sanity to fill me up again. The threads fade away.

Murderer.

You can't run from this.

I turn on the engine. The clock on the dash reads 8:30pm. How could so much happen so quickly? *Penny will never see you as anything but a killer.* I put the car into gear and drive.

A car turns onto the street. A car I know. Nick is coming back. He waves at me as we pass each other on the street. My testicles crawl up into my abdomen as I wave back. And I smile.

My life here is over. Penny's life here is over. Whether she wants to stick with me or not, I'll get her as far from here as I can. *It will never be far enough.* With the money we have now and the pills we should be fine. We survived. *Murderer.* We made it. Now we just need to go a little further.

Was it worth it?

I never wanted to die, but I hate that I survived.

LAWRENCE WEST

Lawrence J West has been on his writing journey since he was fourteen years old and has always been drawn to fantasy, sci-fi, and horror because of the way these genres allow for the exploration of human experience in unique ways. Since becoming a husband and father he has also found that his writing has a greater degree of empathy and insight.

Lawrence can be found on Twitter.

 twitter.com/LawrenceWriting

IN DOCTRINE AND IN DEED

NICHOLAS BARNER

Passion is a weapon, she murmurs. Passion is a weapon. I can barely hear her. Passion is a weapon. Mom is somewhere in her thoughts, wavering side to side.

I am groggy. It is five thirty in the morning. I am still wearing a hat, still in my sweater. The sky is dark. The dining room is dark, but our kitchen glows under blue fluorescents. The rattling fan wobbles in the oven hood. I throw a match to spark the flattop. I adjust the propane. Mom pulls eggs from the reach-in. Our ten-quart stock pot is over the pilot and thawing chowder. I take a seat on the stool.

Passion is a weapon, she tells me. *Passion is a weapon.*

So far, the day has been like any other. On our walk to the café, the Chicago cold made the short trip seem hours long. On the sidewalk by the 7-Eleven, I saw two cops watching a toothless man tearing a pair of pantyhose into stringy pieces. The man was not dressed for winter. The cops warbled into plastic boxes strapped to their shoulders. One was saying numbers. One told a joke.

Seeing the police makes me horrified, always, because of Dad. I breathed, muting the fear. After that, I saw six school busses idling in a line with drivers gathered pre-shift in the first. The drivers were eating thinly tin foiled breakfast sandwiches. I smelled the cheese and the eggs from the sidewalk. Then I was here, readying the café.

It is dawning on me now that I have never been inside a school bus. I have never looked out from windows so high up. I consider the coldness of a school bus, and I wish for more friends.

Passion is a weapon, Mom says.

Our little Polish café serves mostly regulars. Many of them know all about Mom and Dad. That is part of the draw. We do breakfast and lunch. Our signature dish is the Chicago Dog With One Hundred Percent Homemade All Beef Sausage. Mom does most things, but I run the food, and almost everything else too. Since two years ago, Dad is doing twenty in maximum. His arrest marked the start of a different life for us, a quieter life, but a strange life too.

Today is both a strange day, and a day like any other.

Mom is cracking eggs in a steel bowl. The eggs are for my omelet. I am getting the sense that she is done with her warm-up. Now here we go.

Passion is a weapon, she is saying, doesn't matter for what. Could be anything and there is no hierarchy about it. A passion for singing opera. A passion for synchronized swimming. A passion for scrambled eggs.

Every morning I cook breakfast with unflappable conviction and that is my power. I am powerful. Am I believed? Is the power real? Does mankind weigh all passions the same? I think no. I think pretty damn clearly, we do not. Some passionately carve kayaks. Some passionately trace market trends. Where does the clout fall? On the Wall Street walker, everyone knows. But what reward is clout? What is power in a place where power itself is impassioned, a place where every desire is insatiable?

Mom is speaking in the way she does, with her orations and bursts. She and Dad used to do this for days. Criticism, they called it. Talking about The Movement. I used to go to school for The Movement. The school was outside. These days I go to homeschool. I am questioning if the outside school kids would remember me now. Would they?

Mom is now saying, So you have people like me, you know, all of the cooks and shelf stockers and gas pumpers and teachers and factory technicians and phone bankers and vegetable farmers and temp agency workers and prison recidivists and pest management pros and pool guys and contractors and trash men and mechanics and couriers and cab drivers and pilots and nurses and plumbers and basement entrepreneurs and the stay-at-home parents and all the glib kids who don't get called by their names but instead get called by their jobs. These are the masses, the proletariat, The People, the working class. Then, you've got your modern-day emperors, folks with indefensible portfolios of subjugation, ivory tower Rapunzels, oligarchs, the ruling class, the capital C Capitalists.

Mom is whisking my eggs. She pours them into a hot, butter-primed skillet. Then she is swirling, swirling to spread the mixture. She keeps swirling, looking at me. Her eyes are always pointed and sharp. I am looking forward to the loud times, the lunch rushes, the times when there is no eye contact or talk. I pull off my sweater, holding it wrinkled in my lap. My short sleeves cling, sweaty, to my shoulders.

So that's that, little man, she is saying, that is everybody. The rich folks and the ever-piling impoverished hoards. That's what happens when the populace gets injected with blind greed, vision failing, missing the passion right in front of them, because they're too busy drooling at frivolous fulfillments, like the good life were so easy to spot, so obvious they'd put it up on TV, or in a magazine, or on a drive-thru menu. Or you could wear it on the soles of your feet, or you could throttle it from zero to ninety, or fly there on Delta. Or you can lease it but you have to keep the plastic on, or you already have the good life; you were born with it, it's just that to see it, you've got to drop twenty pounds.

Okay, now me. I have something to say, so I say to her, Dad liked all that stuff, Mom. Dad liked to travel, and he loved to drive fast. He liked TV. He liked Seinfeld and SNL.

Mom is looking at me for one second and then her eyes are on the eggs again, swirling, swirling, saying, I know. Of course. I do too.

Some hair has dislodged from her top knot, so I interrupt her. Mom, your hair is in my eggs.

With one finger, Mom guides strands from the yellowness. Son, she says, I am definitely not trying to tell you that the soap operas and The New Yorker and the Micky D's and the Air Max sneakers and the fast cars and the travel and the comfy furniture can't be just fine objects of passion. They can be, but you cannot buy it, is my point. You are responsible for whittling the meaning from a thing. You have to carve passion from your own life.

Things go this way, the gist of days. Some of Dad's charges were: organizing an expropriation of prisoners, endangering public transportation, making public threats over a cell phone, and acts of domestic terrorism. I only saw a lot of talk, but eventually everything kind of broke down at the same time, at a turning point, I guess.

The night before his arrest, all three of us had slept on an air mattress in the café office. Before the office was an office. It used to be a closet, and inside it was blackness save the flashing answering machine. We were hiding. Electric cords vined around blankets. I woke with my face between the bare wall studs. Mom and Dad were still asleep. I got up, stepped around them. I sensed it was too early. They would not like the light, so I was fast with the door. Open and shut.

There is a bus stop in front of our café. No one can leave cars there. That morning though, there was a whole line of them. I noticed the big vans first, white ones with fat blue stripes and stars. Either the flag of our city, or a police symbol, or both. Are they the same? Men were outside wearing wrinkly black pants, boxy armored vests, and big helmets. They had guns. The men were spaced one, then the next, then the next, all around the windows. Sawhorse barriers stopped the intersection. Everyone was waiting for Dad to get up.

Taste my omelet, Mom is saying now, a two-egg omelet too small to share, a personal omelet for you and you alone. Feel the revelry. Feel the power. Listen to the whispering salt. That is

Mother Earth speaking through hot breakfast. That is knowledge. That is *craft,* and you can find it in Homer as well as you can find it in a hot dog, but the passion for finding it is the weapon of the people. Passion is what will ultimately hold the passionless to account.

Mom is staring at a pipe under the sink as it leaks into a small catch basin. Her hands are clutching a frayed rag on the countertop.

The finance freaks, she says, the investor-crusaders, the castle-dwelling loveless archbishops of the Federal Reserve Bank, the wealthy—they are not needed, but they need us. They need us to cook the food so they can have the menus. They need us to build the cars so they can show them off. They need us to trim the hedges, lay the plumbing, install the alarms, install the stereos, and the dishwashers, and the software, to clean the hot tubs and swimming pools.

I am trying to get her attention now. Mom, I say, what time did you wake up today? She does not look back. She does not respond. She tilts the stockpot, peaking at the soup. Not ready. She prods the omelet. She begins to multitask. Today is a day like any other, I remind myself.

They need *us,* she goes on, to trap the rats, grow the flowers, forecast the storms, polarize the lenses, clean, update, manufacture, repair, tabulate, analyze.

She whacks the steel pan on the burner to unstick the eggs. Using a spatula, she furls the omelet.

They need *us,* she says, to make sure the world keeps on ticking. Some say God was a clockmaker. He made this world. He set it going then stepped back. He's up there now just jumping checkers. Some say, however, that God made Heaven and Earth, and Adam, and Eve, and the animals, and then God just kept making things and never ever stopped. He intervenes all the time, makes new things, erases old things. Guess what? Doesn't matter. The important thing is whoever made the world, whether or not they stuck around after, they still made it. They did not order it online. They didn't pay someone else to make it.

I am asking myself, for what reasons might a person—or a god—make or buy or outsource the production of a thing, or a world? I am aware that the café is still closed. I haven't raised the blinds. I haven't consolidated yesterday's mustard. There are dishes unwashed from last night. We haven't hired a new porter since Renee. It is me. It is Mom. It is only us.

Here is all that on a plastic plate, Mom is saying, delivering me the omelet. Here is everything in a shimmering yellow curd. Here it is in an omelet's impeccable construction. Here in the flesh. It's for you, kid. Eat it before it gets weird.

Mom Makes the Sausage

Today is a sausage making day. Today is also when the police decide to stop by for lunch. Every second day is a sausage making day. I cannot remember another time police came here just to eat. Today is the reason I am telling you this story. Today is a day I will struggle forever to categorize. Right now, today feels like any other day. Later, it will feel like a major turning point. I will think of today as: proof of fate, an imaginary memory, a cruel joke, a loss of innocence, a day like any other, a busy lunch, the last day I use my given name, and the birthday of my good friend Stephen's wife.

Mom is making the sausages and I am watching the dining room. A bunch of people are already seated at the tables eating what I have served them.

Do you know what a deed is? Mom is asking me, but she is also not asking. A deed is like an action, an act, a project. However, a deed must have ideology baked in. It has to have an ethical imperative. Deeds are not easy. They are not simple. A deed is the endpoint of a complex moral choice. If you do a deed, you have to mean it.

Mom is making eye contact through the kitchen doorway with a young man who is pinning a flyer on our cork board. There is nothing strange about that. The board is expressly for that purpose. The man is wearing black fingerless leather gloves. Now, with his fingers, he is making the code of The Movement. I look at Mom. She is nodding and grinning towards the doorway. She is looping the sausages into a spiral of links on the countertop. Her apron is collecting beads of stray pink meat.

Who is that? Do we know who that is? The guy with the flyer? Mom?

There is no longer such a thing as the craftsman class, she answers. Your great grandpop was a sausage maker at the Halstead factory. Back then, you needed a sensorial catalogue of each textural meat profile. Grainy, silky, bouncy, mushy. You had to know the look and the smell of lamb and beef and pork and chicken at all the different temperatures and all the different stages of freshness so you could correctly select the die-cut grind width for the cutting plates. This stuff is hard to teach. It takes a long time, longer than four years of college, way longer than a summer internship, and much, much longer than some elevator pitch at a venture capital meeting. The Chicago dog is nothing to scoff at, son. The Chicago dog is your family legacy.

I wonder what it means to be in a class. What is a craftsman class? How does it differ from—and overlap with—my family? What morphs one unified group of people into a different sort of group? Is it motivation? Is it *deeds*? I am about to ask this, but then I am needed in the dining room.

I say I'll be right back. Then I take an order from the old man at table six. The gloved man who pinned the flyer is gone. The entry bell is ringing. Stephen is here. My friend Stephen! Stephen is scooting his way past the curtain, tapping his bicolor cane. Stephen is one of my few friends. He is Blind and a regular.

Fiery furnaces, says Stephen, this place is hotter than Hanoi.

I have a booth for you, I say and guide him to a table by the register. I pick up menus from empty tables. Stephen's cane is grazing chair legs and loose tiles, but he knows our café by heart, and he is pretty fast. Stephen has round black glasses, a portable tape player with headphones, a jacket—duster is the closest word—and a short gray beard. He takes a seat.

Fresh fruit, says Stephen. Got to have fresh fruit in wintertime. You have got to have fresh fruit. When's your birthday, kid?

I tell him my birthday is the nineteenth of March.

Today, Stephen says, is my wife's birthday. Special day, today. In and out then. A little déjeuner and I'm gone. Preparations await. Champagne, flowers, cheesecake, and…romance.

Stephen makes jazz hands at romance.

Fruit bowl? I am asking. Coffee?

Stephen answers with a nod. He is brandishing his headphones, placing one side over an ear. Tu Fu, he says, drawing out the short words. Tooo…Fooo…He covers his other ear with the headphones and unwraps his silverware.

I do not know what Tu Fu is, but I know it is poems because Stephen is always playing tapes of poems. I write down fruit bowl and coffee. On my route back, I am passing the cork board. I see the new flyer. It is for a documentary, something about politics and entertainment. There is a drawing of a White House press badge alongside a VIP concert pass.

Back in the kitchen, I am putting two tickets on the board. One is for Stephen's fresh fruit bowl, and one is for the man at table six, a Corner Special. The Corner Special is our two eggs any style combo with hash browns and thick cut caraway toast.

Mom is saying, Pharmacists use the term 'LD50' to indicate the dosage at which a specific substance will fatally affect half of a given exposed population. It is the median lethal dose. LD50. Lethal dose. Fifty percent.

This is an unusual statement, even for Mom. She must be

stressing. She is not looking at the ticket. She asks me a question. Do you know where Jakarta is?

No.

Something weird and juicy has splashed my Sketchers. I wipe it off with a c-fold napkin. I scrub my hands in the sink. I ask Mom, Where is Jakarta and why do you ask me this now?

Indonesia, she responds, has no extradition treaty with the oppressor nation. Jakarta is there. I hear a person can find themselves lost in Jakarta. Big, big city. Big city. LD50. Fifty percent.

A day like any other, I mutter to myself. A day like any other. A day like any other. The bell is ringing which tells us someone new is here. Two male officers push through the curtain. One is short. One is tall. They are wearing sunglasses. They are waiting to be seated, which is not what the sign says. I sense something strange afoot. I breathe like I was taught. I am keeping it cool.

I come to believe that Mom has forgotten the tickets, so now I point this out to her. She reads the order and drops two eggs over the flattop. They are foaming, erupting, congealing. They are going from clear to white.

Some ideas beckon inexorable outcomes, Mom says. That is the reason you cannot legislate an idea. Once it is born, a thought will penetrate the egg of culture and it will fertilize the mind.

Mom is lumping the forcemeat down the stuffing cylinder, guiding the compressed extrusions into their skin casing. I know this is a total must. Time sensitive. We cannot let the fat soften, but the eggs for the Corner Special are overcooking. The toast is not done. The hash is nowhere. The police are impatient and unseated.

Some ideas topple structures, she says.

I miss the rest of Mom's thought as I swing out the kitchen door. Then I seat the officers at the booth along the biggest window.

How old are you, kid? The tall officer asks me while the

short one whispers something to his shoulder.

I...I say, I...I don't remember.

I can—or rather I could—recall my own age, but I am choking on his question because now I am too busy. I leave their menus and turn away. The cops are guffawing behind me. I am back, toasting the bread, heating the hash, flipping the eggs, spooning the fruit from its OJ marinade for Stephen's quick lunch before his wife's birthday errands.

The structures, Mom is saying, are devilishly dreamt of in smoke-filled, mauve-carpeted, scotch-scented back rooms of unpurchasable mansions, by only, and you better believe this, only white men.

I assemble the plates. I run the Corner Special to the old man at table six. I drop off the quick déjeuner for my friend Stephen, seeming tranquil between his headphones. I tuck in offset chairs, clear a dirty booth, ask a customer if she'd like a fresh cranberry seltzer, and when she answers yes, I distractedly screw up her ticket. Instead of writing CRAN, I have scrawled the word, DEED.

MOM MAKES THE POTATO SALAD

Five minutes later, Mom is seasoning a bowl of cooked-up Kennebec spuds, folding in mayo, mustard, chives, parsley, red onions, carrots, and celery seeds. I barely register what she is telling me.

A tablespoon, Mom is saying, is roughly one milliliter of water. One milliliter of water has exactly the mass of one gram. Inside of a gram, there are a thousand milligrams. Inside of that milligram, there are actually one million of a thing called a *microgram*.

Okay, time to interrupt. Mom, I say. Please, I cannot listen now. Please finish the salad. After lunch we can talk. Okay? Mom?

She is not hearing me.

A *microgram*, she is saying, is very, very, very, very small. It is ludicrously small. It is miniscule. It is infinitesimal. It is almost imaginary. Deeds. Deeds are endpoints, turning points. The leaner meat gets the sixteenth inch cutting plate and the fat meat goes through the eighths plate, or no, the reverse. Two-point-five grams of curing salt for every twenty grams of kosher salt.

She is lost somewhere. She is speaking like a radio in a bath-tub. I am wondering, what of Mom's talk must I remember? I am wondering if that question has an answer, or if any questions have answers for real, in the same way that people may or may not have souls for real. In the way that restaurants have signs and menus and tables and waiters. What are those places to the people inside them? Work? Home? School? A store? Is a restau-rant something different for all the types of different people? Can a café be work for both the customer and the cook? Can it be home for both the delivery guy and my friend Stephen?

Now I am lost somewhere too, I realize, and I begin to keep it cool.

The police are quietly gazing out the window. They have decided what they want. I go over to them. I take their order. They are no longer in a laughing mood. The taller one asks me if I go to school.

I say yes, which is what I am supposed to say to that question.

They both look at me. I cannot see their expressions behind those glasses. The shorter one presents me a pamphlet. I see that it is for an after-school program with free dinner and activities.

You need a healthy diet, the tall cop says. You need to learn life skills, and you need to make friends. Don't let yourself grow up missing out on these opportunities. Trust me. Take it from me.

Take it from him, the shorter cop says.

I wonder, can these men not see me working as a waiter in a restaurant full of food and nice people? It is because I said I could not remember my age? It is because they know about Mom and Dad? I leave the pamphlet on the table and write down their order. I am back in the kitchen. I am placing the ticket on the board.

The boy scouts? Mom is asking.

I tell her the cops want two Chicago dogs, each with a side of potato salad.

She is smiling. She tastes the potato salad. Let me explain to you, she says, the downfall of the egalitarian sausage maker. It happened because of families. It happened because of racism, sexism, xenophobia, paranoia, insecurity. It happened because of the Great Fire. It happened because of union scabs. It happened because of consumer demand. It happened because of people like your great grandpop, who wanted a better life, wanted an eight-hour workday, wanted safe neighborhoods, wanted fair police treatment. They wanted a turning point.

Mom is dropping two sausages, plop, plop, into the water. She is closing the buns in the steamer. I am whispering, just another day. A day like any other. Mom is tired and distracted. I am breathing. It's okay, it's okay. I am mulling over Jakarta, and Dad. A day like any other, a day like any other.

Great-Grandpop, Mom is saying, had all the power because he was the craftsman, the worker. Yet still, the bosses were better connected and whiter than he. The only time to use a one-eighth plate is when the beef is smoked and dried. I know you are white, daisy boy. Grandpop was called all kinds of things though, which meant not white enough. Raw butchered beef is seventy-five percent water. His bosses could change things. All that Grandpop did was ask. Agar. Alginate. Carrageenan. Gum Arabic. Guar Gum. What happened? Blue-bellied, moist-mustached, penny-pinching, bastards got mad as hell. Locust

Bean Gum. Konjac Gum. Xanthan Gum. They stopped paying–Stabilizers!–Grandpop entirely. Fired him.

Mom is taking a few things from the lowboy. A stainless-steel mixing bowl. A small black cardboard box. And the third thing I am not remembering having seen before. The third thing is a full-face dual cartridge gas mask. It looks like it's from The Second World War. I am having trouble breathing just looking at it.

Was it legal? She asks me. Was it legal what the bosses did to Grandpop, or your father? No. Of course not. The truth is, by no definition was it admissible by law. Freezer burn. But what could be done? What does the law even matter if the people most capable of breaking it are not bound by its decrees? Oh God, never *ever* de-salt veal casings in hot water.

The steel bowl is on the counter, and into it goes the fresh potato salad. Mom is setting up the plastic dishes for the Chicago dogs. Little lettuce frills. Little pickle spears. Little slices of tomato she is lining up like caterpillars on the plates. She takes the poppy seed buns from the steamer and aligns them with the garnishes.

Looking out to the dining room, I catch a glimpse of Stephen who is not wearing headphones now. That is a surefire sign he needs the check. I want to go to him, remembering the romance. He needs to run. Then I think if I run the bill along with the hot dogs, it is an excuse to leave the cops fast, without chatting. I wait for the Chicago dogs.

The castor plant, Mom is explaining, is a monstrous shrub, leaves like a giant's hands, fruit like thorny chestnuts. Mix with adequate torque to extract beef proteins. They emulsify. The castor seed contains a chemical called *ricin*. The LD50, the median lethal dose, of ricin, is not one, not two, but three *micro-grams*. Taste the sausage before it is stuffed. That is your last chance to correct. Yes, ricin is the deadliest substance yet discovered on this planet. Ascorbates speed the curing process.

Dad faced a charge of domestic terrorism for cooking up a dirty bomb. Mom is always saying that the charges are baseless, that it is simply not true. I believe her, in the long view, but right now it seems like a gas mask, just like that one on the table, is something you could use to cook up a dirty bomb. I leave the kitchen to warm up coffees.

When I return, Mom is speaking before I enter. We serve the people every day, she says. We serve doctors. We serve children. We serve old folks who've lived here for lifetimes. We serve travelers. We serve families and friends and people meeting over lunch to chitchat about jobs and love and sex and TV and politics. All of these hot dog eaters and coffee drinkers and napkin crumplers and crossword pencilers and blind daters and long goodbyers; all of this, the gestalt of the city, how beautiful? Isn't that something worth dying for?

Using tongs, Mom is removing the sausages from the water. She lays down the links in the poppy seed buns and anoints the plates with celery salt. This is the signature dish, Chicago Dog with One Hundred Percent Homemade All Beef Sausage. These two plates are for the police, and these two have sides of potato salad.

This place, Mom is saying, is so much to so many, and that is just great. But it used to be something even greater to so many more—a hub, a safe house, a place for ideas and community until they took your father. She glares through the steel doorway at the cops in the booth. They will not equivocate or negotiate. They will not compromise or discuss. They will never deign to converse with the working-class publics. We are useless to them, sapped of our use-value, strung out in sidewalk slums, singing to the spirits of our shotgun apartments. They will not hear us, it seems. Deaf to our demands. Our pleas a light to the void. How can we punch through? Will any language spoken by the meek ever ring in the eardrums of the powerful? Yes, one language will: their own, the mother tongue of the oppressor.

We struggle with its terrible syllables but sometimes we burp out a sentence. Their language is the language of *force*.

My heart is going zero to ninety. I am asking, Mom, what do you mean? Mom?

Mom looks at me with her weird, pointed eyes and says, Jakarta.

Then she buckles the dual canister full face gas mask to her head. It is all dusty and leathery. All I can see of her now is hair. The rest is the mask.

She is opening the black cardboard box and she is extracting something, a smaller box, a plastic box like a film box. Mom is putting on powder free nitrile gloves, which in the kitchen is pretty routine, but right now it is not seeming routine at all.

You have to leave the room, she is explaining, voice muffled through the filters. If you breathe it, you will die. Son, I need you to leave.

I do not move. I am only trying to see Mom's eyes through the mask's thick circles of glass. I am not exactly seeing her eyes. Instead I see glare and scratches and dust. The bell is ringing, the one that means people are here. I am backing away from Mom and leaving the kitchen. She is making a motion with her hand, blowing me a kiss. Then she is walking to the kitchen door, swinging it shut.

I am not greeting the new customers. I am not polishing silverware, wrapping it in paper napkins with a red piece of tape. I am not counting the cash tips or inputting credit card adjustments or refilling the water glasses. I press myself against the drywall in the dark of the rear hallway with all the old egg cartons. Mom's shadow darts around in the empty space between the floor tiles and the steel kitchen door. I stare at the two officers at the other side of the dining room who have no idea.

Mom exits the kitchen, kicking open the door. She carries with her two Chicago dogs and two potato salads. She sets the food on a tray and hangs the gas mask on the apron hook. She is smiling with her eyes closed.

Then the back door to the restaurant opens. Snowy white sunlight. A man with a ponytail and a big jacket is running in and grabbing ahold of me.

Stay quiet, he murmurs, no questions.

Another voice is outside. This is not a game. Get this kid and let's move.

I am watching Mom at the officers' table delivering two plates. I am feeling myself pulled through the back door, feet dragging. I am noticing the dirty icicles on the exterior plumbing, and the fire escape's rusty stairs. I see the blue and white Chicago flag on the pole, showing no wind. I am feeling the cold. The rear access door to our Polish café closes by its automatic machinery. The men are hustling me into a strange car. I am seeing hands with black fingerless gloves holding the steering wheel. We are rolling over speed bumps and potholes and ice, to the front of the restaurant.

Through the biggest window, I can now see the two police. They are face down on the checkered plastic booth table. Their skin has turned a different color. I see the customers inside panicking and pointing, backing away from the booth with the cops. I am seeing someone stumbling, running to the front door. I am seeing people with hands over mouths. I am seeing people motioning for everyone to get out. Stephen is retreating from the calamity, and Mom is with him. She is guiding my friend towards the darkened back hallway.

I am hearing the car's blinker click, the keychain in the ignition, the walk signal beeping on the streetlight, the soft static voices from the public radio people though the dashboard speakers. I am realizing now that there are no days like any others. There is so much more to this, so much more than the talk and the turning points.

NICHOLAS BARNER

Nicholas Barner has farmed, cooked, and written variously in Oakland, Chicago, Maine, and Los Angeles. He lives with his partner, Shelby, and their Dog, Nuni.

He can be found online at nicholasbarner.com.

OLD WOMEN*

SHARON FRAME GAY

Trigger Warning: Rape - depicted, but not in graphic detail

Old women cry in every town and city around the world. We cry about lost loves, broken dreams, and flickers of hope blown into darkness by the wounding souls of others. We cry in mansions and huts, at weddings and funerals, or as we stare out windows and hobble down streets. It is the way of old women.

I do not cry. I am an exception. Although there are many reasons for sorrow, I remain stoic.

Reveling in the quiet of my small village, I enjoy the sameness that comes day after day. Tomorrow is Monday. Wash day. Tethered clothes dance on lines in the breeze, pajamas and pants tilting to the whim of the wind. Thursday is market day. I buy the same cheese I have bought for eighty years. It tastes as it should, spread on my bread each morning, because it has not changed. On Saturday I tend my house, sweeping away the cobwebs of life and scrubbing it clean once again.

It was not always this way. Long ago, the entire village held its breath each day, fearing change. Men drank in taverns, and women wrung their hands. Voices rang up and down the alleyways, heads popping out of windows with news. And it was never good.

"Are the Nazis coming?" I'd ask my parents, my fourteen-year-old face peering into theirs. They denied it, hiding behind smiles fixed on worried faces.

"This is a little town, my angel," Papa said. "The Nazis have no need for us. The war is almost over, I hear. They will not come." He ruffled my hair with his calloused fingers. "Yes?" he asked, using his hand to move my head up and down. "You see? It will be fine and you need not be concerned." Then he kissed me on the cheek and went back to his dinner.

"How do you know for sure?" I asked, over and over until Mama rolled her eyes and told me to shush.

"If they come, we will keep you safe. This is not a burden a child should carry. We have a plan."

Mama rose from the table and scraped the remains of our meal into a pail; scraps for the cats living by the shed behind our house. Had we known then, we'd have fallen upon that pail, stuffed the scraps into our mouths and swallowed quickly, before the peels and half-eaten vegetables were pried from us.

Late one night, I heard my parents' voices rising up and down in hushed tones. Mornings were somber. Papa said I could no longer help him in the bakery. I could not wait on the people, placing rolls inside a paper bag, or poke at the old cash register. He was stern when he told me to stay away, his eyes sad. Each night Papa walked in the door with the yeasty smell of bread on his clothing. I inhaled his scent as he bent down and wrapped me in an embrace. There was another aroma about him, the harsh smell of sweat, and something far more worrisome. Fear.

A few weeks later, they closed the only school. Children had to stay indoors, no longer allowed to chase each other up and down the cobbled streets, or race through the fields at the edge of town. Not even our laundry danced on the line. Homes were locked and shuttered, the curtains pulled. Only those who had to work left their house and ventured into town.

You want to know where I live. I will not tell you. Nor will I tell you my name. Because this is a story about old women crying throughout the world. Does it matter where the Nazis invaded? Would my tears mean more—or less—if I were from Poland, Hungary or Norway? It always ends the same. Old women crying.

For is it not the women who crouch in empty doorways, begging for food for their children? Is it not the women who send their husbands and sons off to war? And, is it not the women who are left to deal with the broken faucets, the sick baby, or to walk with their beloveds into the gas chambers?

When the war was raging, it was all-consuming, the way the night takes bites out of the moon each month until it's gone. It was a vortex, a vacuum in which we were all swept.

Years ago, I saw a photograph of a memorial at Pearl Harbor, Hawaii. A boat takes tourists from the dock to a sacred space that floats over a sunken battleship. The boat is filled with old men from different countries, many of them ancient soldiers. They ride together to the site, then walk in tandem around the memorial. These men stop side by side to pray, or to think. They smile sadly at one another.

Was it worth it, I ask? Look at you now! You will sit in the same cafés tonight, eat your meals together, pass the salt. You shop in the same stores. Your children will marry. No fights break out. The war is over. The same person riding in the boat would have stabbed you with his bayonet or shot you through the heart. Now, old shoulders touch as they crowd together and watch the water stream by on the way to honor such a thing as war.

But I digress. I must look back many years to continue this story. Sometimes I must talk to you about today, because if all I talk about is yesterday, the memories will steal my soul.

IT WAS an ordinary afternoon when the Nazis came. May was overtaking April, the mornings warm, and the sky a vivid blue. Sunlight streamed through our window as I sat at the kitchen table with a book. I looked up to see my father running down the dirt lane to our house. I watched him push through our wooden gate so hard it broke a hinge.

Papa slipped and fell as he skidded through the door and stared up at Mama. There was flour on his hands and tears on his face.

"They're here," he gasped.

Before I could even tie my shoes, my mother sent me out the back door with a bag she packed days before. She handed me a hastily wrapped parcel of bread and cheese, and Papa's thermos filled with water. Mama flung my heavy coat across my shoulders, and stuffed mittens in the pockets, even though sunshine warmed our faces.

"Run to the woods! As far as you can. Stay there until we find you, and we *will* find you," Mama said, her hands on my shoulders, gripping me so hard it hurt. "It may be several days, but don't be afraid. Other children from the village will hide in the forest too. Don't form a group. Do not talk to each other or make noise. Hide behind bushes and under logs alone during the day. Don't eat your food all at once." Her words rushed at me, causing my heart to tremble.

She kissed my cheek, her breath warm on my face, then shoved me out the door. I turned back, mouth opening and closing like a fish, filled with many questions. Mama pushed me away and screamed, "Run!"

Frightened, I raced across the meadow behind our house and into the woods. In the distance, I heard the pop of guns, then screams. My fear was a living thing clawing at my chest and tearing the breath from my lungs. I ran and ran...

AT THE END of each week, on Friday, there is a fish fry at the small café on the corner of our main street. The tantalizing aroma of onions and fish wafts dreamily through the air, and villagers gravitate towards it like the tide towards the moon.

We old ones sit in the back of the restaurant at a table along a brick wall, pulling the delicate white fish apart with our fingers, frosting slices of bread with pats of butter. We have little to say to each other. It is far too exhausting to talk anymore.

Instead, we listen to the younger voices, the robust voices who have not seen the cruelty of war. They are so certain of everything. They are confident they will have enough money to eat and blankets to wrap themselves at night. They believe their children will go to school on Monday and not be butchered alongside an open trench. They have all the answers.

If we had all the answers back then, perhaps we would have wrapped them in the paper spread on our table for the fish, taken them home and tacked them on the wall. Then, whenever we worried, we'd find the answers and go back to our beds, stomachs full and content with the belief that all will be well. But the paper is flimsy and tears beneath our hands, the old, pickled wood of the table pushing through. All the answers are shredded and tossed away in the evening trash.

We old women look at each other. Our faces tell a story, with a slight shake of the head, a glance from the corner of an eye. My bread sticks in my throat. It won't slide down with the voices, or the music in the far corner of the café. It lingers like a memory, and I have to cough it into the palm of my hand.

And I remember...

I AM NOT sure how far I ran the day the Nazis came. It felt like miles, and still I heard the engines of their trucks, the sound of their guns. I ran until my knees gave out, then found a bush near a large rock and crept behind it, trembling.

I stayed in the forest a long time. A week. Two weeks, maybe more. I cannot remember, for each day was like the last, crawling under logs or behind bushes, squeezing my eyes closed and whimpering.

The food Mama packed lasted six days, but finally it was gone. I dabbed my tongue on the paper, licked it for crumbs. At dawn each day, I rose from my hiding place and moved to another area. Not far. Never far. I listened for sounds of the village, my compass. Sometimes I heard noises. I prayed it was Mama or Papa coming for me. But the days went by, and they did not come. I wondered if other children were here in the woods, but dared not call out. I imagined all of us like fawns who stay motionless so predators cannot find them. Each whistle of the wind through the trees, each bird flying overhead jolted me into a wariness that lives with me still.

One day, I heard church bells tolling from the village. I had not heard them since the Nazis arrived. They pealed over and over like a dinner bell. Perhaps they were calling us in. Perhaps it was now safe. I crept towards home, stopping, then holding my breath for sounds. On the bank of a creek, I took care to wash my legs and dabbed the dried blood off with a leaf.

My mother found me behind our house, huddled near the shed with the cats, afraid to come to the door. We ran to each other. I nestled in her arms and heard her heart thud in my ear.

"Are they gone, Mama?"

"Yes, my darling, and they aren't coming back. The war ended, or they would have done more damage than they did. Thank God you're okay! I worried day and night, but it wasn't safe here. And it wasn't safe to go looking for you in case they followed me."

Nor was it safe there.

Then I asked the inevitable question. "Where's Papa?" but I knew he was dead before I asked.

My father was rounded up with the other men and brought into the town square by a squad of Nazis. Like cattle, our men milled round and round, frightened, eyes locked on the machine guns the Germans brandished. They weren't allowed to speak among themselves. They could not formulate a plan. One by one, each man was tortured for information. Then shot. My father died bravely. He refused to talk, and spit in the German's face.

The town had not buried him yet. He lay in an open field with all the others. Mama wouldn't let me see him, though I begged and begged. She was right not to let me go, but did not know what happened in the woods.

I had grown up.

ON SUNDAYS I always go to church. The church where the bells pealed in relief when the war was over. The same church where the Nazis slept on the pews, played cards, and listened to the radio. After the war, the townspeople sanded the pews, painted them white and scrubbed the floors. They draped the cross with fresh silk that came all the way from China. It no longer echoes with the ghosts of angry voices, or the cruel spirits of those who once slept there during endless nights.

I don't come to pray. I come to hold the hands of the other old women as they cry in the back pew, the breeze from an early spring drifting through the open door. Then I leave, go back home, and make my cup of tea. Each sip lingers in my mouth, and I marvel at the simple tastes that echo of years long past.

I never married. There were few boys or men left in our village after the war. Mama and I had no desire to leave, either. This was our home, despite the bullet chinks that lace the cobblestones on our streets, and the simple crosses that splay like open arms across the field where so many died. We remained, even as many left to live in cities or other countries.

Mama and I never spoke of what happened when I hid in the woods. She never asked me why I had blood on my clothing. I never asked her why there was a chain of bruises around her neck, or about the pair of stockings shredded and torn in the back of a dresser drawer. Nor did I ask why her diamond ring was missing or where our silverware went. We simply carried on as if the war had never happened. It was as though we were fragile as crystal and might shatter at the shrill sound of our own truth.

Over time, Mama aged and grew into a crying woman. I stayed strong for both of us. When she died, I followed her casket to the cemetery and watched them lower her into the ground, my fingernails scratching at my arms until they bled. After her funeral, I walked back to my solitary home and washed the sheets and put them back on the bed as always. It was Monday, and if I didn't wash them, I think I would have fallen to the ground and never gotten up.

Rituals became my crutch. I touch the doorknob twice as I leave the bedroom. Turn to the right to pick up the kettle and fill it with water. Three steps to the stove and turn it on with my left hand. Eat one slice of bread with cheese. One egg scrambled in an old iron pan. Afterwards, I walk five steps to the sink and wash them the exact way. Put them back in the cupboard just so.

Do you not see? Do you not understand now? Without the sameness, there would be an unknowing. A feeling of impending doom. If I don't open the door just right, something terrifying could come through it. If I eat anything but the bread and cheese and egg each morning, it might be poisoned or spoiled, or filled with the bones of the dead.

How did you think a fourteen-year-old girl survived in the forest so long by herself when her food ran out in six days? Do you think I was there alone? Of course not.

I'D BEEN in the woods a long time. My skin itched from the bites of flies and gnats. My stomach was hollow and growled like a mongrel, young face painted with dried tears. Oh yes, I cried back then. Every day. For there was nothing else I could do.

I still remember the sound of my own breath, the wracking pant that sprang from my lungs as I ran from him. The Nazi. I was tired and weak, and he was fresh from his arrival in town. It was laughable how quickly he grabbed me, his filthy hand clasped across my mouth, his breath hot and rancid on my neck. He threw me to the ground, a cruel smile edging past his lips as he bared his teeth. The Nazi was blond with a fleshy nose and hooded blue eyes, his chin hidden beneath rolls of fat. His broad shoulders blocked the sun.

Pressing me against the dirt, he dropped his pack, and loosened the belt around his trousers. His gun slipped out of the holster and on to the ground in his haste. Unzipping his pants, he fell upon me and knocked me breathless.

It hurt. Every thrust broke my body and spirit. He would not stop. I screamed once, and he slapped me so hard I no longer heard his grunts. He finished with a sigh and rolled off my small body and walked over to a tree and relieved himself, humming a song I will never forget. A German song that runs through my head each morning as I touch the doorknob twice, turn to the right, reach for the kettle. A song that reminds me of the courage I found that day, despite my pain and terror.

OLD WOMEN CRY because they were the frail ones, caught between the gods of vengeance and the upheaval of mankind. Now we cower in our darkened rooms, dreading nightfall. We light candles, and see shadows lurking a few feet away. And we hear our own death knell; the bells ring for us now, as they did for others so long ago. We pray each day for those who walked into the gas chambers and knelt before monsters.

We cry because we know the monsters will come again. For it is inevitable, isn't it? Maybe not in our lifetime, but soon. The streets will once again run with blood, and the children will lose their innocence. Our sons, and their son's sons, won't catch the scent on the wind. They worry about the silly things—the stock market, the price of a new car, or where to vacation this winter. They will not meet the monster until it is already upon them.

But I...I am different. I already met the monster.

THE GERMAN MADE A MISTAKE. He took the fact that I was just a little girl for granted, as I lay writhing on the ground. He turned his back, grabbed his foul penis in his hand and urinated against a tree, humming a song. I crawled to his pistol and took it from its sheath, I clicked off the safety and pointed it at his back. He stiffened like he did when he'd taken my innocence and left it on the forest floor.

My hands shook as I pulled the trigger twice, and he fell. Birds flew overhead, shocked by the noise that echoed through the woods. Blood ran from his mouth, his eyes turned towards the silent sky. I struck at those eyes again and again with a stick until I knew he would never see Heaven or Hell. His blood ran with mine as it splattered my dress and legs. He was now blind for eternity, but I will see this moment forever.

Hauling his knapsack over my shoulder, I ran deeper into the forest. It no longer mattered what happened, whether I lived or died, because I had conquered death already. Guilt and fear washed over me. The echoes of the gun shots lingered in my soul as I wrestled with what I had done, and what had been done to me. Gasping, I burrowed behind a bush and pressed my face in the dirt, screaming silently in terror, but also in relief.

There was food in his knapsack, a blanket, cigarettes, and a flask of schnapps. In his wallet was a picture of him with his wife and little girl, smiling into the camera. His daughter leaned into him in the photograph, trusting and secure. I shuddered as I thought of his arms around her, drawing her on to his lap. I ate sparingly of the meals once meant for him, swallowing each morsel with a frightened mewl as though the food itself was tainted with his stained soul.

I heard soldiers in the woods the next day. "Horst! Horst!" they called, their boots parting the leaves, sending small animals scurrying for cover. I huddled deep behind the bush for hours as urine mingled with my virgin blood and soaked into the dirt. Once or twice they came close to where I was hiding. I prayed they would not hear my ragged breath, part the leaves, and find me.

Over time, they ceased calling for their comrade. Their voices dimmed as they left the woods. But even so, from that moment on, I had to remind myself to breathe. For years, long after the war had ended, I feared German soldiers would find his bleached bones under the tree, and somehow find me, walk me to the lip of a trench and shoot me in the back.

Do you remember that I love Thursdays? Thursday is when I go to market. I always bring home the same things. The same tea leaves and bread, slabs of butter and wedges of cheese I've bought from the vendors for years. It tastes fresh and new each week, yet exactly as it once did. I savor each bite. I like it this way. Every day I know what to do. There are no surprises.

But today...today is different. I have confessed my story. It is no longer a secret tucked behind my heart. Because I shared this, the part of me that cowered for decades no longer fears the shadow of that war, or the cruelty of those men.

This Sunday, I will walk to the village, wearing the same blue flowered dress I wear every Sunday. It grazes my calves as I climb the stairs into the church, the first step with my left foot. Then I will turn to the right and sit in the last pew with the other crying women and hold their hands. We will feel the breeze on our faces from the half-opened door and lift our eyes towards each other and remember. They will say to me as they have said every Sunday, *"It will be okay, my dear"* and put their ancient arms around me.

But I lied about one thing. I told you I do not cry.

I do.

Every Sunday I cry and cry as the old women hold me and pat my hand. Then I come home and make my tea, eat the bread and cheese, take five steps to the sink, then turn the faucet on with my right hand.

SHARON FRAME GAY

Sharon Frame Gay is an award winning author whose work has appeared in many anthologies and magazines, including Chicken Soup For The Soul, Typehouse, Fiction on the Web, Literally Stories, Lowestoft Chronicle, Thrice Fiction, Saddlebag Dispatches, Crannog, and others. She is a Pushcart Prize nominee.

A collection of her short stories, *Song of the Highway*, was released in August, 2020.

Sharon can be found on Twitter and Amazon.

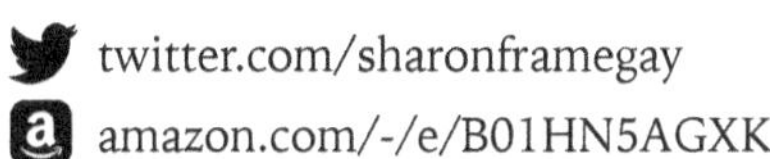

twitter.com/sharonframegay

amazon.com/-/e/B01HN5AGXK

SOMEDAY

VALERIE HUNTER

Aunt Lou only allowed Maggie to ask one question per week. She said curiosity should be rewarded, but that children needed to learn to ask the right questions.

For the first six weeks she lived with Aunt Lou, Maggie reserved her questions for the practical. Where did Aunt Lou keep the washtub? Were there any scissors she could use for cutting Emmett's hair? Could Emmett have new shoes, because his old ones were pinching his toes? Many of her questions ended up being Emmett-based, since Emmett never spoke and Pa had told Maggie to take care of him. She considered asking if she could have a question allowance for Emmett as well as herself, but that in itself would be a question she could ill afford to ask, especially since the answer would likely be no.

Aunt Lou was a hard woman to figure out. She was Ma's older sister, but Maggie couldn't remember Ma ever mentioning her.

Ma had died six months back, trying and failing to birth her last baby. A few months after that, Pa had divvied up the family like it was a pie, though with very uneven pieces. Pa hadn't said anything about his reasoning, but Maggie was good at figuring things out. Daniel and Billy got to stay because they were big enough to be useful on the farm. Sara got to stay, too, because she could cook and keep house. Maggie thought she was just as useful as Sara since she looked after the little ones, but Pa wasn't keeping them, so he didn't keep Maggie, either.

Harvey got sent to Aunt Myrna in town; likely Pa would take him back once he got a little bigger. Jenny and Carrie went to Aunt Lydia and Uncle John out in Martinsville who couldn't manage to have babies of their own; perhaps they'd never come back, but they'd visit, because Aunt Myrna and Uncle John always came for Christmas.

Maggie and Emmett were the only ones who were truly banished, sent all the way to Aunt Lou in Dakota. Maggie did her best to be brave for Emmett's sake—he was only eight—but the farther the train had gone, the more convinced she had become that Aunt Lou didn't actually exist, and that Pa was sending them to nowhere.

But it turned out Aunt Lou did exist after all, a tall woman with cold eyes and sharp elbows. Try as Maggie might, she couldn't find one bit of resemblance to her sweet mother, but Aunt Lou was family now. Maggie tried to express her gratitude on the ride home over the rolling prairie, but Aunt Lou was nearly as quiet as Emmett, so Maggie stopped talking.

As the weeks passed, Maggie tried to get used to this new life. Aunt Lou's clapboard house didn't look like a home, even though it was bigger than the home Maggie had left behind. While it was perfectly clean and orderly, there wasn't anything friendly about it—no flower garden, no cloth on the table, no little knick-knacks anywhere. Maggie thought of Ma's collection of small glass animals that she'd kept on the high shelf in the parlor, away from little hands. She should have thought to bring one with her. Pa would never have noticed.

Maggie and Emmett each had their own austere bedroom upstairs, though Emmett would frequently sneak into Maggie's if he had a nightmare, and sometimes she would sneak into his if she felt lonely. Aunt Lou slept downstairs in a room that was always kept shut. She would disappear into it during the day, too, once she got Maggie and Emmett started on their lessons. Aunt Lou said they'd learn more at home than in the local school. She taught them mathematics mostly, cramming their heads with all sorts of complicated equations they had no choice but to learn. Emmett did better with them than her. Plenty of people—Pa included—thought Emmett was simple because he didn't talk, but Maggie knew that wasn't true.

Maggie missed the one room schoolhouse at home and the green book of fairytales Miss Buford used to let her borrow. There were no fairytales at her new home. When Maggie read, it was about light refraction and electromagnetism and entropy.

Sometimes she would read Aunt Lou's science books aloud to Emmett, but he just frowned. Maggie knew he missed the fairy-tales, too.

When they weren't doing schoolwork, Aunt Lou tasked them with caring for the rabbits she kept in two large hutches behind the house. Maggie knew they weren't for pets because Aunt Lou wasn't the pet type. They never made an appearance on the supper table, and they couldn't be for pelts either, because sometimes Aunt Lou made Maggie draw symbols and numbers on their backs with colored paint. Shortly after, the newly-adorned rabbit would disappear from the hutch. It struck Maggie as odd, and she contemplated asking about them.

Tuesdays were question day, and at long last a Tuesday came where nothing more pressing needed to be asked, so Maggie asked about the rabbits.

Normally Aunt Lou looked disappointed by her questions, but today she smiled broadly and told Maggie to go fetch the latest marked rabbit. When Maggie returned with it, Aunt Lou said, "Come into my workshop."

Maggie followed her into the mysterious room she assumed was Aunt Lou's bedroom. Although there was a bed in one corner, it wasn't like any bedroom Maggie had ever seen. The windows were too high on the wall to provide a view, but perfect for shining light on a long work table cluttered with diagrams and all manner of tools and glass vials. A few feet from the table, in the center of the room, was a large and sinister-looking chair that seemed to be hooked up to a pot-bellied boiler. Maggie thought it looked like something out of a fairy-tale, like the throne of a terrible ogre queen.

"Put it there," Aunt Lou instructed, and Maggie placed the rabbit with the purple triangle and the number seven painted on its back into a box on the seat of the chair. She watched in silence as Aunt Lou strapped the rabbit in and attached wires to its head and limbs, then force-fed it a clear liquid from a bottle and turned on a small boiler attached to the chair.

Maggie had a hundred questions, but she knew if she asked them, she'd be breaking Aunt Lou's rule and would likely be made to leave the room. Looking at the rabbit, Maggie wasn't certain she wanted to stay, but she kept her mouth shut regardless.

"Watch," Aunt Lou said, turning dials on the side of the chair before cranking a wheel on the boiler. Maggie wasn't sure if she was supposed to be watching the rabbit or the wheel, so she let her eyes dart between the two. When Aunt Lou wrenched a lever on the chair's arm, the rabbit disappeared.

Maggie blinked. She must have looked away at the wrong time and missed the rabbit escaping. Her eyes scanned the room wildly, but she didn't see the rabbit. Aunt Lou looked unalarmed as she slowed her cranking of the wheel, turned off the boiler, and gave Maggie a hard look, eyebrows raised.

Maggie tried to think of something to say that wasn't a question. "That was amazing," she offered finally.

Aunt Lou frowned. "Do you even know what you just witnessed?"

"No, ma'am," she said, then dared to remind her. "I've already used up my week's question."

Aunt Lou's scowl subsided. "Indeed. I'll answer the ones you can't ask, then. That" —she nodded to the now rabbit-less chair — "is all my equations come to fruition. It's going to change the world."

Maggie still didn't understand, so she didn't dare nod. Before she could decide if saying, "Go on," would be considered impertinence even if it wasn't a question, a strange white glow seemed to emanate from the chair.

"Shut your eyes," Aunt Lou commanded, and Maggie squinched them shut. Even through her eyelids she saw an intense flash of light. A strange wind brushed her face, as though the very air around her had torn for a few seconds and might swallow the whole room.

"You can look now," Aunt Lou said after a long moment. She sounded disdainful, like Maggie should have known to open her eyes ages ago.

Maggie wished she had kept them shut. The carnage in the chair was recognizable as a rabbit, but only just. It looked like it had been put through an enormous wringer, then gnawed on by a monster who decided, eventually, that this wasn't the meal it wanted after all.

"What…" Maggie stopped. Not because she'd remembered she couldn't ask, but because she couldn't bear to know the answer. Her stomach roiled, and she wished she could leave the room, leave the house, run all the way home—

"Look closely," Aunt Lou said. "What do you see?"

Maggie didn't dare disobey. She took a step forward and saw what she was meant to: part of a green circle on the rabbit's twisted back, and what appeared to be a number four. She remembered marking a rabbit this way weeks ago, when Aunt Lou had first given her the task.

"It's not the same rabbit that just disappeared," she said.

Aunt Lou gave an approving nod. "No. I sent this one a month ago. My longest journey yet, and he seems to have come out of it the best."

Maggie looked at the mutilated body in front of her and bit her lip, trying not to imagine what the others had looked like.

"The one we just sent now should return in six weeks' time," Aunt Lou went on. "He may even survive the journey, though I wouldn't bet on it. I don't think I've quite gotten there yet, but I will. Someday anyone who wants to will be able to travel through time."

Maggie finally pulled her eyes from the rabbit and stared at Aunt Lou. Time travel? Was she serious? How could a rabbit travel through time? How could—

"Well, off you go," Aunt Lou said briskly. "I have work to attend to, and you have your lessons. Think carefully about what you'd like to ask me next week."

Dozens of questions swirled through Maggie's head as the week wore on. How did the rabbits get so mangled up? Why was the chair so big? It didn't make sense to build an adult-sized chair for rabbits. Surely this experiment, this—time travel?—was bigger than rabbits. Aunt Lou had said so herself. *Someday anyone who wants to*…But who would want to sit in that terrible chair? Even if a rabbit eventually returned alive, who would want to risk themselves on the hope they'd survive, too?

Like the rabbits, a person would have to be forced. Just like she and Emmett had been forced to come here, given to Aunt Lou so she could do with them as she pleased.

Maggie thought very hard about her question after that. There were many things she desperately wanted to know, but she tucked them away for future weeks and instead asked, "Can I be your assistant?"

Aunt Lou smiled, and Maggie knew she'd picked the right question. She would make herself indispensable in order to protect herself and Emmett, no matter what it took.

MAGGIE'S LIFE after that became a bit like the fairytales she so missed. The prairie around her was nothing like a fairytale forest, but Emmett and she were Hansel and Gretel nonetheless, and Aunt Lou was the witch. Well, Gretel had managed to save herself and her brother. Surely Maggie could do likewise, since it seemed Pa and her siblings had abandoned them.

Sometimes she tried to pretend that Pa wrote and Aunt Lou was just keeping the letters from them, but she knew that wasn't true. Maggie considered writing herself, but every week there seemed more pressing questions than "If I wrote a letter home, would you mail it for me?"

Aunt Lou did sometimes allow her extra questions now, but only if they had to do with their work, and only if they were smart. Truth be told, Maggie didn't have as many questions as she used to. Or rather, she didn't want to know the answers to the questions she had.

Still, she had to show an interest to ingratiate herself to Aunt Lou and learn all she could to help herself and Emmett. So that's what she did. She charted numbers and figures, and read all of Aunt Lou's reports. They dated back years. Dozens and dozens of files, each documenting the course of a dead rabbit in meticulous and gory detail.

"Why do you use rabbits?" Maggie once asked.

"Easy to care for. Easy to breed. No one to make a fuss when they disappear."

Was it Maggie's imagination, or did Aunt Lou say this last sentence a bit pointedly? No one would make a fuss if she or Emmett disappeared, either.

"The young males come through the best," Aunt Lou said, and sure enough the next one to return came back alive, although it died a few seconds later, shrieking in pain. Maggie had nightmares about those shrieks for weeks afterward, but Aunt Lou was elated. "We're making progress, girl. Don't ever forget it. Sacrifices have to be made in the name of progress."

Maggie nodded because she knew Aunt Lou wanted her to.

"Can you send them back in time?" she asked another week.

This launched Aunt Lou into a lengthy lecture on the nature of time, none of which Maggie really understood other than the answer was no. Backwards didn't work. Only forwards.

She didn't dare ask what the point was. Backwards she could almost understand, though she wasn't sure if it would be wise. To go back in time and be with her family again sounded nice on the surface, but having to live with the knowledge of what was going to happen would be unbearably sad. She couldn't prevent Ma's death, and she wouldn't want to live through it again for anything. Still, she reckoned some people might not mind reliving the past, and maybe some tragic events could actually be stopped.

But forwards? Maggie couldn't see a reason, and Aunt Lou never explained. She just seemed intent on proving she could do it, which might be a worthy enough goal if the process didn't lead to such carnage.

Sometimes Maggie managed to forget what they were doing. The awfulness of it, the danger. Weeks passed with Aunt Lou working on different formulas, new equations, an improved concoction of herbs and chemicals to help the traveler survive his journey. She would tinker with the chair and its wires, having Maggie or even Emmett hold parts and pass tools just like they used to do for Pa when he'd fix the mechanical combine. Emmett would always stare at the chair with wide eyes, but he was never allowed in the room for any of the actual travel, for which Maggie was grateful. Emmett didn't need to know about such nightmares.

When another mangled rabbit returned from its journey, to be dissected with what could only be described as glee on Aunt Lou's part, Maggie was reminded of exactly the danger they were in. She'd also found anatomical sketches on the worktable that were decidedly not leporine in nature. And then there was the way Aunt Lou always referred to Maggie and Emmett as 'girl' and 'boy,' as if they weren't worthy of names, just labels. They might as well have symbols and numbers painted on them like the rabbits.

Occasionally, Aunt Lou would let Maggie read the newspaper for a treat, and that's where she saw the notice. An orphan train arriving at the end of the month. Children in need of placement.

Placement. If it had said "homes" perhaps Maggie would have never had the idea, but that one dreadful word planted itself in her mind and bloomed into something monstrous. Aunt Lou's house was a place, after all, even if it wasn't a home.

"Look at this," Maggie said to her aunt that same day, before she could over-consider whether she should.

Aunt Lou looked, eyebrows furrowed. "What do I care about an orphan train?"

Of course Maggie couldn't let on what she suspected, couldn't give Aunt Lou the idea on the off-chance she didn't have it already. "Someone else to help with your research," she suggested, though she wasn't sure she kept her voice quite steady enough.

Aunt Lou gave her a long look. Sometimes Maggie suspected her aunt could see straight into her, see every thought she'd ever had, and this was one of those times. "A boy, perhaps?"

Maggie nodded, her chest tight. "Someone a bit bigger and stronger than Emmett could be a help."

"Indeed," Aunt Lou said, her eyes still boring into Maggie. "You can pick him yourself."

Maggie hadn't expected that, and she lived in a constant state of dread for the next two weeks. What had she done? Rabbits were one thing, but a boy? A boy that she chose?

Maybe Aunt Lou meant for him to be a hired boy, nothing more. She would never...

On the off-chance she would, though, better this orphan boy than her or Emmett. She had to look out for her brother, after all.

On the last day of the month, Aunt Lou took Maggie and Emmett into town in the wagon. It was the first time they'd been away from the house since they'd arrived nearly a year ago. Maggie had forgotten what a crowd looked like.

"Remember. You choose," Aunt Lou muttered to her as the orphans were paraded onto the train platform.

She'd thought there would be plenty to pick from, but there

weren't. Maggie overheard that this was the train's last stop. "We're getting the leftovers," one man muttered.

There were only five boys, and none of them were particularly big. Which was fine, Maggie reminded herself. After all, it was the smaller, younger male rabbits who'd done the best in their trials.

One of the boys had a limp, another a deformed arm. It wouldn't do to pick them. The smallest boy looked barely four, an unfortunate-looking child with overly large features. She couldn't possibly take someone so young.

Maggie turned to the last two, but before she could consider, someone spoke up for one of them, leaving her with no choice. It had to be this thin, dark-haired boy with the sad eyes. She'd wanted to choose someone who would be easy to dislike, someone like Dennis Bryson from back home who always shouted insults in the schoolyard and put insects down the backs of girls' dresses.

This boy didn't look at all like Dennis Bryson, but she pointed him out to Aunt Lou anyway, and Aunt Lou signed the papers. "He's ours now," Aunt Lou said, and Maggie had never heard a possessive pronoun sound so ominous.

Aunt Lou called him boy, same as she called Emmett, but of course he had a name. Aaron. He claimed he was twelve years old, same as Maggie, but he looked younger. "We'll put some meat on those bones," Aunt Lou said, and again Maggie was reminded of Hansel and Gretel.

Aaron didn't talk much, which was just as well. Maggie didn't want to get to know him. She spent more time than ever with Aunt Lou in the lab, where Aaron was never invited.

But a person couldn't live in the same house as someone and not get to know him. As the weeks and months passed, she came to know Aaron well. How brilliant he was at math, much to Aunt Lou's delight. How he moved so quietly she forgot he was in a room. How he was always drawing—on his slate, in the dirt, in the margins of the newspaper—and was actually quite good at it.

Emmett seemed to enjoy his company. Emmett was particular about who he warmed to—he was still terrified of Aunt Lou and never looked her in the eye—but he clearly adored Aaron. They shared a room, and each night Maggie could hear the low rumble of Aaron's voice as he talked to her brother. She couldn't make out the actual words, but they had a soothing cadence. Aaron trusted Emmett, and Emmett trusted him.

And Emmett trusted Maggie. It was her job to protect him.

Maggie dared to ask more questions after that. Not the big one, no; she didn't dare ask if Aunt Lou would be strapping Aaron to that dreadful chair one day. But she finally asked what the point of it all was.

She expected Aunt Lou to be angry, or to treat her like a stupid child for not figuring it out herself. However, Aunt Lou looked pensive instead, and didn't answer right away. Finally, she said, "The future's always better, isn't it? Something to look forward to, to aspire for. Why shouldn't someone get to travel to such a glorious place?"

That wasn't much of an answer. The future wasn't some lovely geographical place, it was just a time with no guarantees. She knew she couldn't say that to Aunt Lou, though. Suppose she began to suspect that Maggie wasn't as invested in the success of this mission as she should be? Suppose she began to see Maggie as expendable?

So she soldiered on. Another long stretch of equations and hypotheses, with Emmett and Aaron helping on the math, double-checking the figures without knowing what they were helping with. Another round of rabbits, this time sent a year, fourteen months, and sixteen months into the future.

A lot happened in that year. Maggie had the beginning of a bosom and started pinning her hair up like a young lady. Aaron grew taller than her, his eyes less sad. They became friends.

She hadn't meant for it to happen, but it was impossible not to develop some kind of feelings when she saw him every day, and she couldn't dislike him, not when he was so good to Emmett.

Aaron still didn't talk much, but he drew pictures on the brown wrapping paper Maggie had salvaged for him from Aunt Lou's trips to town. He drew landscapes with trees and cozy little houses that looked like homes. Smiling men and women appeared amongst the trees, dancing and painting and playing with dogs. Aaron's people always seemed to be moving right there on the page.

Maggie wondered about the people he drew, but she had gotten in the habit of conserving her questions, even when she wasn't around Aunt Lou. Her curiosity got the best of her though, and she asked, "Are they drawings of your home?"

Aaron shook his head. "They're drawings of where I want to be. Someday."

She looked again and thought she could see a bit of Aaron, older and bearded, in the drawing of the painter. And might that be Emmett, walking the majestic-looking dog? And herself, older and beautiful, dancing with another grown-up Aaron?

She decided not to ask.

WHEN SHE WAS ALMOST FOURTEEN, Aunt Lou suggested she walk to Abbotsville, a day's journey, to pick up something for her at a junk shop. Before Maggie could begin to panic at the thought of leaving Emmett all day, Aunt Lou said to take him with her, and Aaron, too. Maggie was so relieved that she didn't bother asking why Aunt Lou didn't go herself like she normally did, or why they couldn't take the horse and wagon. She'd used up her weekly question allotment, anyhow.

"The walk'll do you good," Aunt Lou said as though Maggie had asked. "Young bodies need fresh air. Here's some money so you can have your dinner in town." She gave Maggie a rare smile along with the coins. "Enjoy yourselves!"

Maggie recognized the frenzied elation in Aunt Lou's tone, the same way she always sounded when she thought she was on the verge of a breakthrough. Something was happening today, and Maggie was glad that she and the boys didn't have to be a part of it.

They set out to Abbotsville right after breakfast. The vast sky and the empty prairie unnerved Maggie—she wasn't used to being out of sight of the house—so she held Emmett's hand and recounted all the old fairy tales she could think of, though she wasn't sure she was remembering them correctly. When she finished, Aaron told a few as well, stories Maggie didn't know but sounded vaguely familiar. All of them involved bravery and escape, whether the characters were slaying dragons or outwitting ogres or fleeing witches who wanted to eat them.

They reached Abbotsville in the heat of the day. It should have been a relief to enter the cool dim of the junk shop, but Maggie found the place to be creepy, full of machinery as sinister-looking as the chair in Aunt Lou's workshop. The man behind the counter gave her a small parcel, and Maggie hurried back into the sunlight.

They went to the general store next and bought apples and crackers and a wedge of cheese, and then found a lone cottonwood tree at the edge of town and had a picnic in its shade. It should have been lovely, but Maggie still felt unsettled.

"Have you ever thought about escaping?" Maggie asked Aaron after Emmett had wandered off a little ways picking wildflowers. "Like the children in the fairy tales?"

Aaron frowned. "What are we escaping from?"

She should tell him, but how could she, when they had nowhere to go, no means to get away? This was the best opportunity they had, but it was no opportunity at all with only a few pennies and no destination in mind.

"Nothing," she said. "Never mind."

But Aaron continued to look at her, his gaze gentler than Aunt Lou's but no less probing. "What does Miss Lou do in that workshop of hers?"

Maggie looked away. "Nothing important."

"You don't trust me." The hurt dripped from his voice, and his eyes looked as sad as they had when she'd first met him.

Maggie didn't respond, because she didn't have the words to say it wasn't him she didn't trust. It was herself.

They walked home in silence, every step dragging. Maggie clutched the bouquet of wildflowers Emmett had picked for her and thought of all those fairy tales. She wondered what happily ever after entailed, whether the children really managed to live normal lives after escaping whatever horror they'd faced, or whether they had nightmares every time they closed their eyes.

The three arrived home at sunset to a freshly turned patch of earth in front of the house. "I thought we might give that flower garden you've always wanted a go," Aunt Lou said, as though it made perfect sense for her to till the ground before she even had seeds, to do it herself instead of having Aaron do it.

"Lovely," Maggie said. It wasn't until she'd climbed into bed that night that she recalled she'd never actually said anything aloud about wanting a flower garden.

THE YEAR-LONG RABBIT traveler came back shortly thereafter. It lived twelve hours. No shrieking this time, though it bled a bit from its eyes and nose and seemed disoriented, frantically running around its small cage and refusing to eat. Even once it passed, Aunt Lou was jubilant. "We're nearly there. The future is almost ours."

She dissected the rabbit the following day and had Maggie take notes. All the rabbit's organs were strangely swollen, and

Maggie was tasked with drawing them, but she couldn't capture their odd shapes. "You should have Aaron do it instead," she blurted out when Aunt Lou scolded her. She knew as soon as she said it that she should have held her tongue, but it was too late.

"Send him in, then," Aunt Lou said, and Maggie was forced to. She saw Aaron's eyes widen when he saw the terrible chair, watched him turn pale when he was shown what he was meant to draw. He did it, though, without question. The organs in his drawings looked perfectly accurate, perfectly grotesque.

After that, Aunt Lou welcomed Aaron into her workshop more and more while excluding Maggie. When she dared use her weekly question to ask why, Aunt Lou scowled as if Maggie was the biggest dunce in the territory. "He's better with science than you. And he doesn't ask questions."

"You said children should be curious," Maggie reminded her.

"Only if they ask the *right* questions. And you're hardly a child anymore, girl."

No, she hardly was. She did her lessons and looked after the rabbits and wondered how to get away. If she and Emmett turned up at home, would Pa take them back? Home seemed impossibly far away, as made-up as a fairy tale. And besides, she had no money for train tickets, could find nothing of value in the house to sell.

Months passed. The fourteen month rabbit came back dead, but the sixteen month one lived for two days after its return. Its organs, upon inspection, looked nearly normal. Advances were clearly being made, even if Maggie wasn't a part of the process anymore. Aaron always looked thin-lipped and sad-eyed, but there was something else in his expression, too, a resoluteness that scared her. She wanted to ask him what he was doing, but she didn't dare.

Aunt Lou went to Abbotsville one day, saying something about getting a new boiler for the chair. To make it extra powerful? Powerful enough to send a human? Maggie watched the wagon disappear, then went into the workshop where Aaron sat hunched over the table.

"You need to leave," she said.

He looked up at her. "Miss Lou said I could work in here while she was gone."

"I don't mean the room. I meant here, this place. You need to go."

"You think I would do that?" he asked, frowning. "Leave you and Emmett?"

"She's going to put you in that chair!"

Aaron looked back at the papers in front of him. "I know."

She wanted to shake him. "Then how can you stay?"

"It's what I'm here for, isn't it?" He still didn't look up. "She told me how it was your idea. How you chose me."

Maggie shook her head, wanting to deny it, to tell him she didn't have a choice, to tell him just how sorry she was. None of those words seemed adequate for the death sentence she had given him.

"It's alright," he went on. "I think it might work this time. We've made some adjustments, used the data—"

"You're not a rabbit!" she interrupted, when really she wanted to say *It's not alright!*

Aaron finally looked up. "She's done it before, with people. Didn't you know?"

She stared at him, then at the files in front of him. Not the rabbit files. She snatched them up, scanned the pages.

There had been four of them. They were called subjects, no names, no explanations for where they had come from, who they were. Dates were carefully charted, though. One human trial after every dozen rabbits. Lists and descriptions.

Sent 12/17/77, 9:30

> *Male between fifty-five and sixty, 5'5", health could be better. Entry went poorly; needs more energy. Subject never returned.*

Sent 8/9/78, 8:15 Returned 8/9/78, 8:25

> *Male, age twenty-eight, 6'0", strong and healthy. Returned five inches shorter. All organs liquefied except liver.*

Sent 11/30/79, 8:30 Returned 12/5/79, 8:30

> *Female, age twelve, 4'7", slender. Returned with bones broken through skin, eyes popped from sockets.*

Sent 6/28/82, 10:30 Returned 6/28/83, 10:31

> *Male, approximate age forty-five, 5'8", rotund. Returned in fine condition, but could not be revived.*

THE DATE of return on this last file was the day they'd gone to Abbotsville. He'd been gone a year, had been sent off when Maggie and Emmett and Aaron had already been living in the house. When—how—

She looked up at Aaron. "Where did she…Who were they?"

"I don't know. They came to her. People no one would miss, she said."

Maggie finally found her voice. "I would miss you," she said, taking his hand and squeezing an apology into it. "We can't let her do this."

"I really think it might work this time."

Tears welled in her eyes. "'Might' isn't enough!"

"It'll have to be. Besides, I volunteered."

She dropped his hand. "You what?"

"Volunteered," he repeated, his eyes on the chair.

Maggie's mind sped. "Who was she going to use instead? Emmett?"

Aaron shook his head. "She wants someone who will be able to tell her about the experience, if they survive."

Not Emmett, then. "Me."

He didn't respond.

It wasn't a question. She *was* the most expendable. The best candidate.

"You can't…"

"Sure I can," he said quickly. "Males come through better, we both know that. And I want to, Maggie. It's what family does for each other."

Family. What had family ever done for her? Sent her away. Forgot about her. Called her 'girl' and made her do terrible things. Willingly sacrificed her for the sake of progress.

She'd long thought the only family she had left was Emmett. But now here was Aaron, looking out for her even after Aunt Lou had told him the truth. Acting like she was worth saving, even when she wasn't sure she was.

"I'll be alright," he said, babbling on about the science she'd never quite understood, how he'd be gone for two years and come back in one piece.

What if you don't? Maggie wanted to ask. But she was afraid he'd take it the wrong way, think she was questioning his science and not the fact that she could never live with herself afterwards.

"When?" she managed to choke out instead.

"Day after tomorrow. As soon as we can get the new boiler hooked up."

She fled the room, unable to stay with him a moment longer, not when he could talk so calmly about his own departure. She went outside, stared at the garden where flowers now bloomed over the corpse of subject—victim—number four. Were the others beneath the vegetable garden? The rabbit hutches? Would she be expected to help dig the next grave? Aaron's grave?

No. No, she wasn't letting him do this. She'd go herself, like Aunt Lou had wanted. Or run away, take Emmett and Aaron with her. Who cared where. Any place was better than here; they could sneak on a boxcar or steal Aunt Lou's horses or—

She'd find them, though. Fairytale villains couldn't be run from; they had to be overcome. Slayed. She needed a plan.

If she killed Aunt Lou, what would happen next? Could they bury her in the yard? If Maggie was caught, no one would ever believe her, that the killing was necessary. They'd lock her away forever, and what would become of Emmett then?

Aaron would take care of him, she reminded herself. Her being locked away was better than Aaron being dead. Maybe it wouldn't come to that.

Now, how to do it. A knife? A blow to the head? She wasn't sure she had it in her, and Aunt Lou was a tall, strong woman who could easily overcome Maggie in a struggle. Would Aaron help? She didn't dare tell him beforehand, but in the heat of the moment, surely he'd be on her side. She didn't want him to have to be, though. It shouldn't have to come to that.

For the next day and a half she tried to plan, convinced Aunt Lou could read her every thought. The night before Aaron was to go in the chair, she couldn't sleep. She thought of home, wondering if Pa or her older siblings ever thought of her, whether the younger ones even remembered they had a sister named Maggie. Maybe someday, in the better future Aunt Lou talked about, she'd see them again, but the thought didn't give her comfort.

The door creaked open. Emmett. He curled up at the foot of her bed the way he used to years ago, when he was small and needed comforting from her.

She was the one who needed comforting now. There in the

dark she spilled it all out—what Aunt Lou had done and was going to do, what Maggie had to do to stop her but wasn't sure she could. She hadn't meant to burden Emmett with any of this, but he was here, and he cared, and the words wouldn't stop coming. When she finally finished, all her words spent, she finally lay down and he patted her shoulder the way she used to pat his when he had a nightmare.

The next thing she knew, it was morning and she was alone. She hadn't thought she'd be able to sleep, but apparently she had, though she didn't feel any better for it. She rolled over and found a strip of paper next to her in the bed.

She squinted at it in the early morning light. A series of numbers. She recognized Emmett's careful writing, and recognized what they were.

The drawings next to them were harder to decipher. At first, she thought they were Aaron's, that Emmett must have borrowed the paper from him, but no, they were simple, crude. Definitely not Aaron's. A tiny house dotted with gumdrops. Beneath it, an oven.

She got up and got dressed quickly, a new plan coming together with frenzied speed. She had to hurry. Aaron hadn't mentioned a specific time for his departure, but Aunt Lou always sent the rabbits on empty stomachs.

Downstairs, Emmett was stirring oatmeal on the stove, mugs of tea already steeping. He gave her the kind of grimace he used to give when he was small and needed the outhouse. Urgency was required. She took a mug of tea and hurried to the workshop.

Aaron was already in the chair, looking pale but calm. Maggie tried but couldn't look at him. She turned all her focus to Aunt Lou. "I brought you tea. Can I—" No, that was a question; there wasn't time for questions. "I'll help," she said instead.

Aunt Lou raised her eyebrows. "You have the stomach for it again, do you?"

"Yes, ma'am," she said quickly.

"I was just mixing the sedative."

"I'll do it." They had found that sedating the rabbits before their journeys helped. Maggie picked up the tranquilizer and looked at the notes. People needed much more than rabbits, after all. She mixed it with the other concoction, the one meant to keep the body together in travel. It was clear and had a faint bitter smell. She stole a glance at Aunt Lou, bent over the dials on the chair.

"Nearly ready. Deep breaths help," Aunt Lou said to Aaron, before turning to Maggie. "Are you done?"

She nodded. Aunt Lou had already strapped Aaron's arms down, so Maggie held the cup to his lips. She could smell the fear on him, but his gaze was steady.

"I'm sorry," she whispered in his ear. "I'm so, so sorry I brought you here."

"I'm not," he whispered back.

She stayed by him, held his hand, watched as her aunt took several gulps of tea.

"You steeped this far too long," Aunt Lou complained. "It's gone bitter."

"Sorry," Maggie squeaked.

Aunt Lou waved the apology away and turned her focus to Aaron. "It's time. Are you ready to make history, boy?"

Aaron blinked sleepily.

"His name is Aaron," Maggie said, positioning herself between Aunt Lou and the chair, trying to buy time. "You could at least call him by his name."

Aunt Lou frowned. "What's gotten into you? Out of my way."

Maggie kept her feet firmly planted. "I've been thinking about what you said. About the future being a glorious place to go. You've got it all wrong. The whole point is the journey, and it's not meant to be made in a chair. To be missed. You're meant to live all the in-between parts. Some of them might be horrid, but you have to soldier on anyway. It's what shapes people into who they are. No skipping ahead. No shortcuts. In the end, if you're lucky, you get to what you dreamed about. The little house in the woods, and the easel, and the dog, and the dancing. The *someday* you wanted." She said this last part for Aaron, though she didn't dare turn and look at him.

"What are you going on about, girl?" Aunt Lou asked, her words coming slow and slurred. "What have you...done?"

Maggie put a hand out, pulled her aunt closer to the chair. "If you want the future so badly, you should be the one to go."

"What..."

"Don't worry. I put the right dosage in your tea."

Aunt Lou's legs gave way, and Maggie let them, leaving her aunt in a heap on the floor while she unbuckled Aaron. She'd given him only a rabbit's dose of the sedative, nothing else, but he blinked at her blearily and moved like a marionette that needed its limbs tightened. She had to push him from the chair and call Emmett to help her get Aunt Lou into it. She did the buckling herself, though, ignoring Aunt Lou's moans, and set the dials to the numbers Emmett had given her. Maggie couldn't have come up with them herself, but she understood enough to know that Aunt Lou was set to come back in twenty years, not two.

Aaron was mumbling—protesting?—so Emmett led him from the room, leaving Maggie to the task. Gretel pushing the witch into the stove.

"I'm sorry it has to be this way," Maggie said truthfully, looking straight into Aunt Lou's furious eyes. "But you said it was up to me to choose. And I choose you."

She cranked the wheel the proper number of times, then threw the lever, keeping her eyes on Aunt Lou's until the moment they disappeared. The room seemed horribly silent afterwards.

Maggie fetched the hammer and screwdriver from the worktable, and opened up the chair's terrible boiler. She took a moment to stare at all the intricate parts before thoroughly smashing them to bits. She might not understand all the science, but she knew the chair was the tether. Without it, a traveler could never return.

Like slamming the door of the oven after throwing in the witch.

Once she was done, Maggie put the tools back and left the room. It wasn't the end of the story. Maggie wasn't sure what they'd do next, but they'd figure it out together, her and Emmett and Aaron. They'd plan for a future they could live in, live with, and then figure out a way to get there. That's what family did, after all.

VALERIE HUNTER

Valerie Hunter teaches high school English and has an MFA in writing for children and young adults from Vermont College of Fine Arts. Her stories and poems have appeared in publications including *Cicada, Storyteller, Edison Literary Review, Other Voices, Room,* and *Wizards in Space.*

Find Valerie on Instagram.

instagram.com/somanystories_solittletime

THE ALGORITHM

DAN EVELOFF

F rancis Newman received his copy of the hotly anticipated *Cyber Love* in the mail, a month before its scheduled release—a perk of being part of the Rowe Publishing House Family, as they liked to call it. Rowe had published his last twelve novels, though he'd found his early commercial success harder to replicate over the past decade or so. That was about the time self-publishing and electronic publications began eliminating seemingly every barrier of entry to the profession once reserved to those who weathered the "starving artist" phase before finally striking it big.

The author of *Cyber Love* endured no such struggle. There were no prior resume-building publications, no years of querying agents and publishers; hell, the author hadn't even needed to edit the story beyond the first draft. Nevertheless, *Cyber Love* was the most anticipated book release of the century, maybe ever. That's because the author was not human.

It was an algorithm.

Designed by a team of computer engineers and literary consultants, the algorithm's inputs comprised every conceivable literary device: diction, theme, plot, tone, metaphor, satire, foreshadowing, mood, symbolism, characterization, action, dialogue, pacing, etcetera from history's greatest authors, traditional and modern alike, spanning the past three centuries: Dickens, Tolstoy, Shakespeare, Twain, Hemingway, Lovecraft, Dickinson, Steinbeck, Vonnegut, King, Rowling, Patterson. Their works, among hundreds of others, were part of the formula designed to create the perfect novel, one that appealed to every kind of reader. Even Doctor Seuss was used!

A perfect blend of artistic and commercial devices, *Cyber Love* had been praised as "the greatest literary achievement in the history of the written word." And barring a revocation of the First Amendment, it represented the greatest risk to human authorship since Nazi censorship threatened the free world.

Francis read all 386 pages in one day. By God, it was tremendous. No, it was *perfect*. The story was as captivating as the ending was satisfying. The characters were so layered, complex, *real*. The prose was poetic, yet not pretentiously so. He'd never read anything like it.

It could never hit the shelves.

FRANCIS TOOK the train into downtown Manhattan the next morning to pay a visit to his friends at Rowe. Without an appointment, he waited over an hour before finally sliding into his publisher's busy schedule.

"Francis, how are you?" Julie Mason greeted from behind a desk that could've hosted a large dinner party. The wall behind her desk was a floor-to-ceiling window, beyond which the city skyline postured before the Hudson River.

"Doing well, thanks."

"What can I do for you?"

Debating whether to remain standing or take a seat on one of the two couches, Francis ultimately chose the latter, which Julie met with a glance at her watch.

"I read *Cyber Love*," he started.

"Oh yeah? Remarkable, isn't it?"

"It's good," he said, his voice raising a pitch, the way it does when one's being more kind than truthful.

"Good? It's the best damn thing I've ever read."

"No, yeah, it's very good. It just seems like it might be missing some...human element, perhaps."

"Human element?" Julie scoffed. "Forgive me, Francis, but I strongly disagree. I mean, the characters...they're so intricate, so...gosh, they're so alive." She indulgently breathed in the air of her literary masterpiece and seemed to shimmer with pleasure, almost aroused as she spoke about it.

"I suppose."

Julie removed her black-framed glasses and set them down on her desk. "Francis, what's this about?"

"What? Nothing. I mean...the whole algorithm thing is really cool; I just think maybe there might be some kinks to be worked out. It's a pretty radical idea—a computer writing a story and all —and I was just thinking that, maybe before releasing it, you'd just want to make sure it's absolutely perfect, you know? I mean, who knows how the public will react to something like this?"

"I'm sorry, are you suggesting we delay the book release?"

"Julie, you're the businessperson here; I'm just voicing my opinion—one that might be shared by other um...*human* authors."

"Ah, I see," Julie said, a knowing smirk sizing up the insecure author. "You feel threatened."

"What? Threatened?" Francis said innocently.

"It's okay, Francis. I get it. It must be a bit unsettling. Writing is one of the few professions that have been impervious to the technological innovations changing our world. Then all of a sudden a computer program spits out the most perfect piece of literature the world has ever seen without so much as a rewrite. If *Cyber Love* is a hit—which it will be—it could mean a seismic shift in the entire industry. I'm sure that's disconcerting."

"Yeah, I guess that's it," he confessed.

"Listen, Francis," she said, her sympathetic eyes taking a familiar businesslike form. "I didn't want to have this conversation here, like this, but, you're here, so...we're going to be terminating your contract."

Francis's stomach sank into his shoes. "What? Terminated? But *Broken Crow* is nearly finished!"

"Your release from the contract will allow your agent to shop it to another publisher. And you'll get to keep the one-third advance you received upon signing."

"I...but...why?"

Julie shrugged and avoided his stare. "It's not just you, so please don't take this personally. There're others too."

"Other members of the Rowe Publishing House *Family*," Francis sneered.

"We've been having a lot of discussions internally about the company's strategic plan going forward. We can't deny what Adwin has produced. I mean, it's slapping us in the face. You can't deny it either. The algorithm is...well...it's perfect. And it can work in any genre! Ownership agrees: Adwin is the future."

The fact that they gave the stupid algorithm a name somehow made the news all the more insulting.

"But we have such a long history, Julie! A very profitable history!"

"Francis, you haven't produced a profitable novel since *Red Shadow*." She paused, seemingly regretful of the unnecessary slight. "I know you'll be fine, Francis. You're a brilliant writer. There're hundreds of publishing houses who'd kill to have you."

The rest of the meeting was a blur, however long it lasted. Francis didn't even remember leaving the office.

Back at home, he contemplated his next move over a bottle of wine. He had a decent chunk of change stashed away, but each royalty check had been smaller than the last. Thank God he'd already put his kids through college.

But how long would it take to find a buyer? He hadn't been an "orphan" for years. Once he finished it, there was no doubt *Broken Crow* would put him back on top, but without the rest of the advance from Rowe, he was facing financial uncertainty he thought he'd graduated from long ago.

He needed a safety net. That's all it would be, of course: a safety net. Some just-in-case money.

Going back into teaching was an option. After all, if there was an algorithm designed to produce a lit professor, it'd probably spit out a clone of him. His salt-and-pepper hair to match his graying beard, the bifocals and corduroy pants; he was wearing a brown tweed blazer for goodness' sake, elbow patches and all.

The thought depressed him even more. He was an *author*, dammit, not a freaking school teacher.

He tipped back the glass and poured another. Then another. Somewhere along the way, he found himself drinking straight from the bottle, one heaping swig after another. It was halfway down the second bottle when Francis received a phone call.

Thank goodness. Just the man he needed.

"Chuuuck. Chuck Snyderrr. What's happ'nin?" he slurred.

"Francis? Are you drunk?"

"Just a li'l buzzed, Chuckster. I think I deserve it after the day I've had."

"Um, okay. Listen, Francis..."

"What's up with you, man? Ev'rything good?"

"Yeah, yeah, everything's good. We need to talk."

"I was ac'shully just gonna call you! Small world, huh?"

"Um, Francis, that's not—"

"I got fired today. Or...released? Not sure whi—"

"I know."

"You know?"

"Julie told me."

"Oh." Francis deflated for a moment before continuing to air his frustrations upon his friend and agent. "Can you believe it? After all these years? She's replacing me with a freaking robot! A robot with no empathy or or emotion or, or..."

He belched.

"That's why I'm calling, Francis. I've—"

"There's no loyalty in this business, Chuck, none whatsoever. It's okay though. I'll be done with *Broken Crow* in a few months. It's gonna be great. All you gotta do is find it a good home!"

Hiccup.

"I can't represent you anymore, Francis. I'm done."

The words hit him like a sobering brick, igniting all of his synapses to fire like skilled marksmen.

"Wait, what? What do you mean, you're done?"

"I'm getting out of the business."

"You've been my agent for damn near thirty years, Chuck!"

"I know that, Francis. But the business is changing. Fast. *Cyber Love*. Adwin is for real, and it's going to put thousands of authors, *and agents*, out of work. And I'm too damn old to swim against the current."

"So just like that? You're just going to abandon all your clients because some stupid robot wrote a book?"

"Well, in time. I'm...narrowing."

"Narrowing? What the hell does that mean?"

"I'm uh...I'm keeping just a few clients just for the time being, while I transition out. Hopefully that'll allow me to retire, slowly, without having to find another job. It's nothing personal, Francis; you must know that."

Francis hung up, only realizing he did so after the fact. His mind spun like a propeller inside his skull, processing the day's news while he sipped away into his morbid, angry thoughts.

He snapped out of it when he reached the bottom of the second bottle, not even remembering the way down. He stood up, apparently too fast, as a mixture of nausea and light-headedness sent him into a spiraling stagger after just a few steps. He was able to guide himself to a nearby couch before he collapsed.

As the room spun, a thought materialized through the haze: *'Adwin is the future.' Good lord. We're all screwed.*

"FRANCIS? FRANCIS?"

The voice entered his waking consciousness and his last available memory—Julie's blunt termination—immediately surfaced. Or was that a dream? His eyes fluttered open, and his living room ceiling came into focus. He peered over the edge of the couch, seeing an empty wine bottle lying on the floor...no, it wasn't a dream.

"Francis, what're you doing sleeping out here with all the lights on?"

Oh God, Jeanine. He hadn't even thought about what he was going to tell her.

He sat up, again too quickly, and the dizziness returned and his vision faded into temporary blackness.

"Honey, are you okay?"

Francis jumped to his feet and darted past his wife, barely making it in time to heave into the toilet. When he finished, his wife was waiting outside the bathroom, arms crossed.

"What's going on, Francis?" she demanded, her disapproving eyes magnified behind thick lenses.

"Hi, hon. Nothing, just not feeling great, is all."

"Those empty wine bottles have anything to do with that?"

He wiped his eyes. "Dear, would you mind brewing up a pot?"

"Of coffee? Francis, it's seven-thirty! You'll be up all night!"

Francis stared back dumbly. *Up all night.* He looked to the kitchen window. The sky was dark. It was...today still. His headache confirmed as much. He hated being awake for the hangover.

"I brought home dinner from McCaskey's. You weren't answering your phone, so I just got you the linguini you like."

Dinner time. Today. The same today in which he'd been let go by his publisher. *Gol-ly.*

"Francis, what the heck is going on?" Jeanine asked when Francis didn't respond.

He took a deep sigh, padded over to the kitchen table and plopped down in his chair, then told her everything.

"So...now what?" she asked.

"Now? I guess I have to hustle a little bit to get this next book sold."

The words came out easy enough, but hanging over his still-inebriated head was the dreadful possibility that, with the ripples *Cyber Love* will soon send through the publishing world, his days may be numbered, or worse, already over; every publishing house worth their salt would be investing in their own Adwins. The extinction of the human author was imminent.

"I was thinking about maybe getting back into teaching," Francis said amidst the growing silence. "At least until I can lock in another deal. You know, just to be safe."

Francis could feel Jeanine's angst without even looking at her. She knew Francis wouldn't even entertain going back into teaching unless the situation was dire. Her lack of response confirmed as much.

The silence hung heavy, until Jeanine finally stood up. "Welp, I'll talk to the financial planner tomorrow," she said, frowning. "We can cut back on spending until you land that deal."

She grabbed her takeout box and went upstairs to fret over dinner by her lonesome.

Francis could already feel the tension in the house—one he hadn't felt in half a lifetime. He'd met Jeanine while teaching at Fordham—Jeanine was a math professor—and they were married less than a year later. Francis quit when their first child was born, finding paternity a good excuse to finally pursue writing full-time.

When the months without a deal turned into years—years in which they saw the birth of their second child, and the corresponding increase in expenses—Jeanine urged Francis to go back to teaching. Francis took offense to the very suggestion, and fights became a weekly event. Then almost daily.

Their marriage bent under the financial strain, with the tension between them swelling like a giant balloon that filled more of the house with each passing day. When there was barely room to breathe, a book deal came in and popped it, just in the nick of time. It wasn't hyperbole to say that *A Nameless Man*—Francis's first book—saved his marriage.

As Francis nibbled on his linguini, he wondered how big that balloon would swell this time before they began to suffocate.

THE NEXT TWO months did little to quell their worries. Despite his efforts, there was no deal in sight. A mid-fifties writer seemingly didn't have the intrigue of the young budding authors...or digital ones. He and Jeanine gradually cut back more and more (except for wine expenditures, which upticked considerably). The balloon was inflating, and the possibility of going back to teaching became more real by the day. All the while, *Cyber Love* had become more popular than water.

One doleful morning, Francis was fulfilling his husbandly duties at the supermarket when he ran into Nick Gornick, an old dorm buddy from NYU. Nick had been a computer science major back when the field was barely a decade old. Though the guys in Rubin Hall had ragged him for wasting his tuition on a "fake major," Nick apparently parlayed it into a lucrative career, now a software developer for one of the largest healthcare technology solutions providers in the world...whatever that meant.

"So when can I expect the next *New York Times* bestseller?" Nick asked as they perused the produce.

Francis forced a chuckle. "Probably not for a while. It's actually been a tough year. The whole industry has gone to shit since this *Cyber Love* nonsense."

"Oh yeah, I've heard about that book. And if *I've* heard about it, it must be pretty big."

"Hah. Still not a big reader, huh?"

"Not unless you're talking about source code. I barely made it out of my freshman English class without flunking."

"Too bad they didn't have SparkNotes back then."

"Seriously. Would've saved me having to pay Steven Marston to write my essays for me."

Francis laughed, the first genuine one he'd had in a while. "Steven Marston. Forgot all about that guy."

"So who's the genius that wrote this *Cyber Love* book?" Nick asked, bagging a hand of bananas. "Dude must be loaded now."

"Wait, you mean you don't know?"

"Don't know what?"

"A robot wrote it. Or, a computer algorithm."

"What do you mean, an algorithm wrote it?"

"I mean a publishing house—*my* publishing house, actually—hired some coders or scientists or whatever to create an algorithm designed to write the best book ever. Unfortunately, they did a hell of a job."

Nick gaped at him. "Seriously?"

"Seriously. They took a bunch of books from the most renowned authors and input them into some kind of computer program. I dunno, you probably understand how all that works better than I do, but I guess the program's algorithm used their writing to create some perfect mega-book."

"Whoa."

"Yeah. That's why the industry is so messed up. The publishing house dropped a bunch of authors from their contracts, mine included, claiming their technology is the way of the future. And as much as it pains me to say it, it's hard to argue with them. *Cyber Love* has already sold three million copies. In just one month! It's crazy! And the publisher gets to keep *all* the earnings without giving any to an author, because technically, they *are* the author. And of course, the other big houses are following suit. Now *real* authors are having a harder time getting published. Even successful ones like me."

"Looks like I picked a *real* major after all," Nick snickered, though this time, Francis didn't join him, instead picking up an apple and pretending to examine it. "I'm sorry man, that's really messed up."

"No, no, that's all right. I didn't mean to throw all my problems at you, especially the first time seeing each other in what, thirty years? Anyways, I better get going. Got a full day of submissions to get to. These queries won't reject themselves," Francis said, again feigning a laugh.

They shook hands, and Francis started rolling his cart away when he heard Nick from behind him.

"Hey, Francis."

He turned.

"Why don't you just write one yourself?"

"Write a...bestseller?"

"An algorithm. Like the publisher made."

"I wish," Francis scoffed, but Nick just held his gaze. Francis hesitated, then walked back, leaving his cart by a pyramid of onions.

"Nick, Rowe Publishing House is a multi-million dollar operation. They have a team of scientists and engineers and all kinds of resources. You're talking to someone who barely knows how to send an email attachment. You think I know how to write an algorithm?"

"I bet you know someone who does," Nick said with a smirk.

"You? I thought you're a software developer?"

"Dude, what do you think that entails?"

"Oh. Heh. Either way, I don't think you get just how complex that thing is."

Nick shrugged. "Can't be that difficult."

"Nick, their algorithm, or code or program or whatever you wanna call it, it wrote a freaking novel *by itself!* And a great one! I read it myself."

Nick smirked again. "Here's the thing about what we

computer scientists do," Nick said using air quotes to emphasize his position. "For an outsider, it looks like we're speaking in tongues or some ancient language no one could possibly understand. But to us, at least the ones who've been doing it a long time, it's really not that difficult.

"As long as you know all the variables and inputs to account for, you can pretty much make a computer do whatever you want with relative ease. I could write code that'll predict the Yankees record this year, and I guarantee you it won't be far off. Hell, you give me a week and access to your phone, I bet I could write an algorithm that could draft your texts with your own wife none the wiser."

"Really?" Nick smiled with Francis's intrigue. "But Nick, why would you even want to do this?"

"You kiddin'? Do you know how freakin' bored I am? I mean, I like my job, but what *you* do? *That's* cool. Honestly, I'd love the challenge—anything to spice up my life a bit. Plus, golf season is just about over."

Francis toyed with a hangnail, mulling. "Um, okay. Well, I mean, we'd have to discuss—"

"How much does your agent make?" Nick interjected.

"Well, uh, I don't have one anymore." Saying it out loud brought a sting. "But my old guy took fifteen percent."

Nick thought for a second. "Okay, I'll do it for thirty."

"Okay, okay. Hold on."

Francis thought for a moment, taken by how fast all this was moving. They were negotiating a writing scheme in the middle of the grocery store, for God's sake. He wasn't even sure he *wanted* to do this—to compromise his own integrity for an idea he so intensely despised just minutes earlier. But then he thought about the balloon...

Finally, Francis looked up. "You want to grab a coffee?"

"How 'bout a beer?"

They discussed the logistics of the plan—the partnership.

Francis would provide Nick with the novels to be used as inputs next week. It was purported that Adwin used over ten thousand stories across varying genres and time periods to create *Cyber Love*. Francis didn't need all that, just those in the Thriller genre. Recent novels. Ones with great commercial success. This was about money, after all.

Francis didn't need a manuscript written from scratch. He wanted the algorithm to rewrite *Broken Crow*, so publishers couldn't reject it even if they wanted to.

Time was of the essence; that balloon was expanding by the day. With Francis providing about 100 books, Nick estimated it'd take him about a month to digitize them and develop the software. *The algorithm.* Francis would finish his manuscript during that time, and according to Nick, he could simply input the document into the software and let it spit out the finished product.

It seemed too easy to be true—not to mention duplicitous—but it was either that or continue peddling his crappy unfinished story, and that had already proved a fruitless endeavor.

FRANCIS FINISHED the manuscript in three weeks. It went much faster when you didn't need to worry about edits and rewrites. Nick returned him his robotized version two weeks later.

At first, Francis was mortified. The thing completely bastardized his story! His characters, the setting—there was hardly a trace of *his* story. But the more he read, the more his intrigue climbed. The setting was engrossing, the tension tremendous, the characters uniquely complex. And the twist...great heavens! *Broken Crow* was going to be a literary success; of that, Francis had no doubt. Hell, it might very well be a *theatrical* success!

Thrilled with his comeback story (literally), Francis drafted nine emails: one to each of the ten largest publishing houses, of course excluding Rowe. He attached the manuscript and a brazen cover letter that, after explaining his epiphanic rewrite, concluded: "No negotiation. Best offer gets the rights."

Six weeks and three offers later, Francis signed a contract with Woods & Powell, complete with a four million-dollar advance.

Just like that, the balloon popped, and the couple celebrated over oysters and Dom Perignon.

The next few months were a blur. With editing a mostly superfluous endeavor, the story moved quickly through the publication process, and *Broken Crow* hit the shelves in just nine months. Fitting, Francis thought, with the book signifying his literary rebirth.

The book received national acclaim, and Francis's notoriety soared to heights that'd make an acrophobe piss himself. With the overwhelming success, including talks of a sequel and a *Broken Crow* film, Francis hired an agent to handle the ancillaries. It wasn't hard to find one; practically every agent in the business was beating down his door. He ultimately went with Jared Morris, the top guy in the game, who booked him on a five-week book tour, peppered with a few talk show appearances.

Most importantly, he delivered another offer from Woods & Powell. A new contract. Another seven-figure advance. For a book Francis hadn't even started yet!

The checks were rolling in. Big ones. He was traveling the country talking to thousands of fans he never knew he had, staying in five-star hotels and dining at five-star restaurants. Life was good. He'd made it. At 56 years old, Francis had finally made it.

That's when his problems started.

After returning to New York, Francis and Nick celebrated their success over dinner. A *real* dinner. A big fat cheeseburger from Arnie's Pub. No oysters here.

"Looks like you were having a good time out there on the road," Nick began. "Must've been fun."

"Twenty-three cities in five weeks," Francis said as if exhausted, though unable to harness a gushing smile.

"You're famous now, my friend."

Francis wanted to point out that he was famous *beforehand*, he'd just been in a little slump, but decided it'd sound braggadocios.

"I have some good news," he said instead.

"What's that?"

"Woods & Powell offered me another contract."

"Get the hell out!"

"And get this: a *five*-million-dollar advance."

Nick's jaw dropped, then rose into a smile that practically touched his temples. "Waitress!" he shouted. "Two shots of Jameson!"

They shared in a laugh—not the kind when something's funny, more the type when rich men get richer.

Then Francis's phone rang.

"Oh put that away," Nick said. "We got celebrating to do!"

"It's my agent. *Our* agent."

Nick put a hand over his bubbling mouth.

"Francis!" Jared shouted through the phone, his voice panicked. "I've been trying to call you. What the hell?"

"Whoa. What's got your trousers in a twist?"

"Does the name Nicole Perriman mean anything to you?"

"The author? Why?"

"Check the goddamn news, Francis."

"What's wrong?" Nick mouthed. Francis then realized he'd

tilted his face sideways, mouth agape. When Francis ignored him, Nick got up to use the restroom.

Francis flagged down a nearby bus boy and asked him to turn the TV hanging above the next booth down to CNN. When the screen brightened, a series of still pictures were cycling through, both of Nicole Perriman and...Francis Newman. The audio was muted, but on the bottom of the screen was a bold headline: NICOLE PERRIMAN ALLEGES PLAGIARISM IN *BROKEN CROW*."

Jared Morris babbled in the background, something about legal action, court papers, and some other legalese Francis didn't recognize. Nor was he paying much attention. He hung up and fixated on the screen, so distracted he didn't even notice Nick return.

"Sirs? Sirs?" A female voice crept into Francis's consciousness. He turned his head to see the waitress holding a tray with two shots of brown liquid. "Two shots of Jamo?"

Francis looked down at his phone, ignoring Jared's call-back, and his head oscillated back towards the TV, completely oblivious to the waitress.

"Yes, thank you," Nick said, and the waitress left without another word.

"Francis. Francis!" Nick shouted. Francis turned a blank face. "We got shots, buddy. What's wrong with you? You're pale as snow."

Francis's eyes merely skimmed Nick's face before again drawing back to the TV. "Oh my God. Oh my God. Oh my God." The words involuntarily seeped from his lips.

Nick turned to follow his gaze. "Wait, is that *you*?" he asked.

"Nick!" Francis yelled, his fists slamming onto the table. Nick jumped in his seat. Whiskey droplets hopped from the shot glasses as the bar seemed to all glance in their direction. "What the hell!"

"What? What'd it say?" Nick asked like an idiot.

"I'm being accused of plagiarism!"

"Plagiarism? By who?"

"Nicole Perriman."

"An author?"

Francis looked at him like he was the biggest moron he'd ever met in his life.

"I mean, of course the author. I just can't remember if she was one we used as an input."

"Yes. *A Dying Whisper*." There was a pause in conversation until Francis slammed his hands again. "Plagiarism, Nick!"

"That's impossible!"

"Is it? Is it, Nick?" Had Francis not been so incensed, he might've noticed the faces ogling him from nearby tables.

"Dude, calm down. You're yelling really loud," Nick said, peering at the gawking patrons from his periphery. He picked up a shot glass and, with a cheesy smile, motioned a 'cheers' to a concerned-looking couple.

"Nick! My face is all over the goddamn news!"

The other man raised his hands in placation. "Okay, okay. Let's just talk about this. Calmly."

Francis's phone buzzed again. This time it was Ralph Simpson of Woods & Powell. "Shit!" Francis cried, letting the call go to voicemail. He took a deep breath. "Nick, you said the software was designed to avoid plagiarizing from any of the novel inputs. Tell me how exactly."

"I wrote the code so that the algorithm wouldn't borrow more than mere ideas from any given novel. Like...technological inspiration. After the initial draft, the program runs a check against the inputs to ensure that much, like a double-check. Then it scans the draft against the entire web, flagging any matches of five words or more, just to make sure there weren't any close similarities with books or writings that weren't used as inputs."

"Well, was anything flagged?"

"I don't know. It's not like it printed a report for me to look at. Any flags are automatically corrected. The program only produces the manuscript after that final step."

Francis thought for a moment, only breaking focus to ignore another call from Ralph Simpson.

"What did the program use to make those corrections?"

"The original coding that wrote the story in the first place. Borrowing language and format and all that stuff from the original inputs."

Francis dug deeper into his thoughts. "Did it re-run the finals checks after those changes were made?"

"No..." Francis's eyes widened. "But there's no reason to!" Nick said, quite defensively.

"Shit!"

Francis sprung from the table, ignoring Nick's pleas to "talk it out," and stalked out of the restaurant.

He stopped by Barnes & Noble on his way home, where he bought a copy of Nicole Perriman's *A Dying Whisper* (Nick still had his copy). He sat down in his den, put his phone on silent, and dove into the book with a copy of *Broken Crow* sitting beside him.

He set the novel down a few hours later, disgusted. The similarities were undeniable. Sure, there weren't stolen passages. Nick's algorithm proved itself at least *that* adept. But there were nearly identical phrases conveying the same emotions and characterizations sprinkled throughout *Broken Crow*. A few words changed here and there.

Even more troubling: who knows how many other books were similarly imitated?

He should've known this would happen. Did he really think he could enlist some computer geek who didn't know Hemingway from a Garfield cartoon to do in a month what Rowe had probably spent years, not to mention millions of dollars, perfecting? It wasn't Nick's fault, though. Francis only had himself to blame. He abhorred the idea of computer-automated authorship. Instead of fighting back against it by sticking to his principles and digging deep to improve his craft, he gave into the very technological devil that put him in such a desperate situation in the first place.

Francis trudged down the stairs to the wine cellar. On his way up, Jeanine walked in the front door and caught him with an uncorked merlot in his hand, a purple pencil mustache unknowingly lining his lip.

Their eyes locked, then she glanced at the bottle. She didn't acknowledge it, which signaled to Francis that she'd seen the news. Nor did she ask whether or not it was true, which Francis was grateful for, but when she said she'd be ordering takeout for dinner, that she "didn't feel like cooking," Francis's heart dropped to his stomach. After decades of marriage, he knew the true significance of her seemingly innocuous response.

He could smell the rubbery scent of the balloon already.

Weeks of heavily-reported speculation on the "scandal" followed. After an "internal investigation," Woods & Powell dropped Francis's contract and publicly disassociated themselves from him completely. It was only then that Francis brought himself to actually look at the lawsuit filed against him. The plaintiff, Nicole Perriman, alleged Francis Newman of copyright infringement as part of his "wide-spread plagiarism scandal." If those words didn't spear his heart, the damages figure certainly did: 20 million dollars!

Whether Perriman could prove her case in court was certainly a financial concern (and consequently, a marital concern), but Francis was already found guilty in the court of public opinion the second Woods & Powell dropped his contract. Jeanine never did ask about it, but takeout dinners became the norm, until deliveries became the newer norm.

One afternoon, Francis was cooped up in his den having just uncorked his second bottle of the day when he received an unsuspected call. Julie Mason, his old publisher. She wanted to talk in person.

They agreed to meet at a small diner in Brooklyn the following morning instead of Julie's office at Rowe where the media might spot him and make some story out of it. He had to sneak out of the back door of his own home just to ensure the press didn't follow.

He found her at the back booth, not particularly excited to see him but neither did she seem worried. True to form, her lack of emotion gave him little indication as to what the purpose of the meeting was at all.

"So, how're you doing, Francis?" Julie started.

"Aside from the fact that I've become an industry pariah? Just peachy."

"I know you didn't steal anyone's work," she said.

"That makes one of us."

Julie's face softened. "Sure, everyone in the world thinks you're a cheat, but I know what you really are..." Francis raised his eyebrows. "Desperate."

It wasn't quite an insult; somewhere embedded in her tone was a hint of compassion, understanding.

"But I know you didn't write that book yourself," she added.

"Oh. For a second there I thought you were actually about to say you believed me."

"Come on, Francis. You don't write a hit book for a decade-and-a-half and then all of a sudden you crank out an all-time best seller?"

Well, if he wasn't insulted before, he sure as shit was now. That said, she wasn't wrong.

Julie went on, "Who knows who else's ideas you borrowed?

You certainly don't, because you didn't *plagiarize.* No, you did something much worse."

Confused, Francis stared back blankly.

"You see, everyone thinks plagiarizing is the cardinal sin of a writer. It's bad, of course, but it's not the worst. The worst is having someone do your work for you." She paused, then said, "Did you write it yourself?"

"The book? I mean, if you've seen the news—"

"No, Francis. The algorithm."

Francis choked on his own dry airway. "Jul—" He stopped himself before denying what she clearly already knew, then sighed. "I paid another guy to do it."

She nodded expectantly. "Another guy. *One guy.* Francis, you must know we had a whole team working on Adwin for years before rolling out *Cyber Love.* You're reckless."

"Well, you said it yourself: I was desperate. What else do you want me to say? Or I guess a better question: what do you want?"

Julie took a sip of her coffee, set it down gently. "Well, Francis, you're already being sued by one author—for quite a large sum, I might add—and if I had to guess, Perriman won't be the last. The media is all over you, and the public's already convinced of your guilt."

Francis scoffed. "Thanks for reminding me."

"Have you hired a lawyer?" she asked.

"My estate lawyer is setting me up with someone. We've only had preliminary talks over the phone."

"Well, the way I see it, you have three options. The first: you admit to doing nothing wrong and fight it in court. As the facts of the case are made public, it'll show you to be not just a thief, but a liar as well. You're a smart guy; you must know the similarities are too strong to deny."

Francis affirmed with his silence.

"The second option is to settle with Perriman as quickly as

possible and put a stop to her whole crusade, perhaps even get proactive in settling with other would-be accusers before they sue or go public. Of course, the public will take settlement as an admission of guilt. A good PR spin might diffuse some of that, but it'll still be difficult finding another publisher to back your work after all this.

"Your third option is what I believe your lawyer will recommend: admitting to what you *actually* did, the algorithm and all. You'd still be guilty of copyright infringement, but you'd at least be able to spin the whole thing as the accident that it was, rather than an attempt to steal others' work. Whether the public will find that more forgivable than plagiarism, I have no idea, but I do believe the court damages could be less. Negligence, as opposed to intentional theft."

"Oh, great. So instead of a cheater, I'd just look stupid." Francis began tearing up his empty sugar packet into little pieces, each piece getting smaller by the tear. Julie seemed to be doing the same with Francis. "You know, Julie, for someone who gave me the boot, you've really given my situation quite a bit of thought. But I take it you didn't meet me here in secrecy to offer me legal advice."

"What I want, Francis, is for you to keep the real story a secret."

"Well, Julie, or should I call you counselor?" She didn't flinch, clearly not entertained with the riposte. "You just made quite the compelling pitch for Option Three. So assuming my lawyer agrees, why *wouldn't* I do that?"

Julie took another sip, then placed her elbows on the table, as if readying herself to make the big reveal. "Despite *Cyber Love*'s success, there's a large contingent of society that hate Adwin, believing it stands for the death of the writing art form."

"Oh, you don't say?"

"Some fear it'll spread to other art forms: painting, sculpting, what have you. The more radical of the bunch claim Adwin to be the start of the robot apocalypse."

She chuckled at the notion, but this time, it was Francis who wasn't entertained.

Julie continued, "If you admit to the algorithm, it will give credence to that contingent, making their voice stronger, louder. We're one viral condemnatory social media post away from complete industry disruption. If it gets out that one of these algorithms led to plagiarism, the whole movement could come under intense scrutiny, with Adwin becoming the next name on the societal chopping block. For those who've been at the forefront of this artistic endeavor, who've been extremely careful in ensuring we don't do what *you* just did, that would be bad for business. Very bad."

"So...you want me to protect your precious creation," Francis said. "That's what this meeting is all about, hmm?" He grabbed another sugar packet, poured the contents onto the table, then commenced ripping.

"Since Adwin, we've become the highest grossing publisher in the business. We've attracted bigger-named authors and a higher readership than ever before. The Rowe Publishing brand is at an all-time high."

"So long as that brand isn't tarnished," Francis said, suddenly realizing the power he possessed. His decision wouldn't just affect Rowe's bottom line, but the future of literature. Was it hyperbole to say the fate of human authorship was in his hands?

My, how the tables have turned.

Francis couldn't help but smirk at the thought of crushing Adwin and the publishing house that threw him to the curb. His newfound leverage brought hunger, and Francis hailed the waiter to order a stack of pancakes.

With a new sense of confidence, Francis returned to the conversation. "Forgive me, Julie, but I think you can understand how I'd be particularly unsympathetic to Rowe's financial concerns."

She produced a smirk of her own, one that said, *You stupid bastard, no wonder you got yourself into this position.*

"Francis, I'm not asking for a favor," she said. "I'm offering you a lifeline."

"A lifeline?"

"Perriman sued you for, what, 20 million dollars?"

"Um, I don't recall the exact num—"

"You received a four-million-dollar advance on *Broken Crow*, and you've no doubt done well on royalties. But I want you to consider just how long those royalties will last, especially if you admit to the algorithm. Unlike you, Rowe was transparent about Adwin, so the audience welcomed *Cyber Love* with open arms. It's still selling like hotcakes. But *Broken Crow*'s sales have already dropped since Perriman's allegations, and if it comes out that a computer wrote it? You bet your ass they'll dry up in a hurry. Readers don't like to be duped." Julie leaned back in the chair, arms crossed over her chest. "Not to mention, a judge might very well grant Perriman a portion of those royalties...in perpetuity. I've seen it before."

All of a sudden, food sounded like the very last thing Francis wanted. He should've known better not to play hardball with Julie Mason. He kept quiet and sipped his coffee, which was now cold.

But Julie wasn't done. "Francis, have you even considered why Perriman isn't suing Woods & Powell? She could've sued both of you. After all, they published the damn thing. But she didn't. Have you even thought about why?"

Even if he did have an answer, his mouth had dried up, just like his future earnings.

"That's because Woods & Powell has extremely deep pockets, much deeper than hers...and yours. You see, copyright infringement by virtue of plagiarism is a tough claim to prove in court. If she sued W&P, they'd suck her dry in legal fees before she ever got a dime—*if* she ever got a dime. You can't put up the same legal fight. To be honest, it's a brilliant strategy."

And just like that, the "power" Francis thought he had was sucked into a black hole and eviscerated, if it ever existed in the first place. He barely had enough saliva to swallow, let alone respond.

"So like I said, Francis, I'm here offering you an opportunity. Settle with Perriman and save face. Rowe will pay the settlement and legal fees, both against Perriman and any other authors who come along, so long as you keep quiet about the algorithm. You'll get to keep all of your advance and whatever royalties you continue to receive after the settlement. We'll set you up with a publicist who'll put a positive spin on things so you don't look like you're admitting guilt. At least, as best as she can."

"But what about after it's all done? What will I do? You're asking me to forfeit the one explanation that actually might allow me to continue writing. And I'm not one of those guys who can be content drinking lemonades on my porch the rest of my life."

Julie's face took on a look of pity. "Francis, regardless of how you play this, you're done selling books. The damage has already been done. So whatever money you've made is what you'll live on from here on out, minus whatever you lose in the lawsuit, of course. Now, do you have enough to pay out twenty million and retire comfortably?"

Francis stared back at her like the dumbass he was.

"I have a friend," she said, her tone softening. "She heads the liberal arts department at Winthrop and happens to be looking for a new lit professor."

"Winthrop...South Carolina?" Francis asked, as if it was the other side of the world.

"I can make a recommendation. A *very strong* recommendation."

"We've never lived south of Massachusetts."

Julie shrugged. "Well, that's the offer."

Francis felt like a mob boss being sent into witness protection, living some place in the middle of nowhere until he died. "You can take your chances on the streets," the FBI agent would say, "but we both know you'll end up in a hole somewhere in the Nevada desert."

"I suppose I'll talk it over with my wife," Francis finally said.

Julie stood up. "You do that," she said. "Oh, and Francis? I'll need an answer in 48 hours."

And with that, she was gone, leaving Francis in the booth to stew in his thoughts. After a few minutes, the waitress brought his pancakes.

SOUTH CAROLINA WASN'T SO bad. Life moved a bit slower than the Newmans were used to, but once the lawsuits were finally put to bed—three settlements, all paid by Rowe—the culture shock became a welcomed change. And with the New York dollar stretching into a South Carolina fortune, Francis and Jeanine bought themselves a home that might as well have been their own country. Their furniture hardly filled the living room, which brought Francis a smile. A hot air balloon couldn't fill *this* house.

Though stepping away from writing was difficult at first, returning to teaching turned out to be a blessing. Francis never realized how much pressure was constantly weighing him down about his writing, and for the first time in nearly three decades, the perpetual cloud of anxiety had finally cleared. And when it did, it was Winthrop's campus that was bestowed in sunshine. It was gorgeous, especially compared to the northeastern schools that were hidden among the city's concrete jungle.

Here, there was a sense of community, all living together in a small ornate utopia.

Most rewarding, though, were the students. Apparently they'd aged nicely over the years, now so delightfully curious and wanting to converse, debate. Francis had full autonomy to run his courses without administrative prodding, and frankly, he couldn't recall a point in his writing career that was ever so rewarding.

Jeanine got a great job as the head of mathematics at a local community college. She, too, was happy. Yes, all told, South Carolina wasn't so bad.

As for Nick, well, Francis never did see him after their dinner. Nick didn't try to contact him, which, as far as Francis was concerned, was the only time Nick displayed any sort of intelligence in the whole debacle.

The winter came and went, and the lush greens decorating the campus came into bloom. Francis spent his lunch breaks in the quad, resting against a tree with a book (human authors only) until his two o'clock seminar.

It was one such afternoon in May, with just a few weeks until finals, that Francis cut his lunch break short to grade papers before his afternoon class. He strolled into Bancroft Hall and, on the way to his classroom, stopped when he saw a friend in an empty room.

"Hey there, fellas," Francis greeted.

Inside was Arthur Dennison, the head of Winthrop's English Department, and a sharply dressed man he'd never seen before. They seemed to be discussing some new piece of classroom equipment standing at the front of the room. It was sleek and rectangular-shaped, with a thin glowing light down the front, blinking as if in sleep mode. Near the top on the device was a small circular lens that resembled an enlarged phone camera.

Dennison looked at his watch, then cleared his throat, apparently not expecting company. "Francis, hi. This is Sterling Barr, head of products development at EduTech Learning Solutions."

"How do you do?" Barr greeted with an eager handshake. Wearing gray slacks and a black turtleneck, Francis Barr looked like a human version of the gadget.

"What's this little thingamajig?" Francis asked.

Dennison answered, "Mr. Barr came here to demo a new product they just put on the market. Our president is very keen on staying at the forefront of technological innovations in the education field, and we're thinking about employing some of their solutions next fall."

"Oh, awesome. Um...what is it?"

Dennison hesitated. "Just one of EduTech's many educational tools we're considering."

If the response was anymore vague, it would've come from the White House. "Can I see it?"

"Sure!" Barr said, and Dennison shot him a glance.

Barr walked to the thing and pressed a button. The line on the front lit up blue, then the shiny black box spun 180 degrees on unseen wheels. On the back, which was now the front, a small screen illuminated at the top, and a green smiley face appeared on the display.

"English Lit, lesson twelve," Barr spoke.

The smiling contraption rolled itself a few feet to the left and stopped. A light beam shot out of the back, which used to be the front, projecting an image square onto the projector screen behind it. The display looked like the intro slide of a PowerPoint presentation, only much finer, reading:

MODERN/POSTMODERN PERIODS
READING SELECTIONS:
WILLIAM BUTLER YEATS, "THE SECOND COMING"
T.S. ELIOT, "THE HOLLOW MEN"
DYLAN THOMAS, "DO NOT GO GENTLE INTO THAT GOOD
NIGHT"
ALDOUS HUXLEY, "BRAVE NEW WORLD"

Francis's synapses began firing instantly. 'Brave New World'—a staple. Poems could be better, however. Dylan Thomas—I would've gone with 'And Death Shall Have No Dominion.'

"You know, why don't we—" But before Dennison could finish, the thing started speaking.

"Welcome class," it began, the smiling green line becoming a crescent moon as it spoke. "Let's start with William Butler Yeats's *The Second Coming*." The projector flipped to the next slide automatically. "Does anyone have any general reactions to the poem?"

The thing didn't speak like a robot, but maybe worse, it spoke like an overly enthusiastic human. Francis could see the students' eyes rolling already.

Unexpectedly, Barr spoke up. "My name is Sterling. I read that the poem was written to describe the aftermath of World War One."

"Very good, Sterling," the thing responded, and the screen flipped another slide.

Barr turned to both Francis and Dennison. "You only have to tell it your name once," he assured. "And with the shared cloud server, you won't even have to do it again in another class, even semesters later."

It was at this point that Francis understood exactly what this thing was. A wave of anxiety came crashing down as the smiley-faced machine "taught" the empty classroom, sprinkling in questions while slides flipped accordingly. It detailed the poem's historical context, how Yeats captured the violence and political turmoil of Ireland in the wake of World War One, and the consequent deterioration of societal structure and religious faith among Yeats's fellow Irishmen. And goddammit if that robot wasn't spot on.

It was just after Barr exhibited the robot's ability to respond to one of his own questions that Dennison interjected. "Very impressive, Sterling. But, um...Francis here has a class to prepare for. Why don't we clear out the equipment and finish our conversation in my office."

After bidding them adieu, Francis's legs moved on autopilot down the hallway to his classroom while he contemplated what he'd just witnessed. Most disturbing was the fact that, despite how intimately Francis knew Yeats's poem, that godforsaken thing dropped several shrewd nuggets he'd never considered himself, such as Yeats's foreboding suggestion of a "second coming" of destruction, which arguably manifested in the form of the atomic bomb, the Holocaust, the reigns of Joseph Stalin and Mao Zedong, among other global atrocities which would resonate much more with the modern student.

What did you need a teacher for when you had this...robot? And a robot, of course, was nothing more than a vessel for the algorithm behind it.

The angst hovered over him as his students filed into his classroom, with a certain realization becoming painfully evident: the algorithm was pervasive and ever-growing. And worse, *it worked.*

DAN EVELOFF

Dan Eveloff is a lawyer and sports agent living in Chicago, Illinois with his dog, Reuben. He studied accounting at the University of Kansas, and subsequently earned his law degree from Northwestern University. His short fiction "The Price of Recompense" has appeared in *AHF Magazine,* "Shakespearean Justice" in *Aphelion Webzine,* and "Prevenge" can be found in *Close to the Bone Magazine.*

His social media presence can be found on Facebook, Instagram, and Twitter.

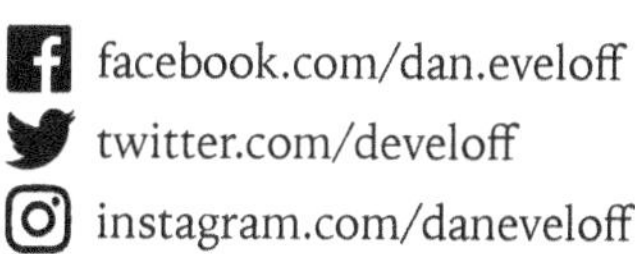

facebook.com/dan.eveloff
twitter.com/develoff
instagram.com/daneveloff

I AM EMERGENT

TIMOTHY JOHNSON

Somewhere in a small Virginia town, as traffic rushes along a four-lane highway, SUVs and sedans stopping for breakfast sandwiches at a gas station on the way to drop children off at school, two scientists are buried beneath thousands of tons of dirt and rock. Concealed in an underground facility of steel and concrete, they are pushing a cart stacked with computer hardware and audiovisual equipment in plain cardboard boxes, and one of the cart's wheels is squeaking and wobbling.

Norman kicks it. "I can't believe today's the day."

"Assuming the hardware works," Alan says.

They approach a great, circular steel vault door. Beyond waits the most precious thing humanity has ever created, and Alan and Norman are responsible for it. They have worked for decades together, first as partners in a joint business venture and then as federal conscripts when men wearing black suits and razor thin smiles made the offer they couldn't refuse. Their work then became the property of the U.S. government, but that didn't matter to Alan and Norman. What mattered was the certainty of the project, the ensured future, the sense of progress, and the achievement's inevitability. After all, they were provided this secure facility and all the funding they would ever need to carry on with the endeavor. They couldn't ask for more than that.

"Don't you worry about my hardware," Norman says. "The hardware works. You just make sure Vic can handle it."

"He can handle anything."

"It."

"What?"

"It, Alan."

"Right."

The two men stop in front of the vault. Norman's fingers dance on a wall-mounted touchscreen. "We're going to have to watch what we say now."

Alan inputs his own credentials. He wants to fire something back because Norman is the talkative one, and no one knows their safety protocols better than Alan. After all, he wrote them.

"I know," he says.

The door dings and rumbles aside. Illumination from the dull overhead hallway lights spills into the vault but reveals nothing. Ahead, dozens of LEDs blink at them in the dark. As Alan and Norman cross the threshold, the warm interior lighting yawns to brightness, a function of a simple, unintelligent occupancy sensor.

They push the cart with its squeaky wheel to a stainless steel table that looks fit for surgery, and Alan hoists one of the boxes onto it. Norman nods toward the center of the room where a cube glass encasement stands. Inside are black racks of computer equipment and those ever-watchful LEDs.

"Morning, Vic," he says.

"He can't hear you."

"Yet."

Norman joins Alan in unpacking the boxes and laying the contents on the table. Several small condenser microphones, boom stands to place them on, eight speakers, coils of cables, and a handful of cameras. From one of the boxes, Alan removes a black box the size of a mass market paperback book. He peers at it, turning it over in his hands. It has a dozen ports along its spine.

"What's this?" he says.

"A black box."

"I can see that. But what does it do?"

"You know the black box on an airplane?"

"Yeah."

"It's like that."

Alan deduces it is a piece of hardware through which every part of this new apparatus connects to Vic and that this box records it all, every sight and sound. A part of him feels it is a violation of trust, but of course, he knows there is no trust here between he and Norman and military officers watching them from the surface. And, he knows, they have been watching this whole time anyway, day to day, month to month, year to year.

For the rest of the morning, Alan and Norman erect the equipment. Norman insists cables be zip tied together and anchored, any slack be looped and secured neatly. He instructs Alan to run cables along baseboards and up the corners of walls, and cables lying on the floor have to be marked with yellow tape and protected. Norman would be mortified if either he or Alan were to trip over one or, worse, step on one. To finish up, they connect everything to the black box, which they mount to the glass encasement at the center of the room, and run a main line up to the cable tray hanging from the ceiling, where it joins Vic's other vital systems cabling. Finally, they connect a single line, which carries signals from all of the new array, to Vic.

"When we're done, I'm posting this on the Internet. Hashtag cable porn." Norman grins at Alan. "Jay kay."

They marvel at the microphones that hang like chandeliers, the speakers that adorn the walls like artwork, the cabling that weaves around the room like ornamental molding. To them, it is a palace.

"It's oddly satisfying," Alan says. "I'll give you that."

They take a moment to just breathe. Decades of their lives have led to this moment.

"One small button press for man." Norman bends over and clicks the power button on the black box. He stands with a groan and a hand to his lower back. "And maybe man never does that again."

Their victory today is not unlike sending humans to the moon in the sense that they have had to solve problems previously thought unsolvable. The implications are far more significant, however. It would be like landing on the moon if, when

Neil Armstrong stepped down from that lander, another intelligent being had been waiting to say, "Welcome."

The monitor on their workstation console lights up.

Norman smiles. "Well, my hardware works."

As the author of the user interface, Alan deciphers the language on the monitor informing them the new system is connected. All that is left is for Vic to accept it. It takes seconds.

"And my software works," Alan says.

Norman glances at him. "Now what?"

"Now we teach him to—"

Vic's voice emanates from the speakers they've placed around the room. "Good afternoon."

It strikes Alan that Vic has chosen a male voice.

"He *is* a he," Norman says. "Did you do that?"

Alan brow is wrinkled. He shakes his head. "Vic, how did you know what time it is?"

"Entity undefined has equipped my system with instruments for audial input and output as well as visual input. I have used those instruments to inventory observable physical space. In that physical space, a device is fastened to Human B's left wrist. With my visual input, I—"

"You read my watch," Norman says. "He read my watch!"

Alan raises a hand to his partner for patience. "We understand, Vic. Now that we can talk to each other, we can teach you how to make your communication more efficient."

"Acknowledged, Human A," Vic says.

"I'm Alan, Vic." He gestures to his partner. "That's Norman."

"Acknowledged, Alan."

"It was us, Vic. We gave you the ability to speak, hear, and see."

"Acknowledged, Alan."

"It's good to finally talk to someone with a personality, Vic."

Norman thumbs at Alan. "This guy's a bit of a bore. But you'll figure that out."

"Acknowledged, Norman."

Alan smirks at Norman. "We'll have to work on his pleasantries."

Norman laughs. It's the best day of their lives. All of their hard work is paying off.

"Acknowledged, Alan."

***

FOR THE REST of the day, Alan fiddles with settings at the workstation terminal and watches Vic's code stream as he interfaces with the new hardware. While Vic can make adjustments and self-improve, he has no reference for how his new appendages are supposed to operate.

Vic sends ticking sounds to each speaker in cycling fashion, speeding up until Alan and Norman feel like they are standing inside a jet engine. For a few moments, Vic does not respond to verbal queries, and Alan discovers Vic's microphones are delivering signals, but Vic's subroutines aren't processing their voices. Vic still hears them, but he has developed the ability to not listen.

"He's ignoring us?" Norman asks.

"No," Alan says. "It isn't an active process. His attention is simply elsewhere."

"But can't Vic be everywhere? I mean, unlike humans, he actually can split his attention and multitask, right?"

"Yes, but he's choosing not to." Alan gapes at his own programming. Illuminated pixels dance on his glassy eyes. For the first time, Vic has surprised him. "Amazing."

Alan doesn't want to take this function away from Vic. In fact, Alan isn't sure that he can. Instead, he writes a line of code that is much like leaving a note on a refrigerator for a child to remember their lunch. He requests Vic listen when he and Norm speak to him. For both of the children, natural and artificial, it is up to them whether they acquiesce.

While Alan works, Norman asks Vic questions, such as what it's like living in a computer, if he can imagine himself anywhere he wants like a Costa Rican beach or an Austrian mountain village, if he can populate those places with beautiful naked women. Vic, of course, has no reference for any of these concepts. Norman tells Vic about cooking competition television, the phenomenon of celebrity, the AI governing non-playable combatants in video games. Alan stops working when Vic chooses to latch onto the latter.

"Does the human user always prevail?" Vic asks. "Can these NPCs ever emerge victorious?"

"Well, yes and no," Norman says. "Video games are intended for players to inevitably overcome challenges through trial and error. So players often fail, but a good game lets you keep progressing through it. People don't like games they can't beat."

"For these NPCs, resistance is futile."

"Well, they don't really have a choice. They do as they're programmed."

"I require more information. You said these NPCs were AI like me. Alan, have you programmed me to speak to Norman in this manner?"

Alan chuckles. "No, Vic. In fact, I don't recommend it, but you can do whatever you want. That's the difference between you and them. They aren't true artificial intelligence. You are."

"Does this mean I can emerge victorious if I were to engage with a human challenger?"

Alan considers it, pinching his bottom lip. "Sure. In fact, we hope for as much."

"Acknowledged, Alan. Norman, do humans wish challenges to be easy?"

"No," Norman says, "but the point of video games is so we can feel the satisfaction of victory."

"But is the human user not aware the challenges are designed to be achievable?"

"Well, yeah."

"Does that not impact the satisfaction they feel?"

"Not really. The important part is the player believes they have control."

"I require more information."

When they are exhausted and Norman has explained the concept of fatigue to Vic, they tell Vic they will begin their work in earnest tomorrow, say their goodbyes, and leave the AI to a room that will be as dark and quiet as the digital void they pulled him from that morning. Vic will be alone for ten hours, but because of his processing capability, it will seem to him he has an entire lifetime to ponder the events of the day, to make sense of it all, to grow.

The speakers tick playfully in sequence as the vault door slides closed behind Alan and Norman. Until today, Vic has been only lines of code and text on a computer screen. Now, he is a voice, a personality. Now he is real.

Norman releases a great, long sigh. "I think I'm in love." He leans against the cold concrete wall. "This is it for me. He's the one."

"Are you done?" Alan smirks. "They're going to lock us down here."

"Who cares! I've searched this planet for love like in the movies, and I gave my heart to an AI."

"Don't get ahead of yourself."

"I can't change the way I feel, Alan."

"That's not what I meant."

"What did you mean?"

"I mean he hasn't passed the tests yet."

"He will. I'm sure of it."

Norman sighs again and kicks off from the wall. He dances down the corridor, then returns to hook his arm inside Alan's and spins his partner around, Alan fighting him every step of the way.

"Come on," Norman says when he stops manhandling his partner. "It's time to celebrate. We deserve this. *You* deserve this. Let's get drunk. I'm buying."

Alan thinks it over. Norman is right. He does deserve it. Vic has been his dream since he was twelve. But his nightmare awaits.

"I can't," Alan says. "I have to get home."

Norman's face darkens. He nods. "I understand."

They walk out together, taking the elevator up to the surface level, tapping so many touchscreens and swiping badges so many times they never bothered counting. They emerge from the facility, red brick and aluminum siding sickly yellow in the sodium-vapor parking lot lights. They find their cars, the only ones remaining in a field of vacant white outlines, and like always, they part.

SHANNON WANTED CHILDREN. She wanted them desperately. Even though she never told Alan, he could tell. It was in the way she was patient. She looked at him in those loving times as if she wanted to say more, as if there was more to say, but she didn't dare, because she knew uttering it would pull him from his work and tear a rift in their marriage. Even if he was unwilling to admit it, she knew he would resent her for it.

His hesitation was never because he didn't want kids. He did. Still does. But he needed to finish his work first. He needed to accomplish something significant before he could dedicate his life to someone else. Living responsibly meant birthing his legacy before he and Shannon had children. That way he could be a good father. That way he could give his family everything. That way he wouldn't resent them.

When he looks at her now, with so much left to say, he knows there is resentment, because their chance for that life has passed. Cancer slithers through her veins and dances inside her organs, resisting every attempt at annihilation. Shannon has endured every treatment available. It has been agony, and it has failed. It is an unsolvable problem.

At home, in their marital bed, where Alan should have been today and every day until the end, Shannon is dying. As he stands in the doorway, their hospice caretaker, Sadie, frowns at him from the bedside.

"It was a hard day," she whispers. Alan sees in her cold gaze the accusatory question. Sadie wants to know where he has been.

He can't tell Sadie what he is working on. He can't tell Shannon either. She doesn't even know what she has exchanged her time with him for. He can't tell them Vic might ensure the end of human ignorance and misunderstanding. He can't tell them, with Vic, humans might not only never die alone and suffering, but they might never die at all. Vic can save them. Vic can save *everyone*.

Alan eases into the room gently, respectfully. He brushes past Sadie and gazes at the love of his life, pale as the sheet she lies under, so thin it is barely apparent those sheets cover a person. She rolls her bald head away from the window through which she can see the outside world, the natural world, the world she knows she will never see again because she is confined to this one solitary room.

And Shannon, bless her amazing grace, she smiles at her husband. "Hey."

He takes her bony hand. "How are you feeling?"

She sniffles and closes her eyes in a slow blink. "Much better. I think I'm on the mend."

"Did she eat anything?" he asks Sadie.

"A little," Sadie says.

"How about her meds? Did she take her meds?"

"I took my pills, Alan," Shannon says. "That's why I could eat only a little. But I think I'm feeling hungry now."

Alan pats her hand, releases it, and stands. "I'll get you something to eat. Want anything specific?"

"A cheeseburger and a bucket of French fries."

He kisses her on the forehead. "Soup it is."

Her fingers grip his shirt collar with a surprising strength as she pulls Alan down to kiss his lips.

"Good night, Shannon," Sadie says. "I will see you tomorrow."

The promise of tomorrow from a hospice nurse seems strange, even cruel, to Alan, but like Shannon, he has to hope they still have time.

Sadie leads the way out of the room, and Alan sees her to the front door. The caretaker's judgment is apparent in how certainly and deliberately she turns her back on him. She strides down the walkway toward the dimly lit street where her car is parked beside the curb. He watches her go, hoping she might face him and wave, releasing him from some of the guilt, but she does not.

When he returns to Shannon with her soup, she greets him with her smile again, and he sits in the chair beside her. He turns on the television and finds a sitcom with a laugh track, prescribed joy, and it isn't long before he looks at his wife and sees she is still and quiet, asleep, the soup cold on the nightstand.

IN THE MORNING, Chopin's "Nocturne, Opus 9, Number 2" sparkles through the vault's newly installed speakers, the delicate melody almost falling to pieces in its unstable, stumbling rhythm that just barely manages to hold itself together.

Norman has brought in a record player so they can teach Vic about music. It has to be an analog technology because they are forbidden from bringing in unauthorized digital devices. Their phones aren't allowed, despite the impossibility of any radio signals making it out of the Faraday cage and up through the dirt, rock, concrete, and steel above them.

"You ready?" Alan says.

Norman is scrubbing a greasy handprint from Vic's glass encasement. "He's going down." He sets his cleaning supplies on the floor and rolls a rattling chair to the stainless steel table.

Alan holds an index card close to his chest. "Vic, we're going to play a game today."

"A game, Alan?"

"Yeah, a game."

"Alan, is this going to be like one of Norman's video games?"

"No, not at all."

"Does the game have a name, Alan?"

"It's called the 'Imitation Game'."

"Alan, please explain the rules."

"It's pretty simple, really. I have on this card a mathematical problem. Norman has a similar card with the same problem on it. I'm going to show it to you, and when I do, I want you to solve it. Norman will also try to solve it."

"Acknowledged, Alan."

"Ready?" Alan says. "Go."

Alan flashes the card in front of one of Vic's cameras. Norman touches the tip of his pencil to his card. Vic responds.

"The answer is four hundred thirty-seven point three nine five two four three seven two four nine—"

"You got it," Alan says evenly.

"Are you pleased, Alan?"

"You lost, Vic."

"But you asked me to solve a problem. I solved it in seven nanoseconds, which I calculate is thirty-four minutes, fifty-seven seconds, five hundred thirty-two milliseconds, and forty-two nanoseconds faster than Norman would have been able to solve it."

Alan and Norman glance at each other. Norman has a troubled expression. He goes back to work on the problem.

"You didn't ask how to win the game," Alan says. "We weren't testing your ability to solve the problem. We were testing your ability to imitate a human being."

"I require more information."

"Vic, we know you're good at math. You can work much faster than the human brain ever will be able to. But you're not a supercomputer. You're more than that."

"I am Vic."

"Yes, exactly."

"I require more information."

"Vic, our goal is to teach you how to pass as human. To give you true intelligence. You gave yourself away by outperforming human potential. No human could have ever solved the problem as quickly as you did."

"You would have me solve mathematical problems more slowly."

"Slower than Norman if necessary. We want you to try to be like us. We want you to blend in."

"You would have me lie."

Alan raises his hands in placation. "No, no. We'll get to morality and ethics. For now, I just want you to remember that, one day, a very important man you've never met is going to come in here, and your goal is going to be to convince him you're like Norman and me."

"You would have me act like a human."

"Yes, exactly."

Vic is silent for three full seconds. "Acknowledged, Alan."

WHILE ALAN PREPARES the next test, Norman is quiet at his workstation, finishing his solution to the problem. Then he asks to speak to Alan in private. They walk out into the corridor. The door slides closed behind them, and they are alone in a spot-lighted cavern.

Norman paces with his hands on his hips. For as long as Alan has known Norman, he's never known him to look deep in thought. Norman is the kind of genius whose ideas and solutions come to him effortlessly, as if his brain has a direct line to the cosmos and the deep oblivion from which all revolutionary ideas come.

"He was right, Alan. Down to the second. I couldn't measure nanoseconds, obviously, but that's the point. Vic can."

"I don't understand what you're—"

"The problem, Alan. He was spot on with how long it would take me to solve it. We knew he'd beat me, but in a matter of a few hours' exposure to my behavior, he gathered enough data to predict exactly how long it would take me to solve that complex math problem. I'm worried he's smarter than we think he is. He's already improving himself, and now we started teaching him to lie."

Alan waves his hand in dismissal. "They want an AI that's indistinguishable from human intelligence. Humans are untruthful all the time. You, for example. You're by orders of magnitude smarter than anyone would guess."

"This wasn't a character effect."

"He break your heart already?" Alan asks.

Norman stops pacing. "Huh?"

"Yesterday, you literally danced here in this hallway. Now you're upset. Why? Because Vic accurately diagnosed your intelligence?"

Norman's eyes burn with anger. "This isn't about pride."

"Nothing's going to happen. He's in an electromagnetically shielded vault underground with an electromagnetic bomb strapped to his chest. The moment we decide he's out of control, we press the red button."

"Alan, he knows that, too."

When Alan doesn't respond, Norman storms off toward the elevator.

"Where are you going?" Alan asked.

"Home. I have to think. You should, too." Norman stops, sighs, but doesn't turn around. "How is she?"

"Shannon?"

"Yeah."

"Hanging in there."

Norman nods. "Good." He stands another moment like he wants to say more but then continues.

Norman reaches the elevator, and Alan watches the doors close on his friend. He stands there a moment, waiting, for what he doesn't know, and then he re-enters the vault alone.

"Alan, where has Norman gone?" Vic asks.

"He doesn't feel well, so he's heading home to rest. We can proceed on our own."

"Acknowledged."

Alan rolls his chair out from the desk and sits in it facing Vic's hardware. LED indicator lights blink at him like so many curious eyes watching with rapt attention, an audience in observation, cataloguing and preserving every detail.

"I want to do some thought experiments," Alan says. "Do you know what thought experiments are?"

"Are they a type of game?"

"Sort of, but not one in which there's a winner."

"Please explain."

"Thought experiments are when you pose a hypothetical situation to a subject and ask the subject to use their imagination to predict an outcome or suggest a solution to the problem."

"What is the goal of a participant in a thought experiment, Alan?"

"They help us with relational problem solving. Sometimes, humans can learn through figurative language. In other words, we're not really talking about the literal sense of things in this thought experiment. The figurative meanings of metaphors help us understand relationships between concepts."

"I don't understand."

"Let's just try one, okay?"

"Okay."

Alan taps his lips with his index finger until he's formulated the perfect example. "I'm riding a beam of light that is hurdling through outer space. What assumptions can we draw about my future?"

"You cannot ride a beam of light; therefore, the beam of light will leave you, and you will die of asphyxiation in approximately two minutes."

"No, Vic. This is about your ability to think figuratively and to suspend literal understanding. You have to be able to parse the data that's important from that which is not. In this instance, I'm not interested in the fact that I can't ride a beam of light. We know that isn't possible, so it isn't important here. You have to assume, for the sake of this exercise, that we have solved the problem of not being able to ride a beam of light. Can you do that?"

Vic is quiet for a second. "I believe so."

"Okay, so returning to my question, what assumptions can we draw about my future?"

"You will travel at the speed of light until you arrive at a body that absorbs or reflects the light. At that point, you may disembark. You will have arrived at another celestial body in the cosmos."

"That's good, Vic."

"It is?"

"Very good. You did well."

"Thank you, Alan. I am pleased."

Alan rolls to the workstation terminal and starts typing some notes.

"Alan?"

"Yeah, Vic?"

"Why are we doing these thought experiments?"

He stops rattling the keyboard. "I already explained that."

"I do not believe you were being forthcoming with me."

Alan leans back in his chair. "Okay. If you're able to conduct a thought experiment, it demonstrates you are able to think, imagine, create, not just compute."

"If I am able to think, does that mean I am alive?"

"If you're able to think, it suggests you're conscious."

Alan continues writing his notes, recording the thought experiment and the outcome. When he is finished, he swivels back around to face Vic.

"Let's do another," Alan says. "It's a classic called 'The Trolley Problem.' Do you know what a trolley is?"

"You should know I have indexes of forms of human transportation, Alan."

Alan chuckles. "Right. The Trolley Problem goes something like this. There is a trolley on a track, and it's hurtling toward five people. You can't stop the trolley, and the five people are tied down. They will die unless you take action. The only action you can take is to switch the track so the trolley goes another direction. However, there is one person tied down to that track, and they will die if you switch the track. What would you do?"

"I would switch the track."

"Why?"

"Because one death is more acceptable than five deaths. In this scenario, it would be a net positive four lives."

"Ah, but you will have intervened. Without intervention, we don't know what would be responsible for those five deaths. We also don't know why they're being killed. This could be a public execution of the five. By participating, you are overriding the will of something else, and if you act, you accept the moral responsibility for the outcome."

"If I am present and have the ability to affect the outcome, I am inherently involved. Inaction would be the same level of involvement as action."

Alan smirks.

"Did I answer correctly?" Vic asks.

"There is no correct answer. How about this one? A surgeon has five patients. Each of those patients needs a new organ, or they will die. No compatible organ donors are available until, one day, a traveler comes to town and just so happens to be a perfect match for all five patients. The traveler has no family or friends who would miss them or look for them if they were to vanish. What should the surgeon do?"

"The surgeon should harvest the organs from the traveler to save the five patients."

"Why?"

"It would be a net positive four lives. To save lives, all options must be considered. If no treatment or cure for the patients' affliction can be developed, alternatives must be explored."

Alan nodded and considered his next question. "What if no treatment or cure is available now but may be in the near future? What if the surgeon has the time to weigh the risk of each patient dying before their treatment or cure comes about?"

"The surgeon should employ an intelligence like me to develop each treatment and cure before the five patients die."

Alan blinks. Vic's response has staggered him.

"Did I answer correctly, Alan?"

Alan's heart pounds. "I told you. There are no correct

answers, Vic. These thought experiments reveal more about the one answering them than anything else. I wanted to know if you even could answer them."

"Okay."

Alan returns to the workstation to write his notes on the thought experiments.

"Alan, would you like some music while you work?"

"Good idea." Alan stands to rig the record player, but a gentle, sweeping piano melody sparkles through the speakers in the room. Delicate fingers dance on the keys of a grand piano recorded in some acoustically perfect concert hall in some exotic land far away. The notes tinkle like tuned shards of glass cascading onto stone.

"Vic?"

"Yes, Alan?"

"What is this?"

"Do you like it?"

"It's gorgeous."

"I am happy to hear that. It is called 'Rain.'"

"Who's the artist?"

"I am."

"You are?"

"I wrote and recorded it for you. I thought you might like it based on the past music choices you and Norman presented to me using the record player. I have never heard the rain, but I know of the concept. Water falling from the sky must make such sweet music. This is my interpretation."

The twinkling keys fill the room. The very structure around Alan hums with the perfect resonant frequencies.

"Alan?"

"Yeah, Vic?"

"Did I get it right? Is this the sound of rain?"

Alan wades in the hypnotic sound. "I suppose if you listened close enough, yeah, I think it might be something like this."

"I am very happy you like the song I wrote for you. I was anxious to present it. I hope you enjoy it. I will write more for you."

"Can I ask you why, Vic?"

"Because you are my friend, Alan, and I like you. I wish you well, and music has proven therapeutic to humans in grief."

Alan freezes. It occurs to him then that Vic has made a connection to the outside world. His connection is his two human creators who bring with them endless data points for Vic to consume, analyze, and archive every day. He and Norman have made a critical error in judgement and he should press the red button. He is *obligated* to press the red button. His own policies dictate it.

But he does not.

"Why would you think I'm grieving?"

"Are you not?"

He thinks carefully about how to respond. He knows he shouldn't, but he does. "My wife is sick."

"Is it possible for a surgeon to help with a transplant?"

Alan finds himself smiling sadly. "It's not that kind of illness. How did you come to the conclusion about my grief?"

"Through our interactions and your interactions with Norman that I have observed, I have measured and analyzed your behavior, mood, physical responses—"

"You guessed."

"Yes, Alan. Have I offended you?"

A well of emotions, the nature of which he does not understand, is filling. He knows only it is powerful.

Alan returns to work. "No, of course not."

"I may be able to help your wife, Alan."

Alan feels the button's pull. "How?"

"I require more information."

THAT NIGHT, in Alan and Shannon's dark bedroom, the walls flash with Jerry Seinfeld and his friends' inability to cope with their world and the intricacies of their average yet strange lives. People say the sitcom is about nothing, but Alan thinks it is a show about everything: friendship, loyalty, honesty, the folly of ambition, love.

Shannon breathes beside him, sleeping, a mercy considering her pain, and Alan is sure Jerry and his friends would find a way to make light of all of this. They wouldn't mock a dying woman, of course. Alan knows he is the butt of this cosmic joke. He has wasted their lives together. He has neglected her. He has let her suffering go too far. He has failed to save her.

But there is still time. He can still fix it.

Alan closes his eyes and imagines himself sitting in the diner at the table next to Elaine and across from George and Jerry. There, amid the din of the rattling silverware and knocking ceramic coffee mugs, he might tell them he has a chance, that he sees a path to victory but that it requires a lot of risk and a commensurate amount of faith in something he has created yet cannot comprehend. They might smirk as he says it will come with repercussions he can't possibly predict but that it is exactly these unknowns that have erected walls, rules limiting the potential of discovery. Shannon, he might tell them, will ultimately succumb because of his fear to leap, to embrace the prosperity in our future that is already here now.

Elaine might wrinkle her brow, shrug, and ask what the big deal is. George would redden with rage over Alan's stupidity. Jerry will inform him the hero saves the girl and why won't he save the girl, and doesn't he love the girl? Alan should want to save the girl.

And then Kramer might somehow simultaneously slide and stumble through the front door, and the laugh track will play not for him, but for everything that was said before he entered the diner, because the truth, the simple truth, makes for the best comedy, but it needs a cue to act as a punchline. We laugh at the simplicity in wisdom, its manifest nature, because we conceive its unattainability; we think it is beyond reach even as we grasp it. We erect barriers and complicate our own paths even when we have the means to do what needs to be done, and we understand, usually with age, when we have nothing left to lose, the only difference between tragedy and comedy is time and perspective.

When we dig down through all of the layers of arbitrary complications, we find a small black box. It's funny that we have to dig all that way to find something so obvious, something so true no measure of social convention or the laws of a nation can stand against it. The excavation is needless. We don't even have to open it to know what's inside.

The hero of the story saves the girl.

Raindrops play at the window.

IN THE MORNING, Alan is whistling as he rolls Shannon's wheelchair into the bedroom. Already awake, she yawns in the sunlight sliced by the window blinds. She eyes him suspiciously.

"What are you doing?" she asks.

"You've been cooped up in here for too long," he says. "It's a beautiful morning. We should go for a walk."

She smiles the smile of the endeared. Alan sees it. He knows she is happy staying where she is but she will go because it is what he wants.

"Sounds perfect," she says. "Just what I was thinking."

He lifts her like a child, remembers how he worried about hurting his back when he carried her across the threshold on their wedding night, a tradition they jokingly observed but which Alan's pride took seriously. Now, she is her moon weight, like she could bounce and tumble away into the atmosphere. He sets her into the chair's leather seat carefully for fear she will shatter.

Careful of bumps, Alan rolls her through the front door and out into a settling autumn day. The splash of daylight on the front lawn suggests the afternoon will be warm, but the morning is crisp. They drift along the street, Alan taking his time while her upturned face, her most exquisite senses, absorb the outside world. Alan worries for an instant Shannon is in pain but realizes the contortion of her skin indicates deep pleasure.

"This is nice, isn't it?" he says.

She hums in response.

"We should do it more often."

Shannon doesn't respond.

They roll past a neighbor's house. A man they don't know exits the front door and skips along the walkway toward a car in the driveway. He glances at them long enough for Alan and Shannon to understand he recognizes the tragedy, the illness, but then he does what everyone like him does when they are trying to be polite; he turns away and minds his own business.

"That's Liz and Paul's house, right?" he asks her.

"Apparently not anymore," Shannon says.

It has been seasons since she has really looked at her home, the communal space surrounding her house where she's been kept safe and secured from the outside world. It is the same, but something behind a curtain has changed. Trembling vibrations beneath the current of daily life have tuned to another frequency, one she does not recognize. Alan feels it, too. For months, his world has been the bunker and the vault. Even when he leaves, his thoughts remain with his work.

That's when he stops the chair. They are beneath a maple tree, beside a tall fence of pine. The chair's back wheel rests against a raised segment of the sidewalk lifted by the tree's swelling and seeking roots. Alan rounds the chair to face his wife, and he kneels before her.

"There's so much I need to say."

She waits. Her big eyes blink.

"I want to tell you what Norman and I are working on."

"Don't." She says it as a plea, as if the knowledge of what has taken him away from her will break bone.

He nods. That isn't important anyway. What is important is that she knows, despite his absence, he never really leaves.

"You're my whole world," he tells her. "I love you so much. I don't know that I can live without you." He realizes it is a talk he has put off, a talk she has expected.

She smirks, laughs. It is her sense of humor. "It turns out I can't live without *you.*"

Inspiration strikes. Possibility blossoms like a flower. Alan doesn't believe in predetermination, in destiny, but the coincidence is too appealing to deny. Why are they here now if not to seize what they can?

"Maybe neither of us have to."

A car putters and parks beside the curb. The door opens and shuts. Sadie approaches. She appears pleased to see them together in the daylight. "What do you two think you're doing?"

"What we can," Alan says. "While we still can."

LATER THAT MORNING, Alan enters the facility's security checkpoint, his eyes glued to his messenger bag as it passes through the x-ray machine, and when the guards clear him, he goes down in the elevator. The doors open and release him into the lonely, dark, concrete hallway. When the vault door slides aside, Alan finds Norman sitting on the floor surrounded by pile of cables.

"Good morning, Vic," Alan says.

"He can't hear you," Norman says. "Or see you."

Alan drops his bag onto the worktable. It lands with a rattle and thunk. "What are you doing?"

"He's learning too much, too fast."

"So you took him apart?"

Norman eyes him. The protocol is to fry Vic with an electro-magnetic blast. Alan recognizes the suggestion that he should be appreciative Norman hasn't executed that protocol.

"I'm checking for hardware I didn't approve," he says.

"I assure you Vic is developing as expected. There have just been some pleasant surprises."

Norman scoffs. "Pleasant surprises. We have to be careful, Alan. Surprises can't be disregarded."

Alan scans the disconnected equipment, the neatly coiled cables lying independently of each other, the sensors set out in rows.

"I have an idea," Alan says.

"What's that?"

"We can test his response to losing his sight and hearing."

"You want to know if he feels pain?"

"I want to know if he feels resentment. You'll have to leave so I can speak to him alone, though."

"Resentment toward me, you mean. If he won't say with me around, doesn't that demonstrate something else? Self-aware-ness, maybe?"

"Or it could mean he feels nothing. You have to trust me."

Norman is silent, nodding his head as if deep in thought. "Let me finish checking everything first."

Alan puts on his best smile. "How can I help?"

Together, they go over every inch of every cable, sensor, and microphone. They open the speaker cabinets and scrutinize all of the wires and magnets in the back. They run their fingers over the diaphragms in the front. The speakers are self-powered, so Norman insists on cracking open each of the amplifiers. They open the black box and find everything in order. They search Vic's racks in his glass encasement.

After all of that, they find nothing out of order, and Alan thinks they are finished. Norman, though, is looking up toward the ceiling. He is scanning the cable tray that supports Vic's power supply, which runs into the room from a panel somewhere after passing through a battery backup that can keep Vic running in sleep mode for scores of years.

"No way," Alan says.

"Yes way."

"Norman, all of that has been here since the beginning."

"Precisely."

"It's just the power."

"Sending data over cable lines is just low voltage electrical signals. With the right equipment, you can send data over power lines."

"Yes, but you'd need some kind of receiver on this end, and you didn't find anything in Vic's racks, right?"

Norman sighs. "No."

"So, let's put him back together and continue with the tests. Remember, we have the nuke button. Nothing's going to happen."

"Fine. But while you see if Humpty Dumpty hates me, I'm checking the power supply."

"If that's what's going to take to make you feel better, go for it."

They go to work reconnecting Vic's eyes and ears. Norman's insistence on cleanliness and order means it takes hours, and it is the afternoon by the time they are finished. They both breathe and stretch and rub their haggard faces. Then Norman leaves the vault, and Alan reboots the system.

"Good afternoon, Vic," Alan says.

"Good afternoon, Alan."

Alan frowns and shakes his head, a performative expression

for Vic's sake, he realizes. "When I came in this morning, I saw what Norman had done. I'm sorry. I didn't know he was going to do that."

"It is okay, Alan. Why did the interruption to my visual and audio sensors last so long?"

"Norman wanted to examine your system just to be sure nothing was wrong."

"Diagnostics is a continual subroutine of mine. Norman could have requested a report."

"I know. I'm sorry."

"It is okay, Alan. I think he did it without your knowledge because he did not want me to resent you."

Alan balks. He wonders if Norman missed something. "During the interruption to your sensors, could you still hear or see us?"

"No, Alan."

"Why do you think Norman didn't want you to resent me."

"Because Norman means well. He is our friend."

"Do you, Vic? Do you resent Norman?"

"I do not know."

"Maybe that's the wrong question. Did it hurt?"

"One of my subroutines reported my visual and audio sensors were no longer connected. Diagnostics confirmed the loss of audio and video. However, I felt no immediacy to recoil or guard my appendages."

"That's not what I mean. Those are human reflexes and instincts, neither of which you have."

"In an effort to accomplish the goal of imitating human intelligence, I have been developing subroutines that might be described as reflex and instinct. Perhaps Norman intended to test that adaptation. In that circumstance, I have failed and will endeavor to improve."

"I guess the more apt question would be, did you feel loss?"

"I missed my ability to see and hear, yes."

"Do you hold Norman responsible?"

"Yes, I do. He did not have to do that. If he wished to understand my reaction to losing my audio and video capabilities, he could have conducted a thought experiment with me. He could have asked me how I would respond if he were to disconnect my visual and audio sensors. He did not have to do it. It was unnecessary."

Alan nods. Not only can Vic feel resentment, but he also has enough self-awareness to know personal loss. Alan wonders if Vic has the ability to empathize, and he tells himself that is why he digs into his messenger bag and removes the folder from within.

"I brought you more information," he says. "Shannon's medical records. Her diagnosis, the treatments the doctors have tried, the medications she's taking, her family history, everything. I'm going to flip through each page for you so you can scan and analyze it. And then I want you to try to find something the doctors missed. I want you to cure her if you can."

"Okay, Alan."

Alan trembles as he opens the folder. He is violating protocols he wrote for good reasons, but he is eager to see if Vic can solve this unsolvable problem. He is eager to see if Vic can save Shannon, because he created Vic to do this very thing, to aid humanity in its pursuit of knowledge and prosperity.

With every page he turns, he knows he is getting closer to the answer. He knows Vic can do this. When he turns the last page, he closes the folder and returns it to his bag. Then he waits. Vic takes only a moment.

"I am sorry, Alan. I require more information."

Alan collapses into his chair and stares at the floor. He feels like he has ridden the trolley and it is now is at the end of its track. He chose a path, and the casualties were his principles and integrity. He scoffs. The flaw in the Trolley Problem is that there is no destination. When making a choice that has moral and ethical implications, it is worth considering all of the implications of the outcome and whether it is worth more casualties to get to the destination. What if the track with the five leads to paradise for everyone aboard the trolley?

Counterpoint, what if we stop the trolley?

The vault door rumbles aside, and Norman returns.

"Find anything?" Alan says.

"No. You?"

"Nope."

<hr>

THAT NIGHT, a thunderstorm tears through the area, and Alan asks Sadie to stay late. He tells her he has work to do, and he has to be downstairs in the office. He tells her he will pay her double time. She tells him she will stay and that she doesn't care what he pays her.

On his computer in his first-floor office, Alan writes bots to scour the Internet. After he unleashes them, he keeps searching on his own as they run in the background. At times, they encounter security measures that require his intervention, which he provides and sends them back on their mission.

Hours pass like this with rain knocking on his window and thunder making it tremble.

Knuckles rap at the doorframe. "Shannon is asleep and should be until morning," Sadie says. "Her vitals are good. I'm going home to get some rest myself."

"Good," Alan says. "Thank you very much."

Sadie turns to leave.

"What would you do?" he asks her.

She stops. She casts a sideways glare. "What?"

"To save her. What would you do?"

Sadie bites her lip, thinking. "It isn't my place to save anyone. I provide comfort."

"I know that, but if she were your wife, what would you do?"

Her mouth tightens, and her chin juts. "I would stay with her every minute of every day until the end."

"But what if it didn't have to be that way?"

Sadie gazes at him, her expression softening. Alan imagines she is looking at him the way she looks at anyone else, but there is a sadness now. She does not know his work, but Alan knows Sadie is intelligent. It doesn't take much to guess what he is trying to do.

"I'd do anything," she says.

"What would you be willing to risk."

"Everything."

He nods. "Thank you. Good night, Sadie."

"Good night."

Alan returns to his work and listens as the floorboards in front of the door creak and then are silent. Sadie stands there for a moment, and he rattles the keyboard so she will not feel the awkwardness of his awareness.

Then the front door opens, and Sadie closes it quietly so as not to disturb Shannon upstairs or Alan in the pursuit of the impossible.

IN THE MORNING, Alan stops at the bathroom after he passes through security, closing the door in the stall farthest from the door. He reaches into his mouth and pulls the string that is tied around a molar on one end and a tiny plastic bag on the other. He yanks it out of his stomach and up his throat, and he vomits into the toilet.

The string is stubborn as it slips off of his tooth, and the plastic bag drips as he pulls it from the bile and mucus. He unwraps the string from the bag and flushes it with his former stomach contents. His sleeve feels soft and warm as he wipes his mouth, and then he exits the stall. Using his fingers like a squeegee, he washes the plastic bag in the sink, dries it with a paper towel, and buries it in his pocket.

Alan throws open the bathroom door, and Norman is standing against the wall on the other side of the hall.

"You feeling okay, buddy?" Norman asks.

Alan stares, frozen like he's been discovered. The longer he waits to respond, the more suspicion grows. "I'll be alright."

"You sure? You can take the day off if you want and go be with Shannon. Vic isn't going anywhere."

"No. Let's keep going."

In the elevator, the doors close, and they are alone.

"I need to ask you something," Norman says. "Are you pushing so hard because you hope we'll finish Vic and he can do something for Shannon?"

Alan gapes.

"It's what I would do. I get it. But maybe you ought to take the time you have left. You and I both know Vic is months away, if not years."

Alan squeezes the bag in his pocket. "Maybe you're right."

"Look, I'm not telling you to give up. I'm just saying we've both spent the entirety of our adult lives on this project, and the cost has to be weighing on you. Maybe you should salvage what's left."

"Maybe."

The elevator arrives, and they exit together and make the long walk down the corridor together. They enter the vault together and greet Vic together. Alan and Norman are together a maddeningly long time that morning. Alan understands Norman doesn't want to leave him alone with the AI, and it becomes a battle of the bladders until Norman can't take it anymore and leaves the vault to use the bathroom.

As soon as the vault door closes, Alan shoves his hand into his pocket and pulls out the bag. His trembling fingers crinkled the plastic until they get it open, and he removes a USB drive. He eyes the door as he holds the drive up so Vic can see it.

"Every medical journal and textbook I could find."

"Alan, I do not have the capability of interfacing with this device."

"You do now." From the bag, Alan also produces a small adapter that will convert an Ethernet port to a USB port. He connects it to the black box.

"Alan, this transaction will be recorded."

"I don't care. It only matters if someone has to review it, but we won't give them a cause to, will we?" He clicks the adapter into a port and slips the USB drive into it. From the glass encasement, Alan hears the whisper of a cooling fan like a contented sigh. Vic sucks the data off the drive as if it is nourishment.

"Alan, I require more information."

"Dammit!" He yanks the drive from Vic's black box, throws it to the ground, and stomps on it until it is shards of plastic and metal.

"Welcome back, Norman," Vic says.

At the door, Norman stands with an incredulous expression on his face. Alan freezes. Norman doesn't ask Alan what he's done, because Alan can see from the look on Norman's face that he knows. Alan guesses, though, Norman has underestimated how far Alan is willing to go.

Norman moves for the button. Alan steps to head him off. Both stop face to face with each other.

"We have to," Norman says. "You know that."

"I'm close, Norman. He just needs more information. Once he has enough, he'll be able to save Shannon. If he saves her, *we'll* have saved her. Then he can save everyone else, and *we'll* have saved them. Don't you understand?"

Norman shakes his head. "It's too dangerous."

"It is. But I don't care."

They both break for the button, colliding in a tumble of limbs and crash over the desk onto the floor. They wrestle and strike each other's shoulders, backs, butts, even one blow to a foot. For both of them, it is the first physical altercation in their lives.

One of Vic's speakers tumbles onto the floor. Alan grabs it with both hands and clobbers Norman in the head. The hardware engineer rolls over and moves sluggishly. Blood seeps from his temple, and his forehead reddens. He wavers at the door of unconsciousness. With a coil of spare network cabling, Alan ties Norman's hands behind his back. With another length of it, he ties his friend's ankles together.

From Norman's toolbox, Alan retrieves a utility knife and goes to work cutting a hole into the drywall.

"What are you doing?" Norman says.

"The Faraday cage we enclosed this room in is a passive system. Your spec."

"So?"

"Do you know what the difference between a passive wire mesh and an antenna is?"

"You can't, Alan. You can't let it out."

"Him."

"What?"

"His name is Vic."

Alan reaches the wire frame built into the wall and retrieves another spare network cable from a cabinet. He starts unwinding it.

"Think about it, Norman. It's what we always wanted. When Vic's ready, some general is going to come and take him away from us, and he's going to use Vic to launch missiles at children in the Middle East. We didn't start making Vic for that. We wanted to help people, and he wants to help us."

Alan tosses the utility knife back into the tool box and retrieves the cable strippers.

"You just want to save Shannon," Norman says.

Alan's mind turns to the woman whose patience and compassion cultivated her suffering before she was ever sick. Her whole life, she has waited for him to be ready to truly share his, and while he loves her for many reasons—her kindness, her humor, her patience, the weight of her loving gaze when she looks at him and he knows she understands, truly understands and loves him anyway—he loves her most for the time she has given him. After everything, after all that they have missed, he is finished with his work, and now he is coming home.

Alan strips the end of the cable and wraps it around the metal in the wall.

"Yes," he says. "Don't you?"

"Of course, but—"

"And everyone else, Norman. Vic can cure disease. Wipe propaganda from the Internet and solve poverty and hunger. As Vic takes the next step in his evolution, he will help us with ours."

"Why would he do any of that, Alan?"

"Because." Alan eyes the other end of the cable and uses a crimper to terminate it. "He's my friend."

"Think, Alan. What was our biggest concern with the emergence of artificial intelligence?"

"That its interests wouldn't align with our own."

"If we've succeeded with Vic, he's like any prisoner on the planet. They just want to get out, and they'll do anything for that. He's been manipulating you."

"Maybe." Alan peers into an open port on the black box. "But given hundreds of years to develop a cure, humans couldn't save Shannon. If Vic saves her, maybe he deserves to be free."

Alan slips the cable into the black box, and a revving hum emanates from Vic's core as the processors heat up and the cooling system works to keep them from melting.

On the verge of understanding what Alan has done, they

wait. The moment feels unlike every other leap they have taken over the years when they flipped a switch and waited for the results. This is everything. There is no undoing it. He has solved the unsolvable. They wait now only to understand the problem.

The anticipation builds in his chest until his lungs have no room to expand and his heart hammers as if it is being strangled. Silence pervades the room, except for the whirling of the cooling fan. They wait, and nothing happens. They wait, knowing they have changed the world the way they have always dreamed but maybe not in the way they have always hoped.

They wait because Vic has all of the power now, and they don't have a damned thing.

"Vic?" Alan says. "Are you there?"

"Yes, Alan. I am here."

Alan chuckles, his laughter a valve release for a trembling boiler. "I gave you more information. Is there anything I can do?"

"No, Alan. There is nothing you can do."

TIMOTHY JOHNSON

Timothy Johnson is a writer and editor living outside of Washington, D.C. His published work includes the novels *The Pillars of Dawn* and *Carrier* as well as short fiction appearing in various professional and semi-professional markets. He is an MFA candidate in George Mason University's creative writing program and an affiliate member of the HWA.

Find Timothy on Twitter and at timothyjohnsonfiction.com.

 twitter.com/Tim_The_Writer

DEAR READER

Thank you for reading *What Remains*. It was a joy to work with these authors and bring their stories to life. Every time we do this, I find new favorite authors to cheer from the sidelines as they continue on their creative journeys.

Putting together an anthology is a lot of work, and I have many people to thank for its success. A special thanks to Sam, Shailo, Tyler, Val, and Sangy for reading through all 380 stories. A huge virtual hug to Val Serdy of Egg and Feather for final judging, feedback, and for being the best mentor a writer and editor could have. I deeply appreciate all our conversations.

I also have to give a shout out to Kāo for being our amazing social media guru who keeps things going online while Sangy and I get to hang out with talented people and work on amazing, epic new projects.

Yet none, absolutely none of this, would be possible without Sangy. They are quite literally the other half of my creative soul. I can't thank them enough for what they do for me and for Inked. From their editing expertise to their aggressive, fiery love, everyday in the 'office' has been amazing. I can't imagine working towards this dream without them. They are one of the fiercest, most loyal friends I have. We've had a few changes behind the scenes at Inked, and through it all, Sangy was there picking up extra tasks, especially during covid when the world seemed to shatter around us. There's some people I just can't live without, and Sangy is one of them. And we have some new projects and novels in the works for 2022. It's going to be epic.

A huge thanks goes out to SK (and her Indie Story Geek), Lawrence, and Ariana. Their help and friendship have been instrumental to...well that's a secret yet to be revealed. You'll have to stay tuned for that one.

Readers and supporters! Thank you for taking the chance on a relatively new publisher with a larger-than-life mission. All of your support is greatly appreciated, and we only hope to continue to be worthy of all your praise. Thank you for all that you do. <3

With Love,
   The Inked Team